PRAISE FOR NICHOLAS MOSLEY

"One of the most fascinating novels of the last generation."
—Joseph McElroy

"Mosley is one of the most interesting and gifted English novelists writing today." —*New Statesman*

"Mosley's very special talent is for describing the sensations experienced within a cocoon of dismay and terror."
—*Sunday Times* (London)

"Mosley is the most serious and brilliant of Britain's novelists of ideas." —*Times* (London)

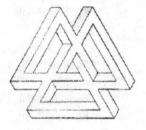

OTHER BOOKS BY NICHOLAS MOSLEY

IMPOSSIBLE
OBJECT

NICHOLAS MOSLEY

DALKEY ARCHIVE PRESS

Dallas, TX / Rochester, NY

Library of Congress Cataloging-in-Publication Data available.
ISBN-13: 978-156478-465-0
ISBN-10: 1-56478-465-7

Printed in Canada

Contents

You know how love flourishes in time of war, women standing on station platforms and waiting for the lines of faces to pull out, men's heads three deep in the carriage windows and arms raised like the front legs of horses on the Parthenon. The men do not want to go to war; they look forward to travel and the warmth of soldiers. The women have handkerchiefs round their heads and are tired at so much weeping; they will run to the arms of American airmen and war profiteers, will be carried to armament factories and farms for the breeding of white feathers. The men will sing sad songs round firelight; move across plains in heavy armour jerking and screaming like crusaders.

Now there is no war. The train stops and the faces fall on top of each other like snow; the women are left with their outstretched arms and pots of honey. You get out on the station platform and are again in the world of paper and thin concrete; go along to the waiting room where there are bodies like newspapers wrapped on trolleys. You put a coin in the slot and pull out cardboard. Mummies are crenellated so that they will look beautiful in a million years.

This was the spring when I had been married half my life and there was this drought, cherry and lilac, the crowds moving round the flower stalls and raising their straw-hats and blazers. And when the call came they moved as one man and lined up on the platform. We had lived in this garden, my wife and I, through a quiet winter. And God came down through the trees one day and scratched himself as if a man had walked over his grave or trod on excrement, and said "What are you going to do?" I looked round the garden and saw a father and a mother and three sons with bronze draperies over their knees and their heads pin-points. We sat in deck-chairs and ate from trolleys. I said "I don't know." I went to the attic where was my paraphernalia of war, my uniform and moths, rats and sleeping bag. My wife came to me: she said "I don't want you to go." I said "I don't want to go." In 1940 there had been planes overhead like fireworks and searchlights that had hit through a thin sky. Men had run across no-man's-land and fallen like keys of a typewriter. I had kneeled to pull at the straps of my luggage as if praying.

And now there was this time, a quarter of a century later, when we looked out and saw the ice-cap coming down from the pole; saw that we had been in our cave too long with our ancestors' bones and drawings like tooth-decay; that we should move out through forest and plain till we came to the desert, and should camp there without food until we were saved from being preserved for a million years.

When you know that love flourishes in time of war—those kisses taken on street corners where you might be killed, barrel-organs outside pubs meretricious as bullets—then, when there is no war, what do you do with these images? You have them from the beginning: are forced out of the tunnel into the football stadium; know the moment before the doors open when you are in the dark; then the roar, with the goalpost and the lion. You lie on the hard bed with your legs in the air; watch for the mouths of nurses and lovers. Nothing is more terrible than war; just the spring coming round again with the bodies wrapped and the need to lance them like pins stuck on a wall-map. And all the old generals and call-boys coming dancing across the stage with feathers in their hair and their tight leather arses. And in the front rows the exhausted people who have to defend themselves against this barrage of boots, spittle, blood, eyes and swagger-sticks.

Perhaps we should strike a medal for all the nancies who once made love possible—those politicians and infants of the spirit—with gratitude from those who have had to sit in trenches and been sick at so much glory. For having so appalled us with their mixture of elephant and tiny baby that now we can take anything; a dozen or a million people can be killed and we do not turn, think we might do the same even; raise our hats and say—Thank you for the lesson; how much do we owe you? For our debt is that of the diamond to the dirt—of incalculable dependency and hatred.

This was the spring when we had been contented so long, chatting to men in grey trousers on lawns, the bourgeoisie, great guardians of the spirit. And at the first call they all put their hands up. The trees I had planted through half my life were now growing; my house in its fields, my sons between nettles and hedgerow. I thought—All battles are now in the mind; we must make our own war. My wife came with me to the station. There were the doors closing and the ghosts three deep in the carriage windows—the ones at the

8

top innocent and the ones in the middle terrified and the ones at the bottom guillotined. They were smiling; afraid of feeling again. The women clung; having to suffer to keep themselves from injury. God was on the platform dressed as a colour-sergeant. He tapped his stick against his leg. I looked to where the bright rails went into the distance and I kissed my wife because I loved her, because we were being separated, because you do not look at the clock when you have to get through the next five minutes. God fussed about seeing the luggage in: he pretends not to notice at such moments. He is on the side of love and suffering. The whistle blew. I stood with one arm raised like the front leg of a horse on the Parthenon. My wife had a handkerchief over her eyes. She said "Take care of yourself." I said "I will."

Family Game

WE USED TO LIVE in a farmhouse, my wife and I, of a kind in which the inside has been painted white and carpets have been laid over yellow tiles and brickwork. Beams sloped at angles above doors and there were steps scooped out like cooking spoons. In the holidays the house always seemed full of children; they haunted it with the thumps and screams of poltergeists, playing games and fighting and banging off walls, indolently torturing one another in corridors. Children are our contacts with the past: spirits were once thought to work through adolescents.

My wife and I have three sons; one of fifteen and one of eleven and one of eight. Their friends, and younger children, used to come in from the village to play these games. At Christmas time life was pushed indoors: fields were sodden so that it was as if we were on an island. I felt myself pursued by these ghosts; defended myself by ignoring them, moved from my study where I worked to the sitting room or kitchen and stepped past the running or struggling bodies as if they were used to being walked through. They would pause for a moment as I passed like the croaking of frogs; then resume after I had gone.

My wife and I used to let the children play much as they liked, believing that if they fought now they would not want to blow up the world later. There is this theory that violence has to come out somewhere, so it might as well come out to the detriment of parents, which is their proper function.

We used to have tea, the family and guests, in the large farm kitchen with the old range boarded up and pipes going through like messengers to the boiler. The children crowded in; the ones that were used to us stretching immediately for food and the ones that were not sitting starving. We tried to help the underprivileged, my wife and I, standing at the back and encouraging equality like a butler and a parlourmaid. This seems to be the prerogative of humans as opposed to that of God; who seems on the side of the beautiful and greedy.

There was a day when my eldest son brought his first girl friend home to tea. This is a difficult time for any father: he is old, his wife busy, he is spry and battered as a boxer. As a professional he knows when to duck; the swings of an opponent come only out of his mind—jealousy and betrayal. To avoid these should be easy. But amateurs do not know the rules; and sons' girl friends are amateurs.

My eldest son's first girl friend was someone of whom we had only heard: he had met her in the village, had fallen in love. She was fourteen; an only child. Her parents were dead; she spent her holidays in the houses of friends and relations. She was with a cousin for Christmas. When spirits are in adolescents, they herald their approach with trumpets.

There is a relationship between father and son that is like love. You see the forgotten part of yourself; you smile and are frightened of it, you want it to flourish and yet know that part of it or you will be destroyed. You and your son walk one slightly ahead of the other down the dusty street like a posse hunting for criminals: you fight with jealousy and betrayal until they are defeated and then, from an upstairs window, someone shoots you.

The family sits round the kitchen table. Father is at the head in an old grey jersey, dark trousers, ruined shoes. He does some pretence of eating more loudly than the others in order to shame them; he thinks this is more helpful than telling them about good manners straight out. Such is cowardice—or the liberal imagination. I put my head down to the small children on either side and gobble: I can make them laugh like this, requiring love like any human. My wife is at the other end handing round cakes as if they were medals; she has this habit like that of royalty to treat everyone as immortal or an adult. The smaller children sit half underneath the table like men in racing cars, their dark hair helmets. The elder children slump. The table has a red plastic top. There are hot buttered toast and cakes and biscuits.

My eldest son and his girl friend had not yet arrived.

The point of a family is that there is space to be free and thus to care. If mistakes are made, then there is time to pick up the pieces and put them together again.

My eldest son's girl friend appeared on her own as if she might have come to the wrong house—a windfall such as an actress with a car broken down or a charity flag-seller. I was coming along the corridor from the kitchen; I had left the tea-party because I had been showing off; was thinking—wouldn't it be better if parents simply betrayed their children and then the children would be free of them? In the doorway was a tall young girl with the light behind her. I put out an arm to guide her back to the kitchen. She wore a black jersey and a pale blue skirt. The skirt ended just below her behind. She had white socks and long black hair. I said "Come and have tea." I walked slightly ahead. My wife was at the stove toasting crumpets. I pulled a chair back. The girl had a young round face with long lashes. The lashes were false. This amazed me. I pushed the chair in and stood behind. There were girls nowadays who pouted and whirled their arms like clockwork toys.

My eldest son was still outside doing something to his bicycle.

I went round talking to the younger children. I pretended I couldn't remember their names. I said "Do you know what happens if you eat silver paper?" There were two little girls from the cottage next door who were scrubbed and polished till the surface had rubbed off them. I thought—At the chimpanzee's tea-party the keeper has to act a clown in order not to embarrass his prisoners.

My eldest son came in. He was tall and dark with hair brushed forward like feathers.

Children do not speak to each other much in front of adults. They wait with eyes cast down like people who have committed murder and are being interrogated. Their crime is deeper than love or happiness; something from their birth, and about what will become of them. My eldest son sat by his girl friend and was as solicitous as a statue. Across the table—I was seated again—there were these lines from four of us forming a square. One line went from my son to his girl friend who were in love, another between my wife and I who were married; there was a diagonal between my son and my wife which was their original crime and ecstasy, and between myself and the girl friend who were ridiculous. Between my son and I was our hunt up the dusty street; and perhaps my wife always grieved for her non-existent daughter. I passed the girl friend some cakes. She had a soft mouth which birds could peck crumbs off. I was not ashamed of feeling this. I thought—We can love ourselves enough now to know our awfulness: girls of fourteen are symbols of the unobtainable. They are birds in the Sahara or eels in the water-tank: they will fight for their lives there. Witches usually choose their own executioners.

I asked—Where was she at school? Did she like it? How long was she staying?

My wife thinks that people would be happier without polite conversation.

I thought—I will go away to the Argentine and live there like God on forged papers. I will sit in the sun and wear dark glasses and read my obituaries.

My eldest son likes intelligent conversation. He asks questions of the kind that are debated on brains trusts and are of interest to dreamers and rulers of the world.

He said "Have you seen the figures about the birthrate?"

I said "Without war or disease, what can you do about it?"

He said "Do you approve of war then?"

I said "Of course I don't approve of war!"

Children are logical. They think an argument is an answer, as politicians do.

My son said—"We'll all be standing on top of each other in five hundred years."

I said "I know who I'd like to stand on top of me."

My wife disapproves of these jokes. She thinks I am flirting with my children. I am.

My second son, who was of an age to appreciate such jokes, began to roll about as if garotted. Bits of bread seemed to emerge from his eyes and ears. He was fair and pink-faced with bright blue eyes; a passionate fighter. I raised my finger and gave myself out like a cricket umpire. In my mind I began my walk back to the pavilion. I thought—I will sit upstairs and watch the girl friend through binoculars: we live so much with our eyes nowadays that we should be voyeurs of the spirit: then we would get less burned—even by sacredness. The girl friend had not laughed. She sat with her hands between her legs; like mimosa.

When my eldest son offered her more biscuits she did not look at him. Her false lashes were like bee-stings. I thought—She will have to hurt him to prove to herself how much she has been hurt.

I said "Do any of you want to play a game after tea? I'll be down after I've done a bit of work."

I sometimes join in their games after tea, especially round Christmas. I do this because I like this, and they want me.

In my room upstairs I sat in front of my typewriter and the keys were like men waiting to be sent out over no-man's-land. I was writing a story at the time about how love only flourishes in time of war; how God has to pack up our suitcases and send us off like a nanny. I thought—I will turn it into a story of a father with children. I felt seeds from my own youth settling on me: mouths like fishes at the top of the long grass and hooks coming down to catch them. God puts the worm on and dents the soft flesh; throws it into the river with one arm arched like a rainbow. God is a fisherman in thigh-length boots like a woman: the worm is a lyre or the lips of a young girl. I thought—We misunderstand this; imagining love has to do with paradise.

Downstairs began again the thumps and screams of poltergeists.

Our house is on four levels—upstairs the bedrooms and the rooms where my wife and I work, downstairs where the children play in the parliaments of the world, the attic where are dressing-up clothes and my old army equipment, and the cellar where in cases falling apart at the seams are my memories and old love-letters.

The symbolism is obvious.

I thought—Should I not want to rescue my son? Throw him back into the water because he is so young?

I wanted to write—With what gentleness does God take the hook out of the fish's mouth and bring up half the stomach! Perhaps on his face is the adoring look of angels.

We are all processes of God's digestion.

Footsteps come along the passage. My youngest son is the one who comes to my room because he is not anxious with me; he only recognises anxiety, being in touch with visions. He knocks on my door and stands staring at the ceiling. He has large eyes. He has forgotten what he has come to say. Birds rush over him. The clouds part at memory.

"Oh! Are you going to come now?"

"In a minute."

"How long?"

"I'll be down."

There is this first impossibility—that a father can be too good. He can go down on his knees and play at elephants and let the children stick spikes into him; then they will be ruined, having nothing better to do for the rest of their lives than dress up in the turbans and silk trousers of mahouts. Yet a father who never kneels will leave behind him only hunters exhausted by expending so many arrows. Either way, the father has to be immolated.

I went downstairs. The elder children were round the record-player. This is a primitive position—the ju-ju man above his bones. There were records with pictures on the covers of boys waiting to be kissed: girls in chain mail and helmets. I wanted to point out—This is one solution to the population problem. I circled round on my broomstick, my own feminine part. The girl friend had one leg bent at the knee and her fingers resting on a table. There was a vacuum about her which others would rush in to fill; then they would stand with their arms up like people in a wind tunnel. My eldest son touched the back of her hand. I said "Well shall we play a game?" They said "What game?" They were like the unemployed waiting on street corners on Sundays. I said "The game in the cellar." Light came into their eyes as if war had been declared; there was cheering and a rush to the colours. I thought—Wars usually start in summer amongst railings and the legs of young girls. I was deprecating as a Prime Minister: no one really wants war.

The game in the cellar was a hide-and-seek in the dark in which there was one catcher and the rest were his victims. The game took place among the junk we had thrown out from our lives upstairs; the ruined furniture and packages around which we crept only in dreams. We, the children and I, pretended to be ashamed of this game since we were too old for it; myself of course by thirty years but the older children too, being interested as they were in politics and birth-control.

We moved excitedly towards the cellar stairs; my eldest son and his girl friend in front, my second son like a bare-fisted boxer of the last century, my third son a faun about to be tickled to death in a wine-vat. I thought—In order to liberate one's children one has to be made a fool of; get a rib stolen when one is asleep or come riding into town one Sunday on a donkey. But what happens then? In the walk back to the cricket pavilion or on the shoulders of acolytes there is the terror of entombment; having achieved defeat or sanctification there is the rest of one's life to get through; one is back amongst the pads and elastic and bits and bridles, the robing and disrobing in the vestry. So you get out your broomstick and become like a woman. I wanted to explain—If the point of life is to die and to be reborn then after a certain age you have to work for it: self-destruction doesn't come easily.

In the cellar we found ourselves a group of seven—the four of the family, the girl friend, and the two small girls from next door. I explained the game: you crept about, were caught, stood still, whispered 'rescue'. You were rescued by someone touching you. I remembered once having written a story about this game: people playing it had become aware that in the room there was one more person than could be accounted for—a hand went on rescuing them after everyone had been caught. I began telling this story now. The children were in the light of an unshaded bulb from the ceiling. The cellar was in several rooms slotted into each other like a puzzle with a central junction where the light was. I acted the story of the ghostly hand with my eyes staring and my hair slightly on end: the story had been called—The Seventh Person. I realised I was frightening the younger children; they would soon be crying. I took the story back; told them it was not true. I thought again—Why do I do this? I need the applause like all public images. The children began to whoop and gurgle with animal noises; put their hands to their mouths and blew. The girl friend was standing as usual with one foot slightly in front of the other and her hands by her side; she seemed to be seen both full-face and from the side at once, like Cleopatra. I said "Turn off the light." The children had become so excited it was difficult to get the game to start: there were croaks, groans, the rattle of ravens. The cellar walls were coming apart like old musical instruments; on the floor were toppling chairs and cobwebbed china. My second son was

17

to be the catcher; he would play to win. The light went out. I noticed where Cleopatra was standing. She had been married to her brother at the age of eleven; had been carried in to Caesar in a carpet. When they took her clothes off they found the marks where snakes had fed. Succubi feed off witches. The darkness was total. I thought—Now I can indulge my fantasies.

I stood with my back against a wall. In the cellar of my mind was the damp and decay of frogs. When you are blind it is like being wrapped in paper. You keep your mouth open and listen for others' breathing.

When I had first seen my son's girl friend she had been in the door with the light behind her. She had not looked at me. My wife and I had been married eighteen years. We were a happy family. I had no daughter of my own. When I had looked at the girl friend across the table she had looked back with grey eyes that were thoughtful and despairing. Still none of this worried me. For youth, for growth, there has to be foolishness and tragedy.

I scraped the back of my hands along walls sharp as razors. I was in one of the large rooms of the cellar where were stored letters from my youth. They tumbled out of boxes white with mould, the pages stuck together. When I had been young I had been in love with a girl in the War Office: she had written on officially-stamped paper. There is always litter in war. The animal noises had quietened down; there was an occasional ghostly laugh or groan from a corner. Someone bumped into furniture, swore, set off suppressed giggles. I thought—One could make this game truly frightening; like watching yourself from the foot of a bed or sitting in a group and pretending to be different people. Then the spirits come down. Someone screamed. Cleopatra had been standing by a table with a marble top; had leaned a hip against it. Her skirt was smooth and blue. When they opened the tombs the bodies collapsed like burned paper.

There was a hand moving over my body, my front. When you are in the dark there is a feeling of vulnerability as if a stake might drive through you. The hand squeezed, disappeared: this often happened in the game. I thought I might pretend to be the ghost; could be taken over like a ventriloquist by his dummy. The hand came back to mine on the wall; tenderly. We had been by yew hedges and had walked toward a fountain. The hand seemed to have come from below; must belong to one of the younger children. In this part of the cellar there was a well; it went down beneath a trap door to water far below. This was a mystery—when it had been dug, what it was used for. We had nailed the trap door in order to prevent the children falling through it. Once they had forced the boards up and we had not known whether or not to punish them. We had wanted to say—It was for your own good we nailed it; to punish you would be for your own good too, but you cannot always have what is good for you. So we had explained it. They had not wanted to have it just explained; would have found punishment easier. But only thus does one grow. From the other side of the room a voice shouted "Help!" The light went on. It was like lovers leaping apart: a white road in headlights. Cleopatra had moved closer; was in a corner by the well. My second son came in angrily from another part of the cellar and said "What's wrong?" My eldest son had his hand on the light switch. He was looking for Cleopatra. My second son watched him. There had been a windy day when two brothers had gathered leaves and one of their fires had not got started. And if Adam could have come along with a box of matches he could have saved them. The light went out again. The two brothers seemed to go on existing as if in a negative; one turned towards Cleopatra and the other towards the game. I thought—Both are necessary. They were primitive drawings scratched on a rock-face.

The hand on mine had been that of one of the small girls from next door. When small children cling to you you have to disengage yourself carefully: to move too quickly could be traumatic. I thought that perhaps I should be looking for my youngest son, who sometimes got frightened and gave early warning of panic like a canary.

My eldest son would be getting close to Cleopatra; had doubtless been looking forward to this game to touch her in the dark. When you are young this has to seem by accident. My eldest son and I were of an age to understand each other; walking side by side, of an equal height, watching the different façades of the dusty street. I would sometimes try to explain: would say—This is what life's like. He would say—It's very complicated. When the light had gone on Cleopatra had looked at me. Her eyes were curious. There were more animal noises and giggles.

The darkness made you put your senses outside you for other people to ride on to. I moved sideways with my back against the wall, one hand in front of me like a statue. I had not really been thinking much about Cleopatra; just of her shell like a nut to be cracked, the child that had been lost to Red Indians and then found again. Nowadays we should not be frightened of dreams: there are holes in rocks that we do not have to jump into. The sea sucks up and down and we just watch it. A hand clutched my sleeve; I thought I must have been caught. When the catcher catches you he is supposed to say 'Caught'; so you know it is he. I put out my other hand and we held each other. With my second son I am not on such easy terms: he is too like me, both seeing ourselves as soldiers. I whispered "It's me." I thought someone might be frightened. The hand holding me could not be that of my second son, since he did not speak. The person suddenly put their head on my shoulder. Till then I had not imagined this; I had only pretended it might be Cleopatra. She had come across in a bee-line. She took her head away. The light went on. You do not think; you become the receptacle of earth, air, fire. I thought—She must have been frightened. We were like one of those Victorian couples stranded by a lighthouse. Having taken my arm away I seemed to be leaning against the waves. My eldest son had his hand on the light switch again. Cleopatra and I were standing close to each other. We were not quite touching. My second son burst in; shouted "Who the hell keeps turning the light on?" The light went off. We were jumping backwards and forwards as if through a looking-glass. I thought—What have I done? I only thought she was frightened. My eldest son was searching. She had wanted help in the dark. It is our job to protect the young; otherwise a millstone is hung round our necks and we are dropped down the well. But my eldest son would not believe this; there would be the moment in the dusty street, the muzzle of the gun in an upstairs window. I began to move away. I should have done this earlier. We had jumped slightly apart when the light came on. We had been holding each other. But my eldest son might not have seen. Children do not notice grown-ups. There was now the sound of someone crying. The back of her hand brushed again against mine. I could not trust what was happening. She had put her head on my shoulder. I could take her in my arms and say—Let us go to South

America; let us sit in the sun and watch the crowds go by. I wanted to touch her skirt. She had had white socks. Her thighs were brown. Strength is in the plane between the hips and the small of the back. We were all trying not to breathe so that no one should catch us. My eldest son's voice cried out "There's a body on the floor!" He sometimes did a pretence of being very English, like a butler. He did this when he was uneasy. Someone called—"It's the Seventh Person!" There were more catcalls, groans. I thought—We are exhilarated by terror. She was pulling at my arm as if she wanted my head to come down to hers. I thought she might kiss me. She was going to tell me a secret. I was a ship and she was an iceberg. She whispered something. My ear was by her mouth. I said "What?" She had whispered—"We're making him jealous!" I pulled my head back. I thought—Our corruption is unbearable. I wondered how quickly I could go. A sense of direction depends on memory. In the darkness the shape of the cellar had gone; I was myself space, form, the future. I stretched my arms out and moved. What had I really wanted? I thought—We live in fantasies like wet shells: sometimes the sea comes in with the sound of the universe. Soon it would destroy us. There had been a child crying. I would go and comfort it while there was still time: I would call for a stretcher, give orders like an old general before an attack. Had she really said—We're making him jealous? The voices of spirits speak through children and Red Indians: old witches appear in the form of naked girls. I should have answered—You must not say that! When a millstone is already round your neck, how can you offend against children? I was in an unknown room, going down a passage that did not exist, towards a well of dark water. On a stage actors can act evil but they cannot act good; good comes from the heart, evil from the senses. The sound of crying came from the ground. I called—"Are you all right?" Perhaps I should go back to Cleopatra. She was an orphan and would want to be comforted. She had come in and found a happy family: of course she would want to destroy it. In her blue skirt and white socks; her mouth with the seeds scattered over it. Someone cursed and fell. The crying turned into a wail. I said "All right, we'll put the light on." At the moment before the attack you are as close as possible to the bombardment; then it lifts and you start running forward. My eldest son said "The light won't go on." I said "Put it on." There was the sound of the switch clicking. I had an impression of a shelter with the exits blocked. I tried to get my bearings. There was soft plaster on my right; the back of a chair, a curve of metal. On the other side a roll of canvas showed its age in rings. My second son shouted "Keep the light off!" I said "Someone's crying." He said "Oh, I see." I bumped into an upright beam like a ship. You staggered and patted blood. The ship was like that in which Columbus had sailed the Atlantic. With men in white shirts and grey striped trousers. You had to begin again; examine every possibility. In the dark men learned only through trial and disaster. There was a blue flash suddenly and a gasp of burning. Someone had been hit: lightning fled down the mast and disappeared into a black sea. The ship became a silhouette. My eldest son said "Good God!" I said "What was that?" Then—"Is anyone hurt?" In the blue light I had seen where the room was; the opposite from what I had expected. Space had been forced into a mirror so that if you moved your hand it had to go the wrong way. I moved quickly while memory lasted; went to the light switch and put my hand on it. There was another hand already there. I jumped. I thought—It is only doing its best. I said "Keep the light off: someone's been electrocuted." I often exaggerate these things. The switch was up. Events moved so quickly. I said "Did anyone take the bulb out?" No one answered. I was moving to where the flash had been. I thought— We must not feel guilty: children always think that we blame them but we don't. I said "Don't put the bulb back. Give it to me. Don't touch the wires. They may be dangerous." My second son said "Where are you?" My eldest said "What's happened?" I thought—He will always be asking—What's happened? I said "Has anyone got any matches?" There was a body on the floor that I kicked against. Someone had said there was a body on the floor before the flash; there couldn't have been, or else they were pretending. How does one know what is or is not pretending? My feet were in a trap. I knelt and put my hands on the body. There was a jersey: bone buttons like barley sugar. She had been wearing a black jersey. She had come over to where I had been standing and had put her head on my shoulder. The earth had opened up and ladders went down into a river. Men worked on bodies by torchlight. I touched her. Did I want it to be one of my own children? I said "Are you all right?" She did not answer. Men killed witches by electrocuting them. I said "She must have touched the connection: keep back now."

When someone is electrocuted you have to do artificial respiration. You undo the jersey and put your hands in and press the ribs and imitate the rhythm of breathing. Then you should put your mouth over hers. The floor was dirty and covered with stones. Her hair was spread out like water. One of the children must have taken the bulb out to play a trick—my eldest son, to catch her, or my second son, so the light would not go on again. Or herself, so that no one should ever discover her. But what was it she had wanted? She had whispered to me. I put my hands under her jersey. There was silk slightly greasy like skin. We had none of us thought about her. Had my son thought about her? What was it like to be in love? There was something kicking far inside; a horse, fallen down a ravine. I put my head down to hear her breathing. There was a distant drum. I said "Go upstairs and get a torch." She was on her back; her heels were on the floor; she was just shaking. My ear was against her face. Her teeth were bared. There was no breath coming through them. I thought I should force her mouth open by pressing my fingers between her teeth. Perhaps then she would bite me. I was sitting astride her and pushing at her ribs; some of her bones seemed not quite to fit, as if they would creak. One of the small children was now yelling; a wolf had come down through the forest and you had had to throw someone out of the troika. I had not wanted to hurt her. The child was running up the stairs banging off the walls like something wounded. My second son had gone up ahead to fetch the torch. I thought—She is a nun: demons live behind walls, come out when there is sacrifice. She had stopped kicking. I cried "Are you sure no one has a light?" I had to move quickly. I had to tell myself—This is real. My hands were not far enough up her ribs; over her breasts. I had to turn her over, sit on her thighs. She seemed to have gone limp. In the darkness how do you tell if a person is alive or dead? I put her cheek sideways so that it was soft against the dirt. I sat with my knees apart. Underneath her skirt there was muscle. She could not have been electrocuted because you have to be standing in water. The water in the well was twenty feet below. Anyway this was a symbol. I had my hands on her skin and was pressing her. I thought—There are various techniques. When I had put my face to hers I had smelled burning. She could have eaten toast. I thought I might pray. You become impersonal when you have a duty. I undid her clothes at the back. The child upstairs was still screaming. I thought—I cannot save everyone. Someone was coming down stairs with a candle. We never have torches in our house, being always caught by thunderstorms. In the first light I saw her hair that was like water. Love is never what you expect; imagination resides in past and future. She was not responding. There is that exhaustion when people do not move: you know you are on your own in the dusty street and the eyes from windows watching you. I was holding her with my fingers round her ribs and my thumbs squeezing her. My eldest son bumped into me; said "Is she all right?" I was on my knees in front of him, my head near the ground. I knew I should turn her over and kiss her.

When the candle reached the bottom of the cellar stairs there were lights moving round us like a demonstration of history. I had turned the girl over and held her face between my hands. I was in the hold of a ship with someone dying: the battle went on above the decks. I heard my wife's voice repeating "What's happened?" We had all been playing this game and someone had kept putting the light on. Then, in order to stop him, someone had taken the bulb out. I was kneeling above the mouth which birds might injure when they pecked it. I put my mouth against hers. I blew. There was the taste of breadcrumbs. My wife was standing over me. I thought—I can do this easier now. I wondered if I should put my tongue between her teeth so that she could breathe there. My wife held the candle. I squeezed her cheeks to get her mouth open. My eldest son said "She touched the wires." My second son seemed to be pulling a rope up out of the well. Or a wire. There was a small crack in the trap door. They sometimes did experiments in the cellar with electricity. We did not stop them, thinking that they had to do experiments somewhere. My wife said "How?" My son said "Someone took the bulb out." My mouth was still on hers. I was not sure if you sucked or just blew. It was like being beneath water; a rose with petals flaking. I thought—I should have done this earlier, then I might have saved her. But we are so ashamed. My wife said "But who took the bulb out?" I said "It doesn't matter." My wife said "Why?" I wanted to say—Our concern is not with the dead but with the living. But I could not take my mouth too long from hers. Back beneath water the bottom of the sea became clear again: I was going down with a mask on, getting breath through a pipe. My wife began going back up the stairs. I said "Ring for a doctor." The candle was on the ground throwing shadows upwards. The children were standing round. I was doing a demonstration of how to bring life into the world.

Her face was so soft. Beams held the roof of the cellar up. My second son said "All the lights in the house have fused." Our house needed re-wiring. All our lives we had waited for this; then when it came we were ready. My eldest son said "I didn't take the bulb out." My second son said "Well I didn't." We were round the camp fire; the Indians were about to attack us. Perhaps she had taken the bulb out, because she had not wanted to be seen again. She had been coming over to me. I wanted to explain—We have to live; there are always children dying. One of my sons said to the other "It must have been you!" The other said "It must have been you!" I shouted "Stop it!" Then I put my mouth back on hers. There was the empty plain and the two brothers with their piles of dead leaves. God had leaned over Adam and breathed on him. I wanted to say—Remember, you think we blame you but we don't; we blame nothing. I had to go back into the position with my back in the air bumping; love has always been a humiliation. People do it in public; God sits behind a two-way mirror. She had been an orphan and had wanted people to befriend her. She had rushed down to the sea and the seagulls had got her. They had snipped off her legs and she had bucked around on the floor. Now she was still. My wife had come back and was standing by me. She said "The doctor's coming." I was moving up and down rhythmically; you forget what you are doing and are interested only in doing it. After a time you get into a routine. I wondered if she had touched the wires wanting darkness or light. When she had whispered I had never answered her. People who are given respiration are sometimes sick; then you have to swallow it. This was a penance I would be glad of. My wife said "Is she dead?" I said "Yes." I sometimes wanted to frighten them. We were in the underground shelter with the world gone. The entrance and the exit had fallen in and the air was not expected to last much longer. Outside the earth was contaminated by fire; soon it would seep down into the well. I wanted to say—All this is quite natural; don't panic. I put my mouth back. It tasted like daisies. I wanted to say—This is how we pass our time. In the shadows a dog squats over the body of its beautiful mistress. Even when there is no hope, you go on trying. This is a good occupation. There are sometimes miracles.

When God arrived in the Argentine he had his forged papers and re-modelled nose and just the clothes he stood up in and nothing else. His clothes were white cotton trousers and striped blazer and a Panama hat. He had had his beard shaved off and wore dark glasses. He looked like someone in hiding after a train robbery.

He lay out on the beach all day and watched the girls playing volley-ball. He read his obituaries. These were mostly complimentary, since he was supposed to have been responsible for the suffering in the world. People like a good drama. Every now and then a courier would arrive with an instalment of the millions he had salted away in a Swiss bank; the couriers were dressed as nuns with jackboots underneath their habits. It was a relief for God to know he was officially dead: it had not been much of a life after all to be always on the run and undergoing plastic surgery. His surface had been liable to crack each time he smiled: he had had to be kept in a dry and even temperature. And when he had emerged there were always men waiting on the steps of the Casbah with their black silk shirts and polished shoes. They had been after him ever since the day he had been found with Adam in the garden. The police were quick on this now, jumping on unsuspecting clergymen. And once you had a record it never left you.

So God sat in his deck-chair and watched the girls on the beach with their limbs flopping out like turtles. One by one they ran down to the sea and the seagulls got them. This was one of the jobs people had blamed him for—together with love, and the population problem. But it had all been done for the sake of the family. Sometimes the volley-ball would land beside his chair and the girls would come up and look at him from under their false eyes. God had not noticed girls much before: he had always remembered the good old days with Adam. He had known they would finally get him—not the police, but the boys from over the river. They would move in with flashing *eyes and teeth like pin-tables. But now he wanted to go out with girls. He was growing old, and hoped to be respectable.*

Sometimes he told the girls of the coup that had made him famous—the meetings in the upper room, the nissen huts that were like a prison, the workmen carrying on their shoulders the sealed instructions to end the world. He had not had much to do with this himself: he had been the brains, but others had done the dirty work. He had sat at the head of the table not saying much, just listening; dressed in his white suit and dark glasses and occasionally knocking off the ash from his cigar. And the ash settled on the fields. They had told him of the creation of new worlds; the defence of freedom. They had put stockings over their faces to make themselves look like women. God had twirled the cigar round and round and said—Gentlemen, I have a better idea. He had taken an envelope out of his pocket and had thrown on the table some picture postcards of the Argentine.

Looking back on it he could see that he had had some luck; you should not entrust the administration of details to subordinates. There had been twelve of them, Jewish, from the University of Heidelberg. The man who had been supposed to betray them had slipped up, and they had almost been eradicated. The plan had been to make life so awful that man would at last become responsible; man had, after all, always worked in opposites. But there had to be some clues left to let one or two people know what was happening. This had been achieved: but only at the cost of suffering.

So now God sat among the millionaires in sharkskin uniforms and the old ladies like commercialised Christmas and he took the girls on his knee and gave them diamonds. And sometimes he read in the papers that one or another of his subordinates had been captured; was serving on an aerodrome or in a committee. He watched the roulette tables which were like green fields and beyond them the sea with the washed-up bodies. This was all that was left of his empire now: the experiment had succeeded, and anyone was free. They could come to the Argentine. It was only sometimes dull never to be treated like a criminal.

So he dreamed of going back to the place where failure had been possible.

One day the boys from over the river came to get him. They had travelled over the sea disguised as princes; came up the dusty street on a Sunday on their horses. They found him sitting in his deck-chair in the sun. They wrapped him in nylon and put electrodes in his head and heart; hung him from a

*crane with an insignia above him. But all this had happened to God before:
he knew what to do about it.*

*On the beach where he had been sitting there was a movement in the hot
sand and eggs were hatched and turtles crawled on the surface. They began
their run down to the sea. God sat in the chair where he had been sitting with
his hat tipped over his eyes and the stick between his knees and his fingers on
the diamond rings twirling them. Love was a hydra; there was no end to
betrayal. He heard the fireworks going off and the dancing in the streets and
he stood up and walked round the back of the crowd as if he were invisible. He
saw his effigy burning on top of the tower and his cardboard bones in cages.
He moved in and out of the shadows quietly appearing and disappearing like
a firefly. Then he went down to the harbour and for the first time in years
looked at the sky. He made enquiries about the next ship to his homeland.
All his luggage had arrived on the quay before him and was in packing-cases
like archaeological specimens. His face had been altered slightly back to its
terrifying look around the eyes; his passport had the stamp on it with the old
photograph neatly fitted. He wore his white suit and his broad-brimmed hat
and his black-and-white shoes from the nineteen-twenties. He paused at the
top of the gangplank and looked back at his safe world; the men with donkeys'
heads and the women insects'. He circled for a moment before disappearing
into the ship; saw a gap in the clouds, took aim, and flicked his cigar-butt
into the ocean.*

A Morning in the Life
of Intelligent People

MRS. MOSTYN LAY IN bed rigid. She had lain like this all night, while her husband had slept beside her. Now she could feel him waking. She knew that when he did, he would flutter for a moment as if he were a child and then he himself would become rigid. The night before they had quarrelled. They had said unforgivable things. Then Mr. Mostyn had gone to sleep, while Mrs. Mostyn had lain awake rigid. She had been like this for six or seven hours: she did not count the two or three she had been asleep. Mr. Mostyn had occasionally snored and she had wanted to wake him, but she had not, because she was unselfish. Also, she thought, when he woke up on his own, she could hurt him more effectively.

When Mr. Mostyn woke he remembered the night before and he was amazed at having had a good night's sleep. He could feel his wife lying rigid beside him. He knew that she would have been lying like this for hours and would be waiting for him to wake so that she could hurt him. She would let him show some tenderness towards her and then would repulse him. He rolled away and drew his legs up. He tried to work out if he should pretend to be asleep, or if by letting her hurt him quickly he could then be unselfish about it and so could hurt her more effectively later.

Mrs. Mostyn felt her husband curl up and she knew that he was awake and was wondering what to do. She knew that if he made the first move of reconciliation and she repulsed him, then he would be hurt, and all through the day he could make her feel guilty. On the other hand since she was the one who had lain awake all night it was not up to her to make the first move nor at once to accept his advances. She saw no way out. She and her husband often became paralysed in this sort of situation, lying side by side in their different attitudes like the tomb of a dead crusader and his dog.

Everything depended upon who did not make the first move. But in this war of attrition, Mrs. Mostyn knew, economic and diplomatic factors were on the side of men. It was women who were heroic and military.

For instance, there were the children whose breakfasts she had to get before school. There was the mother's help who looked on her as a model wife and whose good opinion she needed. Faced by the appearance of either of these forces she would have to make a move and then Mr. Mostyn would defeat her. On the other hand there was his need not to be late at the office.

Mr. Mostyn calculated that if he did not shave and pretended to be too hurt to have any breakfast then he could stay in bed ten minutes longer than usual by which time the children would be coming down and would be making demands on Mrs. Mostyn. Then, if she responded to the children, he would have outlasted her in bed; and if she did not respond, he could jump out of bed and make a fuss of the children and thus imply that she was a bad mother. Also he could dash out of the house without any breakfast and ask his secretary, who was pretty, to feed him. Or he could cook a special breakfast himself downstairs. In both cases he would be implying that his wife did not look after him.

Mrs. Mostyn heard her children moving about upstairs and realised that time was running out; she would soon have to move or lay herself open to the attack of being a bad mother. She thought how unfair it would be to be defeated simply because she was a woman; and looked around for a special weapon from her woman's armoury. She might just have time, she thought, to lean over and be tender to her husband and then, when he was vulnerable, to withdraw from him. By this means, since she would have made the first move and been unselfish, she would not need to feel guilty. What she would be doing would be simply to make up their quarrel. So she put her arm round Mr. Mostyn.

Mrs. Mostyn was a very beautiful girl of twenty-eight who had once tried to be an actress. Her career had been interrupted by her marriage. She had short black hair and the ability to make her eyes go liquid. She had long thin legs and a thin body; breasts and arms gentle as a wood-carving. She wore a transparent nightdress to her thighs.

Mr. Mostyn felt her arm coming across him and had an experience as if he were about to be tortured. This sort of thing had happened before; their love-making was a change of battle rather than an alleviation of it. But, as always, he felt desire; and with this the impression that he might after all be immune—that spirits might fight for him as they had done for crusaders. He thought that he might be able to roll over on top of her, take what he wanted, and then leave her without being vulnerable. So he put his hands round her hips and buried his head on her.

She immediately became inactive. She put aside her plan to withdraw and waited to see if he would force her to make love. She did not know if she wanted this—she sometimes thought she did—because then she could remain aloof and make out he was brutal; also it might really give her pleasure. But she did not know if she wanted pleasure. This might make her vulnerable. But in any case she knew he would not force her, since they were both people dedicated to non-violence. Still, she could hint that it was a fault that he did not. Though if he did, she knew she would leave him. She became confused. She pulled his head from her breast and gazed at him with eyes that were like a waterfall.

Mr. Mostyn, inundated, felt a battle lost but still believed he could win the war. His masculine weapon was endurance; also a mind that could analyse more profoundly their complex motives. He began caressing her; but from a distance, as if she were a puppet. This was one of his pleasures. He put a hand down and found her legs tight shut: looked up and smiled at her brightly. He knew she might want him to take her by force, but then he would expose himself: also, he did not know if he could. He would be safer, as always, in martyrdom. It was she who would then appear to be frigid, and would feel guilty. So he let his hand lie on her and gazed tragically at the bedspread.

Mrs. Mostyn felt him drifting away, so opened her legs slightly. She did not want him to go because then he would seem martyred, and she would feel guilty. As soon as she opened her legs he rolled on top of her and entered her.

Both Mr. and Mrs. Mostyn had believed that in sexuality as in everything there should be nothing outside man's intelligence and control and that the aim of sexuality was to produce simultaneous orgasms. Accordingly they had worked out a system whereby they should let each other know of their progress—a language like that of the deaf and dumb, since speech was unsensual. Mr. Mostyn pulled back his head and raised his eyebrows; he saw his wife's eyes closed and beginning to tremble. His own desire grew. He became still. He wondered what she had done about her diaphragm. He should have asked her before they had begun. She usually put the thing in at night, but last night they had not been on speaking terms. He felt angry because he could not now speak to her, and she had not made it clear to him. Neither of them wanted a baby, but she might risk it just to spite him. Her fingers were on the small of his back pressing him. He felt his own orgasm coming. He wanted to cry out that he loved her. He had a vision of strangling her. He decided he would have to withdraw. He became split by emotions which seemed to be tearing him apart like horses. He bared his teeth and shuddered. He wanted to shout against God, like an unbelieving victim.

Mrs. Mostyn had earlier put her arms around him in order to tell him that she was forgiving him. She wondered if he knew she had put in her diaphragm. She had done this the night before because, in spite of their quarrel, she always did what he wanted. But it was too late to tell him now. She also wanted to see if he loved her enough to risk having another baby. Neither he nor she wanted a baby, but if he risked it it would prove he loved her. Her mind was brought back by the pressure of her orgasm starting. Always at these moments something beyond her seemed to take over; she had wanted to attract him and then withdraw in order to remain inviolate; but now what involved her was overwhelming. She clung in earnest; opened her mouth; dug her fingernails into his back. For the moment she loved him; his long spine like mountains. She thought he had finally given himself to her. She said to herself—I will change. Then he withdrew. She could not believe this: she went after him with her hands crying. He was hanging like someone half-way down a rock-face; she could not reach him, his teeth were bared, she felt herself falling. The one small tree on the cliff had broken; she was still holding it, her love, but was tumbling over and over. She would hit the rocks on the bottom. She felt her life lost irrevocably. A body sprawled on the shingle.

She began to cry.

He said "What's the matter?"

He was looking at her as if through a microscope.

At the bottom of the cliff she wanted to stay dead. She could not climb the ice again.

Mr. Mostyn remembered he had wanted to hurt her. He now felt remorse. His own life had rushed out like a bucket into a gutter. He lay on top of her and shivered. They had once loved each other so much. What had gone wrong?

He said "You gave me the sign."

When she cried her shoulders rose and fell attractively.

He said "Darling, do look at me!"

He thought that now might be the time to say how much he loved her; that he would never again fight, never withdraw; that they would have more children and he would cherish her for ever.

She suddenly gave him a violent push in the ribs.

He felt as if a spear had gone through him.

She said "The children."

There was the sound of footsteps coming downstairs. He wanted to remain on top to show his power simply by weight. He could pretend that her pushing him had made him paralysed. But if the children arrived and found him on top of her then she could make him feel guilty—both he and she believed in Freud. Whereas if he jumped off her and walked stiffly to and fro he might still make it seem that she had done him some injury.

When the children arrived they saw him in his nightshirt—he wore a nightshirt because this was physical—and they rushed straight past him and jumped on the bed. He thought how unfair it was being a man, since although he was the more attentive parent—he was sure of this—the children still went past him and showered love on their mother. He reached for his trousers standing bandy-legged as if in pain. He did have a pain, where he had pressed on her hip-bone. The eldest child was a small girl with dark curly hair; the younger, also a girl, was curiously unlike either of its parents, having straight fair hair and a round face. Their mother enfolded them and her voice became gentle as plucked strings. Mr. Mostyn pulled on his trousers: he noted that his wife never used that tone of voice to him. Also when she was with the children she became uncharacteristically physically abandoned: now, as she leaned over to hug them, her nightdress pulled up so that he could see her behind. He wanted to tell her that to do this was bad for the children; but he could not do this in front of them. She was so sensual. He thought that he might say later—Do you have to use the children?—and then smile enigmatically, so that she would not know what he was talking about. Or he could explain that her demonstrations of affection were nothing but her own narcissism.

Mrs. Mostyn climbed out of bed and put on a dressing-gown. The children had clambered all over her and had pulled her hair; it was always the mother, she thought, who had landed with their emotional demands while the father could go quietly to the bathroom. She tried to push the children back upstairs; they ought to be being dressed by the mother's help. But girls were so hopeless with children nowadays, they seemed to have no control. It was true that she and her husband had told the girl that they did not want any strictness, but there must be some way of doing things without all this rushing about in the mornings.

Mr. Mostyn was in the bathroom shaving. He tried to remember the unforgivable things that had been said the night before. They had been having a purely abstract discussion about the different roles played in the psyche by intellect, feeling, intuition and sensation. He had suggested certain preponderances in her—that is, that were likely to be found in the female. He had suggested that women were concerned with intuition rather than sensation; and to this she had taken violent exception. She had thought he was casting a slur on her sexuality. In a sense he had been; but there was no reason for her to have thought this. It was a man's job after all to analyse and clarify; and it was typical of a woman to take this personally. In retaliation she had attacked him for being an intellectual, on which of course he prided himself, but which in this case she was using as a slur on his sexuality. Whereas it was after all he who always wanted to make love, so how could he be an intellectual? Mr. Mostyn looked into the mirror and saw his bright face with dark curly hair at the sides going silver; his spectacles streaked with shaving soap.

The brush rolled off the shelf and fell with a plop into the water. There were some mornings when even physical objects seemed possessed; as if there could be evil spirits.

He noticed in the cupboard above the washbasin the round plastic case in which his wife kept her diaphragm. The case was empty. He realised that she must have had the thing in all the time. He felt a sudden rush of tenderness; she must have been ready for him to make love even when they had quarrelled. He smiled. He thought that now he could forgive her. It was up to the man, after all, to use his powers of rationality: he had areas of free will which were unavailable to the woman. And she was so young; in many ways still a child. He thought of her soft body; her eyes like waterfalls.

He thus decided that when he came down to the kitchen he would be cheerful and would talk to the children and would be kind to the mother's help. His wife would have cooked him eggs and he would tell her how delicious they were. There was a shirt he had asked her to wash, and he would thank her. He would take her in his arms and tell her what a good wife she was.

When Mrs. Mostyn arrived downstairs she found a pile of dirty plates from the night before when they had quarrelled. She could not remember what the argument had been about, but she knew that she had accused him of not being sensual. She noticed his shirt lying dirty on top of the refrigerator; she had promised to wash it. She was suddenly sad. She knew that she was not a good wife; she had these moods; he should have married someone more compliant. And it was true that it was she who often did not like his making love. She thought that she would wash his shirt at once and have it ready by the time he came down. She sprinkled some soap powder in the sink and put the shirt in. They had been together such a long time now; ten years; it would be a pity to break it. At the beginning they had really been in love; she had admired his energy and his loneliness. She had had a small part in a play about the Greeks: he had said he had never before met an actress. He had asked her to marry him almost at once. She determined to make it up to him. She noticed the milk heating on the stove: butter bubbled in the frying pan. She looked round for clean cups and plates. There were none, because of the night before. She would have to take his shirt out of the sink in order to wash the crockery. She screwed the shirt up and laid it back on the refrigerator.

When Mr. Mostyn came down he noticed his shirt where it had been the night before but it seemed dirtier than ever, she must have screwed it up and deliberately thrown it on the refrigerator. He decided that he would stay out late at work that evening; would get in touch with a girl he had met recently and perhaps ask her out to dinner. In the meantime it was essential for him to remain calm and loving. Otherwise his wife could hurt him. He might pick up his shirt with finger and thumb and drop it into the waste-bin. Or he could wait till she asked him if he wanted an egg and then say—Oh no thank you—and boil an egg himself. But it was first necessary for her to ask him—Do you want an egg? Till then he would stand and whenever she came near him would move out of her way with exaggerated courtesy.

Mrs. Mostyn found her husband suddenly in every corner of the kitchen waiting until she almost bumped into him and then smiling as if demented. And this was just as she was trying to get the eldest child off to school. She had been about to ask her husband if he wanted an egg; but now she had to take up so much time circling the table to avoid him. She knew he had seen his shirt and was disappointed it was not washed; but this was unreasonable, because it would in any case have been too wet to wear this morning. She decided to ignore him.

Both Mr. and Mrs. Mostyn heard the children coming down the stairs, this time together with the mother's help. They were about to be trapped once more by their reputation for unfailing courtesy. Mr. Mostyn looked round for something unpleasant to say quick: if he got the timing right, she would not be able to answer him. There were the breakfasts for the children—they could be being given too much or not enough—but it was not clear what she was giving them. He sat and hummed. He did not like the way she turned her feet in when she walked. She had not brushed her hair. She put a cup of milk on either side of him. The children were almost at the door. He said, simply, "You are a bitch," in a pleasant voice, and felt better. He had never said such a thing before. He had at last been decisive. This was a masculine prerogative. He immediately regretted it.

Mrs. Mostyn could not believe it. The children had come in so she could not answer him. She did not want to anyway. She would pack a suitcase and leave that morning. She could not go to her family because her parents lived in Australia. And her bank account was overdrawn. But she could go to Rome, where there was a producer who had said he could always get a part for her. Her husband was lucky that she was such a gentle person, or else she might have done violence to him. To call her a bitch was unforgivable; much worse than violence. She realised she was on the point of tears: might have to go upstairs and pretend to commit suicide. She would lie on the bed with her hands folded and her skin the texture of lillies; people would stand at the foot and stare at her. They would blame her husband for her death and none of his friends would speak to him. The mother's help would leave, and call for police protection for the children. It would be in the papers. There was a tear rolling down her cheek. But she must at all costs prevent the mother's help from seeing this. They had always kept up appearances. On the other hand, it might be better if it was seen. Then he would be shamed publicly.

The mother's help, Janet, whom Mr. and Mrs. Mostyn imagined thought of them as a model couple, in fact did not think of them much at all, since she was a girl of nineteen and Mr. Mostyn was thirty-nine and Mrs. Mostyn twenty-eight. It seemed to her that as a married couple they were always acting and pretending to be cheerful whereas in reality they were getting on rather badly. Janet certainly did not want to think of marriage herself just yet; besides, she was having trouble with her own boy friend. When she had come into the kitchen the morning had seemed much the same as any other: Mrs. Mostyn had had her back to the room and was reading from a cookery book, Mr. Mostyn held a knife and fork above an empty plate and was smiling. Janet had said "Morning all!" and Mr. Mostyn had said "Morning!" She had gone to get her packet of slimming biscuits.

Mr. Mostyn saw that his wife was crying. This was unforgivable, because it was shaming him publicly where he could not hit back. All the unforgivable things of the night before had been forgivable but now she had trapped him. So he had to make it up to her. He had after all once loved her and now she was crying. He felt himself going backwards and forwards across the table like a ping-pong ball. If the mother's help had not been there, he could have gone round the table and kissed her.

Why did she want a mother's help? other wives didn't. He would now be late for the office. Someone had put the daily paper on top of the marmalade. He looked for something to wipe his hand on. He jumped up. He was going to kiss Mrs. Mostyn. He might still hit her.

He realised he was wiping his hands on his half-washed shirt.

He flung it into a corner.

Mrs. Mostyn had seen him coming round the table and did not know if he was going to hit or kiss her. Then he seemed to go berserk, and was throwing things about the kitchen. She had been trying to transfer an egg from the frying-pan on to a plate, but she had to defend herself and the egg fell on to a newspaper. Mr. Mostyn put his hands in his hair and his face went red: he was like a judge, she thought, beneath a wig. Then he dashed out of the room, knocking a chair over.

Mrs. Mostyn went to her children and held their heads close. Her face became sharp; her nose delicate above a lengthening upper lip.

Mr. Mostyn had run out of the house to go to the office. He jumped into his car and gripped the steering wheel. In front and behind him were cars parked very close: he could only move out by banging them. He turned the key and the engine revolved sluggishly. He wanted to butt his head through the windscreen. He jumped out and ran to the car in front and tried to push it: it rose up on its springs like a donkey. He pulled at the handle of the door which was locked. He went back to his own car and started it and rammed the car in front: the bumper of his car got wedged. He went into reverse and the car in front came with him: he rammed the car behind. A whole row of cars seemed to go banging backwards and forwards as if in an orgy.

Mr. Mostyn switched the engine off. He thought he might take his wife by the throat and bang the car with her.

A taxi went past with its flag up and a strap round the flag. Mr. Mostyn jumped out and chased the taxi. There was a main road where the taxi stopped. He caught it and stood with one hand on the door: gave the address of his office. The taxi-driver pointed to the strap around the flag. Mr. Mostyn opened the door and climbed in. The driver got out and came round and said "Get out." Mr. Mostyn said "This taxi is not occupied." The driver got hold of Mr. Mostyn's arm and pulled. Mr. Mostyn pulled. They emerged on the road holding on to each other and waltzing. Cars in front and behind hooted.

Mrs. Mostyn had gone upstairs and had taken down a suitcase. She opened drawers and looked at her clothes. She was going to Rome, where there was this producer. She would need trousers and summer clothes and her dress with the frilly sleeves. This was at the cleaners. She sat on the bed. If she spent tonight with a friend, she could pick up the dress and go tomorrow. In Rome there would be a room hung with fish-netting and spears: a bearded man playing folk songs. There would be women with hair like woodshavings, couples reclining on cushions and smoking. She noticed on the mantelpiece some drawings by her children. They were of square houses with blue swirls coming out of chimneys and windows like crosses. Beside the bed was a bottle of sleeping pills. She had an appointment with the hairdresser that morning. The children were going to the dentist tomorrow. Outside, cars hooted. When Mr. Mostyn came home he might find that she had murdered her children.

She put her head in her hands. She had not felt like this for years. She wanted someone to help her.

She went to a corner of the room where there was a cupboard. Standing on a chair, she reached to the top and pulled down a hatbox. Opening it she felt behind loose lining and pulled out a bundle of letters. They were on faded paper with the leaves stuck together like wood. She unfolded a letter and began to read it. The writing was tall and spidery.

> I have a terrible compulsion to do as much hurt as I can while I can. I think this is what love is, an attempt to get what you can't and then to destroy it. There's a shred of sanity left which tells you what's happening; but this doesn't help, it only means you can't escape it.
>
> So I want to tell you how much I love you; and that whatever has happened, you mustn't blame yourself. Remember—it has all been worth while.
>
> It isn't our fault that everything works in opposites.

She sat for a while with the letter in her hand: then picked up the receiver of the telephone.

She dialled the number of her husband's office.

Mr. Mostyn had emerged from the taxi and handed the driver a ten-shilling note. The driver waved his hand at it. Mr. Mostyn smiled; leaned forwards and stuffed it in the driver's pocket. The driver saluted. Mr. Mostyn ran lightly across the pavement. He held a handkerchief to his mouth which had been bleeding. He paused in the doorway of his office; looked to the left and right. Then he went next door into a post office. At a counter he said "Any letters? My name's Harris." A clerk looked in a cupboard with pigeon-holes. Mr. Mostyn drummed his fingers. The clerk came back with a letter addressed to J. W. Harris, Esq. Mr. Mostyn took it. When he was in the street he opened the letter, which was typewritten, and read—

My darling,
Imagine a room high in a building overlooking the Borghese gardens, a wide window with red blinds open on to lovers on the grass, a high lovely room with gold and blue cherub ceilings, gold painted doors and mirrors, heavy velvet curtains and a tapestry round the bed, a gilded double bed with an uncomfortable mattress and a thin bumpy bolster, a girl in tatty pyjamas sitting up in it, not happy, not unhappy, typing to someone she fancies.

Mr. Mostyn put the letter back in its envelope; went into a call-box and dialled the number of his home. The number was engaged. He wondered whom his wife could be telephoning.

When he was in his office his secretary brought him a sheaf of papers and laid them on his desk. His secretary was a young girl with a very short skirt and a patent leather belt across her behind. Mr. Mostyn opened the file of papers. There were photographs cut into shapes and pasted on to huge sheets of white cardboard; columns of print down the sides and circles with handwriting in red pencil. One of the photographs was of a young man with white hair sitting on a lavatory: his knees were raised and he was naked, and he had two church collection bags strapped against his chest. A caption underneath said *Mervyn Harper by Charleton Dodd*. Mr. Mostyn read the column at the side. The telephone rang; he picked it up and said "Yes?" and then "Ten thousand in Germany." He began writing in thick and neat handwriting.

Mrs. Mostyn had dressed and gone out. She thought she would take a short walk before either getting her tickets for Rome or going to the hairdresser. It was a fine day. When she had telephoned her husband he had not yet arrived. She found herself walking close to the British Museum. She went in. She had not done this for some time, although she lived so close to it. She went through the main doors and turned left towards the freizes from the Parthenon. There was a maze of cardboard screens and then the long room with the white light. The sculptures were facing inwards because this was a museum: in their original positions facing out no one had seen them. Everywhere were men and horses fighting; their heads and necks pressed together as if in love. The men and horses were sometimes centaurs. There were bodies without heads; hooves kicking where thighs had been. The torsos were soft; she wanted to touch them. Notices told her not to. Penises had been broken off leaving holes. There were lines above hipbones like lyres. Once, when he had been lying with her, he had said—You make love like war; like horses on the Parthenon.

In one of the rooms she had come through there had been colossal Egyptian statues of gods sitting smiling.

He had said—There was a moment when the world stopped smiling.

In the long white room a negro had come up and was standing by her.

He had said—Horses and men became inextricable.

The negro spoke to her.

She said to the negro "Yes, isn't it marvellous!"

She thought—They always come and talk to you.

He had said—Then men and horses separate again.

The negro had small pink eyes and a mouth like a sofa.

Mr. Mostyn sat at his desk looking at a photograph of a small thin man bound hand and foot who was being held up by bayonets. The men with bayonets wore American-type uniforms. The man's wrists were pulled up behind him so that he was pressed forwards and bent. The scene was a jungle with thatched huts and an army truck. The man was naked. He was photographed from the back, so that attention was focussed upon his legs and thighs. Mr. Mostyn noticed after a time that the man had no head.

Mr. Mostyn's secretary came in, and he said "Try to get Mrs. Mostyn."

He looked out of the window and saw the narrow and busy street. He thought he might take his wife and their younger child on a holiday soon to Italy. Their elder child, at school, could stay with friends. He noticed his wife coming along the street escorted by a policeman. She was wearing her pale blue leather coat and was carrying a leopardskin handbag. Her black hair was like a helmet. The policeman was walking just behind her. Mr. Mostyn's heart began to thump; he backed away and stood out of sight beside the window. After a time a buzzer went and his secretary's voice said "Mr. Mostyn, your wife is here." He said "Show her in." He found himself sitting behind his desk in the position of a prisoner; his fingertips on the hard surface and his mouth too anxious to smile.

His wife had put heavy make-up on around her eyes. She came across to his desk and leaned with one hip against it. He said "What is it?"

She said "I'm sorry."

He said "What about?"

She went to the wall and stood with her back to it. She held her hands by her side and gazed at him.

He said "We've absolutely got to stop behaving like this."

She said "Yes." She made her eyes go liquid.

He said "You take things so personally."

He began putting the photographs back in their file.

He said "What were you doing with that policeman?"

He went to the door of his office and locked it. He turned off a switch on the speaker to his secretary. He stood in front of her and started taking her coat off. She watched his fingers as he undid the buttons. Her face was interested, as if her body were being garlanded.

She said "A man kept following me."

He said "Did you get rid of him?"

She said "Yes."

When she was half undressed he took her by the shoulders and led her to a chair. He said "You are so beautiful."

He knelt and pressed his face against her. It was as if he were going beneath water. She looked down. Her face was like the prow of a ship.

He said "At least, we still feel something."

Later he went to his desk and took the photographs out. He looked at them.

He said "Do you ever think of him now?"

She said "Who?" And then—"Yes, I sometimes think of him."

Nietzsche is a hero of this time, who declared that God was dead and imagined himself to be God, who preached the exuberance of man and ended at the mercy of women, who saw the necessity of war and was sick at the sight of it. He knew with sanity that you cannot be sane either with illusion or without it and so you go mad. And so he did. It was he who bought God's tickets for the Argentine; standing on the station platform with the handkerchief round his head; then going back to take the rap for twenty or thirty years, knowing everything but not talking, pacing in his upstairs room and a mother and a sister listening below and all the worshippers taking down his footsteps. He saw that God had to die and that man would go mad if God died; but man had always been mad so what was the difference. At least God would be safe in the Argentine. So Nietzsche signed the confession and said that he had murdered God and the police took it all down and did not believe him. It is a habit of criminals after all to make false confessions.

What had made Nietzsche say that he had murdered God was, the police alleged, a visit he had made to a brothel in Bonn twenty years earlier. There he had caught syphilis, did not marry, and went insane. This was one solution to the population problem. But it still would not have been easy for a young man brought up by a mother and a sister to climb those stairs and find the cashier in tight black underwear and all the little balls and cylinders whizzing above her. There is the small hole you speak through; she puts the money in a drawer and presses a button and something very small comes undone; you look down and can't see any difference. She says—What is it, boys, did it get lost in the wash? You have to be something of a hero. When Nietzsche went up the stairs perhaps life was better in those days—perhaps there was one of those German blondes in straps like a horse being put aboard a steamer. But still there would be the ring of the till, the romance of communications and industry. Young men were happier even then lying in the long grass and waiting for the hooks of young girls to come down; God in thigh-length boots like a woman. But this was no answer to the population problem; worms propagate in geometrical progression. All the young men still had to line up on the platform.

When Nietzsche was young he joined the army as a nurse because he gloried in war and wanted to stop men killing. He looked after the wounded for three days and then became ill, because wounds were so unpleasant. What is glorious in war is all the cavalry in their tight leather arses; their thighs indistinguishable from women. And when you sit underneath them they kick their legs up in a row and there is that glimpse of darkness. When Nietzsche fell in love he sent his best friends to propose to the girls so his best friends tried to marry them. When you fall in love you don't want to get what you want, or how could you be in love with it? You wait in the garden and get your best friend to betray you.

I once went to Turin to see the place where Nietzsche went mad, travelling through battlefields where I myself had once fought, the farmhouses like a children's playground and ridges falling like torn paper. We had all been young then and had not wanted to die; had jumped up as one man and stood on the platform. In Turin it was as if we were on leave again with the sun on the stones and palaces like pre-history. The point of war is that it is so wonderful when you get out; you stop banging your head against the wall and the jailer brings you porridge. Nietzsche came to Turin one winter after he had dreamed that God would not be inflicting pain on the world any more; that man would have to fetch this for himself if he wanted it. Nietzsche took lodgings in Via Carlo Alberto next to the square where there were statues of heroes of the Risorgimento, who had fought and died for human freedom. What Nietzsche had said was not that man had to surpass himself but just that if he did not then everything was over. So Nietzsche went into the square one day and saw an old cabhorse being beaten by a driver. He knew that all battles were in the mind; that war was useless. So he went to the cabhorse and put his arms round its neck and cried there. The cabhorse perhaps had one of those straw hats over its ears like a T.V. comic. They took Nietzsche away and handed him over to his mother and his sister. They rewrote some of his books to say the opposite of what he had intended; and downstairs listened to his footsteps. Sometimes when people came to visit him they had the impression that he was not really mad, but only pretending.

There is now a plaque on the spot where Nietzsche went mad, saying how he had triumphed in the fulness of the human spirit. His house is an antique shop in which there are Chinamen running lances through the throats of children. In the square is the statue of the horse with an upraised leg; a line of soldiers leaning against their bayonets. In a palace is the museum of the Risorgimento; a monument to the furious will of soldiers. Opposite is a modern art gallery with flowers made of green sponge-rubber: behind, a courtyard of ancient balconies and bookshops. On the plaque is Nietzsche's face with his huge moustache like a scrubbing brush: he looks out on the world he so much loved and hated. He had the illusion that you could do away with every illusion and so he did. Perhaps he had worked it all out twenty years earlier when he went to the brothel at Bonn—that a life's work can only be completed if from the beginning you know what to do about it. Then people can say that you go mad through the triumph of the human spirit. And they can still dream of their armour and drawn swords while you stand by the bonfire and watch your effigy burning. And when they look into your eyes they will have the impression that you are not mad but only pretending; that somewhere behind you too are the brassbands and banners of angels.

A Hummingbird

THE TOWN OF TAMANET was destroyed by an earthquake a few
years ago and now there is wasteland along what used to be
a promenade, the ground curving whitely over stones and
sand-dunes to a fringe of palm-trees and the sea. The air is thick like
traces of grease left on a wind-screen. The Atlantic comes in in high
rollers and the sand goes down steeply and where they meet forms a
trough where the surf seems to be feeding. On the beach are a few
Europeans from the houses rebuilt by the harbour and some Arab men
in white robes and Arab girls in bathing dresses with bare legs and arms.
This is the new Africa, with the old largely eradicated.

I was on holiday with my wife travelling in a small hired car like
a violent toy. The road to Tamanet crosses the Atlas mountains over
a pass high and rocky and descends in layers to a hot plain with fruit
trees. I had not intended to stay in Tamanet because the earthquake
had made news round the world three years ago and my wife is affected
by this sort of thing: she had frowned over the newspapers then as if
struck for the first time by death and suffering. She had said—Isn't it
awful about Tamanet!—as if this were some personal loss: and I had
answered, as I usually do—There's this sort of suffering everywhere;
why do you pick on Tamanet?

We have these conversations which are those between husbands
and wives and are like the sand and sea washing each other.

So coming down through the fruit trees and into the warm wind
I said we would drive through Tamanet and go on to a town in the
south, though it was dark and we were tired from so much driving. I

had wanted to stay in Tamanet myself because I had never before seen a town destroyed by an earthquake. I am interested in anything odd, as well as beautiful. The road was narrow with crumbling edges: boys were hitting donkeys into the bushes. When I had said we would go on my wife had not answered. I said "Are you all right?" She said "I do feel a bit ill." I said "Then we'll have to stay in Tamanet." When I am on holiday I usually want to press on, as if to fall behind on schedule might lead to some disaster.

She said "No, I know you want to get on."

I said "It's I who've always wanted to stay in Tamanet!"

She said "All right, we'll stay then."

My wife usually wants to find somewhere that she likes and to settle, to get to know the place and the people.

I said "But it's you who didn't want to stay in Tamanet, because of the earthquake."

She said "I'll do what you like."

I said "I want to do what you like."

When we have these conversations which are husbands and wives in troughs it is because we are tired, we have not been looking for the enemy. The enemy is the desire to fight in order to be martyred and to get comfort from this. Usually we spot it from a distance and defend ourselves by separating till the raid is over. But this is impossible in a foreign country in a small car being shaken like dice.

My wife has a gentle face with short brown hair. When she is feeling ill or car-sick she becomes white as moonlight.

I said "Of course we'll stay in Tamanet then: it's just that I rather wanted to see these places in the south."

I know when I am doing this. We have been married for eighteen years.

My wife does not like my driving fast; so sometimes I drive fast for a moment and then slow violently and say—Sorry!

I said "Sorry. This is because we're tired."

The guidebook said that there was one hotel in Tamanet, an encampment of prefabricated buildings that would not hurt in another earthquake, they would flutter down like a card-house. The guidebook said that the food was good: the hotel was run by a Frenchman.

The town of Tamanet had no houses any more, there were streets with street-lamps in an area of foundations. Everything on top seemed to have been taken away to a museum. A crossing had green and red lights and nothing round it. A smell of dead fish came from a factory.

A tidal wave had come in with the earthquake. There had been a wall of water in which fishes had been seen swimming vertically.

Down by the sea were the prefabs like beach huts. We stopped the car on the sand-dunes and seemed marooned. The hot wind was like a bath; you wound up the windows to keep cool.

I said "Why did you really want to stay in Tamanet?"

When I turned on the light to look at a map I caught sight of my face in the convex driving mirror and I was all skin and forehead and no hair; a protuberance like an eye at the bottom of the ocean.

Dinner that night was a five-course meal with wine. We sat with polished glasses and white napkins and beyond the windows the sea ran like ghosts. Large whales sometimes got washed up on this shore having lost their way in the mist. My wife and I touched legs under the table. We can still do this after eighteen years.

I said "We can't help this afternoon. If we didn't have times like that, it wouldn't be so nice in the evenings."

She said "How do you think the children are?"

We had come on this holiday after a more than usually strenuous Christmas. We have three boys, one of fifteen and one of twelve and one of eight. We can get away during term-time because we send them to boarding school. We feel guilty about this; but excuse it by saying that they grow up better on their own. They probably do. We had seen them off on station platforms with their faces packed three deep in the carriage windows as if they were going off to war.

My wife said "You go on to the south tomorrow. I'll be all right here on my own."

I said "You can't stay here."

I had wanted to go to the south alone, because when travelling in Arab countries there is always an impression of an adventure round some corner, an image of a black-eyed girl with her face half covered in a doorway.

She said "Why not?"

I said "You wouldn't be safe."

She said "You know you want to go on on your own."

After dinner we walked along the beach. We held hands and our feet sank in the soft surface. In the dark my wife's hair falls smoothly and makes her look young again. The sand-dunes went up on one side into a small ridge topped by eucalyptus trees which waved like demented arms. On the other side the sea shot out its tentacles; dragged the land back like a maiden.

I said "All right, I'll go on. I'll be away two nights. That'll mean driving about four hundred miles. You will be careful, won't you? Don't go too far from the hotel. And stay where there are lots of people, like the beach. Wear a hat or something and put your hair up. And keep your arms covered."

I was not really worried. People only get into trouble if they want to. We make gestures in order that they may not want; and perhaps to excuse a lack of feeling.

She said "There was a marvellous Arab in front of the hotel."

That night I lay awake while the sea ran and the moon made shapes like children's faces against the window. We did not make love. I wondered if I might really meet an Arab girl in the south; if we would go through a doorway to an inner courtyard with fountains. I thought— Desires are chained to their opposites as if to a rock; to be suffered or wait for the vultures.

In the morning we said goodbye as if I were off on some exploration. My wife stood on the pavement above the sand-dunes and raised one hand in benediction. She said "You will be good?" I said "Of course I'll be good!" I ran down the path towards the car. The eucalyptus trees overhead were machine-guns.

My journey took three days. I saw the camel-markets of the south, the men in dark robes with eyes like swords, the houses painted on the sides of rocks and the darkness in half-opened doorways. One night in a town with mud walls in a maze I came across an Arab wedding-feast. There was a crowd on tip-toe. I was beckoned from the door. I looked behind me, not believing this. But I was invited in as an honoured guest, because a stranger. I sat cross-legged among a row of chiefs; ate rice and yellow meat from bowls in a courtyard with fountains. I watched dancers with women's bodies and bright boys' faces from a tribe of gypsies, trained as prostitutes. I nodded in time to the music; dipped my fingers and was spattered with rosewater. I thought—This is why men build empires and go out into the desert; to get away from their loved ones and comfortable homes and to sit on floors with Arab chiefs and watch prostitutes.

Driving back along the coast the next night there was above me the signalling of eucalyptus trees. I thought—Ours is a good marriage because we can be together and yet separate like this; are not tied, which is the modern infancy. We are close by being apart. We are right to risk this, because there is no life without opposites.

In Tamanet there were the streets with no houses again. Thousands of bodies had been bulldozed under the rubble.

At the hotel there was the reception-bungalow and the Frenchman behind his desk like a football coach. He had a bald head and a large green eye-shade. There was the dining room by the sea where we had sat three nights ago like a honeymoon couple. We had said—We do love one other. My wife was not there. The bedroom bungalows were at some distance from the dining room down neat paths like an army barracks. The ghosts in the sea were still running. There was a light in our bedroom. I thought—We will make love tonight. For a moment I had been anxious.

The day we had arrived, also having dinner had been a party at another table with a man at the head in the uniform of a soldier or policeman. He had had a brown tunic and a brown face and a thin moustache like boot polish; a thick belt tight at the waist but which left the rest of him sagging like something in an attic. The people with him had watched him and flattered him. He had watched us; and had once asked the Frenchman who we were. Later, the Frenchman had told us he was the local chief of police.

The Frenchman had raised one eyebrow and had added—One must keep friendly! He had drawn a finger across his throat.

My wife had said—Vraiment?

My wife is sometimes drawn to danger like a lonely person to drunkenness.

When I opened the door of our room she was standing between the two beds facing the wall and smoking. She does not usually smoke.

There was nothing on the wall, it was the end wall of the bungalow and was slatted like a boat. Beyond it was the sea. When she heard me she looked up and did not smile. She did nothing. Behind her was a table with papers on which she had been writing. My wife writes stories for children's magazines. I looked behind me and felt guilty. I was someone still hunting after the quarry has gone to earth.

I said "Aren't you pleased to see me?"

She took some time to put out her cigarette; inside a tumbler, which went black with smoke.

I said "What's happened?"

She came round the bed and stood close to me. I saw she was frightened.

I said "You're joking!"

She said "No."

I took her by the arms. We live so much with our cleverness now that there is almost an excitement with fear.

She said "You won't be angry?"

I said "No."

I thought—I will try to be.

She said "I must tell you."

Still holding her, I took her to the bed and sat down and twisted my face up. I thought—I'm pretending.

I said "Quick."

She said "Something happened."

I thought—This is too ordinary; like a telegram announcing a death.

She pulled at my arm. I wanted to say—I suppose you met a man on the beach?

She said "I went for a walk and there was this man on the beach."

I said "What man?"

She said "Nothing awful."

I said "Did you—"

"What?"

"Oh for goodness sake!"

There was this coldness coming up from my stomach, heart. I thought—Is she in love with him?

She said "I didn't—"

"He assaulted you?"

"In a way."

"What way?"

She said, "I mean, it wasn't like that."

I jumped off the bed and stood with my teeth clenched. I thought— This is real. Isn't it?

She said "Oh I knew I shouldn't have told you!"

I said "Of course you should have told me!"

I thought—I do feel jealousy: am I gratified?

"Well, I went out for a walk on the evening of the day you left. There was this man on the beach. He was trying to be nice. Really. He didn't come up for a time. Then he told me it was dangerous to bathe."

When my wife talks she sometimes pauses at places which make no sense, like a cripple on a gangplank.

I said "Were you going to bathe?"

"No."

I thought—I can bear anything except her making it ridiculous.

I said "You did the whole thing?"

She said "Of course not!"

I sat down. I thought—Well that's all right then.

Just before, I had had the feeling that I might have had to kill someone.

I said "What did you do?"

"Just talked."

"What about?"

"Mohammedanism."

"Mohammedanism!"

"He asked me if I would have tea with him at his house the next day. But I said No."

"And you didn't?"

"No."

"Was this before or after he assaulted you?"

She said "Oh I knew you'd be angry!"

I walked about the room. I looked at the walls of the bungalow which were like the cone of a loudspeaker. I thought—Did I really think that I might have to kill him, or only after I knew I needn't?

I repeated "But nothing happened."

After a silence she said "What do you mean?"

The cold came in again. I thought—All right, I will prove this.

I said "Go on."

"Well, I did go on the beach again. This was the next day. I suppose I shouldn't have. But I think in the end it was all right."

She waited. She seemed to be doing this to hurt me. I thought—She will have to hurt me, in order to stop herself feeling guilty.

She said "Why are you looking at me like that?"

I said "What am I looking like?"

"He asked me to go for a walk along the beach. I thought he was trying to see if I trusted him. I thought I had to show I trusted him. Don't you think?"

I said "This was the second day. Nothing happened the first?"

She was twisting her hands up; was about to cry.

I said "I'm just trying to get it straight."

She said "It was all right along the beach. Then he said there was a short cut through the eucalyptus trees."

I registered—The eucalyptus trees. This might have been funny.

She said "Then he took hold of my hand. Oh I know I was stupid!"

She was holding her breath as if under pressure.

She said "I saw—"

"What?"

"In his eyes."

I repeated "But nothing—"

She was shaking. I put out my hand and touched her.

I said "What in his eyes?"

She said "An animal."

I imagined his face coming down through the leaves; the bad breath feared by the hunter.

I wondered—How dark was he?

I said "He pulled you?"

"Yes."

"Did you struggle?"

"Yes."

"He held you?"

"Yes."

"On the ground?"

She didn't answer.

I said "Did you go to the police?"

I thought—At least she doesn't love him.

She said "No."

"Why not?"

She frowned, as if over some purely abstract problem.

She said "He was a policeman."

I imagined myself exclaiming—A policeman?—with incredulity; outrage; the timing of an actor.

I said "Not that fat policeman?"

She said "Which fat policeman?"

"The one at dinner."

She thought for a moment and then shouted "Of course not that fat policeman!"

I wanted to say—Then why a thin one?

She got up to light a cigarette; backed away as if the smoke were chasing her.

I thought—I will walk up those dusty streets and will meet him beneath a lamp-post.

"Did he kiss you?"

"Yes."

"But nothing more?"

"I've told you."

"But how do I believe?"

She put her head in her hands; seemed to push against rubber.

"What stopped him?"

"I asked him not."

"What did you say?"

"Please."

"And what did he do then?"

"He said—you would if I weren't—"

"A policeman?"

"No!"

"An Arab?"

"Yes."

I shouted "He's ten centuries out of date there!"

I was pacing up and down as if action had been decided on.

Then I thought—This will make an extraordinary story.

She said "Then he said—your husband will be doing it with girls in the south."

There had been one girl at the wedding feast I had attended with her hair cut short and a face as if made out of lapis-lazuli; a thin brown body and transparent trousers.

She said "You didn't, did you?"

"No."

I caught sight of myself in a mirror and I was like a dinosaur by a lake of ibises.

She said "He told me about his life. His mother and father were killed in the earthquake. He was eighteen. He ran out on to the beach and saw everything moving. The sea was coming in in a wave. There was a boat rowed vertically. He was picked up and thrown against a breakwater."

I thought—Like an octopus.

"Before this, he had had such a terrible time with the French. When they caught anyone they used to take them in for questioning. They tortured them. He said that when he was a boy he was taken and he never forgot it. Then when there was independence he and his friends wanted to get the French and *couper la gorge*"—she moved a hand in front of her throat—"but they didn't, because of what they thought about Mohammedanism."

I said "What did they think about Mohammedanism?"

She said "That we mustn't hate one another."

I said "That's not Mohammedanism."

She said "He said it was so awful not to be able to see any Europeans without hating them."

"And you were the first one he didn't?"

"Yes."

I threw my head back. I wanted to say—So we all have to love one another.

I said "What happened then?"

"We came home."

"Together?"

"Yes."

"Did you separate in front of the hotel?"

"No, by the trees."

"When he attacked you did he touch you?"

"What do you mean?"

"You know what I mean."

"No he didn't."

I said "Well if he had I might have killed him."

She said "Don't be silly."

I shouted "I'm not being silly!"

I looked out of the window. There was one bit of dialogue I wanted to remember: when she had said—He was a policeman; and I had said—Not that fat policeman?

She said "Don't be angry!"

I said "I'm not angry."

There were people moving from the bedrooms towards the dining room; the sound of the sea and cutlery like a ship.

I said "We'll go and have dinner."

We went up the dark paths lit by stones; sat behind the thin glass against which the sea blew and the ghosts ran towards the town that had disappeared. I wanted to ask again—He didn't touch you? either to make sure, or out of convention.

I said "What else did he say?"

"He said he couldn't understand Christians. They were all such hypocrites."

"And what did you say?"

"I said there were some who weren't."

"How?"

"That we believed this too. About non-violence."

I wanted to say—That's our prerogative.

We were eating fish cooked with almonds and butter; a white wine thin as wood shavings.

I said "And you've made all the difference to his life, and so on."

She pushed at her food quickly.

I said "All right, all right, I can imagine."

The Frenchman came in and sat at a table close to us. He held a newspaper in front of him like a steering wheel. I wondered if he knew and the chief of police knew that my wife had been into the eucalyptus trees; that I was the clown left at the front of the stage at the fall of the curtain.

She said "He asked me to write to him. To send him books. He wants to learn English."

I thought—We give them our countries and our wives: do we have to add dictionaries?

That night when we went to our bedroom there was the impression we were strangers; that I had gone with my Arab girl to one of those caves behind the courtyard, my wife young again and golden; the full body and bright boy's face and myself a visitor from a northern country; strapping on my equipment in the dusty street and going to do violence under a lamp-post. She lay on the bed with the openness of women who trust in their bodies; who are painted nude and stare down at themselves with repletion, one hand on a thigh and the other trailing and the body compact as bread. I thought—She wants me to hurt her. I took off my clothes. There was guilt fluttering behind her eyes and mouth. I touched her gently and she watched me and then stretched up to me. She seldom did this. I thought—There is nothing to be ashamed of here; there is perhaps no love without power.

Afterwards I thought—You let the day take care of itself; live like lillies.

In the morning there was breakfast in the dining room above the white rubble and sand-dunes. When the sea had come in it had pushed over the stones and withdrawn satisfied.

My wife sat with her quiet face above the butter and thin bread so sharp it cut you. She did not ask anything. I knew she wouldn't.

I said "Well we must get on today. We'll go up to that other place along the coast, where they made that film, you know, that epic, with slaves and triremes and whatnot."

She said "Othello."

I said "Oh, Othello."

I looked out of the window at the white mist.

I said "How did you leave it with him then?"

She said "Leave what?"

I said "Did you say goodbye? Were you going to see him again?"

She said "Not without you. I said I wouldn't meet him without you."

"Why?"

"He said he wanted to meet you. He thought you must be very nice."

For a moment I threw back my head and pretended again. I wanted to say—I am Iago.

We did our packing, which was as if we had stayed in the place for years. Our movements got slower.

I said "Did you say we would?"

She said "I said I didn't know."

I thought—The categories are simple: there are bad people like us who can do good, and good people like us who go on fighting.

When I paid the bill the Frenchman sat at his desk and his head was like an egg that you crack and it runs over the egg cup.

We put our luggage in the small car like a toy. We sat with the bonnet pointing over the sand-dunes.

I said "What do you want us to do?"

"I don't know."

"You want me to decide?"

"Yes."

I put the car in gear and drove round in front of the hotel where there were no houses but just the lamp-posts like a ballet-set. I stopped the car in the position it had been in before.

I said "Where will he be?"

"On the beach."

It was a bright windy day with the eucalyptus trees like fists and the sun a glass breaking. I climbed out of the car and hitched up my trousers and thought I should have a wide-brimmed hat to pull down over my eyes. We began walking across the sand-dunes, my wife and I, one slightly behind the other, in the formation of a barb or a posse for the hangman. I thought—This is too easy; what if he had really raped her? You keep your eyes on the ground and walk carefully so as not to lose sweat. We were going past the trees that were white like medicine. I thought—But violence only happens when you want it.

On the beach were the huge rollers coming in in tiers. There were a few Europeans from the houses rebuilt by the harbour. Arab men in white robes were looking for flotsam: girls in bathing dresses had bare legs and arms. I wanted to say—Does he hang about on the beach to tell all the girls that it is dangerous?

I saw him from miles away like a child on the edge of a paddling pool; a small brown figure in a brown landscape, one toe in the sea telling it to go back, patrolling it. He was in uniform and had a stick beneath his arm. My wife and I were walking across the sand with our feet sinking in the soft surface. He seemed to see us immediately because the air became still: there were memories thrown across distances like girders; of men travelling over continents, jungles, ice-caps; intent and tip-toeing for such a meeting. He waited and then began stepping towards us, his legs cut off at the knees in a mirage. I was ahead of my wife, not knowing what to do with my hands, stiff and smiling as an archaic statue. I thought—People carry guns for something to do with their hands; like masturbation or smoking. He did carry a gun: a rifle with a white sling over his shoulder. I thought—What if he really shoots me? My wife should go in front like women should go into no-man's-land but never do. My wife went in front. When she walked she moved with a swing like a kilt marching. When he was close he was a boy with a peaked cap and a uniform too big for him; the scrubbed look of a hero. I had glanced away from him at the last moment; to be too confident is to deal with animals. When I looked up again we had all stood still and were facing each other and he had a small beautiful face with large brown eyes. I thought—He is like a hummingbird.

My wife said "Mon mari."

I said "Bonjour."

He spoke in a French which I found hard to understand.

When I held out my hand he took it quickly like someone tempted to steal and put something back again. He had white teeth and a surprisingly pink tongue. I thought—They have pink tongues. He was like a southern Italian. I was far above him with my huge head from the bottom of the sea. I was to be cut open for my oil, my ambergris.

My wife said "Nous partons ce matin."

I said "Nous sommes venus à dire au revoir."

When he spoke I had to look at my wife. She speaks French badly but always understands, as if translating with not her mind but her senses.

She said "Did you have a nice trip in the south?"

I realised that he was asking me if I had had a nice trip in the south. I said "Oui, très bon, merci."

He waited. His smile expected miracles. I thought—Not only our wives and dictionaries, but now polite conversation round the breakfast table.

I said "L'architecture c'est très interessante, les maisons, rochers, les peintures decoratives sur les toits"—I waved my hand—"J'ai eu de bonne chance, j'ai encontré une grande fête de noces où je suis invité"—I looked at my wife. I thought I had suffered enough. I said "How do you say it?"

My wife said "De mariage."

He answered quickly as if he understood not with his mind, but his senses.

My wife dropped her eyes like a mother proud of children.

I said "Well it was nice meeting you. Il faut que nous partons maintenant."

I held out my hand again. I thought—He is not asking anything; this is a bargain.

He said in French "I hope you will come back. It has been a pleasure knowing you."

I understood with my mind, my senses.

When I turned away I was still walking like the unarmed man in a riot. The riot was in my mind. I thought—The smile on the face of the archaic statue is the knowledge that one might be shot in the back. It might have been easier just to have shot each other. Otherwise, it was always so difficult not to be condescending.

We were going back past the eucalyptus trees which leaped like drugged fakirs.

My wife said "Did you like him?"

I said "He was all right."

We sat in the car side by side and looked out where the town had once been, the hill teeming with violence and shouting. A few donkeys now stood like tombstones. I started the car and we went off past the harbour and the smell from the factory. There was the sea with the waves fighting. I wanted to say—It is only in the mind that we want to murder—but this wasn't true. My wife sat beside me and I wondered why she wasn't holding or squeezing my hand. I thought—When you go out on the dusty street the eyes remain behind closed doors and you have to do it all on your own; other people only come out to collect the bodies. I put out my hand and touched her. She put her hand on mine. I thought—Civilisations rot with too much culture. The car began to climb towards the mountains. The sea was below. I wondered if I would ever feel anything again.

There was once a Christian governor of Cyprus called Bragadino who was a good and holy man and who surrendered to the Turks on the understanding that he would be given his life and freedom. This was at the time of the Crusades, when men fought with passion and for piety. The Turkish commander was a politician and an epileptic: he promised Bragadino that he could have his life and freedom then cut off his nose and ears and ordered that he should be flayed alive. But all the time he was being flayed Bragadino maintained such a sweet and seraphic expression that several people watching him were converted. And even when his skin was completely off his angelic smile still continued. This gave the Turks the idea of stuffing it and selling it back to his family. His family bought it and put it in a church, as a moral and religious precept.

The crusades were a proper time in which to observe human nature—the pursuit of holiness for the sake of money, the use of torture for the sake of identity, a time of passionate care and commitment. Those who distributed pain were politicians; those who profited, saints. Either way life was not easy; unless you died young, which was recommended.

There was another such incident at this time, performed by women. The crusades were an excuse for men to get away from women, who pushed them out into the cold like seaside landladies. There was a King of Cyprus who went away to war and left behind a wife and a mistress. The former was barren; the latter as usual, pregnant. As soon as the king had gone the wife imprisoned the mistress and hammered her like a mortar with a pestle. This was to produce an abortion, in the pursuit of morality and religion. But the point of the story is that the child flourished; only the mother died. And the father of course too; who was caught with another of his mistresses and castrated.

When babies have their first experience of love they are already as grown men; green things in the hands of older women, lying on their backs and watching themselves being tickled; the endearments like the forearms of *executioners. They are called duck, rabbit, turtle; the seagulls come to get them. For every baby born, there are the million or two dead children.*

Perhaps the worst torture at this time happened to an Arab who was condemned by a Mongol to eat himself. He was sat down at a table with a napkin round his throat; was served feet first, perhaps; would have had to tell his host how delicious they were, such is Arab hospitality. And there were still the great delicacies. You close your eyes and open your mouth and in nanny pops them. And the eyes. He would not have got as far as the eyes: he would not have been left even with the smile of Bragadino.

The baby crawls across no-man's-land with its limbs shot off by the drug its mother took to keep it happy. It hopes that one day its mother will come to punish it, because then it will know who it is again. It looks out on a world in which slaves walk round with their hands pierced and hung round their necks like identity discs. It is by pain that caring is demonstrated: we were taught this at Sunday School.

So we wait for the aeroplane to come over the mountain, the stars on a clear night so beautiful. Once men found it easy to be hurt; now they have to advertise in shop windows. They ask for someone to order them; to lock them on the wire floors of cages. Sometimes they dream of walking forwards again like mad archaic statues. But first their hair falls out and then their teeth and their spectacles in piles. They have the vision of the sky opening again. This has always happened at the cost of the skin being stuffed; the million or two dead children.

Public House

ONE WINTER I WAS doing research work in the reading room of the British Museum and I used to go for lunch each weekday to a public house. This was of the kind where students and young businessmen jostle over chicken sandwiches and beer, their arms and talk as impersonal as machinery. This suited me, since I like to feel anonymous in a crowd. I occasionally tried to hear what some of my neighbours said, but I seemed able only to catch laughter or exclamations just before or after words, so that intelligibility was as hard to come by as the pin-pointing of an exact present.

One day there came into this pub a couple, a man and a girl, who stood out from the rest of the customers because of their self-absorption and exposure. The man was tall like something grown out of its shell; he had spectacles and fair hair and was almost middle-aged but not quite, because of some vulnerability about him—a daddy-longlegs. The girl was self-contained and dark-haired and beautiful; she was young but at the same time mythical, like Cleopatra. One or the other would arrive at the pub first; would peer round tables and over screens with the gaze of people intent on hidden music; would go out into the cold or into the rain again to wait because like this they were closer to each other and more comfortable than being distant in warmth. They were in love. They seemed a definition of this term—like dinosaurs of extinction. Love is out of date now because it is annoying to others; exposure causes embarrassment.

A London pub at lunch time has a masculine air; there is an activity of elbows like bow-strings being drawn back at Agincourt, feet are on duckboards and glasses are grenades in the hand. There is a roar of agreement as if in a Paris *salon* that Dreyfus should be shot. I did not like the people in the pub. But I think I am happiest when I feel people are against me.

I was working at the time on a historical book on the relationship between men and women. What interested me was man's view of woman as either goddess or mother or prostitute; and woman's acceptance of these roles for the sake of her identity. I was studying in particular Christian attitudes at the time of the Crusades, and contrasting these with attitudes in classical Greece and Rome.

When the man and girl came into the pub—they would have met out of doors and come in holding on to one another—there were not only the ordinary manifestations of love, the clasped hands, smiles, the gazing on one another like hypnotists; but a further dimension as if they were actors trying to make reality more real than it might be. They seemed to want to prove that love was real by demonstration—an existentialist proposition. And yet they were oblivious of the people around. I had remarked in my work how romantic love seemed to have withered as a result of self-consciousness: the couple seemed not to be unaware of this, but to avoid it. It was as if they were constructing, or honouring, something called love which was separate from themselves; as if they were artists.

The girl had a small dark face surrounded by a fur hat from which her gold eyes looked out. I thought of Anna Karenina at the railway station; her first appearance there and the last, because her end was foreshadowed in the beginning. In the girl's eyes was a depth like a well; you could drop a stone down and listen for ever. When she walked she strode with long legs as if she were skating. When she took her hat off you expected snow to scatter.

The man was older than she. He wore a black overcoat and a brown muffler and seemed always to be looking for somewhere to put his gloves. He did not take his coat off; he wrapped it round him as if he also were waiting for a train. But I could not think so romantically of the man. I was jealous.

The couple ignored the other people in the pub, who ignored them. There was something narcissistic in their rituals: they held hands too long like opera singers, had to keep time to their hidden music, were dragged forward and back and lost momentum. There is an instance in *The Valkyrie* when Wotan and Brünnhilde have to step towards each other across a stage and to keep pace with a drawn-out climax; their movements are absurd, but also beautiful. The couple were like this.

I usually had a book propped on my knee for something to do between eating. I used the book as a shield, just lifting the pages and shaking crumbs off.

I had noticed the couple for several days before I watched them closely. I think I became interested then partly because of my work. I had had the idea that men wanted to see women as goddesses or prostitutes because these are men's own projections and they have to find objects to accept them or else their own nature becomes unbearable. I remembered a fairy story by Oscar Wilde in which Narcissus looks into his pool and asks the water what it thinks of him; and the water answers that it sees its own reflection in his eyes.

I did not at first hear much of what the couple said. They did not speak much. When they met there were a few of the murmured non-senses of love; I heard him once say that she looked beautiful and she answered, as if it were a poem—Oh so do you! She had a voice which sometimes bubbled like a fountain. Then they would sit and hold hands underneath a table; rock backwards and forwards as if playing chess. Eventually time would be running out and they would have to order food. I think that they half fostered their absorption so that they could remember time suddenly and feel tragic; he could get up and go to the bar with the Furies after him, and she could watch him disappearing from a distant shore. At the bar he would widen his eyes and gaze at the top row of bottles; live in memory of the table he had just left. Then he would return, and the girl would greet him as if they had been apart for years. They lived in a myth, which was real to them. I began to build up some imagination about their lives. The girl wore a wedding ring. She sometimes carried gramophone records. I thought she might be a music student. She would play the harp or flute.

The man might be a second-rate conductor. He would fall off his rostrum, flailing at windmills.

At any rate they were both working in the vicinity and were using this pub to meet in at lunch. I did not know why they had nowhere better to meet. The girl was married; probably the man was too. They were not married to each other. I thought—Perhaps all love has to expose itself, since it exists in memory and expectation.

One day when the pub was more crowded than usual and there were no more free tables they had to come over to one at which I sat. This closeness was unnerving; I was suddenly faced with my imagination, like acquaintances meeting in a nudist camp. The girl in close-up was even more beautiful than I had thought; she was in her twenties, probably a mother. Her skin had that quality of the self-possessed; there were no rivers under her eyes for her to cry down. The man had a clown's bright gentleness; he waited for the tea-tray to fall about his head.

I held my book on my knee. It was a book about the Etruscans. The Etruscans were one of the few people of the ancient world who had treated women with dignity. On their tombs husbands and wives lay in each other's arms. This could not have happened with the Greeks and Romans, who were homosexual.

I did not really want to hear the couple talk. The impression that I had of them was that of a silent film. I liked the self-absorption and fluttering of eyes and the long pauses; the impression of white horses rushing across deserts. Speech, self-consciousness, had killed love. You could not lie on a grassy bank and spout Shakespeare.

The man was saying "You cook for him. Clean. Does he expect you to have feelings?"

He had a drawling, upper-class voice, slightly fading at the edges.

Just before this, when they had come in, he had touched her cheek with such triumph.

He said "Anyone can have feelings. On a Saturday night, with you-know-what and a bath."

The girl shook her head. She was eating a chicken sandwich. He waited for her, but she did not speak. I thought she at least might preserve her poetry. When she looked at the man her eyes had the ability to go liquid.

He said "What are you thinking?"

They did not seem aware of myself. They spoke to one side of me.

The girl said "I'm totally destructive."

The man shouted with laughter.

He said "Of course. The difference between you and others, is you know it."

She shook her head.

When they leaned towards each other they were like blind people putting print into a machine: they could not know what would come out of it.

She said "How are things with you?"

He said "We're in different rooms now."

She raised one eyebrow.

He dropped some food on his lap and swore.

She said "How are the children?"

He said "They've got a new girl friend. In pink tights."

Her eyes were pearls cutting down through her eyelids.

He said "How is yours?"

She said "Oh, she climbs all over me."

I do not remember much more of this first conversation.

I had been interested in them because I was lonely: I cared about love. One sees so little of it. Also I had this theory that only in a mixture of cynicism and romanticism was love possible. But I had not expected it in others. I did not know now if I liked it. I wondered how much from myself I projected on to them. Such processes are in the unconscious.

The couple did not come to the pub again for some time. This was around Christmas; I thought that they must have gone to their separate homes. I missed them. I was living so much on my own that this friendship of phantoms was important to me. I did not have a girl friend at the time. I loved women; but because I could not easily have myths about them I think they sometimes feared me. And perhaps I was afraid of them, that they might destroy me.

Then one day the couple were in the pub again before I had arrived. I was so pleased to see them I almost acted as if I knew them; greeted them like one of the characters in their story. I had already begun to think of them as characters in a story—both the one that they seemed to listen to like hidden music and the one that I was even then thinking of writing. They gave this impression of something being constructed by artifice; which they watched unfolding passively, yet also created. I believed that all life was like this; and they were people uniquely who recognised it. I recognised it myself, and so was involved in their story. But perhaps we could never let each other know; like spies in a foreign country.

But I thought I would be brave and sit at their table.

They were in one of their silences in which love existed like a charge between thunder-clouds. I was still half cynical: I thought that people who acted love so openly must underneath be devouring. When I sat at their table the man looked at me and for a moment I thought he might recognise me; but he recognised nothing. The girl, as always, was sensual. She had taken her coat off. There is a girl in a Moravia story who is very young but when she takes her clothes off has the voluptuousness of an older woman. This girl was like that. The two of them were under some strain. They seemed to hover slightly above their seats like hummingbirds. I thought they might be meeting for the last time. I put my beer down quietly. The man was doing his rocking-chair act; a Cezanne in the evening. The girl's lower eyelids had gone slightly up as if heat had contracted them.

The man was saying "If we went off with each other we'd break within a year. There's a love that destroys you, which is what you've got, and that frees you, which is what you haven't. If you want love then you have to be both together and apart. This works. The other doesn't."

She said "You don't really want me."

He said "I do." Then—"You'll see one day."

They were not eating. Their food remained on their plates like the helpings which come back to children at lunch and tea and supper.

She said "I want us to have some sort of life together. I think love is a common world which you build from day to day. If you don't have that, you don't have anything."

He said "We've got everything."

She said "We've got nothing."

He looked exhausted. He had wrapped his coat around him as if in cold. His mouth was stiff and his words were difficult to enunciate. He said "All poets have always known, that you can't have love by grabbing it. You've read the books. For God's sake."

She said "I'm not a poet."

He said "You are."

She looked like Judith going to Holofernes.

He said "Once society did it for us. Now we have to do it ourselves."

She said "What?"

He said "Make impossibilities."

She said "What's the point?"

He said "To maintain ecstasy."

He spoke like someone making a confession under torture.

She said "All right keep your beautiful marriage."

He did not seem to hear this. He put his head back and closed his eyes.

He said "One does build from day to day. But one adds, one doesn't destroy."

She said "You risk nothing. Nothing'll break you."

He said "Or one loses the lot."

They were silent for a time. They seemed refugees preferring to die than look over the hill to the promised land.

He said "Why don't you leave him then?"

She said "Because you don't want me to."

He said "I do."

She said "I think I have a great capacity for love. I could give myself totally."

He said "You do it then."

She said "I can't bear deceit."

She spoke in her operatic voice.

He said "All life is some bearing of deceit. That's human nature."

She said "I don't believe that."

He said "Ducky, I know you don't."

She said "What?"

He began to tremble.

He said "Like Anna Karenina in the railway station. You spread a little happiness around."

She stood up. She said "That is unforgivable."

I wanted to say—I thought of Anna Karenina!

He said "Oh sit down."

She opened a bag and took out a pair of keys and put them on the table.

The keys lay there like things untouchable except by pincers. I thought—So he did have somewhere to take her. He paid no attention to the keys. I thought—But she won't be able to go now. She went to the door. I thought—He'll go after her. He did not even look up. She went out. The keys remained; one with a shaft like a gun barrel.

I wondered for a moment if I might follow and see where she lived: then I might make a date with her.

The man finished his sandwich. I wanted to say to him—Just because it is impossible, doesn't mean you stop trying!

After a time he stood up. He was the exhausted soldier after five minutes' rest on the march, strapping his pack on and setting out for the firing line. I thought he might still go after her. But he went to the bar and ordered another beer. And when he came back I saw that he was smiling. His was one of those faces that you turn upside down and it comes out different; the clown becomes the cossack. I wondered how he did this. He sat beside me again. His face had become gentle: a cunning child's.

I thought of my story about this man and the girl who looked at themselves in mirrors, who moved the opposite ways from what they intended. I might make the man be living like myself alone up four flights of stairs: the girl coming to make love mornings and evenings. They would use their lunches purely for public purposes; needing an audience because observers influence that which is observed. Or perhaps they did not make love at all, being so concerned with their maintenance of ecstasy.

After this there was another gap of a week or so in which neither of them came to the pub. I felt as if I had missed my opportunity to speak. The man of course had picked up the keys and had put them in his pocket.

Then one day the girl came in on her own, stepping as usual with long legs as if on ice, peering serene and purposeful and still with no rivulets beneath her eyes. I sometimes think this look of hers was simply because she was short-sighted. There was nothing unusual about her coming in alone; the man would follow. I waited with my book propped up. I was reading Suetonius. In Suetonius, men and women do little except murder one another. I suppose at first sight I am not very noticeable, being short, shorter than the man—though I look quite like him. The girl gazed across at me and I thought she might recognise me; but she did not; she went to the bar and ordered her sandwich and fruit juice. But she did not go to wait in the cold. And after a time the man still had not followed. I wondered whether they had arranged their usual rendezvous or whether she had come in just by chance. After a quarrel they would both be proud; they would not telephone to make it up. They would prefer to wander in the streets on the chance of casual meetings. I thought I was getting to know them now. In a casual meeting there would be no resentment nor triumph: they would hope for miracles. But still the man did not come. Her face began to look as if it were being hit. I tried to imagine her with her husband and child or children. She would go out each day to study music. Her husband would be a thickset man with well-cut hair. They would sleep in a bed with a canopy like a sea-shell. She had finished her sandwich and still the man had not come. I wanted to talk to her. She was standing picking the petals off daisies to see if she existed.

I thought I could ask her to have lunch: tell her all about the conductors of hidden music.

She waited three-quarters of an hour and then went out. She had looked at the door often. I had not spoken to her. I think she was too sad. Grief is private, because so exposed.

Then the next day the man came in alone. He was so unselfconscious that you could feel his wondering about himself; looking round tables, over partitions, and asking what he was doing there; making the observations that other people would make if they had been interested. He pulled off his gloves and scraped them down his sides. I thought perhaps he was one of those artists who would burn his life's work because he did not have enough wood for a fire; and this would be convenient for him, because his work was not good enough. The girl did not come in. I did not think she would. I thought that their luck had run out now: or perhaps they were purposely missing each other for the sake of their guilt and ecstasy. He ordered his beer; tapped on the counter. I wondered if he knew what was happening. I thought—He is being forced to be responsible. I have these theories. His sad face flashed like a lighthouse. I wanted to say—She was here yesterday; you should ring her up. But I did not. He did not ask me; he did not ask anyone. I thought—We all have our self-destruction; mine is that I don't tell him. He was so noble he would go to the scaffold smiling. He waited, and then went out.

And then I regretted bitterly not speaking to him, because it was on some trust in my doing this that both he and I depended. If we were working for love, I thought, then it was just some chance as this that might effect it. I was a stranger: love is a matter not of arrangement but of grace: I could have said—She was here yesterday—and then he would have telephoned her. Love is impossible for people in it but not for the stranger; there is the ghost on the street corner, the face in the dream, the accident by the church yard. The happy outcome of love depends on the chance good-will of others. I knew this. All the other people in the pub were working their arms and mouths like oil-drills. Within love is the curse of opposites; you cannot force them, you can only let them grow. But the stranger can break in and impregnate them like a sperm. I had not done this. I had been jealous of him.

I wished to God I had taken hold of him on the bridge of a ship in the gale and had said—Angels do sit on the masthead!

After this there was a spell of cold weather in which the pavements froze and all the young men came into the pub happy because their legs had nearly broken and they had just missed being run over by buses.

Then the man and girl came in together again one day having met just outside; they reeled through the door as if into a bedroom. I thought they were really going too far this time; their hands were groping over each other's backs, sides, coat-tails. I thought—They are too old for this: God sits behind a two-way mirror. Their smiles had gone into skulls with pleasure: they were climbing up each other as if on a rock-face. I wanted to say—Go out into the street again; you can do it better in private. I did not like them then; they were making me feel deformed. The pub was too crowded to sit down. The man was saying over and over again "Oh I do love you!" and the girl was saying "Oh so do I!" I was standing by them in order to get more beer. The young men had their tankards up like boxing gloves. The man and the girl were still clinging to each other. There is a moment in making love which is like the end of a four-minute mile: I wanted to jostle them and shout—Keep going! She was saying "I don't know how you can ever forgive me." He was saying "I never have anything to forgive you." She said "You are so marvellous!" He said "So are you." I wanted to shout—Come on, ref, break it up ! I had to push my way between shoulders. I said "Excuse me. Thank you."

He was saying "That had to happen. Didn't you know? You have a genius for love. If you hadn't hurt me, where would we have been? Or if I hadn't hurt you. You're too good. I know you can't bear deceit. It's I who am wrong. I'm trying to change. You're forcing me. It's your instinct, which is true, and my knowledge, which knows this. But look, it can't be easy. We're trying to do wrong, and doing right, and this is impossible. But we can. How do you break things? There's something happening. But we have to go at it backwards. There's one racket, power, and another, love. But love is total; it leaves nothing out. It runs you. What do you think life's like? I'm not going to say any more. You can't expect miracles. You trust. Don't you?"

She said "I trust you, absolutely."

They went to a table and sat stupefied. Every now and then he opened his mouth and then shook his head. Their hands were under the table like elephants grasping buns. There seemed to be a curved drop of concrete in front of them.

After a time she said "How are the children?"

He said "All right."

I do not remember this time how they left; whether they or I went first, whether I watched them out of the door still reeling like wounded soldiers. I remember his giving her back the keys. I think I saw them still at their table as if in some final tableau; the curtain going down and up concealing and revealing them; the crowd standing and moving for the exit. The life of characters in a play is only in their performance: in the empty auditorium are ghosts.

There was another long gap. It became so long that I thought they must finally have settled to go to their room instead of eating chicken sandwiches. Or they might have quarrelled again. I thought—I know the rules; he was wanting to have his cake and eat it; but you don't go on for ever getting more loaves and fishes.

In the spring the atmosphere of the pub changed from a Turkish bath of elbows and overcoats to the bright stillness of a linen cupboard; the doors suddenly opening on to cherry-blossomed streets and cars bright like axes. I had quite given up hoping to see them again. I sometimes dreamed of them because I did not know the end of their story. I wanted to write of them coming across each other again in the distant future. And then one day the girl did come in once more, alone. She was without her coat and fur hat and was dressed in jeans and a striped cotton jersey. She had had her hair cut. She looked like a boy. For the first time in the pub all the men noticed her. She had the sensuality of opposites—the youth and experience, the leanness and voluptuousness, which invited both protection and sadism. Her hair was in a fashionable style shorter at the back than at the sides: you could pull it like bells. There was a large label on the seat of her jeans. She was looking round the pub and not really expecting to find anyone. She was there for the memory. I think I knew then that I loved her: that I could now speak to her. It was not that I had really been afraid before, but simply the power of imagination. I stood. There was a feeling in my throat as if I had put my hand between her legs. Then I saw a man who had come in behind and was staring at her. She had her back to him. This was a man I had not seen before. He was elegant with dark curly hair. I knew that he was to do with her. She had not noticed him. He seemed to be waiting for her, or driving her, as if she were a pony: or as if he were a footman behind a queen. So I could not speak to her. I wanted to tell her that he was there. I knew her situation so well. Then she turned. She recognised him slowly with her short-sighted eyes. She did not move her feet; she swivelled her body, so that her back was still half to him. I thought—She is having it both ways. There were diagonal creases along her jersey and jeans. She said "You!" He smiled. He was different from the other man: he would not need to bang his head against walls to come out smiling. She had opened her mouth and pearls were cutting down her eyelids again. He said, copying her—"You!" He had a voice like a madrigal. Her face began to change—first into the look of being hit which I had once seen when she had been with the man (her man; I felt as if I were standing in for him; this other man was obviously her husband) but then into something hawklike, almost predatory; her top lip lengthening into that of a Red Indian. The husband wore a grey suit and white tie; he looked as if he were picking up a sailor. He said "You didn't expect me." Then—"Do you meet him here?" I thought that her

man—the original man—might be about to come in: I could go out
into the street and warn him. Then I could at last step into their drama.
But I stayed where I was. She said "Did you follow me?" She stood with
her head slightly back as if the smoke was in her face with which she
sent out signals. She said "Do you have people following me?" She did
not sing now; her voice had a slight accent; as if from a flat land with
wheat fields. He went on smiling. He jingled money in his pocket. He
repeated "Do you meet him here?" She waited; a chieftainess with her
eyes on the hills. Then she said "No." He said "Do you promise?" She
said "Yes." I thought—She cannot bear deceit. They looked at each
other. They neither of them believed.

I found myself getting up and going out with half despair, half
anxiety. I felt something bruise about what I had felt about love: I also
wanted to see if the man was coming. I had been so happy to see her;
I myself was in love; I was in the street on a bright spring day looking
out for someone to meet me. I thought—We can no longer be shocked;
we find ourselves on corners, beneath windows, and we do not know
how we got there. But we would rather be there than anywhere else. I
might lay down my cloak in some puddle—for her or for her lover. I
might think I was waiting for my own girl with dark hair. But I was not.
Ultimately we make no contact; not with anyone, not with ourselves. I
was in the street for a breath of air. I turned back to the pub. My beer
and sandwich were on a table. The girl and her husband were at my
table. I said "Excuse me." She still did not recognise me. She was after
all short-sighted.

She had such a beautiful skin with a glow coming from the inside
as in Venetian paintings. Her husband said "Why do you come here
then?" The blackness of her hair made her mouth red and her eyes gold;
colours were built up in layers by time and by tradition. He said "You
never go to pubs." His watch-chain was gold: he was rich: perhaps the
other man was poor. The husband said "Well?" I wanted to say—Tell
him you meet a girl friend. She said nothing. She crossed her legs and
pulled in the small of her back. In this position she showed off her body.

He said "I know you meet him. You were hoping to meet him today.
Why do you lie? You were once honest. He won't come back. He won't
do anything for you. How can you love someone who doesn't love you?"

She said "I wasn't going to meet him."

He said "I love you. I'd do anything." He took hold of her wrists.

I thought—Crash the tables, knock over the beer mugs.

He said "You are so beautiful."

A look of peace had come over her face. She stared down at his fingers as if they were bracelets from a lover. I thought—She is in love with pain; she will get it from him.

He said "Come and have lunch."

She said "I've had lunch."

He said "Here?"

He looked round the room with its clanking of human machinery. He seemed amazed. Then he noticed me. He was the only one of them who ever did notice me; as if it were his duty to distinguish natives.

She began to pick his fingers off her wrist. They were burrs from a hedgerow. He had leaned half across her lap. She placed his hand on his knee. He said "Do you love him?" She said "Yes." I began to pick up my books. I thought—They are well suited. There was the look on her face of an eagle above fur. His was a neck with the crowds going over him; he would live full of medals and of glory. I did not want to stay for the end. You know when it is the end because of the change in the music. Everyone gets up and leaves the cinema. She and her husband would lead a good life, the seashell above their bed and the dinners for six people. You avoid the National Anthem and find yourself in the street. It had been raining. You copy the people in the film; take a deep breath and go off to the sunrise.

I tried to analyse, after I had gone, what it was that had happened. I do not know about marriage—I have not been married myself—but it seems to me that what men want from women is a mixture between doll and mother so that they can push the doll around and make her pretty and then, when she cries, ask the mother to punish them. Which she does. This is perhaps the best a woman can do for a man—to be pleased at his weakness. But it is impossible. What a woman wants from a man is a mixture of god and victim—then he can be pitied—but she only tolerates someone who is cruel. This is safe. But neither a god nor a victim is cruel.

I returned to my own life; my own impossibilities. My work at the

British Museum came to an end. I made plans to go on a trip to Rome, which is another story.

It was on one of my last days at the pub that I saw the man come in again—her original man, the musical conductor. He had brought a woman. I knew the woman was his wife: he had not even bothered to get her to follow him. She wore dark glasses. She had a face of delicate and strong melancholia, the good contours slightly gone, as if from rain. Her dark glasses were worn to hide something underneath; not from the sun, but the rivulets people cry down. The man was holding her by the arm. She did not look round the pub, did not seem interested in it. He took her to the bar. I saw that she might still be beautiful; was tall and drawn as a film star. He asked her what she would drink. She looked round the bottles and said she would like water. She must be his wife, to ask for water. He leaned right over the bar to make this special request for her. He drummed with his fingers. I remembered all these mannerisms of his: I thought—He will suddenly look round the room and remember he has been here before. Perhaps he even wanted his wife to ask him—Have you been here before?—so he could pretend to be amazed, and say—Yes. She had short brown hair; she drank the water as if it were precious to her. The man looked round: at the oak fireplace, the hunting prints, the elbows like machinery. Perhaps he had remembered he had been here with a girl. His wife suddenly asked him "Did you meet her here?" He said immediately "Yes." I could hear this quite clearly. I had come to the bar to order beer: I had no illusions that he would recognise me. He still gazed round. Perhaps he heard the birds singing. He said to his wife "You knew then?" He put a hand out and patted her behind. She remained motionless. Then she made a face as if there was something bitter on her tongue. He said "Oh that was a long time ago." He chanted this. The woman drank. He said "Do you want me to talk about it?" She did not answer. He hummed. I suppose he often had to have these conversations with himself, having no one else to talk to. He looked towards the door. This was where they had come in, had clung as if under a waterfall, had climbed up each other's rock-face. His wife said "Why did you bring me here?" He said "To exorcise it, ducky." He said this very quickly. Then he said "Don't you want me to exorcise it?" I wondered if she ever answered. He drank some beer. I thought—He will always enjoy his beer. His wife said "Do what you like." Then she smiled. I thought—These people surely cannot last; they will be overwhelmed by what they are doing.

≈   ≈   ≈

I did manage to forget about the couple then. They lived on at some level of mind because they were still symbols of what I believed about love—of its complexity, even of the necessity of this—but they became unreal to me as people. I thought that they had possessed for a moment some secret about love; but they had betrayed this.

I finished my book on the relationship between men and women: I went to Rome; travelled through Italy. When in Turin I wrote the story about the man and the girl at their future meeting. But this became mixed with a story about myself, and had to be fitted into a larger context. I remembered how I had had the impression that I was a character involved in their story as well as they in mine; and none of us yet knew the endings.

Then some time later when I was travelling in Morocco—a year or so, I do not know; we become confused about age; we do not want to remember it—I saw the man again. I did not at first recognise him: I was not sure where I had seen him before. I thought he might be a colleague from a previous metamorphosis; an academic, perhaps, or a fellow-officer in the war. He was wearing shorts and a dark blue shirt and was holding a beach ball. He was pouring with sweat. He was standing in front of the plate-glass window of a hotel. This hotel had been put up by the government to attract tourists; it was on stilts over the beach, an edifice like a whale. In the plate-glass my vision was doubled; as if the man were standing both inside and outside himself. I was not staying in the hotel; I was in the Arab part of the town, in a room above a cafe. I still did not quite believe, after I had recognised him, that he could be the man in the pub: you see someone in unexpected surroundings and you have no way of fitting him in. The face is no help; everyone has a face; you have to wait for something mutual. He has to be as uncertain as you, in order to create accustomed surroundings. The man had a large rather muscular body on thin legs: Englishmen abroad seem to stand like birds. The plate-glass window reflected the beach; the wind blew sand against it, the lines of waves came in in tiers, they made a trough where the man was standing. I was at some distance, staring at him. His face was redder and more aquiline. I tried to reconstruct what I remembered; his figure a windmill amongst overcoats and elbows. There were three children in a group beyond him waiting as he held the ball; they were boys, bronzed and indolent. I remembered that he had said he had had children—or that might have been in the story I had written. There is something primitive in a group of boys by the sea; they wait to be engaged in some contest with horses and fighting. Beyond them was a young child, a girl, playing alone in the sand. She had dark curly hair and was tiny. I knew it was the man and yet I could not prove it; if I spoke he would not know me, and he might not want to remember the pub. Yet there is always the chance of talking to strangers in a foreign country, and I had despised myself for never having spoken to him before. I thought I could just go up to him and say—I sat next to you one winter; you won't remember me. It was extraordinary how much he sweated. I went up to him and said "You won't remember me. I used to see you in a pub." People make a show of recognition; raise a hand and let it hang above your shoulder. He said "Yes I remember." He had that drawl. I was touched. I thought he might say—Fancy seeing you here! He held out his hand. I took it. I thought—He is confusing me. I said "Do you really remember?" He said "No!" He laughed. I remembered his way of enjoying embarrassment. I said "It was a pub called—" I mentioned its name. I did not want him to get away with it. But he looked delighted. He shouted "Oh!" as if the sky had reopened for him. He said "Then you must meet—" He turned and waved his hand towards the hotel. I thought he was suggesting that I must meet his wife. I remembered I had never really liked him. He said "What are you doing here?" I said "I'm writing a book." He said "Oh you write too?" When he was interested it was still as if it were only in himself. I said "I once wrote a story about you." He said "About the pub?" I said "No, about a journey up through Italy." I thought this at least would interest him. He said "I wrote a story about the pub."

He was looking towards the three boys. He did not want to introduce me. He began again. "You must—" but he often did not finish his sentences. He looked at the hotel. I thought I should say—It's all right, I won't tell your wife about the girl in the pub—but then I remembered his wife knew already. I thought—He expects people to drop off trees for him. He said "Do you know this coast?" I said "No." He said "I was at Tamanet after the earthquake." I said "I know." He said "How?" I said "I mean, I know there was an earthquake." He shouted with laughter. I thought—People must sometimes land on him like apples. He said "I meant, I once wrote a story about that too: you might have read it." I said "What was your story about the pub?" He said "It was told by a man who had seen us that winter." He banged his head. He said "But you can't exist! Or you're myself. You see how this is impossible!"

The three boys on the beach were waiting for him to play with them. They resented the intrusion of the stranger. I could not place the small girl with curly hair: there was no other family on the beach, and she did not seem to belong to them. The boys were pushing at the sand with their toes and picking it up and hopping on one foot. I waited for his wife to come out; she would be wearing dark glasses and would trust the sun like a lamp she knew would not burn her. He said "Don't go!" I had not intended to go. I wanted to involve myself at last in their story. He threw the ball to the boys where it landed in a pool and splashed them. The small child suddenly put down her bucket—she had been building sandcastles—and ran towards us. She moved with her legs kicking sideways as children do by the sea. She ran right past: I thought she must be running to her mother. I saw that the girl had come out from the hotel. I had not expected this. It was as if she, too, were reflected in my memory double. She was walking towards us and she seemed to have nothing on. There was the way she walked as if on ice, her long legs bending very little at the knee, her boy's and woman's body, the black hair that made her colours so remarkable. She appeared to be seen from two directions at once—both full-face and in profile. The Egyptians had painted like this; with the legs and head sideways and the body straight to the front. You can only get the whole of a person by this sort of art, deception. We all seemed to have been waiting for her. She wore a two-piece bathing suit spotted like a leopard. The boys by the sea seemed holding the reins of horses. The small child had jumped up into her arms. The child was her daughter. The spaces between us were confused; there was a light separating and connecting us. I thought—There are people in the unconscious who stand like this: I am frightened of something so powerful and empty. She seemed to absorb all the light around and turn it to gold. The man said to me "Do you remember—" He mentioned her name. She stretched out her hand. The boys in the background had not moved: I thought—they might have been done some great injury; the sons of a tribal king with no wives left. I told her my name. The man said "He used to sit next to us in the pub that winter." The girl said "Yes I remember!" Her whole face lit up. I burned with it. I said "Do you?" Her voice had bubbled over. The child in her arms was struggling to get free: the man took it: it pressed itself in front of his face like a screen. She said "You used to be reading books in Latin." I said "Yes, how clever of you!" I knew I was still in love. I wanted to ask—How did you get here then? I had not expected them to manage it. I had always known that they had possessed some secret. They had not betrayed it.

One of the boys was coming over to us. He was the eldest, tall with dark hair brushed forwards like feathers. He went up to the woman and said "Are you going to bathe now?" He said this gravely, as if he were her tutor. I noticed again how her face seemed exposed; something peeled, translucent. She looked at the man and waited for him to speak: he was tickling the child. The child was fighting; was trying to embrace him. I wanted to tell them how happy I was to find them; that they had proved something that I had hoped but not believed about love. I wanted us all to stay on this beach for ever. I said "How long have you been here?" The man said "About a month." The girl turned to the boy and said "All right, I'll come." This was in her operatic voice; a decision to embark on a long journey. I could not bear that she should go. She turned to me and said "Are you staying?" I said "In the town." I got the impression then that she was asking me to rescue her. I did not understand this. The boy waited. She moved towards the group; their backs to the sea and the reins on their horses. There is an image of a queen being lifted on the shoulders of acolytes, before she is placed on the pyre. They reached the edge of the sea and stood there. I thought—Perhaps she cannot swim. The waves beyond were taller than she; like the steps of a building in an earthquake. She walked into the water and turned her back and fell into a wave. The boys moved cautiously round her. Then she began to swim. She swam expertly. The man was still holding the child; the child was snapping at him. The man pulled his head back. I thought—They should not be doing this in public: then—All this has happened before. I wanted to ask him how he had managed to achieve love; what he thought would happen later. The others were swimming out to sea; her arms and feet like moonlight. I thought I might offer to hold the child for him; I am good with children. Then he could join the others. But he put the child on his back and called out "Hold on tight!" The child stopped struggling. It put its arms round his neck and clung there. The man waited for a moment and said to me "What was your story?" I said "About the future. A meeting." He said "Good." The child was strangling him: he put his tongue out. He seemed so often to be acting. He said "We'll be seeing you then." He ran down to the sea with the child on his back kicking as if he were a pony. The waves were much too high for them, the heads of the others were far out like oil. I wanted to shout—It's too rough! But I thought that they would always be people who would run into danger, because of their secrets about love and what was possible.

I became interested in the idea of importing pornographic literature into China. I went to General Manager of the Central Agency and I said— General, this is the age of psychological war as opposed to violent war and we have this material. Once we flogged children and slaughtered enemies and this was a solution to the population problem. Now we all work for the peace of the world and will be standing on each other's heads in five hundred years.

The General hitched up his trousers and transferred his cigar-butt from one side to the other.

I said—I refer to the story of Dr. Paragon and the Belgian schoolgirls. Dr. Paragon, graduate of Heidelberg, winner of the Nobel prize, is called on to take charge of a girl's school where previously all has been chaos. The girls are lined up on the deck of an aircraft carrier; they wear nylon suits and have boots halfway up their thighs. Dr. Paragon says—Now girls, we have to have some discipline in this establishment. We have to be perfect. Otherwise, we will be standing on each other's heads in five hundred years.

The General picked up his golf bag and knocked some balls into tumblers.

I said—There was one particular girl, a Russian beauty, with a big black moustache and slanting eyes. Dr. Paragon said—step forward please. She was shaved and had wires attached to her eyeballs, throat, and armpits. She was strapped in a chair and people came to look at her through a plate-glass window. She demonstrated intelligence by finding the way through a maze to a piece of cheese. The cheese was the moon. Dr. Paragon said—Be careful; this is a force that will destroy the universe.

The General said—Where can I get this material?

I said—After this all the girls became excited; they wanted to rush out and bomb the mainland, give birth to babies without legs or arms. They turned their backs and Dr. Paragon pinned medals on them; they had to walk up and down between tables. Dr. Paragon sat on the deck of the aircraft carrier and the dark sea rose underneath him. He said—Gentlemen, we are working night and day in commerce and industry; forty per cent of our national income goes on war. But modern methods of destruction simply cannot keep pace with the ancient world: the Chinese carry babies on their backs instead of golf clubs. We have got to return destruction to the place where it has always been—that is, in the unconscious. So there will be a big party tonight. Put on your false eyelashes, girls, and stick feathers up your arses.

So all the sailors and airmen went down to their dressing rooms and prepared their arms and powder. They formed a long line and came out kicking on to the deck of the aircraft carrier. There were dark patches in their sky; it was impossible to tell whether they were men or women. Spectators lay on their backs and gazed through telescopes. The General took the salute: Dr. Paragon sat cross-legged just beneath him. The General opened and shut his mouth, but the words came from Dr. Paragon. He said—Gentlemen; we have now solved the population problem: there are no more differences between us: there will be nothing to stand on in five hundred years.

A Journey into the Mind

Hippolyta was a half-American half-Italian girl who lived in Rome overlooking the Borghese gardens. She was rich, and her flat was often full of the poets, drug-addicts and hairdressers that are symbols of the fashionable world. Hippolyta was a large girl of twenty-eight who walked with her eyes half closed and her hands pushing behind her as if she was in a gale. She was separated from her husband, who was a minor Italian aristocrat and lived in the country. They had little communication with each other except on the subject of their two-year-old child, whom they used as a weapon with which to fight and keep themselves going. When talking to her husband on the telephone Hippolyta would laugh slowly until he was in a frenzy and then she would hold the receiver out for the amusement of her friends. Her husband's voice buzzed like a trapped fly. When Hippolyta herself was in a frenzy she would hit her fist against her body like a parachutist searching for a failed ripcord.

I had come to Rome to do research work for a book. Rome was a place where once cruelty had been normal; it had been necessary for grandiose society. I did not like Rome. Hippolyta's flat was close to where Caligula had once walked and had watched men being kept alive in tiny cages. I had no friends in Rome. I had been given Hippolyta's address as someone who would put me up and feed me. I was told that she was kind to stray writers. Approaching her flat was like coming across fields towards a castle; a crenellated building round which traffic swam in a moat. I had imagined Hippolyta as powerful and matronly: when she opened the door she was this tall thin girl with the way of pushing herself off furniture as if on a ship. She said "Hullo"; then—"Excuse me, my husband is on the telephone." She went along a passage to a kitchen where she sat on a marble-topped table beside a toaster. She did her slow laugh into the receiver; held it out to me. I heard her husband's voice a long way off yelling as if from a satellite.

Hippolyta had been brought up in Los Angeles by an American mother and an Italian father; had been orphaned, had come to Rome as a girl. Los Angeles is a place without a centre; a civilisation spread out like spilt milk. Rome is the centre of law, order, religion. I forget what Hippolyta told me about her childhood; someone had been neglectful, someone weak, someone cruel. Most origins are ambivalent; can produce either a saint or a devil. Discussions about origins are boring unless concerned strictly with what is to be done; like discussions of motorists about routes.

In the kitchen Hippolyta's child, the two-year-old, sat in a high chair while its mother and father failed to communicate. It emptied a bowl of soup on to the floor. It was one of those children that cannot be distinguished as boy or girl—a pudding-basin haircut above a face like a war-leader. Hippolyta seemed still attached to her husband by the umbilicus of the telephone; although separated, no one had cut her free. I thought—Her lifeblood will run back to her destruction. The child poured more soup on to the floor and looked alertly to see what its enemies would do. Hippolyta lunged either to hit it or to love it; the child might have liked either. But Hippolyta could not get far enough because of the cord of the telephone. I took a dishcloth and wiped the floor.

Afterwards she said "You shouldn't have done that."

I rinsed the cloth and hung it on a plastic clothes line.

She said "Do you like my kid?"

I said "Yes."

When she spoke she had her half-American half-Italian accent that was somewhere in the Atlantic on the ship on which she rolled.

She said "I'd be dead without that kid."

In her drawing room were silk-covered chairs and high windows looking over the garden. It was spring and the trees were like low clouds. There were children riding on ponies. Lovers lay on the grass. I thought— Hippolyta has health, money, good looks, a child; so she wants to hurt other people and destroy herself. Rome lay beneath us with its rooftops and turrets. From its fountains horses struggled as if from an earthquake.

She said "What are you doing in Rome?"

I said "Writing a book."

She said "What on?"

I said "A biography of Nietzsche."

She said "Would you like to stay here?"

I thought we would get on well. She had this bright flat, a bed, a drink, a view, a gramophone.

That evening she gave one of her parties. Her guests were like the ones invited to a wedding-feast—locusts who settled and stripped the country bare. There were neat men with glittering eyes and spurs on their shoes; women with their heads down by their arms, the Anthropophagi. Here Caligula had walked with his white head and monkey's body. His method of execution was to inflict innumerable small wounds so that his victims did not know that they were dying. Hippolyta did not seem to belong to her party; she was like the owner of a castle in occupied territory. The room became a battlefield; white arms stretching for wine and spilled food. I thought—Romans and Americans can conquer the world; they manage to kill their fathers and mothers. I went into the bedroom and found Hippolyta crying. The room was peculiarly bare with just a single bed and a cot for her child. The child was sleeping.

She shouted "These fucking people, who do they think they are?"

I said "Your friends."

She said "They come in here, bust up my home. Don't they think I've got any feelings?"

She began hitting herself so hard I had to hold her.

I thought I should try to love Hippolyta.

Back in the drawing room at the centre of the remaining guests was a poet, a man with a beard and no fly-buttons and his trousers held up with string. I saw him as Hippolyta's familiar; an incubus who fed off the moles of powerful witches. He was waving a bottle of brandy and was singing "Ee-yi-addio we've won the cup." I had been introduced to him earlier: he was a famous poet, on a lecture tour for the U.S. Cultural Services. I thought that if I could get rid of him I might save Hippolyta. I sat down opposite him and stared below his waist, where straw was coming out of his trousers.

He said "Don't you ever speak?"

He began swearing and pulling at his trousers.

I thought—His job is to upset bourgeois morality and prevent the bomb going off.

A few people were trying to have breakfast. The poet had taken himself out and was holding himself in his hand. I thought—If you imagine yourself outside yourself you can produce slight hysteria. In the Borghese gardens the lights in the trees were like explosions. There was Titian's picture of sacred and profane love. The latter was clothed and the former naked. From the brown hairs of the poet the tiny face of a young bird peeped out.

He shouted "Your adversary the devil!"

I smiled at him.

Hippolyta said "Aren't you two getting along?"

The other people at the end of the party had left. Hippolyta put the gramophone on. She played Handel. The poet was going to sit it out. Thus he sat on the steps of embassies, on the runways of aerodromes, on the sides of mountains. He would leave no mark, like St. Theresa.

The child came in. It wore a short black nightdress. It smelled of urine. I thought I might love the child, which could be useful. I lifted it on to my knee. I thought that if it peed on me I would be holy. I needed to be holy in order to defeat the poet. I put my cheek against the child. The poet had spilled brandy over himself. Inside all his sacking his thin body might go up like smoke.

I said "Why don't you put a match to yourself?"

I picked up the child and took it through to the bedroom. It cried. I looked in the bathroom and found a tube of toothpaste. I took off the top and gave the tube to the child. The child squeezed it and stopped crying. The toothpaste lay all over it like wounds.

Hippolyta shouted "Are you insane?"

I said "I'm making it happy."

Outside the wind blew the lights out in the trees.

I said "Shall we go to bed?"

She said "You want to go to bed?"

I said "Yes."

She said "Why?"

I said "People do."

Hippolyta had changed into a short tight skirt as if she were going shopping. On top she wore a loose-necked jersey so that she looked like brussels sprouts.

She said "But I don't want to go to bed."

I said "I don't think anyone does, but they have to."

She said "What about him?" She pointed along the passage towards the poet.

I said "I'll see."

I went back to the drawing room. The poet was sitting in the middle of an Aubusson carpet in a pattern of flames. His face was red as a satyr's. He was striking matches from an old box in which all the heads of the matches had been burned. I got a new box and gave it to him.

He said "Are you a fascist?"

I said "No."

I went back to the bedroom. I thought—I must put an announcement in the papers in the morning.

Hippolyta said "Is he all right?"

I said "Yes he's all right."

She took my hand. She led me along a passage to a spare room. There was a bed like Napoleon's tomb. I thought—Love is a matter of the will: you have to prove it.

She said "You're sure?"

I said "I'm never sure."

We lay on the floor beside Napoleon's tomb. There is always the hope that it might be impossible. All life is impossible: you hope for reality.

Or you wrestle like men on television, simulating pain and watching yourselves in mirrors.

Hippolyta began to laugh, as she did with her husband.

She said "That was fine."

In the middle of the night I thought I smelled burning so I went along to the drawing room and there was a small pile of ashes where the poet had once been.

In the morning I went out before Hippolyta was awake and I walked in Rome among the fountains where men struggled with horses. There is ancient Rome which is like a room wrecked by spirits and Renaissance Rome which has the spirits locked up in people's faces. Water pours out of their mouths and breasts and penises. I wanted to say to Hippolyta— We know about love; we have read Stendhal and Proust; as soon as we get one foot over the windowsill we want to be back at home reading. So what do we do? I sat by the Trevi fountain where the lines above the old men's stomachs were like lyres. There were flesh-and-blood young men with transistor radios round their necks as if their hands had been cut off and hung there for identity. I thought—I am involved in a battle with myself. There is a route from the Trevi fountain to the Piazza Navona through narrow streets lined with the facades of beautiful prisons. The Pantheon is a shell with a hole in its roof; the sound of the sea comes through. In the Piazza Navona are the horses again pouring with sweat and the men hanging on to them. I had telephoned Hippolyta to meet me for lunch. She was in the restaurant before me.

She said "I didn't think you would come."

I ordered the best food and the best wine.

You sit out on the square beneath flowering shrubs and awnings.

Her hands pulled at a napkin.

I said "Have you seen how all the statues have black eyes?"

She said "That's the weather."

I said "I've been thinking about the origins of the Christian church. In ancient Rome, hell was not to die but to be kept alive. So they put men in cages. When Tiberius was emperor, he got babies to suck him off. He is admired in academic circles. The Christian church was dedicated to the idea that power was useless, so it got power, because everything else was worldly. Tiberius died by being given a poisoned mushroom in his food: he was sick, so they gave it him again in an enema. This was Roman efficiency—having it both ways. But they had the wrong thing."

Hippolyta said "Boom-de-doom, put it on ice, you'd make your fortune."

I said "When Nero gave recitals he had to lock the doors of the theatre and kept his audience prisoners for weeks. They got so bored they pretended to be dead, and were carried out in coffins. Only Romans have ever been so bored; except ourselves, who also build empires. The

Christian church knew it was no good just not wanting power, you had to have it to learn humility. This had to happen inside you, too, because they were pulling down the Coliseum. So you imported lions to eat yourself at home. This was healthy. Nietzsche said that war was ennobling, became a hospital orderly, and went to bed for two weeks."

Hippolyta said "When you come out on that little balcony, wow! we'll all be cheering."

I said "Will you come with me on a journey up through Italy?"

Hippolyta said "You want me to come on a journey up through Italy?"

I said "Yes."

She said "Why?"

I said "Because I like you and you've got lots of money."

Hippolyta said "I haven't been out of this town for five years. D'you know what happens every time I try? I get half way to the station and bang! I'm on a stretcher."

I said "Haven't you got a car?"

She said "Yes."

I said "Darling Hippolyta."

We ate pasta in layers with thin cheese; fish in a wine sauce and mushrooms.

I said "There was once a Roman Emperor whose neurosis was that he couldn't get out of Rome, so he dressed up as a girl and had himself raped by his bodyguard."

Hippolyta said "Is this true?"

I said "Some of it."

She said "Why are you going?"

I said "I want to go to Turin, which is the place where Nietzsche went mad."

She said "Why do you want me?"

I said "I have a power complex. I compensate for my lack of love by making people feel guilty, like Christ and St. Francis."

That night I made Hippolyta lie on the bed. She always wanted to be on the floor, like Roman frescoes.

I thought—Nowadays perhaps one destroys oneself because there is no other way of learning humility.

Afterwards she said "I'll do anything."

In the morning she was wearing a leopard skin coat and white knee-length boots. She might have been leading a borzoi.

I did not think I could get her into the lift, which was like a diving bell.

She had a suitcase like a piece of modern sculpture, which was exactly like a suitcase.

I said "Lean on my arm."

The street was hot. We sat in the car and both wore dark glasses like people in a film. A whole city had been built just outside Rome exactly like Rome, in order to film it.

She said "Where are we going?"

"To Turin."

She said "I don't want to. You don't want me. Why are we going?"

I said "We've got to."

We drove out past the housing estates that were like children's bricks. Beyond them the ruins were tumble-down and beautiful.

Hippolyta said "My father was a weak man and my mother despised him. He was a banker. He used to stand on a platform next to Mussolini with his legs apart as if he was peeing. My mother loved him and saw through him and she went to bed and wouldn't get out of it. Do you know what made her die? He had an affair with an actress."

We were out in the hill country north of Rome; the fields like quilts.

I said "This is the country where the Etruscans once lived. They were peaceable people who loved music and dancing. They thought women were superior to men because women's knowledge was instinctive while men's had to be learned. So the Romans wiped them out, because they were not homosexual."

Hippolyta said "I was a virgin till I was nineteen. Then I had to pick up every man I could get hold of. This was to revenge myself on my father, who made a pass at me in a taxi. He told me to open my mouth."

I said "There was a moment about 450 B.C. when everyone in the world stopped smiling. Up till then there had always been people walking forwards like archaic statues. Then Pericles built the Parthenon and the men on the friezes fought with horses. It was supposed to be better not to have been born." Hippolyta said "When you grow up you want to destroy yourself and you have to get other people to do it for you. So you pick another man who's weak, which is why you marry. You feel better. Or you die."

I said "You won't die."

We were going past country in which I had fought in the war. Several of my friends had been killed. We had been sent out from school into a valley of machine-guns; had had medals pinned on us by old men in night-clubs. We had none of us wanted to go to war; had done it because it was proper and we were frightened.

Hippolyta said "But if you have a strong mother and strong father you still feel guilty."

I said "I was taken prisoner for a moment near here in the war. We all wanted to be prisoners, so we would be in our wire cages and safe."

Hippolyta said "What happened?"

I said "I got away."

We drove along the autostrada where the cars came past like bullets. You were not allowed to stop, or if you did, you would be hit and pushed over.

Hippolyta said "I think my father was impotent."

I said "I thought he was a banker."

The road ran over the hills like a roller-coaster. The landscape was made of plywood. It was painted with flowers and dark green trees.

I wondered if we were going on a journey into hell. All adventurers had had to go to hell—Odysseus, Dante. Heaven came at the end like a cup on prize-giving day. Then you had to give it back, to be put away till next year.

Hippolyta said "I feel so sorry for men. No one loves them."

I said "Do you ever see your husband now?"

She said "I sometimes see him."

I began to imagine this as a journey into Hippolyta's mind. She was a princess locked up in a tower. Women had to be rescued by men riding across water-meadows. She was shut up by her father and her mother. She spent her days spinning cloth and her nights tearing it apart again. She lived with eunuchs and dwarfs. The journey would go across this landscape where I had fought before. There would be some repetition of history.

I said "Dante went into hell after he had seen a twelve-year-old girl on a street corner."

She said "You're too good. I need someone like my husband."

I said "I'm not good."

I began to imagine this as a journey into my own mind. War is the only chance of nobility: without it, there are only the standards of fashion and money.

She said "Are you married?"

I said "Yes."

She said "Tell me about your wife."

I said "The first time I met my wife I fell in love with her and asked her to run me over."

Hippolyta began hitting her fist against her leg.

I imagined Hippolyta walking through the garden and her father coming down through the trees and wanting to make love to her. But he had wished her to be perfect.

We stopped for lunch at a restaurant across the road like an aqueduct. Hippolyta went to wash; pushed herself past pin-tables. Cars whizzed underneath. I imagined the screech of tyres; the smell of burned rubber.

We ate hamburgers and green tomato sauce. They were like sponge-rubber.

She said "Where are we staying tonight?"

I said "Pisa."

She said "Why Pisa?"

I said "I want to go up the tower."

She said "One thing's for sure, you're not going to get me up that fucking tower."

She bought some magazines which she tried to read in the car. There were pictures of people being tortured in the far east; a man bent forwards without a head; an artist on a lavatory; some models with holes in their dresses so their behinds were showing.

I said "Nietzsche saw that men did not want to get any better. They only wanted pity, which kept them torturing each other and pleased. The only way to stop this was to be ruthless. This was correct but unendurable."

She said "I don't want to go to Pisa."

I said "No one wants to go to Pisa."

The road turned left towards the sea. The country became littered with villas like war.

She said "If I go up that tower I'll throw myself off."

I said "Nietzsche saw that men were despised by women. Men wanted to be loved by breaking down, then they became women and women became men in comforting them. The only way out was not to want to be loved. Then you were self-sufficient. Also loved."

The outskirts of Pisa were an industrial town with painted pipes like modern sculptures. Tourists moved with reins of cameras round their necks. In the war, there had been the choice between death or the destruction of some monument.

I thought—When we were helpless there was still freedom.

You go into Pisa past trees and a long wall and then into the green and white playground that is the tower and the cathedral and the baptistry. All along one wall are stalls selling relics—jugs and dolls and busts of saints. The buildings are like sideshows put up for the summer; in the winter there will be bare patches on the ground. People scratch their names on the walls and lie on the grass and make love. Fathers and children play with beach-balls.

I parked the car and walked with Hippolyta past the row of stalls. The saints were Napoleon and Shakespeare and President Kennedy.

The buildings were soft as if they had been sat on. Photographers set up their cameras at some distance from the tower and people posed with one arm out as if they were propping it.

Hippolyta said "I'm not going up."

I said "Try."

She said "You'll have to scrape me off the ground with a shovel!"

The entrance to the tower was down a few steps like a well. The tower was at its angle growing out of skin. It had six rings and a knob at the top. It leaned over a box-hedge in a curve like pornography. I thought—They are always above life size. The staircase went up inside.

I said "Imagine it's your daddy."

We went down the steps to the entrance. You touched the hardness. The ground was white stone. Hippolyta almost got through the turnstile.

I said "This is a fairy story. None of it is quite real."

She said "Do you think you're God?"

In the tube the staircase went round and round and you put out your hand and there was that tickling sensation. Hippolyta followed. She said "I'll get to the first landing and then that's the lot." There were some young girls in shorts going up just in front; they had hair down to their waists and their behinds stuck out. Hippolyta hit at the wall with her fist clenched. We came to an opening on to the first balcony; a platform went round the outside and there was no railing; beyond pillars was a glimpse of the sea. Hippolyta said "I'm stopping." I said "Come on." The stone sloped away to the fall. I put out a hand. I said "You're reborn." We went up past the second landing: on the third the angle seemed steeper; it gave the impression that the tower was revolving so that we would be flung off. Hippolyta was hanging on and had her eyes shut; she was in her gale again. She said "I can't move." I had gone to the edge and was looking over. I have a bad head for heights. I thought—This is for myself. I set off to walk round the tower. You go down the slope and are on one of those rockets at the fair. You are pressed outwards and your girl friend is on top of you. The crowds were on the grass below like hair. There was an area cut off by corrugated iron where the tower might fall: as if it had already fallen, and a grave had been marked out for it. I found it difficult to move; I pushed in my own particular gale. When I got back to the staircase I found Hippolyta had gone. I feared she might have fallen. I went and looked: in dreams you can fly. I found her a little way up; she was sitting. I said "Dear Hippolyta." I sat down and held her. She said "I want to go home." I said "You are brave." I kissed her. I wondered if the girls in the shorts would be at the top. I wanted to get there and then it would be over. I thought—I am mad now. The walls of the staircase were peculiarly smooth. We had more glimpses of the sea and sky through portholes; they showed the earth at an angle as if the ship would sink. I began to say to myself—Get me out of this; I move through each day as if it were my last. I took Hippolyta by the arm. She was a large girl who should have been good with babies. I thought that she might go back to her husband now and be happy there. On the sixth landing were the girls with the camera-straps round their thighs. The cameras were out and they were shooting. Below us on the grass bodies were strewn. I thought we could go no further. All life is a struggle; then you come to the end of it. Hippolyta had fought her way up and had sat down again. She had a round face with a mouth that turned down slightly. Her skin was smooth and her cheekbones wide; she might have been a dancer. Her hair was the colour of spun glass. Somewhere out of sight to the left and right were the roofs of the town and the sea. I said "We'll rest here." I could not think what else to do. I could go back to my home. I could make peace. I thought—Wars have no outcome: it is as bad for the victors as the vanquished.

I set off again around what I thought was the top of the tower. I thought—I can jump off myself; it would have been the wind that had pushed me. We all come to this; on top of the world, on the hard bed of the hospital or in the arms of our lover. I heard voices from somewhere above. I remembered there was still the knob on the tower. I began to walk round to find the steps to go up. I came back to where Hippolyta sat: she had come out on the balcony and stood with one hand over her eyes. I said "Are you all right?" She said "I'm going home." I said "Yes." She said "I'll ring my husband and he'll come and fetch me." I said "Yes." There was a small separate staircase through the wall. I said "I won't be long." I climbed. I did not think that Hippolyta would be hurt. I thought—You take a risk, then break it: this works. The staircase opened on to a platform with huge bells close to the floor. The clappers were like gun-barrels. There was a perimeter of arches; people stood facing the stonework. It was as if they were peeing—or waiting for some annunciation. They had earphones on. They were listening to machines that told them the history of the tower. The tower had been built at such and such a date and then had subsided: objects had been dropped off it to prove gravity. There was a strong wind blowing. A white light was at the top of a mountain. The cathedral was at its angle so you could see the curve of the world. When you are high up you have the impression you are near to God. I thought I could hear angels. I saw a girl with long black hair with her back to me. I knew her: I had been in love with her a long time ago. I had not stopped loving her. She had long legs and a short skirt and a body set like a bone in a socket. She was with a man with dark curly hair who must have been her husband. There was a small child with them; with straight fair hair and a round face. The child was playing with a ball. The ball was bouncing and I was afraid it might go over. I wanted to protect the child. The husband and wife were quarrelling. I thought that if the bells suddenly rang, we all might go over. I leaned on a railing and looked over the roofs towards the sea. The girl was sitting underneath a bell. The child went up to the very top of the tower where there was a parapet above the arches. The child threw the ball down. The ball bounced and went over. The child leaned after it, like myself. The girl's husband went up to the child. There were all these people round us listening with their earphones. I went up to the girl and sat on my heels and said "Hullo." She widened her eyes as she so often did, being short-sighted. She said "What are you doing here?" Her face seemed different: we never remember the faces of people whom we love. I said "I'm going to Turin." She said "Why Turin?" I said "Will you come with me?" She looked at me with eyes that went like water. I said "It's the place where they keep all those people who are mad." What was different about her face was that it was so exposed: it had always been beautiful. I said "We could go there." She looked away. Her husband and child were on the arches above: he was holding the child's hand and pointing out landmarks. Below there were voices. I wondered what had happened to Hippolyta. Hippolyta was all right. The girl said "I have my commitments." There was this extraordinary smoothness under her eyes as if no tears came to furrow them. I stood up. I wondered if I should walk backwards to the stairs as if in the presence of something divine or dangerous. I said "I have missed you." She said "I've missed you too," I wanted to say—I told you there would be miracles. I tried to work out how much longer I had in Italy. Her face was brown with a red mouth and bright gold eyes. These colours were held by the black light around her. She said "Are you staying here?" She sang, as if fountains were running over. Her husband and child were coming back down the steps. I thought— What more can be done for us? There was suddenly the sound of bells and we all ducked and put our hands over our ears. The sound was not from the bells themselves, but from a van in the street below which was advertising. The girl's face looked as if fire were being poured over it. I thought—it is beginning again.

≈　≈　≈

You go through a small door from the street and there are nuns to conduct you through what might be the Garden of Eden. I carried my camera and notebook.

The Institute in Turin is an enormous work of charity where suffering people from all over Europe come to live and die and be mad; an organisation not so much to change human nature as to come to terms with it, to try to cure it of course with all the best equipment and technology but ultimately to recognise that this is impossible; to show that suffering has to be used in order to make life bearable.

The Institute is religious, and at the centre is a chapel as big as a cave with hundreds of nuns praying. There are side-chapels with relics of the founder: his hair-shirt, his spiked belt, the lash with which he flogged himself. The founder was a holy man who relieved much human suffering. He knew that one had to take on suffering oneself in order to produce ecstasy. He had no money: he built hospitals which housed two thousand people: the money came in afterwards. You go in the dark to produce miracles.

The nuns take you round like tourists. You prepare for hell; are offered snapshots of heaven. After the relics and spikes and chapels and the cave with its bats praying you go into a world like a modern housing estate. Here is demonstrated serenity through suffering. In small gardens with apple trees are the men who are mad: their faces have turned to stone, they stand festooned with saliva-webs. Their expressions are wholly violent or wholly passive; they have nothing to do with humanity, which is paradox. The mad women are cocottes; they sit in high chairs and wave spoons; they are babies who dream of being mothers. The colour of the mad is white. Madness is in extremes like logic.

In another part of the Institute are the children on whom have been visited the sins of their fathers. They have no legs nor arms; they walk with the fins of fishes. Out of the slime thus climbed our heroic ancestors. You watch them and cannot think what to do. There is nothing to say about suffering, only to do it.

In another part are the very old who want to die but who cannot because life keeps them in beds like tiny cages. The crowd passes in the street below; sometimes looks up and tries to imagine their predicament.

All round is cheerfulness; the bright light at the top of a mountain.

In the centre is the hum of the machine that keeps life going. Life is a factory, of which suffering is only the setting. Boilers consume each day enough flour to feed five thousand: the loaves and fishes appear, but the world remains hungry. There are machines for washing sheets like the printing room of a national newspaper. Cleanliness is near to God; the killing of microbes.

Those who run the place have the good faces of people changing sex. Monks are delicate as birds: nuns strong as Roman emperors. They are happy. Sadness, they click their tongues at.

I thought—If the world is a mechanism driven by pity there are now branches in every country. The work spreads. There is no budget nor board of directors. As soon as a gift arrives it is used, and when there are no more gifts you increase your commitments. All this is evident; it is just refuted by intelligence.

I walked back through crowded streets at lunch time. I was going to meet the person with whom I was travelling. I had been doing research-work for a story I was writing: the story was to do with Nietzsche. Nietzsche had said that one has to break out of pity. He said that one should act as if events recurred; as if what happened to one once went on happening for ever.

On my way to the restaurant where I was having lunch I passed the spot where Nietzsche had gone mad. There is a brass plaque to commemorate this, saying how he was a hero who struggled with the human spirit. His sad furious face looks out from his moustache. Opposite is an art gallery which exhibits sponge-rubber; behind, a courtyard selling books and music. In the square is the king with his upraised sword; a victim of Risogimento.

Our favourite restaurant in Turin has a coat of arms over the place where Cavour once sat: the room is decorated in cream and gold and there are red plush chairs and chandeliers. The person whom I loved was there before me. When she looked up there was that black light around her; her hair making colours inside her transparent skin. I said "Sorry I'm late." I sat down. I said "What are you eating?" She always chose food carefully, having the gift of preferring one thing to another. She said "Costolette Valdostano." I said "I'll have that too." I put my hand on her leg. I said "And for wine—." I chose it. There was a waiter who knew us and who took our order. She said "Did you have a good morning?" I said "Yes." I wanted the waiter to come so that I could have a drink. She said "Tell me." She broke bread ceremoniously. The waiter came and poured out two glasses and I drank. I said "I also saw the place where Nietzsche went mad." There was a stillness about her as if all life went on inside. I said "But I don't think any of this is of importance to you." After a time she said "Why not if it is to you?" I wanted to tell her about all life being inside her; but she sometimes became jealous if I talked about things other than herself.

The night the President died teams stood at the foot and the head of his bed and were ready with diagrams to tell him what was happening. They took him to hospital in a cavalcade with the mayor in front and the family following and the track all lined with bookmakers. In the hospital they took his heart out and left it lying on the table like a baby. Soldiers stepped forward and offered to give up their lives; said goodbye to their wives and families. The teams passed each other in the passages laughing and tearing their masks off.

When the President reappeared he still had wires trailing behind and men had to follow him and stamp on the ends like fuses. Sometimes the wires acted as aerials and the President danced and played a guitar. Once the wires trailed across a high-tension cable and his hand shot up in a salute. A line of airmen came past kicking like chorus girls.

They had to have him back for repairs and they experimented with a thermometer like an explosive banderilla. He spoke softly and when he got to certain pauses his eyes lit up and numbers flashed. He made statements about the time, the weather, and the histories of ancient buildings. At night he was taken down and hung up by the neck: men came to empty out his pockets.

In the meantime they were working on a totally mechanised President which would do away with the necessity of a dead one. They had simulated all his physical organs and had got his eyes lighting up; they had not quite managed yet his way of collapsing over a table. They took him to pieces again and found a message with a map reference in the ocean. A fleet was sent out and picked up a bottle a few hundred miles off target. The report of the analysis was negative.

When the mechanical President was ready they wheeled him out for his first conference and propped him in a chair and sat him so that he would exhibit cards in his window and blow a whistle. His forehead was polished and he had had a few more bristles stuck in his wig; they had sprayed his smile on with fixative. The pressmen got excited and stampeded and took photographs of each other's feet on their faces. A lever was pulled and the President lit up and sparks flew to and fro between his spectacles. This demonstrated how he could be in two places at once, and worked out the speed of infinity.

Soon there were mechanical Presidents in every small town; President kits were marketed that could be made by a child with the help of an adult. You could climb up inside and sit in the President's stomach; slide down a shute into a pool between his legs. You could sit in a silent room where the President's heart had once been—but this was empty. Someone turned the President's head round so that it faced the wrong way: they painted his shoulder-blades like breasts.

But the public got tired of the new toy: the paint began to peel, and starlings roosted in the porticos. The tape recorder that played sweet music had become scratched until there was a noise like a ship in a gale. Sometimes the President's eyes still flashed and his mouth opened for children to throw balls into; but then this jammed, and a piece of paper was stuck over it. Sometimes in the rain there seemed to be tears in the President's eyes; and once in a wind he was heard to groan. There was a referendum on the question of another repair or of his disposal; but no one would take the responsibility. Everything was in the hands of local authorities now, and they had lost the name of his manufacturer.

Suicide

I HAD BEEN INVOLVED in this ecstatic love affair, so I naturally thought of suicide.

I had the idea that all great lovers committed suicide—Romeo and Juliet, Tristan and Isolde, Othello and Desdemona. You put a penny in the slot and first Juliet did it and then Romeo and for your money's worth Juliet again. They gave value in the old days. And Tristan and Isolde—I could not quite remember—they had been on a beach—had been experienced—and had managed it several times too. About Desdemona I was not so sure; she had been young, and had had to get someone to do it for her.

It had been a cold summer. I was living in London in a bed-sitting room at the top of four flights of stairs.

There were peculiar outbreaks of violence at this time. A professor of Greek murdered his father at a crossroads; in Spain, a matador stuck his sword through a horse.

In my bed-sitting room there was a wash-basin with old razor blades piled like footprints. I thought I would jump out of bed one morning and do it quickly. I would touch my toes, knees bend, then cut my wrists. You are taught to be bright and early.

I was in this bed-sitting room away from my wife and family. I had become too content; had got middle-aged around forty. I had thought I should go out like Tolstoy to die in a railway station.

The person with whom I was in love used to visit me mornings and evenings. She was learning to do pottery; would call in to and from work. She would climb the stairs with the footsteps that I had so much longed for; that I hoped might not materialise, that would send me into despair if they did not. I sometimes planned to be in despair before she arrived to get it over with; but I was always enormously happy when expecting her. Then I was sometimes sad when she arrived. I do not know why love is like this: you want what you haven't got and when you've got it you don't want it. Perhaps it is because love is at the heart of things, like the particles that jump without reason or location.

I tried to explain to her about Romeo and Juliet. These desires are in our unconscious; we go to great trouble to make them real. Romeo and Juliet need not have died; they had had to prove their commitment.

She did not believe me.

When she came in in the mornings there would be that black light around her which had been there the first time we had met. She had been standing in a museum against a background of bookshelves. I would usually still be in bed. She would draw the curtains and make me breakfast. I had a gas ring on top of a stove that looked like Cleopatra's needle. She would kneel and make coffee and take croissants from her bag. We drank out of yellow cups like sunshine. She wore a dark jersey and jeans. She sat on my bed and when she swallowed she made a noise like heat going down. I thought how I had had everything in life I wanted now—A wife and children and the person with whom I was in love. I had always wanted everything.

She would say "What's the matter?"

"Nothing."

"Why are you sad?"

"I'm not."

"Do you want me not to go to work then?"

"No I don't mind."

"I won't if you don't want me to."

There is this malaise about love in which one wants to lie in bed and watch it. It walks round the room like a nurse, untouchable.

She said "Do make up my mind."

I both wanted her to stay so that we could make love and to go so that I would not be vulnerable.

I said "You go. We must keep working."

I thought if I said this she would stay.

She said "Well if you want me to I will."

She kissed me. I jumped as if currents were passing through me. I wondered if I were acting.

She said "Look, I'd better stay."

I said "No. Or we'll both feel guilty."

She said "But I don't want to go."

I said "I'm doing this to make you stay."

We always worked in opposites. The only difference between us and other people, I thought, was that we recognised this and they did not.

Not that this made life any easier.

I thought—If I had asked her to stay then she would have said she had to get to work or else feel guilty, but now she is staying and we feel guilty anyway. There is no solution; opposites are infinite.

She said "Then shall I go?"

I said "It doesn't seem up to us."

We lay on the bed. We did this when there was nothing else to do.

I thought—The question is not what is acting and what is not, but what is or is not proper acting.

I said "Then let's make love."

She said "I'm afraid I haven't brought my thing."

I had known she was going to say this. That is why I had been cautious from the beginning.

She did this because of guilt and in order to hurt me. She had once said—I know I do it to hurt you.

I thought—Why not?

I hung my head over the edge of the bed and appeared stricken.

Sometimes when I was like this a look of peace came over her face as if we were a Pieta.

I said "Then go."

She said "I'm sorry."

I thought perhaps things were easiest for women when men were collapsing.

She said "I'll do the washing up."

"No"

"I want to."

"I don't want you to."

She paused by the door. One of the most difficult things in love is to get out of a door. I had the advantage, because I was not the one who was leaving. But I would have the terror after she had gone.

She said "I don't want to go."

We had these farewells like Hector and Andromache; half in tears, smiling, on ramparts above a battlefield.

I thought—The terror is real. That is why no one wants reality.

I said "I love you."

She said "I love you too."

We had to say these words that would make the parting not final but would let it be final if we wanted this.

After she had gone I banged my head against the wall. Once I had banged it till it bled. Then I had felt better. All the razor-blades were in place on my washbasin. My room was tiny with just the bed that took up most of the space and a table and the stove like Cleopatra's needle. Because it was shaped like a needle, I could not get my head into it.

I got out of bed and sat at my table and looked at the blank sheets of paper in my typewriter. The keys were like men waiting to be sent out over no-man's-land.

I was still writing my book about how love flourishes in time of war; how men leave their families and go off on crusades for salvation. They get indulgences from hell, which is to do with order and stillness.

I thought—All love is moral; that is why you want to die in it.

When you are writing you spend much of your time dreaming or doing crossword puzzles.

I had once known a man who used to torture himself in attics. He had tried to crucify himself, but could not manage the last knot. So he had built a machine to do this for him. He was a mathematician. He had not been found for three days.

The person with whom I was in love had used to meet me at lunch time in a pub. The pub had been crowded with young businessmen with elbows. She would come in with her fur hat and muff. She had two faces or personalities—one when it was difficult to see me which was happy, and the other when it was easy which was sad.

I thought—I have always known life is impossible. Stories are symbols in which impossibilities are held.

The pain sometimes got so bad that I had to get up and lean over the basin. I tried to be sick. The problem was not how to kill yourself but how to stay alive. I thought—We need someone to come along and shut us in small cages. I had too much disgust with myself. But if I had not, I might have died.

I thought I might cut a wrist quickly and see how much blood came out.

Someone knocked at my door.

The woman who came in to clean each day was always fussy about the basin.

I said "Who is it?"

A voice said "Plumber."

I said "Wait a minute."

I did not want to be caught in my pyjamas.

I tried the taps, and hot and cold water came out.

There was a trap door in my room that went up into an attic. There were a lot of huge pipes there, some of them leading nowhere like ventilators on a ship.

I said "I was just getting my clothes on."

The plumber said "The things some people do."

He was a thickset man with a ladder.

He put the ladder to the trap door and went up. He had a light with a wire trailing behind him. Huge shadows rushed on the walls.

I said "Is anything wrong?"

He said "Water water everywhere."

I put the electric kettle on in order to make tea. I had an idea that plumbers drank tea.

He said "It goes down here, comes up there, but what happens then?"

The friend of mine who used to tie himself up in attics had once broken free and had come through the ceiling like a fire-bomb.

The plumber said "Do you play football?"

"Yes."

He said "I and my sons play in the same team."

I said "I've got three sons."

His face appeared at the trap door. He said "You know, I thought you had."

I handed up the cup of tea. We were like two climbers on the north face of the Eiger.

He said "Have you got a basin?"

I said "Directly underneath you."

He began sucking on a pipe and spitting water out. The water went into his tea. The edge of the pipe cut his mouth which bled.

He said "Are you a writer then?"

I said "Yes."

"Do you use a typewriter or write by hand?"

"Both."

"Do you believe in God?"

I was half-way up the ladder. There was a big tank with white plastic round it. I thought—If you sat in it, you could get your temperature down to zero.

He said "You shouldn't have any more trouble."

Water suddenly began pouring out all over him.

He said "My son earns forty quid a week."

The water splashed on the thin plaster ceiling. He wrestled with wrenches. His shirt was open and his chest bare. He sweated.

He said "How do you explain suffering children?"

I said "You don't. You do something about them."

He suddenly came down and picked up his ladder. He said "Let me know if you want anything else."

I said "Thanks."

He disappeared.

I went to the washbasin and hot and cold water came out. I sat down at my typewriter again. In the old days, when you were in love, there were all the conventions to make things difficult. Now you had to do it yourself. There were sculptors who made machines that blew themselves up in the desert: painters who exhibited excrement. My friend who went up to attics had wanted to turn himself into a mobile. He had got hold of a piece of string. I thought—We have lost the idea of a loving God.

I wondered if I should ring up the person with whom I was in love. I could say that I could not see her this evening. Then she would be upset and I would feel safer. Or if I did not ring up, she might be worried.

I went back to the basin. I pulled my wrist so that there was a lump of muscle and tendon. You clenched your fist and all the veins appeared in diagonals. When you cut them you had to grab your arm quick in order to prevent pain. The razor blade fell from your fingers.

I thought—Love is not what you feel it is what you do. You put a hand here, raise a leg, there, manipulate machinery. Or you give yourself up and go back to earth again.

I thought of going to my wife and children.

The person with whom I was in love used to stand on tiptoe to kiss me.

I wanted help.

I was holding a piece of string. It had been made in India, where hungry people scratched on dry ground for burial. If I went out of the window, I would dangle like a pawnbroker.

I thought—We are front-line soldiers: we don't want to fight, but we are too stupid or too brave. It is people at the base who hate and stay alive.

I decided I must do the thing quickly. I picked up a razor-blade and made a pass with it at my wrist. You put your hand into boiling water to prove you are truthful. I hit at my wrist again. I found that I had cut it quite deeply. I leaned against the washbasin.

In the old days people had no vegetables in winter. Monks flogged themselves. Children had enemas and leeches.

A lot of blood had come out over my jersey and trousers. I wondered if I really might die. You committed suicide for love; but you did not get love because you were dead. What are adored are torturers and the successful.

I turned on the tap to wash with. No water came out. I thought—Plumbers are useless.

There was not much pain. I had wrapped a towel round my wrist and twisted it. The flesh ached deeply. Once you have done it there is nothing else to do. That is why you have to go on doing it. I walked round the room. When you know that torturers and the successful are loved, do you let yourself be crucified? I thought I should get down on my knees and crawl like a dog. When the person whom I loved had come this morning and had been kind I had wanted to die. If she had been cruel, would I have fought her and been happy? The pain got worse.

I pulled at my groin.

I went to the cupboard and took down a suitcase; it fell, jerking my wrist. The blood welled out. Inside the suitcase I kept a vest which she sometimes wore. I buried my face in it.

I thought—If love exists only before and after, then in relics you have the beatific vision.

I heard the telephone ringing in the hall downstairs.

I thought that she might be ringing up to save me. Or to tell me she could not see me.

The boarding-house was on four landings and men on all floors popped out when the telephone rang. We stood facing inwards on our various landings as if waiting for an annunciation.

The landlady called my name.

I ran down the stairs so fast that I slipped and flung a leg out and smashed a bulb in the ceiling. I wondered how I could explain this.

My wife's voice said "Hullo."

I said "Oh hullo."

She said "Oh you're in."

I wanted to say—Yes I'm in.

She said "I've got the children."

I wanted to say—I know you've got the children.

When I want to annoy my wife I do not answer her, because she puts her questions in such a way that they are not questions but statements to annoy me.

I said "How are you?"

She said "We're in London. Can we come and see you?"

"Yes."

She said "When?"

"Now."

There was a long pause and then she said "Are you all right?"

I ran upstairs and slipped again and lay on my stomach. My wrist seemed to be pumping. I had to clean the blood off the basin without any water. I had to have more towels. I emptied all the clothes out of my suitcase and started wiping the basin with my pyjamas. I thought I might be arrested for murder. I could leave my own body in the suitcase in a waiting room.

I had the room clean and tidy long before they arrived. I sat on the edge of the bed and tried to think of something to do.

When they came up the stairs it was like a fight in a western film, people cannoning off walls, crashing through bannisters, demolishing matchwood. They all seemed too large for such a narrow room: they were Alices with arms and legs up a chimney. I had to crawl backwards over my bed. I was so pleased to see them.

My wife said "What are you doing?"

"Writing."

"Didn't you get my letter?"

I said "I haven't been downstairs. I spend all my time writing."

My wife hadn't been to my room before. I thought she might be interested in the sort of place I was in.

My eldest son said "What have you done to your wrist?"

I said "Cut it."

My second son said "What on?"

I said "A razor blade."

We all had to keep standing up like people in a lift.

My second son said "What are you writing?"

I said "A story."

He said "The biography of Nietzsche?"

I said "No, that's in another reincarnation."

My wife did not seem to be interested. It was as if she had brought all our children just to dump them here.

My eldest son said "But why are you here?"

I said "So I can write. There's this story."

He said "About someone in a bed-sitting room?"

"Yes."

My wife said "We've got to get to Harrods."

I wanted to shout.

She said "Can we get a forty-nine?"

I said "Can you?"

My eldest son said "Isn't it really quite a sensible thing to do to go mad?"

I said "Not sensible."

He said "I mean for a writer?"

I began talking energetically. I said "Just because you know something is likely or even inevitable doesn't mean you ought to do it."

I thought—Who am I talking to?

My wife said "Surely, you don't think too much about yourself."

I said "Who doesn't?"

She said "I'm reading a book about General Birdwood at Saragossa."

I said "General Burgoyne at Saratoga."

They were carrying a lot of parcels. They held them like bagpipes.

I said "A plumber came here this morning. The water was running perfectly beforehand and after he'd gone it stopped."

My second son said "Is that true?"

I said "Not quite."

My wife said "When are you coming home?"

I said "I don't know."

She said "Let me know."

I said "I will."

They collected their parcels. They seemed on a trip to the south pole.

My wife said "I've got you a present." She took out a woollen jersey.

I said "That's terribly kind!"

I held it up by its sleeves. It was like the jersey which I was wearing, which was a present from the person I was in love with.

I thought I might cry.

She said "Well we must be going."

I said "Have a nice time."

My sons were embarrassed.

They went downstairs like ambulance men.

When I was alone I did not think I would try to work any more. I thought I might kill myself with surfeit.

There were people who were trying to become more like machines. This was not difficult. It was only difficult to be human. I thought—I will write a story about what people are really like. We imagine we move according to cause and effect, whereas in reality we are particles with velocity but no location. Or if we have location we have no velocity. We can be in two places at once. If we are together and go apart, then there is energy: if we are static, there is not. These are the conditions of being human. Our minds and our stories find it difficult to grasp this. But a writer should try to describe what is true.

I thought I would ring up the person with whom I was in love and ask her to save me. This might destroy us.

Every other art was concerned with complexity. It was only literature that seemed infantile.

I might rush into the street and catch my wife and family.

I got half-way down the stairs and then I slipped again. I lay on my back. I thought I should take things easy.

The telephone was in the hall. You dialled very quietly so that all the men on the landing would not pop out and wait for messages.

She took some time to get to the telephone. Her voice was distant. She said "Hullo?"

"Hullo?"

"Are you all right?"

I said "No."

She said "Look, why didn't you tell me you were in a state? Then I'd have stayed this morning."

I said "But you didn't stay."

She said "But you didn't want me to."

I said "I know."

I began pressing the receiver hard against my ear.

She said "Look, what is the matter?"

I thought I was going to scream.

She said "Hullo."

I said "Yes?"

She said "We can't go on like this."

I felt the relief beginning. I let my breath out.

I said "Like what?"

She said "I get exhausted."

I wanted to bang the receiver down.

I said "Will you come to the pub and have lunch?"

She said "Well, I had thought of this, but now I don't know. I don't know where I am with you."

I said "Come to the pub."

She said nothing.

I said "See you in twenty minutes."

I ran up the stairs. I took care not to fall. It was difficult getting my wrist with the towel round it through the sleeve of my jacket.

The pub was the one we had used to meet in during the winter. It was now a bright spring day. I thought I might now write my story. I thought—Stories are our only freedom.

Going into a place that in the past has meant much to you is like meeting a piece of yourself. I had forgotten what I had been then. I had had some secret. We had been going to transform the world.

There was the table at which we had sat. Two high-backed chairs like tombstones.

She was there before me. Her small face looked out of its lair.

Sometimes she was the different person from the one I remembered: as if she had a twin sister.

This is common in mythology. It is to do with schizophrenia.

I thought I knew what to do when this happened. You had to be careful.

It was not that she looked different: she and her twin sister were identical. It was just that there was a difference in relation to me.

Her sister often did not speak. She would sit with liquid eyes and let me touch her.

Then she would turn me to stone.

I said "What are you thinking?"

One should never ask—What are you thinking?

All the men were there in their summer suits.

I was sitting beside her.

I said "Do tell me."

She drank her fruit juice. There was the noise of hot iron going down.

I thought—I know what's happening.

I said "You destroy things by not talking. Talking is an exorcism."

I ate my sandwich. We had not been back to the pub since the winter.

She said "All right I'll tell you. It's just that I sometimes feel I'm taking on too much. You were all right this morning. What's wrong now?"

I said "What is wrong?"

She said "On the telephone."

I said "What on the telephone?"

She said "I did my best for you."

I said "Yes."

She said "But all the time I think I knew I was cheating."

I said "How were you cheating?"

She said "I have to protect myself."

I said "Oh ducky you protect yourself!"

When there is self-mutilation there is this feeling of peace spreading through the universe.

She said "I'm not going to talk if you go on like this."

I said "What do you mean you were cheating?"

She said "You don't really want me."

I said "You mean you knew it was over?" I stood up.

She said "Yes." Then—"Don't put it on to me!"

I thought—I am putting it on to her.

She said "I come whenever you want me. I have a lot of other things to do."

I said "Do them then."

She shouted "You can't go now!"

We were both standing. We had never minded what other people thought.

She said "I thought you needed me."

I said "I don't."

When she was angry her face became fragile.

She said "I'll kill you."

I said "You kill me, ducky. I'm an old soldier."

I sat down. We were never good at getting away. We hung about like people wounded.

I thought—I will regret this terribly. In a few hours I will not even understand it.

She stood up and took my keys out of her bag. She put them on the table.

I thought—So she's going first. I'll be magnanimous.

I thought—She'll never make it.

She said "Goodbye." She went to the door.

She always turned round in doorways.

She did not turn round.

I thought—I did not think that we could make it!

Then—How brave!

She went out.

I thought—I've freed her.

I went to the bar and got more beer. Blood was pumping in my wrist.

Later, I went into the street. It was a warm day with the trees like bells. When you have done violence there is this drug, order, that comforts you. I thought that what I could now write about was the need for meaning and morality. We did not know what we were doing, we did it. We were sleepwalkers listening for bells. Freedom was duty. I could. go back. Perhaps I had finally committed suicide.

In an arena on a Sunday afternoon the elite of the fashionable world come to eat ice-cream and throw cardboard on to the sand. They wear clothes with holes at the knees and elbows; sit on stone benches and feel injury. Around them are the advertisements for lung cancer and cirrhosis of the liver, made of white enamel and pitted with bullet-holes. Teenagers cry and moan; a nanny comes on with a guitar to comfort them. At the entrance of the gladiators the noise has risen beyond the range of the human ear: visions are seen of blue dresses above a grotto.

The mannequins wear tight silk trousers and have pigtails at their necks. They walk up a gangplank and pirouette; swing cloaks and turn on the audience with contemptuous eyes. The audience wants blood: at moments of extremity it wets itself.

At a bugle a door is opened and the clowns jump out of the ring: in comes the spangled lady. She is wide at the front and narrow at the back and her rear legs go faster so that she overtakes herself on corners. She is the old war hero in a wheelchair: she moves plugged in like a Hoover.

The technique is to remove each garment one by one while a gramophone plays religious music. The audience is in the dark: they have leisure now in the afternoons. The place of honour is reserved for a President from South-East Asia. The artists have to appear bored. The hero goes past and gets his horn stuck in the barrier. The mannequin stands with one hand on his hip and blows kisses to housewives. The bull sees the saint with the long auburn hair and the crowds at his feet in the valley.

At another bugle horses come in and jerk at the knees like bicycles. Men stand on handlebars and flip between oil-drums. Horses are armoured and are the masculine part of women; if you get close enough you can drop lighted matches through their peep-holes. Barbarians once swarmed across Europe and brought civilisation to decadent Rome: they defended the marshes from *the peddlars of bottles and ice-cream-cones. Now a man lowers his head and gets a woman up against a barrier. A woman likes to see that a man is brave: she lowers her head and spurs him on to ecstasy. By leaning on the shaft and twisting she can produce disablement as well as pain. As the man gets his horn under the belly, the woman has him by the back of the neck. The crowd roars. The contest may end through impotence. The blood makes gay colours against the rosettes. Politics is an attempt to make men pretty.*

When the bugle goes again the boys come running down the road in their white shirts and black tights and thighs like marrows. They can get these to inflate and balloon them. They carry fireworks in small paper bags; are careful to hold these away from them. The suicide watches the blood drip on to his shirt: sometimes it goes through the ceiling. He dabs with his hands, and the orchestra responds to him. They make rendezvous through addresses on the walls of lavatories.

When the prima donna returns for her last performance her skirts are tucked up and she has difficulty in getting through the barrier. A man likes to throw flowers at what isn't there; an ankle, the red cloak of oblivion. He rushes towards that taste of dark hair; then is past, on his knees on the gravel. A boot is on his neck: they make you dig your own grave now. The transvestist turns away and trails his coat: the victim knows that the best he can do is to take the world with him. There is the button to be pressed and sewn; the millions to die for the one sinner. The girl stands under a lamp-post with her stomach out: she wants to be wounded, but the boy is very tired. The blade slips in. He recognises, in love, this reversal of everything normal; his rape by Europa, the sword beckoning to the garden, the spittle separating from dust. Sometimes the blade appears through the walls of his chest and gibbers there. A surprised look comes over his face as if he were being chaired. They hang on to each other, the man and the woman, because to withdraw is unhealthy according to psychologists. You wait for doctors with choppers to release you. You begin to remember where you were born on the wide plains round Salamanca. The girl has her clothes disarranged and is being examined by police. The bull is on his back with his feet in the air. A team of lovely horses come to drag him. They go six times round the walls of Troy. Then he is hung up and the girl's father comes to castrate him. This is the prerogative of fathers. Rape is so difficult to prove. There is a big rent in the girl's trousers, which she puts her hands over provocatively.

Life after Death

WALKING THROUGH STREETS LATE at night I saw a crack in the sky and a red arm coming through with the fist clenched like a foetus.

I was approaching the corner where I had a flat at the top of a row of tall Victorian buildings. I had become accustomed to these impressions at night; as if layers of protection were being peeled off leaving the spaces between me and the world raw, with blood running down the faces of buildings.

My flat was in a house with steps up to a portico. I looked behind to see what the portents might mean. I had spent the evening alone, as I spent many evenings at this time, since I had been involved in an unhappy love affair and did not need human company. I saw my reflection beside me in a plate-glass window. I was something elect and prehistoric, waiting for the ice-flow.

A car was parked outside my house and men were standing on the steps. I thought I would walk past: I had my hand in my pocket as if there was a gun there. I had no name on my clothes; they could not identify me. I was slightly manic at this time. At the bottom of the steps I slowed: I had been sure they were waiting for me. But you do not believe it when you are there.

They were men in overcoats with buttons down the middle. They had blank faces. I thought I could duck and hunch my shoulders. My hand in my pocket held my bunch of keys. One had a smooth barrel.

I said "Are you waiting?"

One of them said my name.

I said "Yes."

They said "May we have a word with you?"

My flat was on the top floor. You opened the street door with one key and then went up three flights to a wall of frosted glass which had a door with a Yale lock and another lock for the key like a gun-barrel.

I said "Are you police?"

I patted my pockets and pretended to be looking for my keys.

There were three men. The car was black with a lamp on the top. I thought—They would have to be police.

I said "Can you tell me what's happened?"

My pockets seemed full of coins. I hid my keys underneath them.

I said "I'm afraid I can't find my keys."

I thought—If they search me, I'll drop the keys down the basement.

They said "You live here?"

"Yes."

"On the top floor?"

"Yes."

I thought—There may be a light on.

I began to go through all my pockets again like a man at a ticket barrier.

I said "Sorry, they've gone. What do you want?"

"We'd like a talk."

"Well we can't go up to my flat."

"Then would you come to the car?"

"Certainly."

I thought that from the edge of the pavement I would see if there was a light on.

We went to the car. They had smooth faces on which no shadows came. As I climbed into the car I felt like a child again. You were driven back to school by strange relations and you counted the miles to see how much longer you had to live.

I sat in a corner. There was a man to one side of me and a man in the front turned facing me and a driver looking to his front going nowhere. I felt like a girl.

One of them said "Do you know Mrs. Harris?"

"Yes."

"When did you last see her?"

"Some time ago."

"You don't seem surprised when I asked you do you know Mrs. Harris."

"Should I?"

I wanted to explain—Surely it would seem artificial?

Then I thought—Victims sometimes incriminated themselves by being too clever for their inquisitors.

"Do you know Mr. Harris then?"

"No.

"You've not seen him?"

"No."

I thought I should say—Has anything happened to her?

I said "Has anything happened to her?"

"Why do you ask?"

"Isn't it natural?"

I was suddenly terrified that something might really have happened. I said "Do tell me."

They said "You're anxious?"

I said "One fears the worst."

They said "What worst?"

They were filling in time: were not really trying to find out from me.

"Are you expecting Mrs. Harris?"

I said "Then Mrs. Harris is all right."

They watched me.

I thought—She must have done something.

I said "Who then?"

I wanted to ask—Is he dead?

I remembered her saying once—I'll kill him.

They were waiting for her to come walking up the dusty street.

I thought—This is because I feel guilty.

Then—But why else should they be waiting?

My heart was thumping.

I said "Mr. Harris?"

I thought—Shouldn't I explain?

One said "Why should you ask that?"

Another said "Yes."

I thought—She sometimes comes up the street looking for my car. She is short-sighted.

They said "You're not surprised?"

"Of course."

"But Mrs. Harris hasn't been with you this evening?"

No.

"When did you last see her?"

"Several weeks ago."

"Can you remember the date?"

"No."

"Why weren't you surprised when you said, Mr. Harris?"

I said "There must be some serious reason for all this."

If she came she might come by taxi but might stop at the corner and walk. She would look up at the window to see if there was a light on. She still had a pair of keys. She might have come earlier and already be there. This was why I had said I had lost my keys.

"We're trying to find Mrs. Harris."

"Yes."

"You don't know where she is."

"No."

"You have a liaison with Mrs. Harris."

I thought—What a word.

I said "What's happened to Mr. Harris?"

"I'm interested in what made you suppose something had."

"You don't come out ordinarily in the middle of the night."

They waited.

I said "Is he dead?"

One of them said "You should think of your position."

I thought—Tonight I went to a film on my own. I had supper at a snack bar. There were yellow lights and stone tables. The waitress would recognise me.

I thought—They must see it's natural I'd think him dead. She had said—He may kill himself.

They said "Where were you tonight?"

"At a cinema."

"On your own?"

"Yes."

"What was the film?"

It was a film I had seen a week ago.

They wanted to find out my reactions before they told me. But people don't have reactions. They just try to do what is expected. Then this becomes too ordinary, and they do something else. Actors cannot act what is real.

I said "Why do you want her then?"

"She'd want to know about her husband wouldn't she?"

"Of course. Why are you waiting outside my house?"

One said "We're asking the questions."

I thought—You stupid actor.

I said "Is the child all right?"

"You know the child?"

"Yes."

Another said "You won't take us up to your flat?"

"I told you, I've lost my keys."

"What are you going to do then?"

I said "Probably go to my sister's."

I thought suddenly—It must be murder, not suicide, or they wouldn't be going on so.

I put my head in my hands. The car had two bucket seats, in the back of which were ashtrays from which if you pulled them all the ash fell over your trousers.

I thought—Then I am an accomplice.

They said "Can you tell us about yourself and Mrs. Harris?"

I said "There's not much to tell."

People who are guilty confess to crimes they did not commit.

"Did you telephone Mrs. Harris at three o'clock this afternoon?"

"No."

"You haven't seen her today?"

"No."

"So you can't help us?"

"No."

"You're saying Mrs. Harris is not in your flat now?"

"Of course she isn't."

I thought—I've known she is there all the time.

A man stretched past me and opened the door.

He said "I should keep clear of Mrs. Harris."

I said "Yes."

I did not understand this.

I thought—I still do not believe it.

I got out into the street.

They said "We'll keep in touch."

I began walking up to my house. I had my hand on the keys in my pocket and was about to open the door. Then I did a sort of dance on the doorstep, hitting my head as if I were crazy. They were watching. I was on my way to my sister's. I came down the steps. I wanted to explain to them—I am mad.

The car drove off.

I thought it might be coming round the block again.

I walked along the street where we had so often walked. I had to protect her. At a crisis, there was nothing else to do.

Being in love is like the day on which war is declared—you stand on station platforms and there is the eternity of the next five minutes. Love is an extremity—heaven or hell. We walked this way after we made love; our arms around each other. I looked to see if the car was following. She might come to the flat after I had gone. I did not know how to stop her. I was going to the main road where there were buses and taxis. I did not know why I was so certain she would come to the flat. I had thought she was already there.

I wondered if I should have asked them what time all this had happened; for my alibi.

The brain goes numb.

If they were following me, I could jump on a bus and then jump off again as they did in films. I did not see how it was possible to be followed. I thought she might be waiting in the dark. It would be terrible if she were not waiting. We always worked in opposites. I did not feel frightened. I thought I should get a taxi and really visit my sister: it was important to do everything properly. It must have been suicide. Once when I had been in my flat I had pretended to commit suicide; I had waved at my wrists with a razor-blade. I wondered if her husband, like me, had leaned against a washbasin. Blood had come out. I had both wanted and not wanted to die. I had wanted and not wanted him to die. When you have been long enough in love, everything becomes double. You become used to guilt; both your own and anyone else's. You forgive, which makes you inhuman.

I had first met her in the reading room of the British Museum. I had been working on a book about the Romans. She would come in each day and at first we did not talk to each other: then we did. It had not been difficult. She had a husband; her husband had been unfaithful; she was looking for a lover. I took her at lunchtime to see the sculptures from the Parthenon; there were the men wrestling with horses as if they were in love. The men and horses were centaurs; they were struggling to be different. I do not think she liked the sculptures. I never could tell beforehand what she would like. She was wearing a short blue skirt and white stockings. I had said—Do you want a drink? She had said—No. I had said—Do you want lunch? She had said—No. She had eyes that went on looking at you after the words had gone. I had said—Shall we go then? She had nodded.

I was in a taxi going to my sister's.

I think she had wanted to be rescued: also to hurt someone, because she had been hurt. A man thinks he wants to make love but what he wants is often just the imagination of it. When it is there what is easier is talk, lunch, alcohol. I had learned she had once tried to be an actress; was now writing a book. We went out of the British Museum past the Egyptian statues with their mad smiling faces. People were only happy when they were unconscious: in love you expose yourself. I did not wholly want to go. I knew what would happen. This was what I had wanted.

When we were in the taxi going from the Museum I felt the bone beneath her short leather jacket. I thought I should explain how she must not fall in love. Of course I wanted her to fall in love. I did not want commitment. I terribly wanted this. She waited in the hall of the hotel. She never said much. Then we were off on our long journey; in our gale. I have always known that in love there was nothing to be done: love is helplessness, and man is accustomed to power. I had taken girls home from offices; power is when you care about nothing, when you walk forward smiling like a mad archaic statue. Love comes into the world with consciousness, with a connection between pain and growth and miracles. This was what I wanted and did not want. I remembered war—the wine and roses and dead children. Only a God would be so ashamed that he would have to want love; to see it involved in death and suffering. Her eyes in the hotel room were watching me. They were dark eyes, going into a well. Perhaps all power has to be unseen: love is a God imposing himself. I wanted to say—Do not be too hard. Her eyes went on and on. She said—What's the matter? I said—You are too beautiful. Her eyes filled with tears. She said—This is very difficult.

The taxi was about to arrive at my sister's. As soon as it got there I would tell it to go back. I did not think there was anyone following me. Or if there was, I could say I had suddenly found my keys.

The second time I had seen her I had said—This is nothing to be surprised at. Her eyes were deciding not to see me again. I thought—Witches are princesses imprisoned in trees: they turn men to stone in order to prevent themselves being rescued. Then they can cry all winter. She said—Tell me what's wrong. I said—All right, I'll tell you. I thought I could do this. If love was helplessness, then you went through the ring of fire. The man who could do this had to have no love, only power. But this was the only way to love. Then, like a god, be resurrected. We went back to the hotel. She did not believe this: she thought she could go on untouched for ever. Witches are women who have their men trapped inside them. I said—Do this. She did it. She had the look of an Arab boy at a street corner. I said—It is all in the mind; you have to get it out into reality. She did what I said. I thought—This is the taboo in the secret place; you cannot speak of it; the marriage of love and power. She closed her eyes. There is a moment at the beginning of a storm when the boats run for shelter. I thought—The marriage is when you are both exposed and invulnerable. There was the look on her face of a person dying in a lifeboat; you press water to their lips and their lips are too cracked to take it. But they live. I thought—Women once were powerless and had to please men in order to destroy them: now they are more powerful and it is difficult to love. So men must tell them what to do. I wanted to say—Is that all right? She would have shouted—Yes!

There was the storm. I thought—It will never be easy. We will always wait for the miracle.

I found myself in my taxi back on the corner by my flat where we used to say goodbye. We were always saying goodbye, because things were so difficult. I paid the taxi and walked quietly towards my house. There was the shop where we used to buy bread and milk: wire fencing like a tennis court. Lights dropped like seeds into pools. She used to stand on tip-toe to kiss me. We kept things difficult to maintain this meaning; ecstasy.

I stood with my back against the fencing. I thought—If there has been someone following me he will be on my right. You stop and his footsteps stop. If they were still watching my flat, they would be beyond the corner on my left. The fencing was round two sides of a garden. On another side was the row of houses in which was my flat: the houses backed directly on to the garden. I thought that if I climbed into the garden I could get upstairs to my flat without being seen. There was an empty flat on the ground floor which I could break into.

I had first to jump the wire. It was about six foot high. I swung a leg to and fro. I had been a good jumper at school. I could vault with one hand on the top. The wire would sag. It might impale me.

I thought I should go to the corner and see if anyone was following. Her husband was a tycoon in the city who had men working for him. He ran a pirate radio station. He was a mythical man of business with many names. His men wore dark blue jerseys and rubber shoes. She had once said—He might do violence. I had said—Let him. There are moments when fear goes out of you as if from drugs.

I went back to the railings and put my hand on the top. I heard a scuffling up the street. I turned. There were boys with a pram. I waited.

When I jumped the whole fencing heaved like a hammock. I was slung in the air. My hand had a spike through it. My bottom leg couldn't get through the one on top. I had too many legs and arms, like an Indian goddess. The hammock turned upside down and flung me into the garden. I was on my knees in a rose bush with a dent in my hand. I thought I had torn my trousers. I was pleased I had not.

It was quite easy; you just put one hand up and jumped.

I moved off into the shadows. Gangsters were men in dark rubber suits dripping with water. I sucked my hand, which tasted of metal. I thought—This is like war: you are most alive when you know what you are risking.

The backs of the houses which bordered on to the garden had french windows and small bridges going across basements. They were like castles with moats. There was no moon. The garden was lit from the backs of the houses. There were forsythia and weeping cherry and dead laurel. You had to get quickly into buildings for protection. I thought—If he is dead she will be free; but will be always haunted by it. One needs a jailor. I reached the back of the house where my flat was: there was no light in the top window. She might not have got there yet. Or she might be sitting in the dark. She often sat in the dark listening to music. There were large french windows on the ground floor but no bridge across. I could see right through to the lamp in the street at the far side: the flat was empty. If the police were still at the front and saw me then I had an alibi: I could say I had lost my keys and thus was breaking into my flat. The basement had railings round it. When you are out on patrol you run from the open and cower under roots; your heart leaps like a forest fire. You watch the clock and it does not move. There was a smaller window at the side that I could reach if I stretched my body across. The basement was like a bearpit: food was thrown in and you couldn't reach it. I climbed up the railings and stretched one hand across to the house. A flare goes up and you freeze. I became stuck. You need a jersey over your face: your hands are diamonds. I had to push up the latch of the window with a knife. I had no knife. You just hold on for a certain number of hours and then you have done your duty. I looked back to where I had climbed into the garden and wondered if I could go back to my sister's and go to sleep. This was like love: one leg over the window-sill and paralysed. I noticed that the latch of the small window was undone. Burglars could get in. If you are doing something dangerous then sometimes providence helps you. In love you possess magical powers. I had always known this. I put my knee across. The bottom half of the window moved when I pulled it. I got my other knee across. I had to hold the window and push it up at the same time which was impossible. I did it. I made a lot of noise. I had to get one leg into the room. I became embroiled again in legs and arms; old men had intestines like rabbits. The edge of the window' caught me and I hopped. I was in a room of dust and rubble. A voice said "Who's that?" I was in the dark. There was the sound of a bed creaking. I was in someone's bedroom. I had climbed in to the wrong flat: I could not have done, because the flat was empty. There was a carpet on the floor. My shoes were making no sound. There was someone living here. I was experiencing visions. When this happened, you had to act quickly. I knew where the door of the room was because all these flats were the same. You went past the bed and then left to the door to the landing. I moved and bumped into a piece of furniture which fell over. I found the door and turned the handle and went out. The person in the bed had not moved; had been too frightened. It had been a woman's voice. I was in a short passage which would lead to the front door of the flat and the stairs. The voice again said "Who's there?" There would be a scream after I had gone. I was at the door of the flat which was made of frosted glass. I could hear a banging noise: imagined lights coming on. I went out on to the landing. I closed the door. Now I was safe. I was in the hall by the entrance. I could say I had just come in from the street. No one could prove anything. No one can ever prove anything: evidence is unreliable. There was a glass panel above the door through which the street lamp shone. But they might be waiting in their car to see if I came in. Then I could not be here. I began running up the stairs. I made a noise, so I stopped and took my shoes off. If the woman rang up the police then they would expect a man to come out of the front door. They were already watching the front door. So how would they have thought I had got in? This was too complex. I dropped a shoe, which clattered. I went on up the stairs. All that was necessary was action. I had to get into my flat without being seen. Then I could bolt the door. I could hide in my attic. My heart was roaring. I got to the door of my flat and there was still no one turning the lights on. There was no light in my flat. I had almost forgotten why I had expected this. She would be waiting. My hand shook so much I could not get the keys out. There was the one with a shaft like a gun-barrel. The door opened on just the small key. This might mean that she was there. Or not. I thought—Of course she is not here. The flat was silent. There was a smell of warm carpets. I saw that there was a fire on. We used to hold our hands out to the fire.

In my flat there is a bedroom at one side looking out on to the street and a living room above the gardens and in between a bathroom and a kitchen. When I closed the door I was back in the home to which one returns after many years; the dream of childhood, the memory of a nursery. I could not turn a light on in case this was seen from the street. I went into the bedroom: there were bed, dressing-table, chest-of-drawers; the chair she sometimes put her clothes on. Objects only come alive when there are people watching them. The bed had not been touched. When you come home you do not mind what has happened; you only care to find the other person. I went along the passage to the sitting room. The silence from the street-lamp made me careful. I had hoped every evening at this time that I would come home and find her. She would be sitting or lying on her stomach. She listened to music on her stomach. I had not seen her for some time. We had quarrelled. She had gone back. I had thought—All love is moral. I went into the sitting room. She was lying on her stomach on the sofa. The electric fire was on and I could see her hair. There were always lights in her black hair. The fire could be seen through the window over the garden. The window was too high; it could not be seen from opposite. She looked up but did not get off the sofa. She had not put the light on and did not wonder when I did not. I thought—We are safe in our turret. I was going to put my hand on her hair. I knew that she would be wondering whether I would be one sort of person or another. Sometimes it is as if I were twins: a cruel one and a kind. The last time I had seen her I had been cruel: I had determined not to be this again. I thought I should kneel by the sofa and stroke her; then she would know me. I knew which person I would find in herself. She turned her face towards me and there was the small beautiful face that sometimes froze as if she appalled herself. Only her eyebrows moved. I did not mind. I kissed her. I thought—I can love now. I did not mind what had happened. I was stepping through fire. There was the softness that a knife might open: roots going deeper than consciousness. I pulled at her. She was wearing jeans. When you love you do not ask; the only choice is between fighting and surrender. I looked up to the uncurtained window where there might be eyes that would see us: there were always faces beyond a window, the shore on which beautiful people walked and beyond them the sacrifice. She had put her arms round my neck and I was breathing life into her. You press at the points which are most vulnerable; feel for the heart and lungs; the body comes alive and is like a hummingbird in front of a flower, the wings do not seem to move but they hold it weightless. I wanted to say—I love you—but we seldom spoke. Talking was only used for exorcism. There was this perpetual ceremony like the offering of gifts. I took her by the hand to lead her back through the fire. You get up after a long time of praying. Love is silence. I pressed hard on one knee: she came up with me. Thus you raise the dead. I could see her face already changing in the firelight. A dead child turns into a woman. In order to raise the dead you have to be ready to die for them. And they have had to do something unforgivable to let you die for. We walked hand in hand to the bedroom. We used to walk like this when we said goodbye. Then we stood slightly apart from each other; there is equality in fighters. You do not want to condescend. She was at these times a myth to me. She had a strong body with muscles. I tried to make the moment stop; to be damned for it. She stood with one foot in front of the other and seemed to be seen both full-face and in profile at once. I thought—All love is this moment before going over the top; I do not want to go; but I will then be her accomplice for ever. We were in the lamplight. I stood on one leg while we bent to take off our clothes. I saw the shape of my leg slightly crooked against the carpet. Her legs were straight and smooth. What is unexpected is the length of the legs and the width of hips and shortness of the body. She was smiling. I wanted to tell her about when the world started smiling. I held her. There is this feeling of pith; of life itself, of death beyond it. You cradle it. I wanted to say—I will do anything: this is what love is: I will die, murder: I will prove it by acceptance. We did our walk to the bed down the moonlit path. Love is water surrounded by air. Out of timelessness you create an eternal present. When she lay on the bed she glanced down gravely as if her body were a landscape. My clouds rushed over her. You use a myth to become unconscious so that there can be a whole. Myths are about courage. She had that confidence that beautiful women have in their bodies; staring down at them from cliff-tops, of which men have to be afraid. The brave are those still capable of fear. You move like risking circuits; hold each end; draw away so that the spark flies between. It might not work. Love is possession and not possession; space has to come alive by magic. I said "I love you." She said "I love you." I could not think of anything else to say. Sometimes her whole face lit with darkness. The sea-anemone does not die but remains opening for ever. She would offer her drink to a dying soldier. And he would thank God for it. You go down into the dark and you must not look back or you disappear. Love is in prospect or retrospect: the present is ecstasy. You must never expect this. God is chained to his rock and a vulture pecks at his entrails. He only gives what there is grace for. She had stopped watching herself: you get to the bone. I took one hand and pulled it and with the other crawled on the rock-face. I had my fingertips over the ledge. When you know what the world means you weep: you lie in the mud and the guard stands over you. You see the earth-crust. Her face began to look as if it were being tortured. They had cut off her hair and wanted gold. Purity appears; you are being transformed again. I thought—Now I am home. But it is still unlikely. You have a shaft to the centre of the earth. There no man has ever been. You do not think you can go on. You wait for nails to be driven through you. All love is unmerited: to force it would be to be martyred or destroyed. You have to trust it. You trust. Then there is the miracle. I went on. Her face was in the last gasp of exhaustion. You are redeemed when you have thought the battle impossible. Then it is won. From a long way off there is the shouting across spaces: you are holding the lines of the head and feet; this is the sky; throughout you is the spark, the energy. This force can destroy you. It can make suns. You are totally lost and totally saved. You are yourself. I had wanted to save her: I wanted to cry out that I was lost. There is that silence when all the birds fly out from porticos: animals rush into the hills. The rock cracks. Iron bands force emptiness into matter. The cry of lovers past each other is heard back round the world. It goes on, endlessly.

I was breathing so hard I thought I had killed myself.

I opened my eyes and found her hair and one dark eyelid.

It was as if she had given birth.

With the weight you think you can never move; your back is broken. You are so light you can fly.

I was in my bedroom with the curtains undrawn and the light from the street lamp opposite.

I thought I would go to sleep for a little before I woke out of my dream.

The taste was sweet like roses.

You go to sleep for a hundred years and then wake up in the garden.

There is a twitching before the body lives: the last kick of the rabbit.

You can never believe that it will work like this again: when it does, it is the miracle.

This does not last. It absolves everything.

I was lying on top of her with our arms spread out. She had this way of remaining beautiful under the earthquake.

She had a look on her face of a bird that has eaten enough to last all winter.

There was nothing around us but air and light.

Her husband had killed himself or she had killed him. The police were looking for her.

They would be outside.

I had never really believed this.

I could ask her what had happened. But I never questioned her.

By making love we would be damned together.

So we had made love.

I trusted.

I thought of the children and was frightened. They were faces against the window.

This is a burden put on you.

There was the sound of a door opening and closing downstairs. Either it was nothing, or they were coming to get us.

I tried again to wake up in my room, bed, carpet, table; my body made of marble as if it were immortal.

You tried moving a limb; were afraid it might break.

She always smiled after making love; like archaic sculpture.

There was more banging downstairs. People seemed to come to the first landing.

Love is involved with death because the smile is in eternity.

I had thrown my life away. I could expect no more miracles.

She said "What's that noise?"

She had not opened her eyes. I had thought she had not noticed it.

I said "I don't know."

Her hand stroked my back.

She said "No one has made love like this."

Soon, I would have to panic.

There were sounds at what seemed to be the door of the first flat.

I did not know if she knew there were people waiting. She did not know that I knew.

I wanted to say—Darling?

Sometimes when I was thinking of something else she would pull her head away and look at me.

I could say—Did you know they were waiting?

Words were a vulgarity.

One's duty was to love those whom one loves.

Each time I tried to speak I drew breath and breathed into her ear.

I said "Did you know there were people waiting?"

She said "What people?"

She jerked her head away.

She had hard eyes.

Footsteps were coming up to the second floor landing.

She said "Them?"

"Yes."

She didn't say more.

I thought—I'll answer the door. We have time to put our clothes on.

I kneeled up as if I were lifting pit-props. The cold rushed in. We had a ritual of saying goodbye to each other.

She said "You don't mind?"

"No."

"Should we get dressed?"

"Yes."

The ritual was kissing her at various parts as if I were adorning her. She never hid herself.

They were banging at the door of the flat below.

She said "Why don't they know which floor the flat is on?"

I did not understand this.

She said "What are you going to say?"

"Nothing."

She kneeled down and kissed me. I might have given birth to her.
We were both dressing.
I said "What happened?"
She said "What happened when?"
I shook my head.
We sometimes became strangers.
I said "I just want to know if I have to say anything."
I thought—We must try not to lose each other.
They did not seem to be getting into the second floor flat.
She dressed very quickly. Like all beautiful women she wore few
clothes. She carried a small bag with little make-up.
She sat on the edge of the bed with her legs crossed.
I said "Shall I let them in?"
"Yes."
I wanted to say—We can't be found like this.
There were footsteps coming up to the top floor.
She stood in front of me and went on tip-toe. She said "I want to
tell you how much I love you."
I said "I love you too."
The footsteps had reached the floor of my flat.
I was frightened.
I said "The thing is, I'm not supposed to be here."
She said "Why?"
I said "They were waiting outside the front door. They wanted to
know where you were. So I climbed through a ground floor window."
There was a knock on the door of my flat.
We were whispering.
She said "You saw them?"
"Yes."
"And you came up specially?"
Her voice sometimes got too loud, as if spilling over.
I said "Yes."
She said "How marvellous!"
I said "I told them I'd lost my keys."
She looked at me as if I made no sense.
I said "If I'd let them come up, they'd have found you."

She said "Yes!"

She sat down on the edge of the bed. She looked miserable.

I couldn't make out what was happening.

I said "We can pretend not to be here. Not let them in."

She said "Is that what you want?"

I sat down beside her.

Her cheek was like petals.

There was another knock.

She said "What are you going to do?"

"Nothing."

She said "All right." She stood up. She looked as if she were going away for ever.

I said "You must tell me what happened."

She said "What happened?"

I mentioned her husband's name.

She said "What?"

I saw then that she didn't know.

I hit my head. I said "Oh you don't know!"

I thought I must have been mad all the time to have thought she knew. But she had been sitting in the dark.

She often sat in the dark.

I felt enormous relief.

I said "Now darling, everything's all right." I hugged her.

I thought—I must tell her.

I said "Something's happened."

She said "Who to?"

I said her husband's name.

I had put my hand on her hair. Was stroking it.

She said "He's all right."

There were more feet coming to the door of the flat.

I couldn't tell her reaction.

I said "When I came back this evening, earlier, the police were in the street."

I thought—How can I ever explain what I thought?

She said "When?"

I put a finger to my lips.

She said "He was all right a moment ago."

"How?"

"He rang up here."

"When?"

"A minute before you arrived."

I said "But the police were here."

She said "But those weren't police!"

She smiled.

She sometimes touched me when she was amused.

I said "No?"

"No."

"Who were they then?"

She said "His men."

I remembered that I had for a moment thought of this, but had decided on the other thing because I was guilty.

I said "I thought he was dead."

She said "No."

I said "What were they doing then?"

She said "He's been looking for me."

I was glad that he was not dead.

I said—"You mean, he sent them round to find you with me"?

She said "Yes. We'd had a fight." Then—"You don't mind?"

I said "I don't mind anything."

I could see that this wasn't the way to put it.

I was thinking—Didn't they tell me he was dead, or did I imagine this? Then—Can I make out that I'm not such a fool; that I really knew what was happening?

I went to the door. I could still act like a hero.

She said "You don't sound overjoyed."

I said "I thought you'd killed him."

She said "Oh I wish I had!"

I laughed.

I said "Shall we open the door then?"

She said "If you're sure."

I said "He wants a divorce?"

"Yes."

I thought—We are like people stuck in an opera.

I went out into the passage. I did not know what I was doing. I had asked for miracles.

They are sometimes not quite the ones you want.

But there's always a point.

She came with me to the door and we stood hand in hand. The footsteps seemed to have gone back down the stairs. The lights were on on the second floor landing.

We were like a husband and wife in nightcaps.

I leaned over the bannisters.

On the landing below I saw a policeman.

It was too late to turn back to the flat. He had seen me.

He began coming up the stairs.

I let go of her hand.

So she had killed him.

Policemen have that way of walking right up to you and almost through you before speaking.

I wondered if I should say that I had killed him.

There is nothing left to do but to look cheerful.

He said "Sorry sir, we've had trouble."

I said "Yes?"

He said "Good evening Ma'am."

I said "Good evening."

I saw that he was registering that she was beautiful.

He said "Burglars."

I said "Burglars."

He said "Broke into the ground floor flat. Didn't seem to go out again."

He was trying to look past me into the flat.

I said "Well he didn't come in here."

He said "May I look around?"

I said "Certainly." I stood to one side. There was everything in the dark. The bed that we had been sleeping in.

We were fully clothed.

He said "Were you in bed?"

I said "Yes."

He said "He seemed to run up the stairs."

I said "How did you know?"

He walked around.

He said "There was a car outside. They didn't see him come out."

I thought—Then I am trapped.

He said "Do you both live here?"

I said "Yes."

She had gone into the kitchen and seemed to be washing.

I said "Couldn't he have got out of a landing?"

The policeman had absolutely pale flat eyes.

I said "Where's the car now?"

He said "Oh, we've moved it along."

I thought I might say—Couldn't they have been the burglars? But one must not cash in on miracles.

He said "Well I won't trouble you."

I said "No trouble."

He went out on the landing and back down the stairs.

She was walking backwards and forwards in the kitchen. She was making coffee. I stood in the bedroom and scratched my head.

I could not work out what it was I should say had happened.

I thought—But perhaps as usual she will ask no questions.

I went into the kitchen. She was still sad.

I said "Darling, I'm sorry."

She said "Oh it doesn't matter." Then—"Anyway, you said such wonderful things."

I said "What did I say?"

I had said—We both live here.

We drank coffee. The noise was like heat going down.

She said "What was all that about your breaking in?"

I opened my mouth. I thought—If I hadn't imagined all this, they would have caught us.

She said "Oh, don't explain."

I held her hand. Sometimes when I did this her face became knowledgeable.

I said "If they had been his men, we were going to let them find us."

She said "But they weren't."

I said "But we thought they were."
She moved away.
I went after her and put my hand on her shoulder.
I said "What we've done once we can do again."
She said nothing.
I thought—She is thinking that to me this was all a game.
I said "Can't we?"
She said "Ah, you always think you can do everything again!"

When I came back from the war there was a silence in my house as if everyone was out picking blackberries. I left my kitbag in the hall and went through the litter of broken toys and fallen petals and I called—Is anyone at home? I knew how when one is at war one's wife is supposed to go off with a black marketeer or newspaper proprietor; I was prepared for this; was ready to go round with orange-peel teeth for a while and other symptoms of jealousy. Jealousy is an excuse for our own misdemeanours: Othello, of course, was in love with Roderigo. In my house I made a noise like searching for children at a tea-party—Coo-ee—and waited for the echo. I thought—After you make the gesture it is sad if there is no one there to hear of it: the cheering crowds fade away and you are the blind man selling matches in the gutter.

I had seen a certain amount of war; the babies with dogs' heads and fishes' feet, the Crusader who smiled so that his skin was stuffed as a moral precept. I had thought—You cannot escape suffering, only turn it into something different. I had visited shrines and brothels in the middle east, had gone up steps on my knees and heard cries of visitation. The cashier had sat in her box and put one toe out to be kissed: by faith you trust it to have been sterilised. She was a dark brown woman with a body like Epstein's Adam: she sat on the bed and played This Little Piggy Went To Market. In this position there is a certain mechanical breakdown: you have to get underneath to look at the shaft. But mechanics in the middle east have a genius at improvisation. I was soon up and on my feet again.

Afterwards I feared I might have got syphilis: such is the outcome of a holy and righteous war. And you have not got with you your Encyclopaedia Britannica. *Something appears—you cannot remember—the size of a lentil or a bilberry. But you do not know what a lentil or a bilberry is. Or nothing appears for such and such a time and then, when it does, it is unnoticeable. This is a relief. Except, of course, when you find your arms round the neck of* a cab-horse; are placed in the care of your mother and sister. But this might happen anyway.

So when I got home I crept through the house and out into the garden and I was terrified as all Crusaders must have been terrified; why else should they have gone off in their armour like the bulls in which victims were once roasted? I feared that my wife might actually have been faithful to me during all this time; might have been sitting knitting samplers for American soldiers; might not have had the lock on her chastity-belt looked at by some middle-eastern mechanic. And then where would I be, with my guilt round my neck like another pair of hands? And having gone to the end of the earth to sin in order that grace might abound; which is a necessity as anyone knows who has to do with morality and religion.

I found my wife lying in bed. I thought—This is an omen. I wanted to say—Look, I have oil on my hands: I have had a slight mechanical break-down. I put a toe underneath her bed; there did not seem to be a lover. I said "How are you?" She said "All right." She had a strong face into which shadows often came. I said "What's wrong?" She said "Nothing." I could see that she was frightened. I thought—She fears I might have syphilis. I would join all those ranks of ex-soldiers and unemployed who sell matches in the gutter; have millstones round their necks like placards. I said "You must tell me." She squeezed my hand. There were furrows on her face down which rivers often ran. She said "I'm afraid I might have syphilis."

I felt relieved. Thus grace was boundless. I could now stay at home for a while and be happy with my wife. Then I could go off again, and carve out some new territory. I thought—The object is to get the best of both worlds. If she had not feared syphilis, how could I not have had guilt with her? I loved my home. I dreamed of my future campaign through Italy.

So my wife started going to hospital each week and I stayed at home and looked after the children. I enjoyed this: all men should take a turn at domesticity. And at the hospital my wife met a lot of interesting people; pop-singers and delinquents and other symptoms of the fashionable world. The doctor asked her in what way she feared she might have got syphilis; and she said—Not the usual. The doctor explained that you did not get it in any other way. But she went on going to the hospital because she was romantic and all diseases were in the mind; so what did it matter that in fact neither of us had syphilis? And the doctor was a Pakistani.

Later I polished my equipment and got out my old maps and looked up the times of aeroplanes and connections. I thought I should soon be off again. In the spring when the crocuses pushed their heads through the hard ground I went to my wife who was sitting in a deck-chair in the garden and I said "Nietzsche said that everything goes round and round; have I told you this before?" My wife said "Have you told me this before!" I said "He said that everything eternally recurs; or rather, that we should act as if everything did." My wife said "Why?" I thought—I have just returned with the children from North Africa: the person with whom I am in love is back with her husband and family; I look forward to Italy: I have heard from Hippolyta, who is happy. I can go again and start at the British Museum. I said "Because this is the only way in which life is bearable." My wife looked disinterested. I said "As if everything that we do were such that we were going to go on doing it for ever."

The Sea

WE WERE STAYING IN a hotel in North Africa by the sea where the noise of the waves came in ceaselessly. I had never lived in such a wild place before. I think that he wanted us to be cut off, but I sometimes wondered about his motives.

In the mornings a mist arose from the sea and it was as if we were surrounded by water. We occupied one block of the hotel which was built on stilts over the sand. The hotel was new and had been put up to attract tourists. It must have been full in summer but in early spring was almost deserted. People came out from the town at weekends, but for most of the time we were the only inhabitants.

Later, there were his three children and mine and that for which we had come here. He had been nervous about his children: he had had an idea that they would be shy or hostile. But I had always believed that I could deal with this. I have a feeling that if one has something to give, then it is usually accepted. I had always thought I would love his children. The eldest was the one I came to know best; he was tall and dark-haired with eyes like his father. His second son sometimes frightened me. The third son often seemed sad, but I suppose this was natural.

My own daughter loved the sea. She was happy all day playing in the sun. We had summer weather. I think she would have been happy anywhere with me; we were close to each other instinctively.

What I loved best about this time were the occasions when we were together as a family out of doors. We would eat meals sitting on a verandah under a ceiling made of straw; there were tables with green-and-white chequered cloths and plates from the local pottery. These were of a dark gold and had lines and patterns in zig-zags. The food was good—shellfish and goat's cheese and dishes of lamb with herbs. There was a local white wine thin as wood shavings. There was always a vase of wild flowers on the table, with small bells of transparent blue. I think that these meals were the happiest times of my life: there was the sun on objects and the light making the spaces between them solid, the sense of expectation and restfulness that comes after pain. I had always wanted to be part of a large family and now I was; though I was obviously too young to be the mother of all of them.

His children were sometimes shy. But children judge by their senses. What is happy is right for them.

I always loved his closeness to his children. I had not known men felt like this.

There was the beach where the rollers from the Atlantic came in and seemed built on top of each other in tiers. Birds hopped just short of the surf looking for worms, their thin legs reflected in the wet. He and his children would run along the beach playing football. They looked beautiful. I find it difficult to write about this.

I sometimes went on my own to an olive grove at the back of the hotel and tried to write poetry there. I have always written poetry. I try to express thus what seems impossible otherwise. I did not always like their playing games. I liked them better when they were still. There is a painting by Degas of young men standing by the sea: they are young and brooding and hold on to horses. The horses are like their unconscious over which they have control. He himself had once used this image. Beaches are desolate. I wished that I could paint; because painting could have expressed this better than poetry.

I have a great longing for order and stillness. I do not like chaos.

I remember the sort of light there had been around him the first time we had met. I had noticed his gaiety, with which he made people laugh. The light was a loneliness and a sweetness about him. We had used to meet at lunch time near the British Museum. We were both married. We had neither of us wanted to destroy, only to build.

When we had come to this place by the sea we had at first been on our own. Even in the winter life seemed to be pushing through dry ground with spikes and thorns; it was a marvel so many flowers could flourish near a desert. I had thought that on our own we would be all right; that what we had come for would be acceptable. There was this hotel on the beach with flowers almost down to the water; a room with a plain oak bedstead and chairs with brown canvas slung as seats. Here we were to stay till summer. He would write. I was very tired. He was extraordinarily attentive to me at this time. He would bring breakfast to me in bed edging diagonally through the doorway with the tray; sit on the bed and talk to me. He would make quite simple things look important; as if bringing breakfast were an expedition. I sometimes did not know what he was thinking. I loved it when he talked; he would often exaggerate, wave his hands as if he were building castles in the air: then say—You know how I exaggerate! He had a way of saying something extreme and immediately taking it back. He thought statements were often true when they were qualified by something of their opposite. I saw what he meant about this: then wondered if he did it too deliberately.

In the evenings we would sit on the verandah with a pressure-lamp between us around which moths came. He seemed to belong to no place and no time. He was free; able to come and go. He would talk as if everything in the world were some kind of symbol. This frightened me.

I wanted just to be still so that a new life could grow.

We had thought a lot about the children. They had been told about us: but this was a difficult situation. We were all trying to do our best; both here and at home. It is not good for children to be separated too long from either parent. The time of the holidays came: it was arranged that the children should join us. I remember them arriving at the airport and standing behind glass screens like the Eumenides. Children are our consciences that we have lost.

He did not pay much attention to my own child at first. I was surprised, because he was so good with children. When he sat at the head of the table I think he sometimes purposely did not notice them; this was another of his theories—that you showed children by example, and did not instruct them. His children ate rather noisily. My child was quiet in the company of the others; she was not usually quiet, but she was much younger and the only girl amongst boys. When he and the boys were out playing we would often sit, my daughter and I, on the verandah in front of our room: we were trying at the time to do needlework, she needed a counterpane for her doll. Or I would read her stories. She had brought a book of fairy stories, but I found these frightening and bloodthirsty and they gave her dreams. I think she found the whole atmosphere here rather frightening; not only the huge waves on the beach and the other children being so different from her but the feel of the place as if we were in another century. Bloodshed had once been normal here; women had been shut away in harems. It was still alarming, sometimes, to be a woman on one's own. At home of course my daughter had been sheltered; at the centre of attention.

The games he used to play with the children often seemed to me to be too young. There was one which was a sort of volleyball over a net of a piece of string between two posts. He and his children would dive and flop about and seemed to revel in the efforts they made even in missing the ball: as if the point was to land hard on the sand on their stomachs. They seemed transformed by the game into people more primitive. I once or twice tried to play; this made him laugh; I was so slow, and would not dive after the ball but would duck when it came near me. I have never been good at games. But he loved this and would come and hold me like he used to do in the days when we had been so happy, when we had not noticed the people around us. We were often oblivious of the children now: I do not know what they thought of this. He would hold me with one hand on my hip and the other on my shoulder. And occasionally these games would transform me too—perhaps into the girl I had been in my childhood when I had been with other girls at school, when I had wanted to be good at games and similar. I think this was a part of what he loved, because it was unlike me. I could still swim well, and I remember how amazed he was when he discovered this. He had laughed till he had almost drowned.

My own child could not play the game on the beach. She was too small, and although she tried to punch the ball and catch it it would after a time hit her and hurt her. But she went on trying with such determination! I saw something of my own aggression in her.

His older children were good at letting her play with them. His eldest son especially was sweet: I had not known such kind children. I sometimes had to stop her exhausting herself.

Then one day he wondered what game we all could play together—
the six of us and of such different ages—and one of his children
suggested a game that they had played long ago but apparently not
for some time. This was a game in which you all ran about and there
was one person trying to catch you; you were caught by being touched
and when you were caught you stood still and the other people had to
rescue you. When this game was mentioned there was a sort of silence
between them; I did not understand this at first, but they soon became
enthusiastic. We went off to play the game in a grove of eucalyptus trees.
I stood behind a trunk and did not run much; the trunk had pale grey
bark on it that peeled. My daughter adored this game: she suddenly
started rushing from tree to tree like a liberated spirit. They were all
wild animals disappearing and appearing between shadows. It was like
one of those paintings of a hunt in the middle ages with men in striped
clothes and the legs of horses stretched in front and behind. The spaces
between the trees became dangerous: they were full of violence and
laughter. I was slightly afraid for my daughter: I looked to see if she was
all right. I thought perhaps they were using her, a much younger child,
as an excuse for their own infantilism. He came up to me and was very
hot, pouring with sweat. He put his face in my hair. He seemed both
ashamed and happy.

There were these pleasures during the day. I had wanted a routine in
which days passed without any limit; the rhythm of light and darkness,
work and play, talk and silence. I sometimes wished we had a house of
our own in which I could cook for them. It was strange that we never
discussed this.

Our nights were sometimes not easy. I have always had trouble
with sleep. Sleep is a blessing that comes perhaps only when you do not
crave it. It becomes so important to me that I see a whole stretch of days
ruined if I do not get it. So I do not get it. I take pills, but I do not like
to do this, and I become anxious which makes things worse. He used
to tell me not to worry; just to lie and read. But I could not do this. I
felt I had to fight for sleep: I do not like my mind going its own way so
easily. So I would lie awake in the dark, and he was patient with me.
But his patience induced some further guilt: it was almost as if I wanted
him to be upset, in order that I could sleep. Otherwise it was too hard

for me not to blame him. I know my own shortcomings. There have been many occasions in which my life has gone in this sort of pattern. Our love-making also became slightly different from what it had been before; perhaps this was not surprising. But I remembered his saying that if ever love-making became easy it would not be so good—that you had to depend on the miracle. I thought that perhaps this was similar to sleep: which has to be unasked for and unmerited.

Sometimes in the morning my daughter would come in when we were in bed. I think she always accepted him. She would jump up as she used to do at home; bury her head in the blankets and look at him through her hair. I was often so doped that I could not pay much attention; but I liked to hear them. He would suddenly lean over and tickle her. My daughter has a small round face with bright eyes and curly hair. She would wriggle and keep her head down. He would then lie and pretend to be asleep. She would try to stand on her head till her nightdress fell around her shoulders. Then she would crawl round the edge of the bed watching him. I think she knew I was smiling. Then she would put her face close to his and pout. He would wake up with a growl and she would leap and become doubled-up with pleasure and terror. It is extraordinary how a child can show all opposites in its face. She would press her skirt between her legs and laugh almost hysterically. He would make his eyes wide as he did when he was flirting.

I found at first it was not always easy to get on with his children. They were very polite: we would have interesting talks after dinner. But I felt it difficult to know them on a deeper level. He himself was slightly formal in spite of his closeness to them. He sometimes seemed to be addressing two or three of them at the same time, or as if he were saying something to one for the benefit of another. I think this was part of his theories about children—that a father should make no personal imposition, but should put things to them objectively and explain. This seemed to work quite well. They talked on many intelligent subjects. I only sometimes missed a certain passion or even prejudice, in which there would not always be two opposite points of view.

He and his elder son seemed to take great pains especially never to conflict with each other. This seemed a necessity for them more important than feeling.

I decided that I should ask his eldest son to come for a walk with me, so that I could get to know him better. I chose a day when he himself was on the verandah writing; when my daughter was happy in the olive trees in the back. He had said he would look after her. (I call him he—their father—because I cannot write his name: I have always felt it impossible to use names for people close to me: a name belittles a person, and perhaps he and the children were the only people I have loved.) Anyway, I asked his son to go for a walk; he looked slightly bewildered. I think perhaps no one before had asked him to go for a walk; they were all so accustomed to being on their own, for the sake of freedom. But he said "All right"; and looked pleased. Then he said, typically, "Shall I put on my shoes?" as if only I could answer this.

We went along the beach towards an old wreck some distance from the shore. This was a relic of war-time. I thought that I would not talk at first, because I did not want to appear simply sociable. But he began talking at once in his polite and careful way; asking how I liked the place, if I thought it a good hotel, as if it were he who were trying to put me at my ease and these good manners were natural to him. He asked if I had been in this part of the world before—and I remembered that his father had once been somewhere to the south of here with his mother; had written a story about this. I had not liked the story. There seemed now almost to be some confusion in his—his son's—mind about whether it had been his mother who had been there with his father or whether it had been myself: he did not quite ask this, but there seemed this slight lack of coordination between his imagination and his thought. This was not his fault, since we gave him no certainty. He and I were walking through the eucalyptus trees. It was a bright day with waves rushing. A smell came from the beach as if something had been washed up there. Whales often got washed up on this shore having lost their way in the mist. We started talking about books. He—the son—had just read *Anna Karenina* and he asked how it was that the love between Anna and Vronsky had gone wrong; he thought that if love was true, it must last for ever. I wondered if he were still asking about his father and mother, or about myself. I remembered his father once saying that I looked like Anna on the railway-station. I said something about love never being easy: about its always containing the seeds of its own destruction. I found myself echoing words that his father had once used. I had not really agreed with these.

I felt a curious comfort in this new relationship with his son. I think there was some extension of himself here that I could be a mother to. I had always found it difficult to be a mother. His son was too old to be my own son; but not old enough for me to affect him. I felt something required of me here that did not make demands; and I was able to give this to him.

I tried to tell him that I agreed passionately with his ideas about purity in love; but that this was a dream only tenable perhaps when one is young because after that there is the need for protection. And then there has to be tolerance, or else there is such bitterness and scorn. These were also phrases his father used. I could see that the son was thinking this too because he suddenly said "But what do *you* think?" And I wanted to tell him then that I did agree with him unconditionally. I said "To be tolerant doesn't mean everything is permissible." He said "No." I was glad he had given me the opportunity of saying this.

We had come down in our walk to the place where the whale had been washed up. The underneath of it was white and corrugated as if acid had been eating into it. I did not want to go too close. He went right up and bent over it. I would have hated him to touch it.

This was one of the moments when I knew how wrong everything was that we were doing.

We were walking back through the eucalyptus trees and had come down to a road which ran towards the groves at the back of the hotel when we heard the sound of a child crying. I had heard it earlier than he: they were extraordinarily slow to notice things. But I had not done anything, because we were strangers in this foreign country. But as soon as he heard it he became concerned; whereas I would probably have passed on. We were walking between stone walls. I remember his saying "Do you hear anything?" and looking this way and that. Then he said "It's a child"—as if it might have been something different. Then he spoke my daughter's name. I had not realised this. I have slow reactions too. I looked over a wall and there was my daughter crouched and crying. I tried to climb over but he had jumped there first. My daughter was in that state in which children seem possessed; she was kicking and pressing her fists into her eyes. He was large and strong and lifted her over the wall like an elder brother. I was terrified that someone might have frightened her: there were men who sometimes lurked in the trees. I held her in my arms, but she could speak no coherent sentences. Her crying went right through her like an earthquake. We carried her to the hotel. When we were approaching he—the father—suddenly appeared: he said "Oh good you've got her!" He had been supposed to be looking after her. I had my face in her hair. I did not see if he looked guilty. His son said "What happened?" He did not answer. They sometimes had these confrontations. He was hot and wild-haired. I was trying to calm my daughter. His son was by my side. We were at the back of the hotel where the rubbish was put out in bins; the lids were half off and there were flies. He said "She got frightened." I wanted to ask—How? But I find it so difficult to ask questions. His son said "How?" He said "I can't look after everything." I took her into the bedroom and sat her on the bed. I thought it extraordinary that he had not been able to look after her. He came to the door and watched. His son came too. I knew it had been difficult for him, because he had been writing. I suddenly felt very alone in a foreign country.

After this I stayed with my daughter more of the time. His eldest son sometimes asked me if I would bathe, and I did, swimming out with them past the line of breakers. With his second son I never managed to be on such close terms; though in some ways he was the most intelligent and the most like his father. He had fair hair and a profile as fine as a Roman coin; he was old for his age, and I think his wisdom was sometimes a burden. He would spend a lot of his time in rock-pools, finding strange shells and sea-anemones which he brought to us in his hands. His third son often joined in these activities: they were close, complementing each other with intellect and instinct. I had very little contact with the third son; I think he was one who was most like his mother. I tried to get these two to join in some of the activities with my daughter and myself—to listen to the stories that I read to her perhaps—but they would not, backing away, always polite but definite. It was not that to join us would have bored them; his second son had a way of saying "Oh no thank you!" almost before anyone had asked him what he wanted; as if he were intent on getting in a riposte. I felt that the youngest son especially would have liked to have been more with us; but was prevented by a more primitive instinct.

When I was with him—their father—at this time, I think we both felt some slight distance between us. We had both got so much of what we wanted—what I had always said I wanted—and this distance was perhaps like touching wood at our good fortune. But in earlier days, when it had been so difficult for us to see each other, our coming together had been such ecstasy: now, when we were with each other all the time, there was a feeling that we had to be slightly separate in order to maintain some memory. He had said—Lovers have to work for this: and then—But usually life does this for them. I had never agreed with him here. But I did notice that it was when we found ourselves in unexpected roles that we perhaps now came together in something of the old way: when he found that I could swim, for instance, and was so pleased; or after we had drunk a lot of wine at meals and would both become for a time the people that we had been ages ago. We would go to our room in the afternoon and then it was as if we were back again in our room at the top of the stairs or having walked from one of our favourite restaurants. The afternoons were quiet and we lay on the bed like children. It was at these times that I did see what he meant about love being contained in some sort of impossibility; that we only possessed it when it was impossible.

I have not explained why it was that we had come to this place. I had been going to have his child. The child had recently been born. It was for this we had gone abroad. The child was with us; it slept in a cot in our room. I find it difficult to write about this, because of what happened later. I try to forget. But I am trying to explain, amongst other things, why it was still not easy for us always to make love.

The day that I am writing about was one of which we had often talked; but like so many of his plans, one that he had perhaps not really wanted. On the beach there were fishing boats painted in bright colours with designs of claws of lobsters and crabs. Fishermen went out in them at night or in the very early morning so we seldom saw the boats used; they sat on the beach looking new and slightly leaning. The children played around them: here again I think his children used my daughter as an excuse to play games that were too young for them. They would climb on the boats and pretend to be pirates; posture and declare how great they were. My daughter was at first rather bewildered, then joined in and became more excited than the others. Acting was so real to her. I remember even his oldest son standing on the prow of a boat with his hand in his shirt and saying he was Napoleon. Their gentle faces became puffed: they were like children who simulate grown-ups by stuffing cushions under their shirt-fronts.

They wanted him—their father—to take them out in one of these boats. I think it was he who first suggested it; but he often made suggestions for the sake of exciting them. He did not need excitement. But once he had mentioned an idea he found it hard to say no. He explained their inexperience as sailors, said that such an expedition would be dangerous, gave the excuse that the fishermen would almost certainly not lend a boat. The children waited till he was finished, did not look him in the eye, then said "Do you mean we can't go?" He still did not refuse them. Responsibility of this kind seemed sometimes to be beyond him; as if he could not take on too much. I understood this. He was writing hard at the time, and the heart is dragged out of you in writing. It is like a birth. We had both of us had a hard winter.

Then one day when they were in the town they saw in the harbour a sailing boat that was for hire—at least they said it was for hire— though this was one of the matters about which the brothers strangely disagreed. One claimed that they had had to ask specially to borrow it. I mention this because he did not settle the argument between them; he only said it did not matter. This was again typical. He did not care about the past, but only about what he called being practical. I did not understand myself why he had not asked the fishermen to take them out; but I think he wanted to do everything himself, to act as a family. They still had to press him. They argued that they could sail the boat quite easily, that they had learned sailing at school, that if they kept close to the shore it could not be dangerous. I could see that he wanted to be persuaded. He sometimes wanted other people to feel enough for him to let him decide himself: he used to say—Decision has to do less with reason than with instinct. He sometimes depended on me for this. This pleased me. But women are often in a certain want themselves.

It was agreed that they should take the trip in the sailing boat. I had played little part in the discussion: I knew nothing about the sea, and I thought I had just to look after my child. But I hated being left out; I always wanted to go with them everywhere. And I did love the sea. He did not ask me then if I wanted to go: I think he assumed that I would not. And I had intended of course to say I could not: but then, when he did not expect me, I wanted to. I had at this time taken to going for long walks in the afternoon; I had bought a kind of carrier in which women in this part of the country carry their babies on their backs. It was an object of great beauty; made of coloured and plaited reeds. I had always loved the idea of mothers carrying their babies; thus the children grow up naturally and have the rhythm of their mothers. They feel that they are wholly looked after and yet are part of the grownup world. I have often imagined the terror of a baby waking up alone. So I was happy carrying my baby: I thought I could take it with me on the sea. I had liked walking in the country with its hard spikes and clear air. My baby was only a few months old: it seldom cried.

There had been one incident, however, that had frightened me. I had been with my baby one day and had taken it down from my back; it had been growing restless and I had sat with it on the ground. I was in a grove of eucalyptus trees. I saw an Arab watching me at some distance. He was squatting, dressed in a white robe. I had thought of feeding my baby: but then the Arab came and spoke to me. I did not mind: I had wanted to make friends with the local people. We talked in French; about the hotel, how long I was staying there. He asked me about my husband. Very stupidly, I said that my husband was not here. I know something of my psychological motivations in all this: I think perhaps I was frightened of being alone in a foreign country, that I wanted to revenge myself for what even now I do not understand. Perhaps it was just to do with being a woman. But I saw something frightening in the Arab's eyes. He came closer; seemed to be encouraging me to feed my baby. I had undone part of my blouse: I think possibly he was only trying to be kind. I got up to leave. He put out a hand and held me. I had to talk to him for some time; to ask him please to leave me. I could not make out what he was saying. I almost panicked. Eventually he released me: but that evening I saw him still fluttering around the hotel, a white shape like a bird.

When I told this to him—the person with whom I was in love—he seemed concerned but I knew that there was something further in his mind, as there was in my own. This was the story he had once written about a similar incident that had happened to his wife—how she had been accosted by a man in this country and how he had thought he should go to the police but he had not, he had eventually made friends with the man. This story had shocked me. I had thought that I would rather die than be such people. Now I knew he was thinking of this; and again, would not go to the police. I did not want him to; but I wanted him to suggest it. I know my own husband would have done this. He did make some suggestion; he asked—"Is there anything you want me to do?" But I did not want him to ask, I wanted him to do it. And by then it was too late, for the man in the trees had stopped appearing. I know I was behaving very ordinarily in this: but it had now become difficult for me to be left on my own. And I had been reminded of things that I had not wanted to remember.

I remembered that we had only come to this place by the sea because of our baby; that perhaps without it we would never have come; and we both knew this, though we never quite admitted it. He had certainly never suggested this; he was always trying to reassure me. He would say—Never feel guilt. But I think that without the baby he would still have been with his wife; I would have been with my husband; and all our children with their proper parents. And I sometimes longed for this: I had a terror at the confusion in which we had cast ourselves. I think this feeling is inevitable in a woman. Any incident that broke through our ordered life immediately reminded me of its brittleness and of the chasm that lay underneath. I realised that his wife must in some way have given permission for him to come; had of course given permission for her children. She was like this; she would not have minded. And I hated this: I wanted a life that was whole, that would have a future and not be impossible. I hated the sort of permissiveness that he and his wife represented in the story; their lack of a commitment to be died for. Sometimes I felt that I wanted to die: that this would be the only resolution out of duplicity.

The night before the projected trip in the boat he was restless and would not come to bed: he stood by the window looking at the sea and I knew that he had his own memories and possibly regrets. It was understood that we never blamed each other. Perhaps he was thinking how he had had to give up much of his work as well as his home: that for a man this was difficult. But I wondered if he realised the vulnerability of a woman. He came and stood at the end of the bed and when he did this it was sometimes as if part of him had disappeared; as if he had become his shadow. This might have been his power over me. He said "Won't you come in the boat tomorrow?" I thought he expected me to say no. I said "Yes." He sat on the edge of the bed. He said "What'll you do with the baby?" I said "Bring it." I think that I said this partly because I knew his wife would not have said this: he had often told me how in spite, or because, of her permissiveness she never joined them on such expeditions; that she would use a baby as an excuse to separate herself from the rest of the family. And of course she might have been right: but I did not want to be like her. I wanted so much for us all to be together. He said gently "I was going to say that we wouldn't go in the boat tomorrow: that I wouldn't leave you." I wanted to say—Why don't you say it then? But I didn't: we never asked this sort of question. He got into bed and held me and told me that I was brave. I sometimes did not know what he meant by this—telling me that I was brave.

The boat was a large rowing boat and had a sail attached. We had come into the town on the early morning bus; the town was at some distance from the beach, and we had walked through the streets to do some shopping. The bazaars were covered with bamboo roofing; bars of light ran up people like ladders. We had had lunch in a restaurant by the harbour and the children had made a fuss about the sea-food. In the harbour there were fishing boats and one or two expensive yachts. The boat that we were to go in did not seem suited to go much out of the harbour. It belonged to an old man with one eye; the other eye was a slit behind which shadows lurked. He helped us into the boat. There were three seats like planks across it and a broad seat at the stern. Our plan was to row out of the harbour and then if the wind was right to put the sail up. There did not seem to be much wind. The boat could be rowed by two people sitting side by side or four people in tiers. The oars had thick stems and narrow blades; were attached to single sticks by rough ropes. He and his eldest son took the oars: there was some laughter about when had been the last time they had rowed: they used phrases about rowing that they remembered from their schooldays. Sometimes in order to impress his children I think he became too close to them; this made them anxious. I was anxious myself: I had not often been in a boat. I sat on the seat at the back with my daughter and my baby. The baby was in its basket: I thought it was safe, I know I should not have brought it. At the front, or prow—I am not sure of these words—his two younger children sat and looked ahead. As we started the boat rocked precariously. But he and his eldest son rowed quite well—I had not expected this—I had feared they might be incompetent. This was one of the reasons I had been anxious. They rowed in short rather violent pulls, as I had seen fishermen do in Italy. The sail remained furled round the mast. Once we were away from the quay there was that extraordinary stillness of deep water; I stopped being nervous and looked over the side. I felt myself becoming part of the rhythm, the pulling of oars, the creak of wood and water. We seemed all to be children again and carried on the backs of our mothers. The oars made a sucking sound. We glided over a transparency that seemed to hold us by surface tension: any violence might break it and send us plunging to the bottom. I could just see the shapes of rock and seaweed. He was wearing a white shirt with his sleeves rolled up; he looked very young. Often in moments of physical exertion he looked young; such as when we made love. He had this feeling of life as a challenge; of something to be risked even if there was disaster. But with him there was seldom disaster. However I did not know what he felt about the sea. I think he was alarmed by it. He was looking round to see if we were going the right way. The pale hills were far behind us, with low clouds placed above as if by hand. The harbour was protected by a long mole probably built by the French in the eighteenth century: it was of dark stone and had small towers with domes. Beyond it the open sea looked wrinkled. They were discussing a new plan—whether to sail right round the headland to the beach by the hotel. The argument was whether it was safe to go so far; we did not know the distance. We had only done this journey in a bus, which took about fifteen minutes. Their method of argument was, as usual, for him to put up objections and then allow himself to be overruled. The children were keen to go on: saying—What was the point of the expedition if there was not some object to aim at? that it was not far. I removed myself as usual; I cannot put my feelings into words, and in this instance I did not know what were my feelings. It was strange how as soon as they had stopped rowing the boat seemed to move up and down with a new momentum. It was like those occasions when you have to stand still in order to hear someone breathing. I remembered then the story he had once written about the catching game they had played in the cellar of his home; they had all got overexcited and one of the guests, a child, had been electrocuted. I thought how relevant this story was to the times now when they became too adventurous in their activities: he had told me that of course the story was not true, it was just a story; there had been some incident, but no child ever died. But I felt the story was symbolic even here, as a good story should be. Now I did not know if it was safe to go on. He and his eldest had stood up and were unfurling the sail: the wind apparently was in the right direction and we were trying to sail round the headland. I did not stop them. I think I was confused; I was used to having decisions taken for me. My husband had always told me what to do: we had fought, but there had been safety. Now sometimes I felt lost in this freedom. The sail had opened and was of rough material like a piece of sacking. He and his son crouched on the side holding ropes; the sail filled lethargically. The boat seemed to be going in a different direction from where it was pointing: I did not know about this, I had not sailed before. I began thinking of the times when we had first met: I had been the one who had always wanted us to go away together, and he had said that if we did we might be destroyed. We had been sitting in the pub in London one day and I had asked—Then what is our point?—and he had said in his voice that suddenly became like an actor—To maintain ecstasy. I had hated this. We seemed to be making some progress towards the headland: the sea was changing to a deep blue. The young children were trailing their hands over the edge and the water kicked up phosphorus. What I did not like was that for him life seemed to depend on complexity and flux: and this was not quite real, it was stimulated. I remember him also saying—But this is the knowledge with which you deal with life. I had denied this too. On the other hand it had been myself who had often refused to face realities, whether in myself or outside.

The wind had increased slightly and we were going round a rocky headland. Another vista opened before us of jagged points. The sail flapped; we seemed to be pointing too near the wind. The sea and the air were working against each other and we were not making headway. His children stood and the boat rocked. They decided to row again. One of the oars went overboard and they had to reach for it.

I remember holding my baby and being overwhelmed by a feeling that I was miles away from home; that I was held prisoner on a vast ocean from which I would never escape. I thought that if we foundered then I would not be able to swim because I had to keep hold of my baby. I longed for the safety of purity and stillness.

He and his son were having a discussion about turning back. The wind was against us: but we were round the main headland and he had an idea that the hotel would soon be in sight. He was standing on a seat trying to look ahead. He said "We might go back" and then "Or we might go on"; almost as if he were mocking himself. It was not that he was unaware of his indecision; he tried to make a virtue of it. He had this idea that fate did what it wanted with you anyway, so your only freedom was to acknowledge this. Thus somehow, he believed, you affected fate for good. He and his son sat down again; they rowed; and for a time I remembered all I had loved him for, his energy, his darkness which seemed inside me like a seahorse. He and his sons were striking out for land like the people in Tennyson's poem—going off for adventure and leaving their women behind. I suppose women always both admire and resent men's courage. This is a split in their own nature. The waves were getting up quite roughly now. They splashed over the front of the boat. I tried to wrap my jersey round my daughter and my baby. I could not think how I had got here. I began to wonder again if he had ever really wanted to come with me to this strange country, or if it had all been fortuitous. I felt that it was; so what was the point? The clouds had come up very quickly now. The wind seemed almost blowing us on to the rocks. I could see he was getting tired. He bent quite close to me each time he rowed and his shirt was open in the heat and his eyes distant. The veins were thick in his arms. I was suddenly very frightened. He had said that I destroyed things but I thought he was a destroyer. The baby had been conceived one day when I had come to his room and my husband had put men to follow me. It was I who had come to his room but it was he who had made love without saying a word; he had had some mad idea that I had murdered my husband. I had trusted him. He said of course he never blamed me about the baby; but even if he did not, I blamed myself. Ever since then I had not been able to go back; I had no choice. I was trapped as on this wide and open sea. I had only wanted to be helped. I thought—Three of them should be able to look after me. But somewhere deeper I felt guilt. I loved my baby with its small round face and straight fair hair. I could not understand how it had made life impossible for me.

We were coming round another headland and in front was the hotel. His two younger children were standing up waving. They acted so emotionally. My daughter remained quiet: she had large eyes and such a determined face. She wanted to be as brave as the others. But suddenly the sea around us altered. We had come round the last headland and were in a different ocean. The wind blew straight on to the shore and there were the rollers. I did not know why we had forgotten the rollers. The water rose in huge movements like whales. Everything suddenly became darker as if birds were scudding before a storm. He said quietly "We should have gone back." I knew he would say this. But we could not go back, because we were too far round the headland. The sea was pushing us forwards and then stopping as if the bottom of the water had fallen out. My daughter said she felt sick. There was nothing I could do. I knew he would be brave, but he did not think of others. I could imagine him standing in the prow and shouting with the rest. I did not know why he had not protected me. They had furled the sail and were not rowing much; we were being blown in on the beach. I had got very cold and was trying to protect my child. We had been a long time in the boat now and the spray and the wind were hurting us. We had seen the fishing boats come in on the beach and they rode on the waves and then the men jumped out and rushed on either side of them. But the men were practised: and he had forgotten the waves. The sea outside the line of breakers was not violent; there was only a swell. But where it broke the water fell and it was like looking down an avalanche. The boat had to be held absolutely straight or it would be hurled and overturned. The beach was always littered with driftwood and dead things. He and his son were trying to keep outside the line of breakers; but they would have to go in some time, there was nothing else to do. We could see the hotel quite clearly; our rooms and the verandah where we sat as a happy family. I was angry because he had risked all this: because he had created it and now was destroying it. He called out to his son to row: they were going to pick up a wave and come in on the crest of it. I did not want to be killed. I saw where the water disappeared towards the beach like a plain seen from a mountain. He became very active; I knew he would; his inaction was only at moments of choice. He stood up and steered with one oar from the side: shouted orders to his children. They were to stand ready on either side and when the time came he was to call "Jump!" and the two youngest were to jump and keep clear and swim to shore. Then he and his eldest son were to jump and hold either side of the boat and guide it to shallow water. Myself and my daughter were to stay in the back. I know he was trying to do his best for us. He accepted adversity so cheerfully, pushing on an oar with the wind in his face like a demon ferrying souls across a river. But he should not have brought us to this hell. We were still hovering just beyond where the waves broke and he was watching and trying to judge which would be a smaller wave; but he could not order the waves, he just smiled, this was what he thought about impossibilities. I felt that he really cared about none of us. He knew I was watching because of the way he stood so still. Then he called out "Jump!" and his two younger children jumped; they began swimming for the shore. They were good swimmers. He and his eldest son rowed fast and caught a wave; they were shouting and almost singing with excitement; it was as if we were a surfboard and they were standing on the sea. They had to see life and death in this parody. The wave lifted us and we were going to be hurled on the land and flatten it. I hung on. I saw swimming almost underneath the boat the head of the youngest child; it had not been able to keep out of the way, the boat was going over it. I could do nothing. I remember the child's wide and terrified eyes. I thought I would never forgive him. I felt something scrape underneath the boat as if it were my own body. I screamed. He shouted "Hold it!" and I remember him pointing to me. Then the boat turned over sideways and I was flung into the sea. I was upside down and water was in my eyes and mouth; I could not breathe, I was in such fear and rage that I wanted to do violence. I was rushed along by a wave; my limbs were flung about; it was as if all the chaos I had always hated had overwhelmed me. I wanted to die. Then I found I was in quite shallow water. I stood. I thought that the boat was going to hit me. It swept past. I was in my depth. The water rushed against my thighs. I had panicked. I was all right now. I did not know what I had done. I saw that at some distance he was holding my daughter. He had her high above his head out of the water and was grinning. She had raised her knees like a dancer. The boat had turned over and was bearing down on them on a wave and he faced it and it hit him and seemed to bounce off; he went down, then the waves took the boat back and he was standing again and still holding my daughter. He was laughing. He had not looked to his own children. I thought his youngest son must be dead. He carried my daughter to the shore and left her there. Then he went back into the waves. The heads of his two elder children were swimming. He shouted encouragement. I could not see his youngest son. The two older ones went past him and then they were all three near the shore. I wanted to tell them that the youngest son was dead. He did not look at me. I think he knew what I was thinking. I thought he would blame me for ever. I wanted to blame him. I was groping beneath the sea with my hands. The foam was in swirls and eyes; I could not see; the ebb pulled everything away from me. The three of them were going back into the waves when the head of his youngest son appeared; he was lifted high, his wide eyes staring above the white foam like a horse's. They all cheered and stretched out their hands; he was fighting with his arms pawing and seemed to be climbing into a different element. They caught him and joined hands and all rushed back to the beach. They were so happy. They seemed demented. I was still standing. I do not think he had thought about me. Perhaps he had wanted me to be responsible for this. When he ran towards me I was still groping under water and he did not notice for a time and then he said "Where is it?" He stood still. He had been fighting hard; was breathing heavily. I had my face down by the water. I thought the water would drown me. He said "But you had it!" He let out a cry. I knew that that cry was against me. He began searching under the water. After a time he took a breath and dived and stayed under. I had been knocked over when the boat had gone over and then another wave had hit me and I had thought I was going to die. I had thought we were all going to die. I wanted to explain—it slipped from my hands, I could not help this. But we never explained. I thought that when this was over I would swim out to sea and drown. I blamed myself. He came up for air and went down several times before he looked at me again. Then I wondered if he would do violence. I wanted him to. I had wanted this before. I think he knew. He went through shallow water to the boat which was lying overturned on the edge of the beach. He ran with high steps as if his feet were burning. The underneath of the boat was striped as if with acid. He put his head under; was trying to turn the boat up. His three sons were on the beach and the eldest was saying "What's happened?" He was always saying this. Then he hit his hand against his head and went into the sea and started looking. The waves were pushing against us and drawing us out. His two younger sons had gone to the boat and were helping him turn it. There was nothing there. I had known there would be nothing there. I did not know what more I could do. I went to the edge of the beach and stood with my daughter. I had looked everywhere. She was shaking with fright and crying. I tried to think that it was his fault because he had taken us. But I could not do this. I thought I would go back into the sea when everyone else had gone. I held on to my daughter. He came running to me once and his face was swollen and he said just—"You had nothing else to do!" I did not answer. I could not explain that I was waiting. I went back and stood in the sea. The colours were of green and yellow plaited reeds. They would not show in the green and yellow water. He was swimming out deeper and was calling to his sons and they were joining him. They did not look at me. They were diving. Some Arabs had appeared and were examining the boat. He shouted at them and they seemed to understand because one or two went into the water, lifting their robes up. His younger son came back and seemed very tired and stood with my daughter. Beyond the waves their heads kept appearing and disappearing like oil. An Arab from the hotel came out carrying a rope. He took off his robe and was wearing a loincloth; the rope was tied round his waist and he went into the sea. Some fishermen arrived and were preparing to get a boat out. He came back once to rest and he bent with his hands on his knees and panted. There was a big weal down one side of his ribs where the boat had hit him. He stood close to me, but he did not say anything. Then he went back into the sea and dived again. The fishermen had got their boat out. I was still standing up to my waist. This went on a long time. I do not know how long. I had been thinking of things to say to him. I had wanted to say—You must blame me—but now I did not want to say anything. All his sons had come back and were lying down on the beach: they were exhausted. My daughter had stopped crying. He was still out beyond the breakers and diving. His sons did not speak. Every now and then I put my hands beneath water and felt there. It had begun to get dark. The world became empty with its deep blue sky and white water. I thought—In death I will find the purity I have always wanted. The fishing boat had gone beyond the waves and they were trying to bring him in. He had been out too long; it was night and they wanted to stop him. But I do not think he wanted to be stopped. They had to have some struggle with him. They were trying to pull him on to the boat and he was resisting them. After a time the boat came back with him. They laid him on the beach. One or two people on the shore had spoken to me: had tried to make me come out of the water. But I stayed there. The moon had come up and made a path straight out into the ocean. I thought that I would swim down it. For the first time I wanted to howl for my baby. I had known that life would catch up with me. I had so much loved life: I had loved my baby. After a time he got up and was walking up and down behind me. I did not want him to speak to me again. I did not think he would. People were talking about coming to carry me in, but he was stopping them. Then he came out into the water himself. I thought that now I should swim. But my legs were too cold. I was paralysed. So he came up to me from behind and took my elbows. He said—"My love, it was not your fault." I did not think it was. He tried to lift me, I would not move. The moon was stuck solid in all my lower half. I knew that he always thought that life could be refashioned and go on, but I thought that it should not. There are some things for which one cannot be forgiven.

I wanted to write you something impossible, like a staircase climbing a spiral to come out where it started or a cube with a vertical line at the back overlapping a horizontal one in front. These cannot exist in three dimensions but can be drawn in two; by cutting out one dimension a fourth is created. The object is that life is impossible; one cuts out fabrication and creates reality. A mirror is held to the back of the head and one's hand has to move the opposite way from what was intended.

You used to dislike happy endings, feeling it is better to have your heart cut out like an Aztec rather than suffer the prevarications of Spaniards. So I have given you an unhappy end like those of your favourite films—the girl shot over and over in snow like a rabbit, the car drowning in a few inches of water. There is also a happy end, though this is less explicit. But you always read books more for form than for content.

Once when men separated themselves from women then crimes were committed by the feminine sides of men and women encouraged them with masculine exhortation. Now men and women face each other and the battle is in the mind: where, in truth, it has always been.

Once upon a time there was a woodcutter walking through a wood and he came across a tree in which a beautiful princess was imprisoned. Now the princess was not really a princess but a witch, and she was sitting in the tree in order to attract woodcutters. So she called out "Help!" in a tiny voice like falling teacups. The woodcutter stopped and asked the princess what she wanted; and she told him that she had been imprisoned in the tree by a witch. Now this woodcutter was not really a woodcutter but a magician, who had come into the wood in order to charm princesses. "I will save you!" said the woodcutter raising his axe to chop her down. "Stop!" called the princess, "I am not really a princess but a witch!" "I know," said the woodcutter; "what would I do with princesses?" He struck her a blow around her feet. She toppled

175

over on top of him, wounding him and imprisoning him with her branches. "Now what do we do?" said the witch. "The usual," said the magician. He rose to his feet and moved round the wood with the princess clinging to his shoulders. She could not let go because she had no feet and he could not shake her off because his arms were broken. They began to perform a series of complex lifts and attitudes; the music following them with careful note of their timing. "Let go," whispered the woodcutter: "I can't," breathed the princess. "Have you noticed," said the woodcutter, "that in ecstasy the body can be lacerated but neither suffers nor bleeds?" "You must be a magician," said the witch. When the time came for the final tableau the woodcutter had to go down on one knee and the princess was to float above him like a bird. "Hold on!" said the woodcutter. "What's the point?" said the princess. They were an apparition of rare and moving beauty; her hair like diamonds, the moss on his neat and sensual face. "What is the point of being a witch and a magician," said the magician, "if we cannot become something different?" The curtain came down. The audience left their seats. The two dancers came in front of the curtain and held hands. They were very tired. They poured with sweat. From the roof there fluttered eggs and roses.

The Streaming Media Guide

Streaming media has irreversibly revolutionised the ways in which media is transmitted and consumed. Most of us engage with streaming media on a daily basis via platforms that deliver our entertainment, such as Spotify, YouTube and Netflix. It has created upheaval in the entire value chain and wiped out industries slow to adapt to it (like video store rental chains) and it continues to evolve. Streaming media is transforming business communications in a myriad of ways, and it is becoming almost as crucial for project managers and marketers to understand streaming technology as it is for media professionals.

The Streaming Media Guide demystifies the technology and features behind a successful streaming media service, especially in the context of how it is used by broadcasters and other media organisations. Common terms and systems being used in this space are presented and defined simply and clearly for non-technical readers. Best practice examples from Michael D'Oliveiro's experiences demonstrate how this technology can be successfully implemented.

This book equips any media professional with the most basic of traditional media knowledge to enable confident conversations in the typical organisation they work in. For technology-based graduates or dedicated broadcast professionals seeking to refresh their understanding, this book provides enough information to form a solid foundation for day-to-day work. Finally, for leaders in cross-functional senior management matrices, information is provided to enable them to understand and exploit streaming media capabilities as a business. This will be the ultimate reference source, guaranteed to be bedside reading for anyone serious about using streaming media.

Michael D'Oliveiro has over 20 years of experience, primarily in the broadcast and streaming media industry, both in Australia and South-East Asia. Well-versed in production, operations and product management, Michael was recently Country Head of HOOQ Singapore, the regional, subscription-based streaming platform.

The Streaming Media Guide

How to Successfully Integrate Streaming Media Into Your Communications Strategy

Michael D'Oliveiro

Routledge
Taylor & Francis Group

LONDON AND NEW YORK

First published 2019
by Routledge
2 Park Square, Milton Park, Abingdon, Oxon OX14 4RN

and by Routledge
52 Vanderbilt Avenue, New York, NY 10017

Routledge is an imprint of the Taylor & Francis Group, an informa business

British Library Cataloguing-in-Publication Data
A catalogue record for this book is available from the British Library

Library of Congress Cataloging-in-Publication Data
Names: D'Oliveiro, Michael, 1973- author.
Title: The streaming media guide : how to successfully integrate streaming media into your communications strategy / Michael D'Oliveiro.
Description: Abingdon, Oxon ; New York, NY : Routledge, 2019. | Includes bibliographical references and index.
Identifiers: LCCN 2018059901 (print) | LCCN 2019004020 (ebook) | ISBN 9780429429750 (eBook) | ISBN 9781138367517 (hardback : alk. paper)
Subjects: LCSH: Streaming technology (Telecommunications) | Mass media–Management.
Classification: LCC TK5105.386 (ebook) | LCC TK5105.386 .D65 2019 (print) | DDC 659.20285/4678–dc23
LC record available at https://lccn.loc.gov/2018059901

ISBN: 978-1-138-36751-7 (hbk)
ISBN: 978-0-429-42975-0 (ebk)

Typeset in Sabon
by Integra Software Services Pvt. Ltd.

To my children Elle, Chris and Ava for being my inspiration.
And my wife Nim for her love and patience.

Contents

Contents

Illustrations

Tables

Acknowledgements

I'd like to acknowledge the help of the following people who made this book possible. Thanks, firstly, goes to my wife Nimmala, who provided an amazing amount of support wherever and whenever needed to help me in writing this book. To my parents, Lina and Monte D'Oliveiro, I owe you a debt of gratitude for encouraging me in my writing ever since I could remember. Thank you, Mum and Dad.

Several people lent their time and effort in reviewing portions of this book. I'd like to thank James Miner, CEO of Video Assure and MinerLabs Group, for his constant encouragement and attention to detail. Given his breadth of experience in broadcast and streaming media, it was great to have his knowledge to tap on but he went even beyond that. Thanks also to Alexandre Yokoyama, ex-Googler and ex-IBMer, for providing his inputs. Despite his current hectic schedule as a mentor to entrepreneurs (and being an entrepreneur himself), he took this assignment on without hesitation. A big thank you to the esteemed Michael Fay, VP of Product and Operations at Akamai Labs, for his passionate comments about content delivery. Thanks also go out to Stephanie Fallon and Hyacinths Pennefather at Akamai for their support. Special thanks also to Derek Yap for the illustrations that were provided despite a busy schedule.

Numerous professionals at senior levels of large media firms gave inputs whilst declining to be named. Nonetheless, their inputs were also extremely helpful in the course of putting this book together. You know who you are and thank you again.

Finally, I would like to offer my most sincere thanks to the editorial and production staff at Routledge and the Taylor & Francis Group, namely editor Amy Laurens and editorial assistant Alex Atkinson, for their kind help and support in making my first book a reality.

Abbreviations

2FA	two-factor authentication
AAC	Advanced Audio Coding
ABR	adaptive bitrate
API	application programming interface
AVC	Advanced Video Coding
AVOD	advertising-funded video on demand
AWS	Amazon Web Services
B2B	business to business
B2C	business to consumer
BOC	Broadcast Operations Centre
capex	capital expenditure
CAS	Conditional Access Systems
CDN	content delivery network
CIAM	Customer Identity and Access Management
CMAF	Common Media Application Format
CMS	content management system
CPM	cost per mille (Latin for 'thousand')
CPU	central processing unit
CRM	Customer Relationship Management
CSAI	client-side ad insertion
CTR	click-through rate
DASH	Dynamic Streaming over HTTP
DBR	dynamic bitrate
DDoS	distributed denial of service
DRM	Digital Rights Management
DSP	demand-side platform
EPG	electronic programme guide

FTA	Free-to-air/Free TV
GB	gigabyte
GCP	Google Cloud Platform
GDPR	General Data Protection Regulation
GUI	graphical user interface
HD	High Definition
HDMI	high definition multimedia interface
HDS	HTTP Dynamic Streaming
HEVC	High Efficiency Video Coding
HLS	HTTP Live Streaming
HTML	Hypertext Markup Language
HTTP	Hypertext Transfer Protocol
IAB	Interactive Advertising Bureau
IAM	Identity Access Management
IANA	Internet Assigned Numbers Authority
IP	internet protocol
ISP	internet service provider
KBA	knowledge-based authentication
Kbps	kilobits per second
LMS	learning management systems
MAC	media access control
MB	megabyte
Mbps	megabits per second
MCN	multi-channel network
MOOC	massive open online course
MPEG	Motion Picture Experts Group
NTSC	National Television Standards Committee
NVOD	near-video on demand
O2O	online-to-offline
opex	operational expenditure
OS	operating system
OTP	one-time password
OTT	over-the-top
OVP	online video platform
P2P	peer-to-peer
PAL	Phase Alternating Line
PDP	personal data protection
PDPA	personal data protection act
PII	personally identifiable information
POP	Point of Presence
PVR	personal video recorder

QoS	Quality of Service
RaaS	Registration-as-a-Service
RAM	random-access memory
RTB	real-time bidding
RTMP	Real Time Messaging Protocol
RTSP	Real Time Streaming Protocol
SaaS	Software-as-a-Service
SD	Standard Definition
SDI	serial digital interface
SDK	software development kit
SI	systems integrator
SIM	subscriber identity module
SSAI	server-side ad insertion
SSL	Secure Sockets Layer
SSO	single sign-on
SSP	supply-side platform
SVOD	subscription video on demand
TB	terabyte
telco	telecommunications company
TLS	Transport Layer Security
TVOD	transactional video on demand
UGC	user-generated content
UHD	Ultra High Definition
UI	user interface
UX	user experience
VAST	video ad-serving template
VCR	video cassette recorder
VOD	video on demand
VPAID	video player-ad interface definition
W3C	World Wide Web Consortium
WCAG	Web Content Accessibility Guidelines

Foreword

All too often (it seems), books written on the subject of 'online video' are created with the sole purpose of drowning readers in a tsunami of industry 'insider' phrases and jargon ... thankfully this is *not* one of those books.

I have known the author since 2007 and whilst he certainly has the industry background to get uber-technical, I was gratified to see that this book was created specifically to help *new* entrants to the streaming media industry to navigate these waters with a comprehensive (yet easy to understand) guide. This book is not just about the current state of the online video space but also '"presses the *rewind* button" to help readers' understand the history and origins of the multitude of platforms and technologies that (today) we all take for granted, but are nonetheless *essential* to the delivery of video over the internet.

In the 20 (plus) years I have worked in the industry, it was always amusing to see vendors touting the 'next big thing' as the definitive 'future of online video' yet 'fast-forward' just a few years and that 'next big thing' would be on the scrap heap – replaced by something 'even better' at half the bandwidth cost of the previous version (for a fraction of the money). A healthy dose of scepticism is needed to ensure that before you jump into these waters, you learn from the mistakes of the past so as not to get caught up in a technology whose time has been (and gone).

Promising careers have been swiftly ended by over-committing business to a proprietary platform or technology that fell out of favour with the consumer (or device manufacturer community). Windows Media Player, RealNetworks, Adobe Flash, etc. The road is long and littered with the careers of C-suite executives who made the 'wrong' choice. 'Those who don't know history are doomed to repeat it' (Edmund Burke).

This is an ever-evolving landscape where hundreds of billions of dollars are getting spent each year to capture the attention of the billions of eyeballs around the world who *demand* a quality viewing experience that they can watch *anywhere, anytime* and on *any device*. Meeting (better yet, *exceeding*) those expectations has always been an enormous challenge. We need to innovate yet *also* reduce our costs of doing business. Consumers are not willing to simply accept 'good enough' (it needs to be 1080p, 4K *(or even 8K)* on their shiny new mobile handset – on their super-fast (5G?) internet service provider.

Innovation and differentiation are the keys to success, yet – *where* do you draw the line? Consumers are a savvy bunch and whilst they love having the latest/greatest viewing experience in their pockets, they are unlikely to put down their hard-earned cash to buy a *solution looking for a problem* (e.g. 3D television). It's hard to know where the line is being crossed between a 'feature' and a 'benefit' (know the difference).

Hopefully, after reading this book you will have a better sense of the complexities involved and have an appreciation for the innovators and visionaries who paved the way for consumers to be able to watch an infinite number of online video clips (or a full-length feature film) from *anywhere* in the world – all at the click of a button.

What a truly *amazing* world we live in!

Matthew H. Sturgess
Regional Managing Director/Head of Asia-Pacific
Verizon Digital Media Services

Introduction

Just press play ...

If somebody had told me in the early 1990s that we would one day be watching TV on a tiny flat screen as we took the morning commute to work, I might have been tempted to say it was unbelievable. Taken in the context of those times – when a typical television set weighed up to 50 kilograms – many people would have agreed with me. Fast-forward to today and an entire new generation of netizens have already grown up not comprehending a world without this prediction in place. In fact, the rapid innovation of online video and audio has redefined not just our entertainment habits as consumers, but also the way we communicate and learn. Officially referred to today as streaming media, it is a culmination of a technology convergence encompassing the internet, software and hardware, as well as new business models that have revolutionised the industry. It's absolutely exciting to be able to engage in content so freely and flexibly wherever you are, isn't it?

It's also terribly scary to try to comprehend how to use it in a professional sense.

The speed of its constant development and innovation has certainly caught us 'off guard'. It is barely two decades old as an industry but it seems that streaming media has already wreaked havoc on those who have failed to anticipate its potential. Before this, television as a broadcast medium had held constant for almost half a century. But the internet and software laid the groundwork first. As worldwide internet usage grew in the mid-1990s, the existence of an online community was already being exploited by enterprising consumer brands. Early video technologies from companies like RealNetworks and Apple capitalised on this by developing the technologies needed to take what was essentially an analogue format and convert it into bytes. This innocuous start led to a significant and historical milestone in March 1999.

Well, it was actually two events in that month that one should look at as a catalyst for the streaming revolution. One was the unprecedented download record of the newest *Star Wars: Episode I – The Phantom Menace* trailer (3.5 million downloads over five days), and the other was ESPNet.SportsZone.com's streaming of the famed March Madness basketball matches. Previously for both events, you either had to be in the cinema (to view the trailer), watch a televised broadcast (if it was available in your region) or be present courtside at one of the colleges to view the basketball match. Watching it on your computer screen allowed a much wider audience to participate in the viewing than before and, arguably, could be a motivation for people to actually then watch the movie (in the case of *The Phantom Menace*) or go courtside to follow more of the action.

Impressively enough for a pre-social media world, the word had spread from offline media to some of the noted online media sites and publicity of the two events led vast audiences online. Little did people know that a consumer revolution had just begun.

When YouTube was founded by three former PayPal engineers in 2005, it served to function as a video sharing site. However, it quickly morphed away from the 'user-generated content' (UGC) that the industry termed it and into something actually meant for entertaining a mass audience. A year later, it was already generating 100 million views a day, with visits from over 20 million users per month.[1]

Services like Hulu in 2008 captured public attention again as the US networks banded together to form a service that could bring traditional TV watching 'on demand' at home. Viewers no longer had to watch a TV show by appointment, since they could watch episodes they already missed as soon as the initial live broadcast of that episode ended.[2]

Cue the hardware.

This boost arrived with Apple's introduction of the iPhone in 2007. For the first time, a smartphone was capable of playing back video using 3G wireless mobile technology and made live streaming of events available for mainstream entertainment consumption even more. People began to find entire sports tournaments available online (the 2010 World Cup being one of them), as well as their favourite destination of UGC like YouTube and DailyMotion, among others. A decade later, the proliferation of the smartphone and its affordability has meant that over 50 per cent of video viewing worldwide is made on such a device.

While the demand from users surprised industry observers and showed potential that streaming video had on an internet audience, no one predicted its growth and ubiquitous presence today. Fast-forward to today and video is consumed on almost any smart mobile device that is connected to high-speed broadband.

Today, we find time to watch our favourite TV shows on the commute or in bed before we turn in for the night. We watch Hollywood movies at the office or during our lunch break. We pause viewing, knowing that we can resume whenever we want to. We stream a digital rental from Apple's iTunes Store and all of us never have to worry about paying overdue fees ('What's that?' I hear you millennials ask). We basically watch whenever there's spare time, coining the industry term Catch-up TV. The fact that we can also watch our favourite TV programmes wherever we have an internet connection has coined another industry term: TV Everywhere (or TV Anywhere, if you prefer).

Streaming media has not only affected consumers. In its course of upheaval around the world it has seen off the bricks-and-mortar businesses that thrived on the physical delivery of entertainment. Video might have killed the radio star but the internet made physical video rentals as obsolete as the dodo – those who grew up accustomed to Blockbuster Video weekends witnessed its passing a decade ago after a well-documented and fascinating drawn-out fight with the web-based DVD rental service Netflix.

Given the ability for Hollywood studios to re-imagine a whole new distribution platform, streaming media has allowed those studios and consumers to get connected immediately, by-passing the middleman (the nervous Pay TV operators). This has resulted in the likes of mobile apps like Fox Plus, which offer titles from 21st Century Fox direct to the public. To placate the Pay TV operators, you still need a relevant Pay TV subscription in order to watch the app. But consider the fact that some time in 2019, Disney will launch its own global streaming media service. All this has happened thanks to Netflix. Fresh from defeating Blockbuster Video, the company quickly morphed their service from DVD rentals only to a streaming media service as well. Not only have such new brands sprung up to take advantage of cutting out the middlemen, completely new industries have been created. Like the content delivery network, or CDN for short. CDN providers like Akamai have built a fair share of their early business by being able to locally cache and stream media content easily from one point out to users anywhere in the world via a vast network of servers.

Perhaps, if anything, the consumption of entertainment has never stopped – it's even been accelerated by the thirst for storytelling that humans crave when they come home at night. You don't need a remote and a five-minute channel-surfing experience anymore to find what you want. Siri listens and recommends. And because you get it straight away, you just cannot fathom why you need to wait for anything. Welcome to the on-demand generation.

Importantly, the interactive nature of the internet has paved the way for media analytics by a host of companies. Did you ever realise when you press 'play' that your interactions are collected to provide real-time information to broadcasters? Today's savvy broadcasters can see what content is popular, on what device and from which country or town it is consumed. The amount of data available is staggering and impressive, if you consider the fact the broadcasters traditionally had no way of rating content popularity except through the use of panel households. A sampled collection of households today is no match for knowing what each and every of your online audience is actually watching. It enables streaming businesses to optimise their content whilst actually generating additional advertising revenue through more intelligent targeting of audiences that advertisers increasingly prefer. Gone are the days when everyone saw the same advertisement. Today, a male and a female viewer watching the same TV show online will receive different ads simply because streaming media businesses know who is logged in and what their basic preferences are. The male viewer is likely to receive sportswear ads since he subscribed to the sports pack on his TV subscription while the female viewer gets an ad based on her age and Facebook 'likes', since she uses her Facebook username to log into her service. The era of homogeneous broadcasting has now evolved into a personalised experience that is more meaningful.

Unfortunately, the proliferation of streaming video as a distribution platform has caught many academic institutions by surprise. Not in terms of technology – this is well documented and taught since the technology behind streaming media is fairly stable even despite the multiple, ever-evolving standards. But few institutions have created anything deeper than the odd elective subject to tackle the business of streaming media. Successful entertainment and marketing professionals have evolved their understanding and adapted their approach but not everyone gets a chance to learn, and self-learning has certainly not been the best way to understand streaming media from the start.

That's where this book comes in.

Making sense of all this from a broadcast business or corporate perspective requires some understanding of the technology and the current trends. If you are part of a larger team and streaming media is still largely a mystery, then you should find solace in this book. Provided you have a basic understanding of computers and how the internet works, this book will help you get up to speed on streaming media, giving you credibility and significantly easing your learning curve as you deal with the day-to-day specifics of streaming media that you manage.

For the senior broadcast engineer or product professional transitioning into a 'new media' or streaming media, this book will help to clarify terms and terminology allowing you to confidently discuss and understand the technology with your more adept peers. Engineers will find the platform or infrastructure aspects of streaming media more relevant for understanding. Product managers will benefit from the product features aspect.

As much as this book will cover all the building blocks of understanding, what it won't cover are the fine technical details that require precise knowledge or qualifications. But since it covers the basics, you can find an area that fascinates you and jump straight into it. Be non-linear, just as video on demand is! Abbreviations abound in this industry and keep growing in number. Besides including the abbreviations list in the front portion of this book, I have made sure to always explain the abbreviations in each chapter as if you were reading about them for the first time.

And, if anything else, I hope you'll be entertained about streaming media along the way.

Notes

1 *USA Today*, 'YouTube serves up 100 million videos a day online', https://usato day30.usatoday.com/tech/news/2006-07-16-youtube-views_x.htm, 7 July 2006.
2 *Business Wire*, Hulu press release, www.businesswire.com/news/home/ 20080312005454/en/Hulu.com-Opens-Public-Offers-Free-Streams-Hit, 12 March 2008.

Streaming media today

Audio-visual media has come a long way since its analogue beginnings and where it stands today is exciting for everyone. There's been more innovation in the past 20 years than in the 100 years before it, as you'll get to understand as you read the following chapters in this book. But before we get any further, we should get the basic terms out of the way.

Getting definitions right

It's common to hear people mentioning the terms digital media and streaming media interchangeably. That's understandable but not quite correct. Digital media can be thought of as anything that has its information represented as binary information. Ones and zeros that are grouped in bits and then bytes. The classic example is the DVD. It may come in a physical form but its information is certainly digital, which is why it's able to store so much information and also why it can offer interactivity via a menu and other selectable features. You can't do that with vinyl records or cassettes.

But with the power of the internet, streaming media offers no physical form to look at, aside from the device you hold in your hands. You don't even need to download a file if you don't want to (but that is an option, as you'll read about later). You can watch something, then pause it and you'll never need to worry about picking up where you last left off. You could pick another device you own and just continue watching from the same point. It's incredibly user-friendly in so many ways and full of possibilities beyond just entertainment.

So there you have it. The difference between digital and streaming.

Just to confuse you, the broadcast industry has a more prevalent term of their own: OTT video. OTT stands for 'over-the-top' and refers to the ability of companies like Netflix or YouTube to stream their content to you using an internet connection that is provided by a different company. This is normally an internet service provider (ISP) or telecommunications company (telco). The term OTT itself can be applied to other services like WhatsApp which, again, provides a service over the internet connection provided by your ISP or telco. There is a connotation here that the OTT company is piggy-backing on the efforts of someone else in a way that also threatens the latter's business model by cannibalising it. WhatsApp threatens telcos' text messaging services since it's free but uses the internet service they provide. So, while OTT perfectly describes what Netflix does, I have simply not decided to use that term in this book. Not out of reasons of being neutral but for professional consistency. Similarly, the direct term 'online video' is also used by many industry organisations and there is nothing wrong with it either. Since this book is for professionals, I've decided that 'streaming' is a more appropriate word to describe this medium.

So streaming media it is. But how did we get to this stage of being able to watch an epic movie in the palm of our hand?

Streaming media today: the basics

A lot of the consumer habits today have similarities to how people have traditionally consumed media back when it was either available in the cinema, on radio, on TV or on video as a DVD. But we don't have to go so far back since the biggest and clearest milestone of that evolution was the public growth of the internet. Thus, I would be inclined to mark this milestone by observing the period right before, during and after it. In effect, we can classify these periods as such:

1. Media before the Internet Boom (1960–2000)
2. Media during and after the Internet Boom (2001–2015)
3. Media Renaissance (2015 to the present day)

Media before the Internet Boom (1990–2000)

Right up to the early 1990s, the creation of mass media like Hollywood movies (as an example) were set in the established process as seen in Figure 1.1. Basically, each part of the value chain was owned by specific entities that specialised in the role they played. Content owners (the Hollywood studios) occupied the role of content creator. They were able to enjoy releasing their movies in three different 'release windows' that did not overlap, and provide consumers with the ability to choose the viewing window of their choice. There were actually more windows (take TV, which would allow Pay TV to get a movie before Free TV did), but this was more or less the way the industry operated worldwide.

Release windows are crucial to Hollywood studios since they offer multiple monetisation opportunities for their movies. Consumers could watch a movie and then catch it on Pay TV and then buy the DVD loaded with bonus features. They could buy the original soundtrack separately to just listen to the music. As part of this ecosystem, the print media played their role in terms of coverage via news or reviews of a movie as it

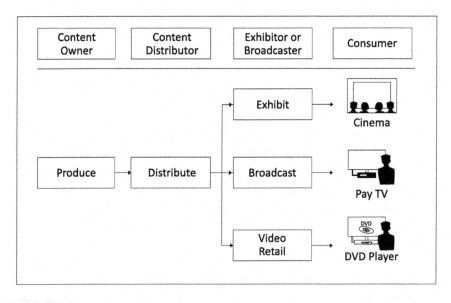

Figure 1.1 Circa 1960–2000: this is a typical production and distribution model for a studio-produced movie that incorporates the three main distribution windows targeted at public audiences

appeared from window to window. If you take into account the other ancillary revenue that Hollywood generates in terms of sub-licensing and merchandising of content you'll understand just how lucrative the industry was, and still is, for Hollywood. This pattern obviously then extends to other countries and their own industries (like Bollywood).

The television industry was likewise entrenched in its own distribution structure. There was primetime television when news and series attracted the most viewers, who had to put up with commercial breaks as a result. Television was essentially viewing by appointment. If successful, a series would extend its viewability on the small screen through syndication. The final step was the DVD box set.

Music followed similar distribution structures, albeit a little flatter. Radio helped promote sales of released singles but both ran in parallel. Singles led to albums and that was the extent of the release window. The only musical event that an artiste could exploit were concert tours and then the cycle would repeat itself.

The consumer had little control in how or where they wanted to view content. Daily schedules revolved around cinema showtimes or the TV guide or the Top 40 countdown. If there was frustration, nothing could be done so acceptance became the norm and, indeed, general behaviour. Once you bought a particular item of media you could do what you wanted.

Media during and after the Internet Boom (2001–2015)

With the rise of the internet, new and innovative players began to exploit it as a distribution medium and allow media to be streamed or down-loaded over the internet, direct to the consumer. Apple was one such company when it launched the iTunes service in 2003. The service initially targeted music lovers and allowed them to buy only one song or an entire album and store it on an iPod. With playback also allowed on desktop computers and laptops, it transformed the way people bought and kept songs. Apple's tagline of '10,000 songs in your pocket' proved irresistible for a new generation of internet-savvy commuters. You could create your own playlist and get ready for your start of the day, joining the masses in urban cities wearing those ubiquitous white earphones.

When movies, TV shows and podcasts followed suit in 2005, the snowball had become an avalanche. Apple's involvement was revolutionary to industry because the company itself now became an e-commerce player, threatening retailers who would forever be saddled with inventory management.

Figure 1.2 visualises this early disruption that Apple set in the market. The significance here is that e-commerce was not a separate window that would come in after the retail window started. It itself was part of that.

Apple's entrance as a digital distributor of media was ominous for the established retailers and rental providers since it provided convenience and easy availability. No one had to worry about stocks running out. You could buy your movie at any time of the day and watch it immediately. All you needed was a credit card or an iTunes voucher. It was the iPhone, Spotify and Netflix that made the greatest impact on streaming media from 2007 onwards.

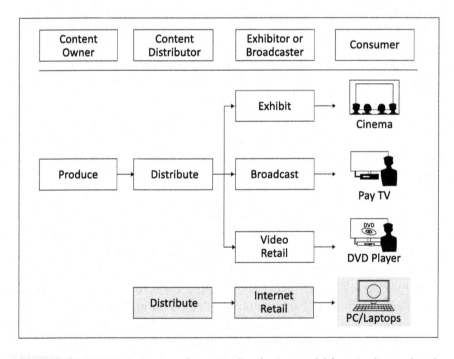

Figure 1.2 1999–2015: the new, disruptive distribution model for a studio-produced movie provided more viewing choices for the general public but also introduced greater competition at the retail level. The shaded boxes show these newer entrants

By the end of 2007, social media had also started to make an impact on the media eco-system, paving the way for start-ups and these platforms to scale up around the globe and become more advanced.

The Media Renaissance (2015 to the present day)

The Media Renaissance is how I'd describe our present state. It shouldn't be compared literally with the original Renaissance in history, which can be defined as a 're-birth' of the arts in Europe inspired by the classics of Ancient Greece and Rome. The comparison between that period and today is really about the social and cultural changes that have been seen as streaming media continues to mature and flourish around the globe. When Apple introduced the iPhone, it did not just shake up the mobile phone manufacturing industry, it demonstrated the beginnings of how media consumption could really be 'anywhere'. With a 3G data-enabled subscriber identity module (SIM) card, you could buy the iPhone from your mobile service provider of choice and take the internet with you at all times. You never had to go online again; you were always online! Mobile operators fuelled growth by launching services and 'zero-rated' data for video viewing (that's industry jargon for not charging data consumption for video to your data quota on your mobile phone bill). Events like the 2010 FIFA World Cup were used to launch such services and drive consumers to early adoption.

While Apple drove media consumption 'anywhere', the business model for monetising this was difficult. Apple's early benefit to consumers only allowed transactional purchases and this still made little sense if consumers had budget constraints. It was also a download-to-own (DTO) model.

Netflix, launched in 1998, pioneered online DVD mailing and followed up this success with a subscription model that allowed unlimited rentals of DVDs each month. The 'no-contract, no-commitment subscription plan' provided great incentives for consumers to try out this service. Netflix fought a drawn-out battle with Blockbuster for over a decade that ultimately ended in the latter's demise as a business and proved industry pundits' view of the disruptive influence that the internet had over the traditional rental model. Also, Netflix's declaration that subscription services would replace rentals and overdue fees catered to consumer sentiments. As if its DVD rentals were not enough, in 2007 Netflix also launched a streaming service, convinced that this was a far better user experience than physical DVDs. The clear advantage of streaming was that no one had to worry about saving space on a device due to heavy video files. In contrast, Netflix was able to use analytics features from consumer usage to optimise how the site would be navigated and how titles could be recommended on a personalised level.

On the music front, it was Spotify that created another innovation by launching a 'freemium' model for its streaming service. You could try the limited service and put up with occasional advertisements, or you could pay a monthly subscription fee and get access to all songs, at higher streaming quality.[1]

Breaking away from industry norms was potentially a financial drag (as of 2017 Spotify is still unprofitable despite annual revenue of EU5.26 billion), but it gave consumers what they wanted: flexibility.

More powerfully, the final step in Figure 1.3 now shows that the ease in creating a medium of distribution has shifted the industry to a more open and accessible playing field. Today, you don't have to be a broadcaster to actually broadcast to people. Anyone can be a broadcaster in the streaming media world.

New uses of streaming media today

Pure-play internet broadcasters

As I mentioned in the Introduction, almost anyone can set up a service and find an audience online to stream to. Success depends really on what you want to do and if there's demand for it. And there's no shortage of pioneers in this area.

The record for 'first ever' goes to a public access programme entitled *Rox*, in April 1995, with an episode called 'Global Village Idiots'. Later that same year, the first fictional series entitled *The Spot* was also released on the internet, supported by advertising this time.

Noted entrepreneur Mark Cuban set out on a visionary path in 1994, when he invested in a company that eventually became broadcast.com. The fledgling company eventually streamed a number of sporting events live in the US as well as other notable public events (including the first Victoria's Secret Fashion Show). At the time of its purchase by Yahoo for $5.7 billion in stock in 1999, it reputedly had 570,000 users.

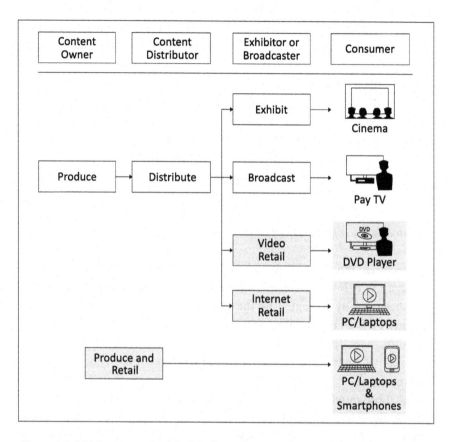

Figure 1.3 2015–present day: the Media Renaissance built entirely new industries for a studio-produced movie to be introduced to the general public, including the rise of pure-play streaming businesses. These also produce their own content. By 2016, Netflix was already streaming to global markets but regional players were starting to compete against it. Industries have also disappeared, particularly the bricks-and-mortar rental chains

ESPNet.SportsZone.com launched in 1995 (as the precursor to ESPN. com) and eventually took advantage of serendipity to stream March Madness in 1999 to basketball-starved fans, beginning the first of its many streaming forays with sporting events, eventually rising to be one of the leaders in US sports streaming that it is today.

Sports aside, niche programming eventually found its place online too. It was in 2007 that legendary website Funny Or Die launched, with its focus on satire or parodies. Its very first video was the viral hit *The Landlord* featuring then co-founder Will Ferrell being berated by the two-year-old titular character. Funny Or Die exploited the interactivity of the web in allowing users to vote for videos as either 'Funny' or 'Die' and spawned numerous imitators around the world.

These internet-only broadcasters are also known as pure-play operators. Colloquially, they are also known as 'streamers' within the industry. Some, like Netflix, call themselves an internet television service. Notably, they are new companies that exist only on the internet (hence the term). Their popularity has resulted in the creation of a new type of consumer dubbed the 'cord-cutter'.

Broadcasters using TV Anywhere

You've heard the term TV Anywhere before. Or maybe in your part of the world it's TV Everywhere. It's the same thing. Traditional broadcasters have been totally disrupted by the rise of the internet and the pure-play operators who have literally taken business away from them. For Pay TV operators who spent decades enjoying revenues derived from expensive TV channel bundles on a recurring subscription, pure-play rivals have resulted in the rise of the 'cord-cutter', a reference to Pay TV's physical 'cable' through which content is transmitted and their subscribers who are turning their backs on the service in favour of streaming media. Cord-cutters are not only early adopters of internet services, they eschew TV bundles knowing that most of the content is not what they want. They prefer an *à la carte* viewing experience even if it means buying from different pure-play operators. Free TV (or free-to-air – FTA) operators have – by virtue of being free – felt the pinch much less but many have innovated ahead of time. The US has a great example in ABC which made bold moves in 2007 to embrace the internet if the right business model and partner could be found. Even then, it took a gutsy personality like ABC's Anne Sweeney to shake up the industry by not only putting the network's TV shows on abc.com but also striking a deal with Apple to distribute them via the iTunes Store as well. The BBC followed suit that same year in the UK by unveiling their iPlayer service, which became extremely popular.

Thus, the concept of taking TV out of the living room and into computers or hand-held devices is what TV Anywhere is primarily all about. Its value proposition is powerful when paired with the Catch-up TV feature, where TV shows are transcoded and made available online hours after the actual TV broadcast. The combination of the two has continued to make broadcasters relevant to audiences. Where critics say that Catch-up TV cannibalises its broadcast counterpart (thereby reducing a show's ratings), its proponents say that Catch-up TV allows viewers to remain loyal to a show because they can literally catch up on an episode and this increases their probability of watching the series they would have otherwise given up on. They also say that ratings should be an aggregate of the viewership on TV and those online. Yet, the main challenge has been monetisation. The majority of viewers expect TV Anywhere services to remain free, especially if it's the online version of its Free TV counterpart. It would be a paradox to charge for viewing on one platform instead of the other. However, even Pay TV operators have found it difficult to charge for their TV Anywhere services since subscribers largely expect it to be subsidised by the TV subscription they are paying. Thus, the low willingness to pay by both the viewer and the advertiser has long made TV Anywhere an anti-churn strategy.

The one exception has been Hulu. The brainchild of several media executives, Hulu was launched in August 2007 and offered one streaming media platform for viewers to watch various hit TV shows from broadcasters like NBC and Fox, as Catch-up TV. Initially an ad-driven service (a legacy of the TV model), Hulu has grown since to be subscription-only from 2016 and become a reference point for other countries' TV broadcasters to use as they plan their own unified platforms.

TV Anywhere and the return of linear channels

TV Anywhere concepts have now come full circle, with broadcasters realising that live and linear channels are still popular, thanks to premium content like sports and news channels which have the ability to provide 'breaking news' at any time. Combined with the rich functionality of an electronic programme guide (EPG), TV Anywhere services allow end users to discover channels and content easily. They can search, look up recommendations, browse the EPG or simply channel surf if they want to.

When US-based Dish Network launched its Sling TV service in 2015, this was billed as a milestone in the industry, with Dish Network effectively launching a virtual, or online only, cable service. The major difference is that its virtual service was considered a 'skinny' bundle, in contrast to the traditionally bloated offerings by the broadcast equivalent. Around the world, this trend has spread, with Molotov launching in France, offering free access to Free TV content but requiring a paid subscription to access the premium Pay TV channels.

In 2017, Hulu began offering 'Hulu with Live TV' with linear channels available from ABC, NBC, CBS, Fox and The CW, among others.

From broadcast to podcast

Since its launch in early 2003, iTunes has been one of the biggest platforms for content distribution, gaining foothold thanks to the ubiquity of Apple's devices and the novel concept of purchasing individual songs, as opposed to albums. Apple's CEO Steve Jobs had personally seen to the broadening of iTunes into areas like movies and TV shows two years later. In 2006, iTunes scored a major coup when Disney's CEO Bob Iger joined Steve Jobs on stage to announce the sale of episodes of the hit TV shows *Desperate Housewives* and *Lost*, for $1.99 each. Looking back, it was only a matter of time before TV found its way online on a device. However, the popularity of the platform did encourage the rise of a unique form of broadcasting by individuals, one that would really spur disruption: podcasting.

Technically, the first podcasts weren't even on iTunes. They were just added to websites as audio files and end users could easily just play back whenever they visited the site. But the iPod's ubiquity allowed podcasting to be more widely adopted, which is fitting since it's actually a portmanteau of the root words 'iPod' and 'broadcast'. iTunes allowed end users to easily navigate to one central place to find all the podcasts they were interested in, by genre or title, and subscribe to their favourite ones. The podcast creators themselves made no major revenue (other than advertiser sponsorship) but won the hearts and minds of a new market of early adopters. Podcasts are a typical example of user-generated content (UGC) that has defined the media eco-system by the end of the Internet Boom.

The only impediment to iTunes was that you had to download the podcasts and sync them to your iPod or iPhone before taking them with you anywhere. That hardly mattered since the benefits of market support helped to overcome that. Car manufacturers soon started offering USB slots to allow iPod charging and even playback through the car sound system.

This has caused considerable disruption in the radio industry, which has no real answer to portable playlists and isn't subscription-friendly.

Spotify has since made major inroads with its freemium streaming service and its popularity has also introduced a competing platform for podcasting, made easier with the fact that Spotify simply streams to your device. There have been many more platforms that try to fill a podcasts-only niche as well as not being tied to a specific client. Player FM is one example that showcases much of the content found on other sites like iTunes or Spotify but focuses on a much better end-user experience. There is no client to download on your PC and simply download their app for other devices. SoundCloud started as a sharing site but now also allows individual creators to publish their own shows with some self-help tools. And you can go beyond that, with blogs being dedicated to finding greats podcasts or helping you find an audience. The streaming age has proven that it's never been easier to be a broadcaster.

Social media as the new broadcaster

Social media has had a tremendous impact in encouraging niche broadcasting. The introduction of YouTube has made UGC scale socially into one of the biggest forms of entertainment and information available today. From the moment YouTube's co-founders uploaded their first video in 2005, the ability for people to entertain each other became possible. Since then, the scale of its growth and popularity is truly representational of a global brand. As of the time of writing, there are over 1 billion users of the service, who navigate the site in a total of 80 different languages. YouTube has also launched local versions in more than 91 countries. This has created consumption that totals over 1 billion hours daily.[2]

Influencer broadcasters

While those numbers are staggering, the monetisation of YouTube with advertising has also helped its many talented individual broadcasters – called creators – become wealthy as their popularity through video viewing has grown. You can 'subscribe' to any creator's YouTube account – called a channel – and get notified whenever they post a new video.

Successful YouTube creators know how to attune their programming to what people want and also know how to build and manage a successful following. Think of individuals like PewDiePie who, at the time of writing, had over 94 million subscribers and is called the world's most influential YouTuber. His primary activity is playing games, although his personality and engaging behaviour are what make him so entertaining. Others, like Rosanna Pansino, have built a following by just focusing on a passion for food but driven by their personality and on-screen charisma. At 10 million subscribers, Pansino has no trouble continuing to indulge in her passion. The rise of influencers and their followers has made them the target of marketeers who are willing to pay additional fees to leverage product placement and other sponsorship opportunities.

Mainstream music artistes like Taylor Swift and Katy Perry have also amassed tremendous views since their fans are clearly digital natives who enjoy YouTube so much. But remember: Justin Bieber himself was discovered on YouTube. Anyone can tap into YouTube's potential and become famous themselves. They just need the right ingredients.

Videos are not exclusive to YouTube, though. Facebook and its subsidiary Instagram have also been promoting videos on their respective platforms but are far behind YouTube in terms of adoption. Twitter, despite its limited scope, is delving into sports streaming as well as UGC but is currently in the same league as Facebook. One notable site with niche success has been Twitch. Founded in 2007 as justin.tv, it has grown massively and is known for its dedication to the gaming community. Who would have known that popular gamers could actually find themselves streaming their activity straight from their PCs or consoles live, and do so to a huge audience? Twitch currently boasts over 144 million unique users a month. The most popular Twitch broadcasters, known as influencers, are not great gamers themselves but possess qualities that allow them to engage with their fans in a highly entertaining manner. Fans actually can – and do – subscribe to their favourite gamer just to be able to take advantage of various digital tokens. This revenue is shared between Twitch and broadcaster.

From niche studios to multi-channel networks (MCNs)

Creators aren't just individuals working on their own. Content owners and companies dedicated to original content production have tapped into YouTube to find new audiences with very professional, targeted programming. Think of studios like Cocomelon, which create 3D-animated videos aimed at children under the age of six. They've racked up millions of views by being focused or niche-driven, which is perfect on YouTube.

There are also bigger companies like the MCNs. They partner with creators to provide valuable services like audience promotion, creator collaboration and even sales outside the YouTube platform, like product placement and branded content. Some even go to the length of creating their own content and thus manage everything. Machinima and Fullscreen are examples of MCNs that partner with thousands of creators.

Which means it is no surprise that Google purchased YouTube in 2006 for $1.65 billion.

Streaming monetisation on social media

Social media is currently largely an advertising-funded space. YouTube has introduced its YouTube Red subscription service in certain countries but that revenue forms a trickle compared to what it gets from advertisers as a whole. In return for providing all the tools you need to upload and promote your videos to its audience, YouTube takes 45 per cent of the revenue gained from advertisers by calculating the price of an advertisement that is shown to 1,000 viewers. This basic metric is known as *cost per mille* (CPM).

For example, the official music video for 'Despacito' by Hispanic singer Luis Fonsi featuring Daddy Yankee has garnered over 3 billion video views from early 2017 to the end of 2018. Given that amount of views, the revenue earned for Fonsi and his record label would be lucrative.

Facebook and Twitter have similar ways of calculating their revenue share based on CPM but have not yet achieved the scale of YouTube although they are making earnest efforts. As of time of writing, Facebook already has a deal in place with the English Premier League to stream all its football matches live in selected countries in South-East Asia, a deal which cost it $240 million over three years.

Educational transformation

Education has transformed from just expanding institutional distance learning to unique websites that have empowered self-learning. Gone are the days when part-time, off-campus students had to converge on campus regularly for intensive tutorials to accompany their mailed lecture notes. With today's universities, live streaming allows for students to participate or at least watch lectures and tutorials via on-demand videos. Within these experiences, course slides are integrated into the on-site video so that students aren't just watching a talking head, but actually digesting presented information. Educational expenses are drastically reduced due to the reduction in, or even total elimination of, airfares and accommodation expenses.

This transformation has resulted in very specific online video platforms (OVP) that are called learning management systems (LMS). An offshoot of this category has been seen in the business to consumer (B2C) space with the launch of sites like Coursera that actually offer online courses up to master's degree level from some of the top-ranked universities in the US.

Others, like edX, call themselves a massive open online course (MOOC) provider that basically offers anything from a master's degree to shorter, self-paced courses to individuals directly or via their employers. The difference is that edX is an LMS that is open source and free, allowing any organisation to tap into it to create a customised online learning site. Founded by Harvard University and Massachusetts Institute of Technology in 2012, edX can be seen as a visionary step forward in how education can be potentially brought to the masses.

The marketplace model also exists and thrives. Marketplaces are where buyers meet sellers without the need for a middleman. These are replaced instead by market-makers who create the ideal online venues for the marketplace model to thrive. Udemy is the best example of a marketplace provider whose courses have enabled individuals to learn anything from basic Mandarin to advanced courses in cybersecurity.

Business organisations are now able to halt investments in their proprietary online learning centres by working with these innovative companies to further the development of their own employees. With thousands of courses to choose from, it makes it easier to just build the integration between Udemy into your company intranet and/or company registration systems and track employee progress through various reporting tools.

Enterprise-based streaming

Internal use cases

While enterprises have been able to work with streaming media providers to outsource their training needs, various other use cases have allowed these same companies to review how their internal and external communications can be similarly transformed.

Take internal communications as an example. If students no longer need to access a physical classroom to be formally educated, why should employees miss an important company event just because they are located a few thousand kilometres away? Why can't they tune in to watch it securely from their workstation or device?

The benefits of streaming media are more than just about being able to 'tune in'. To end users, the interactivity options allow for internal chat/messaging, sharing, questions to the speakers and – if metadata is used – to follow indicated highlights in a video timeline that should not be missed. To the organisers, features like quick polls, user ratings and slide-show synchronisation can create better engagement during the event. The video player analytics provides insights into how engaging the content is, what causes drop-offs, issues in the network and overall interest levels in the live stream versus the on-demand version of the video. Should you build up a library of content, recommendations can also help newcomers navigate and understand what's meaningful for them. The possibilities are really tremendous.

External use cases

Of course, external use is something that is just as exciting. All brands strive for more engaged users since this potentially generates loyalty and repeat purchase. Lifestyle brands are particularly suited to leveraging streaming media. Apple integrates video in its website to show consumers exactly what each new product contains in lush, unhurried detail. No 60-second constraints exist on the website yet there is an understanding that they shouldn't be long. Apple's 'halo' effect is such that it even adds the actual public keynote events as on-demand videos since these are highly sought after by fans too. Apple knows that video is the only way to inform users about a product so that they can make a purchase decision – which is hopefully 'yes' or 'when I save up'.

On a more functional note, Dell computers has made it a hallmark for their customers to be able to buy a computer online according to their own specifications. But Dell also provides great post-sale support and enhances it with plenty of 'how-to' or 'explainer' videos like how to update system software or how to install a chassis into a data centre rack. These explainer videos allow customers to complete installation of their purchase and avoid unnecessary (plus expensive) call-ins in their call centre. When done professionally, explainer videos help to create a better experience and empower end users with knowledge that increases their adoption of their product.

Start with good content

Now that you see the potential for streaming media, it's important to revisit what is the most important fundamental in the business of content creation and communication: well-written content that is well produced. Creating this takes time. Importantly, it should always be written or prepared by experienced professionals. You can do your part by ensuring that you retain good scriptwriters to begin with. They can be hired via the production company you're working with or independently. Make mandy.com your starting point for good talent. In the case of a live event stream, there may not be a scriptwriter *per se*, but the emphasis then is on a high-quality production. Make sure you select a team that is not only experienced but also has a good showreel (aka video portfolio) as their calling card.

Key takeaways

- **For content owners:** opportunities abound for you to find your audience but creating a niche is important so that you stand out from the crowd
- **For corporates (internally):** it may not be necessary to build everything yourself; rather, leverage proven consumer sites to give your employees more choice in internal training
- **For corporates (internally):** don't neglect the power of streaming media to communicate, especially in an interactive way. This allows employees to engage with you and each other
- **For corporates (externally):** leverage streaming media to inform, engender better brand affinity and lower your in-bound customer service calls at the same time
- **For everyone:** don't underestimate the value of professional production values in engaging your audience

Notes

1 While Spotify pioneered streaming, it was not the first subscription-based music service. eMusic launched a year earlier using a download feature.
2 YouTube press webpage, www.youtube.com/intl/en-GB/yt/about/press/

Streaming media technology today

When you watch a streaming service, it's either from an app or a browser. But the service itself is an assembly of different but connected platforms. These are hardware like servers, but with all kinds of different software driving them. You'll hear the term 'platform' being mentioned often. Our platform. Their platform. Platform integration. If you're a broadcaster with plenty of servers hosted on your premises, that's your platform too. It's basically infrastructure (cables and power supply), hardware (the servers) and software (applications that you will access) designed to do one or more things really well and do it at scale. You could be the marketing department of a major multinational corporate and you're getting production services from your IT business partner. Or you're getting a broadcast feed that you want to stream live on the internet. Either way, the first 'platform' starts with you, the owner of the content that is going to be published on the internet.

Do you need to build your platform from scratch or rent it from the cloud? If you're producing live events and streaming them you might need basic hardware like cameras and encoders (more on this in Chapter 8). Beyond that, you might need a server to store end-user login information and a server to store the webpages for your site. You'll need to store and deliver the content. The list goes on. Your engineering team informs you they can build this for you, but only if you have the right budget.

Do you really want to invest in servers and build dedicated software that needs to be maintained by a team of engineers? Unless you have the scale of Netflix or YouTube, the answer is 'probably not'. And if you work in a large organisation, getting your procurement team involved to examine your request for capital expenditure will trigger a process that is necessary but probably too lengthy.

So, what do you do next?

What is cloud?

'Cloud' is simply a concept of a specialised data centre with servers and software that you can tap into, but don't actually own. You don't even need to lease the hardware. You simply store files and process them, relying on a (ideally) pay-as-you-go model. It's an affordable model since you don't even need to think about estimating peak usage periods or cyclical demand. Your cloud service provider does all the planning for you. This works both for the needed hardware and software. In the case of software, the advantage is that the software is not standalone but delivered 'as a service' and updated more often for your benefit. It doesn't need to be downloaded and stored on a server for multiple users, although you may need to pay additional fees based on extra users beyond an allotted allowance.

Cloud services like storage are also disaster-proof by virtue of being backed-up elsewhere on our planet, like a different region or even multiple regions. Because of this, their service 'uptime' or availability to your organisation is nearly 100 per cent. Clouds and platforms are integrated – and communicate to each other – via an application programming interface (API). These are protocols and definitions that are documented and shared to enable a standardised form of communication.

From an accounting perspective, on-premises equipment is purchased under a capital expenditure (or capex) budget. This has implications on the company's balance sheet since hardware suffers some form of wear and tear, and you need to write off a percentage of the asset's value each year, reflected as a loss in your balance sheet. With a cloud model, the licence fee you pay is simply taken from the operational expenditure (or opex) budget and nothing else gets affected. You will need to get procurement involved but it would be an easier discussion overall and procurement would simply help you get a better deal. The bottom line: other than the initial hardware needed, a cloud-based model saves you tremendous time and money.

Public cloud and private cloud

These are the two main types of cloud infrastructure. In a public cloud you're actually sharing space with other customers. You content or data could even be shared on the same server within the same rack. This isn't a problem for most customers but some are nervous about even entertaining the idea of 'sharing' space (mainly due to internal policies). In that situation, public cloud isn't for you even if it's cheaper. Examples of public cloud are Amazon Web Services (AWS), Google Cloud Platform (GCP) or Microsoft Azure. AWS is currently the market leader in several territories and overall globally.[1] It is so big that it hosts a lot of the services that streaming media giant Netflix uses. Then there is also Amazon Prime Video as an internal customer. This positions AWS as a feared competitor. Microsoft Azure has been a very close second in the industry, if only because of the sheer size of Microsoft itself as an internal customer. GCP has been steadily growing in stature as Google starts to tout the external availability of its internal-facing cloud platform.

In a private cloud environment, you still don't get your own data centre (that would be too expensive) but customer content or data is segregated specially from others. It could be on a different floor or specifically away from potential competitors.

Online video platforms (OVPs) often use a public cloud environment but in a different way. They assign dedicated servers in the cloud provider's environment to serve their needs, and subsequently that of their customers. So, they combine the best of both worlds: scalability with security. Because OVPs want to make money by providing a solution to you, they will partner strategically or even exclusively to obtain cost savings for you as a customer for basic services like storage and transcoding. But you still obtain the benefit of being able to use as much or as little of the cloud's storage or compute power whenever you want to. Before we go into an OVP, we need to break down another basic building block: media files.

Media types

Video

Video is basically an audio-visual recording of up to 30 frames (or still pictures) a second. When captured in the earlier days of filmmaking, you could literally see the frames being visible in a long roll of photographic negatives and these were kept in large reels for safe storage. Today, everything is either digital or file-based, or – if it lies in an archive in a vault – in a tape format. The current industry standard of video is high definition (HD), with Ultra High Definition (UHD) being seen more commonly. They are also known as 2K and 4K respectively. Table 2.1 provides a good comparison.

In streaming media, it's important to note that the missing variable to Table 2.1 is the bitrate file that the video player can play back. For some reason, if the device in your hand can only play back video at a very low bitrate (due to a bad internet connection or a device's processing limitation), then you technically won't get a 'high' definition experience. We'll come back to this.

Video containers and compression formats

In technical terms, video is stored in a container, which can be described as the unique way that all the elements of a video file are kept or 'contained' together. Let's use the analogy of writing a letter to someone. You write the message on a letter that you fold to fit into the envelope. So, the letter is the equivalent of video compression, while the envelope is the equivalent of the container. You need subtitles in English, so imagine that being a postcard that also fits into the envelope. The envelope is what your receiver sees and all it has to do is open it to see the message. By reading the letter and the postcard together, it now understands the message completely. The most common

Table 2.1 Basic video standards still in use today. Standard Definition has two main standards, including NTSC (National Television Standards Committee) which is popular in the US and PAL (Phase Alternating Line) which is popular in Europe. The latter is shown here for brevity. Most countries in the developed world are already transmitting commercially in HD

	Standard Definition (PAL-based SD)	High definition (HD or 2K)	Ultra High Definition (UHD or 4K)
Height (in pixels)	720	1080	2160
Width (in pixels)	576	1980	3960
Aspect ratio (width to height)	1.33:1	1.78:1	1.78:1

container is MPEG-4, which uses the file extension .mp4. It was developed by the Motion Picture Experts Group (MPEG).

Video compression concerns the use of compression technology (known as a codec which is short for 'compress-decompress') to help compress large video files without compromising video quality noticeably. Everyone, from consumer device manufacturers to the streamers, uses a codec standard and the most widely used is called Advanced Video Coding (AVC). It is also more popularly known as H.264. If you stream media for commercial purposes take note that the use of H.264 is protected under various patents and involves royalty payments. For more information about payment classes and applicable amounts, visit the MPEG-LA website at www.mpegla.com. It is the body that acts as the patent pool from the various patent holders for H.264. The good news is that if your video is distributed for free, you'll currently not (and probably never) need to worry about royalty payments.

As a response to concerns about royalty payments, Google launched their own codec, known as VP8, which is housed under their WebM project. It is open source and royalty-free but has faced concerns that it may not be on par with the quality that H.264 provides. This is an ongoing debate and you can read more about the codec at www.webmproject.org. Google also chose the Matroska format for its containers. Similarly, a consortium led by the Mozilla Foundation and Xiph.org Foundation has tried to promote a codec called Daala as a superior alternative to H.265. Daala works within the Ogg container but lacks widespread industry adoption.

Table 2.2 The main video containers and their preferred audio/video codecs in use today. In reality, codecs can be paired with different containers, as in the case of H.264 which is the most widely used codec in the industry today. This table is not intended to be an exhaustive source

Company	Video container (and file extension)	Ideal video codec(s)	Ideal audio codec(s)
Google	WebM (.webm)	VP8, VP9 & AV1	Vorbis & Opus
Matroska	Matroska (.mkv)	None, open to all	None, open to all
Microsoft	Advanced Systems Format (.wmv)	WMV9 & VC-1	WMA10
MPEG	MPEG-4 (.mp4)	H.264 & H.265	AAC & ALAC
Xiph.org/ Mozilla	Ogg (.ogg)	Daala	Vorbis & Opus

With the world currently transitioning to 4K video, the concern is the video files will only continue to grow larger, consuming more storage space and bandwidth on the internet. As a response, MPEG-LA has announced their High Efficiency Video Coding (HEVC), or H.265. Google has also moved on to VP9. Both these codes are designed to keep videos compressed even more efficiently.

Audio

Audio is critical to a good video experience. Movies and TV shows invest a huge amount of time in ensuring recorded dialogue, recorded effects and music are mixed into the right balance. Audio playback technology has evolved from the humble beginnings of just a mono playback experience – a single track that contained everything – to the more sophisticated stereophonic (or stereo) experience, where two tracks are played from left and right speakers respectively and produce an overlapping experience that is more impactful than mono. Stereo has since moved on rapidly, with a six-speaker experience possible on a technology called Dolby 5.1 (yes, the .1 is actually a speaker too) both in cinemas and its home sound systems. When broadcasters started offering HD on TV, many carried Dolby 5.1 where possible. This was usually only provided if the content provider themselves supplied a master copy with Dolby 5.1 available. As a streaming service, this is important to include since most homes already watch streaming services on a living room TV.

Audio compression

In streaming media, audio is also stored in the MPEG-4 container format. Like video, audio also uses compression standards and the most common one is called Advanced Audio Coding (AAC). Unlike video, audio is compressed in smaller file sizes with differences that are imperceptible to most people. For example, streaming audio that is compressed in 96 kilobits per second (96 Kbps) may not sound much different compared to streaming audio compressed in 192 Kbps. Interestingly, music streaming service Spotify uses the aforementioned container Ogg and the compression standard called Vorbis. This is part of the same WebM project initiated by Google. Besides being free to use, it's also known for its high quality.

Media streaming protocols

Websites are written in fairly simple code called Hypertext Markup Language (HTML) and this hasn't deviated much since the early days. Besides code, protocols are necessary for the web. Website pages are delivered to browsers via a protocol known as Hypertext Transfer Protocol (HTTP). That has also stood the test of time fairly well. It works by allowing a server to serve a page requested by a browser. The protocol is considered stateless. The server doesn't really care if the browser gets the page. The opposite of that would be stateful. Here, the server would establish a connection with the browser and deliver the requested webpage, and make sure it arrived intact. It would then disconnect itself from the browser. With so many requests potentially being made for a webpage, it made sense to rely on HTTP's stateless protocol as opposed to a stateful version.

The problem with any kind of richer media like video and audio was that there was a lot of data to be compressed and delivered to browsers. It would be a bad experience if all the video and audio data could not reach the end user, so several companies ended up resorting to streaming protocols that relied on a stateful connection as the answer. In doing so, they created their own proprietary technology involving the use of specialised servers and video players. They also used this as their competitive differentiator when doing business.

Progressive Networks was one example in 1995 when they released the RealAudio Player. It smartly tackled audio streaming first before following up with the launch of the RealVideo Player in 1997. Progressive Networks soon renamed itself RealNetworks to capitalise on the household popularity of its players, which had seen a surge in consumer adoption. Most older readers would remember it because you had to download its software if you wanted to upload or play back content. The streaming protocol developed by RealNetworks was called Real Time Streaming Protocol (RTSP). An updated version called Real Time Messaging Protocol (RTMP) was later introduced and this became the de facto standard for stateful connections that could produce good-quality video experiences. RealNetworks used its own container, identified with its .rm file extension.

A formidable opponent to RealNetworks was Macromedia's Flash video format and player. This came in the .flv container and also used RTMP. As its popularity surged (thanks to adoption by YouTube), Adobe acquired it. Adobe leveraged the fact that broadcasters that wanted to use its technology had to buy a combination of server and player software, based on a licensing business model, just like RealNetworks was doing.

The closed nature of Adobe's and RealNetworks' products were a concern early on in the 2000s. Fortunately, a consortium of industry players realised the benefit that HTTP could bring, plus a second innovation called adaptive bitrate (ABR) streaming. In 2002, a team called the WG1 Special Streaming group showed how traditional HTTP servers could be used to deliver streaming media, without the need for expensive software.

A bit about bitrate

In streaming media, the big factor in quality is the bitrate of a video. This is basically the number of bits that are in the video when it's playing back each second. The more bits there are, the more detail is available and thus, overall picture quality improves. But there are different device screen sizes. The device has a limitation due to its processor (also called the central processing unit, or CPU) and can usually be strained if several apps are opened by an end user at any one time. Adding video doesn't help. The internet connection plays a big role too since it determines the download connection speed that a device can achieve.

Upon someone pressing play, a video player downloads the packets of data comprising the video file and stores them in the device (usually in the random-access memory, or RAM storage) to ensure enough is downloaded so that initial playback can begin without undue delays. This feature is known as a 'buffer' and it uses algorithms to keep adjusting itself. But if the internet connection is terrible, the buffer runs low on video data and will need to stop to refill again. This could happen frequently if internet connection speeds fluctuate (which they do), or if the device's CPU itself gets worked up handling too many instructions. This results in the dreaded buffering pauses that we're all familiar with.

Buffering was common in the early days of the internet, because only one video file with one bitrate speed was available. If you had a connection that was allowing you to download 5 Mbps (megabits per second) but you were trying to play back a video that had an 8 Mbps bitrate, then you simply didn't have what the experts would call 'enough bandwidth'. The result would be the video player being disadvantaged and looking to buffer for an extended period of time than was considered acceptable. It had no choice. Conversely, if too small a file was created, its playback would result in a display resolution that would be too low for those on powerful computers and high-speed broadband. Think of a smaller file that might fit an iPhone 5 screen resolution but would be inadequate for the iPad Pro. The iPad Pro end user would be frustrated too. Their video would look blurry or soft. Ultimately, what killed many video experiences was not the blurry video but the actual video in 'buffer' mode at crucial times while watching (like perhaps just before a goal was scored).

But if internet connection speeds were unreliable and so were the device processors, there had to be a better way to be more accommodating and not choke the whole player.

HTTP-based adaptive bitrate streaming

An innovative answer was to have several versions of the video that could be played back. The video player would start by streaming the low bitrate rendition of the video. The video player would then detect more information very quickly, the first being the available internet speed, and the second being if the device's processing capability was also powerful enough. Given those two variables, the video player would continue to request a larger bitrate rendition or a smaller one. It would be important to make these changes almost invisible to the end user so it would be avoidable to have a very big gap between the bitrate size. Each step up improves quality but jumping up from one bitrate to a much higher one would simply be jarring or very noticeable to the user.

This was the birth of ABR technology. ABR is sometimes also called dynamic bitrate (DBR). Don't be fooled by claims made today by vendors or OVPs that they support ABR. That's like car manufacturers saying they support comfortable seats! It is the foundation of how a good user experience is derived today.

Within several years, HTTP-based protocols appeared. Microsoft announced its format, known as Smooth Streaming, at the 2008 summer Olympic Games in conjunction with Microsoft's new Silverlight player.

Apple introduced its standard in 2009, called HTTP Live Streaming (HLS – a bit of a misnomer since it's available both for live and on-demand streaming), and this became the internal standard for all Apple mobile devices. Google also accepted HLS for its Android phones, making HLS a formidable opponent to Smooth Streaming, which was adopted by Netflix for desktop, as well as Microsoft devices. Not to be outdone, Adobe tried to stake its claim in the space by introducing HTTP Dynamic Streaming (HDS). This competes with Apple and Microsoft since HDS works only on Flash Player.

The fragmentation of these formats meant that streaming media services had to transcode their media files several times to cater to different formats. In response, the MPEG developed a standard that they hoped would be adopted as one global reference. This was introduced in 2012 as MPEG-DASH (Dynamic Streaming over HTTP). Table 2.3 gives you an idea of the fragmentation still currently being experienced in the industry.

With ABR, many versions of the video will be created in different formats and bitrate versions. When it comes to the latter, these smaller files are known as profiles or renditions and they basically represent a range of files that start with the smallest version and then step up incrementally larger than the previous version. Table 2.4 shows how numerous these can be. The first versions are for the screen sizes. One video file size is never suitable for the multitude of phone or tablet sizes out there. As mentioned before, it might be big enough to be seen on the iPad Pro but too big for a smaller-screen iPhone. But what about the formats? There are potentially four to choose from so this means quadrupling the number you need to generate.

In an ideal world, the major competitors would just need to adopt one standard and that could well be MPEG-DASH. Thankfully, Microsoft has stopped developing Smooth Streaming in an apparent show of support for

Table 2.3 The current fragmentation of streaming of protocols may soon be ended if MPEG-DASH can eventually be adopted. Until that happens, transcoding is still required to meet various playback requirements

Organisation	Protocol type	Player	Major devices	Major browsers
Adobe	HDS	Flash	PCs and laptops only	Internet Explorer and Edge only
Apple	HLS	HTML5	iOS and Android	All except Opera
Microsoft	Smooth Streaming	Silverlight	Xbox One and Windows 8 or above	Internet Explorer only
MPEG	DASH	HTML5	PCs and laptops only	All except Safari

Table 2.4 This table shows how may files you need to transcode to in order to satisfy different device screens, internet speeds and video formats available today. This table shows 20 variations but in reality this could be exceeded

	MPEG-DASH	Smooth Streaming	HLS	HDS
Very small bitrate			x	
Small bitrate			x	
Small–medium bitrate	x	x	x	x
Medium bitrate	x	x	x	x
Medium–large bitrate	x	x	x	x
Large bitrate	x	x		x
Very large bitrate	x	x		x

DASH, while HDS is becoming very rare as Flash video support is being phased out by modern browsers. This leaves DASH and HLS as future competing protocols. Some say that is still one too many.

Apple and Microsoft apparently agree. In 2015 they proposed a Common Media Application Format (CMAF) instead to MPEG for consideration. Notably, it proposed that the video container standards be unified in one version known as fMPG. In 2016, Apple announced that it would support fMPG but the CMAF proposal is still a long way from helping DASH become a single streaming standard in the industry. You still need to transcode and store multiple copies of the same files, mainly HLS and DASH.

What is an online video platform?

Since the mid-2000s, the OVP has become a buzzword for anyone planning to launch streaming media services that resemble what YouTube or Netflix does. As we read in Chapter 1, they can go beyond just entertainment needs since OVPs can help any organisation that makes use of streaming media (both with live streaming or on-demand media), including enterprises, global lifestyle brands, government agencies, hospitals and even churches. This is because the main goal of an OVP is to help you, as the operator, to manage your content and get it in front of end users. It does this by allowing you to orchestrate workflows to take your content from where it's stored, to a device for viewing by the end user, often with ways to help you monetise your content as well.

OVPs operate on a modular architecture. This means that they control and operate the core part of your overall platform that starts small but then extend it by integrating, or plugging into, other specialised platforms to create a turn-key solution (a complete solution). This means that they can easily expand their value by integrating with another service provider. As mentioned before, like all good cloud-based services, OVPs are hosted in the cloud on a licence-based model so that you don't spend money purchasing hardware or one-off software. The primary benefits are enormous since you never need to maintain software and its updates. The OVPs do. Secondarily, you will never need to worry about technology changes impacting your roadmap. An OVP should be the one to introduce innovation in the industry and convince customers to come along and upgrade in order to remain relevant. To understand the complexity of an OVP, Figure 2.1 should illustrate this well enough.

Some of the more well-known OVPs today are Brightcove, Arkena, Deltatre and Kaltura, among over a dozen other active ones. Brightcove is the runaway market leader with a strong offering across different industry sectors, and is the only OVP that is publicly listed. Arkena is a large media

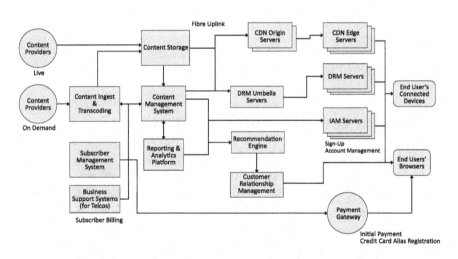

Figure 2.1 A system architecture diagram showing the building blocks of an OVP. The core of the OVP is the content management system, which then plugs into other adjacent services that are required by a customer. This extensible requirement is a must-have

company that straddles traditional broadcast services whilst offering a strong streaming media suite. Deltatre is like Arkena, but goes even further by providing app development services via its newly acquired subsidiary, Massive Interactive. It also has a great reputation for premium sports-based live streaming. Kaltura is the only major open source platform for streaming media too (it's the founder of the Open Video Alliance which promotes open standards for streaming media on the internet). Several OVPs have also been purchased by major telecommunications companies or cloud providers as investments as well as for their internal use. These can provide a measure of guarantee to a customer since a few of the smaller players have ceased business recently. In reality, almost all of them provide the same services and simply have strengths of their own. To determine which OVP is a good fit for your needs, you will need to understand its building blocks. Fundamentally, here is what a good one should provide you with:

1. Content management system (CMS)
2. Cloud storage to keep content safely
3. Cloud transcoding to convert content easily
4. Video player to enable content playback
5. Video player analytics and reporting

There are other areas that an OVP can manage and these will be discussed in the corresponding chapters.

What is a content management system?

A CMS is a specialised web portal where you can access your incoming content and orchestrate workflows to process them for delivery to the end user. It starts with the 'ingest' of content. You'll hear this term over and over again when discussing OVPs with engineers or with the content operations teams. This sounds prosaic but it aptly describes what it does – a system accepting media files inside its environment. Or simply just storing them. It doesn't just stop at files. For continuous media like a live stream of an event, this is usually a video signal that has to be encoded into RTMP by an encoder, and then allow this stream to be monitored by the OVP.

When ingesting on-demand content, you can also convert or transcode it according to defined settings. Or you create your own customised settings. But there's so much more and the depth of features can be mind-boggling. One of the more important elements is the dashboard that shows you essential information. This could be the amount of content that you are transcoding (measured in minutes) or storing (measured in gigabytes, or GB) since you are probably paying your OVP for such usage. Other aspects of the dashboard will relate strictly to the video analytics of your end users and their engagement with your service (number of unique users, number of videos viewed, etc.).

What basic things you can do with the OVP's CMS depends largely on the vendors supplying it. For example, not all OVPs provide a video analytics dashboard or perhaps it could be very rudimentary.

Managing collections

Content taxonomy – how you categorise and display content – is extremely crucial and this requires a blend of understanding what the consumer wants and what you think might be worth curating as a matter of good taste. Take a category such as 'latest releases'. This makes sense if you're managing an entertainment-based or news-based service. People love to try out what's new, particularly if they've been anticipating its arrival. When managing a corporate training video library, that might not be the most important collection to highlight. Sales teams might only be keen to know the latest product training video in order to understand what are its relevant selling points that they need to be informed about. Field marketing teams might be more interested in the latest research findings that your strategy team has commissioned about your users. Either way, once you know what needs you're catering to, your CMS should be able to allow you to manage content accordingly. It could be literally as simple as tagging the latest action movie that you've just received. This movie would be assigned to the 'latest releases' collection and also the 'action' collection. Your end users might be visiting the former category on a Friday night. Bored males might peek into the latter anytime they visit your service. Having content in the right collections is crucial. A lot of it is useful, thanks to metadata.

Creating and managing metadata

Metadata is a mystery to most people. At its most basic, metadata is information about a movie or TV programme that is visible or invisible to viewers. It could be the title, synopsis or the cast information, for example. Viewers see this when they surf a Pay TV channel and press the 'Info' button on their remote. When browsing on a smartphone, the same information is also presented. Additional information is shown like the price of the movie if it's available for rent. When they are plotted, metadata could easily end up using over a dozen fields. However, much more metadata exists that is not shown publicly. The simplest analogy is to describe how you use your passport when you travel. There's a lot of information about you which you can read in the very first few pages. There is also information collected when you have visited foreign countries. However, there will be information that is readable from your passport's embedded chip that conveys more information for authorities, visible only to them.

Metadata helpfulness goes beyond just providing information. In the case of YouTube and similar services, this includes keywords that help in discoverability, i.e. features like search engines or recommendation engines. They trawl content for metadata and add it into suggestions for viewers. The bottom line: metadata is helpful to anyone using your media and you need to make it comprehensive.

This is an example of metadata that would typically exist for a movie if you bought the online rights to it and wanted to stream it from your websites for a fee. The customer-facing metadata would be:

1. Official movie title (provided from the studio)
2. Year of release (provided from the studio)
3. Main genre (drama, sports, comedy, etc.)
4. Sub-genre (legal drama, crime drama, period drama, etc.)
5. Short synopsis (as provided from the studio)
6. Cast (as provided from the studio)
7. Director (as provided from the studio)
8. Censorship classification

And the list goes on. Some of the metadata that would exist for an operator once it's ingested into their OVP would be:

9. Unique content ID (alpha-numeric ID used by the content owner)
10. Stereo sound availability (Stereo, 5.1 stereo, etc.)
11. Subtitles available
12. Audio tracks available
13. Licence window – start date (when they are allowed to start showing it online)
14. Licence window – end date (when they must stop showing it online)
15. Retail price (the price set for retail)
16. Keywords/tags – the more you include the better

And the list goes on. It is not unusual for broadcasters to have in excess of 50 fields to capture all the metadata that exists for a particular title.

Creating and managing key art

As a content owner, if you have taken the trouble to produce or distribute something from scratch, your marketing team will be looking forward to promoting it as much as possible. This includes posters, web display banners, press kits and more. For that to happen, they need to create the official images in high resolution. This is known as Key Art. The direct result of key art is that a version of it can be shared with streaming platforms for use as the official thumbnail images that are displayed for selection. You will need to create a portrait or a landscape version for adaptability. In many instances, you may also be licensing your content or syndicating it to a third party. You will then need to create guidelines and put in place an approvals process so that you have final say over how the finished image looks. It's your asset, so you must protect it.

An OVP should be capable of generating the source of the key art from the video itself. If you own the rights (or the rights-holder grants permission), you should be able to generate countless options to choose from and then select one as the source for your marketing team to build on. Sometimes, simple thumbnail options will do and the OVP will allow you to do this easily during the transcoding stage.

Cloud storage

Your original media files need to be transcoded or converted into the smaller ABR files that are meant to be viewable by the end user. The first step that an OVP will take is to store your file and make a copy in its cloud. If your OVP is using the public cloud providers mentioned above then you don't need to worry about the content being backed up. It will be. If your OVP has its own data centre – which will be unlikely but never impossible – then you need to find out if content will be backed up and how. But this should be something you never need to worry about if it's stored in AWS, for example. Alternative arrangements are for you to store the content via a direct relationship with AWS, although OVPs will probably have preferential rates that still work out to be affordable for you if they offer it. If you get a good storage deal with one cloud provider but your content delivery network (CDN) is a different provider, check if egress data fees apply. Egress data is incurred each time the stored content is pushed by one cloud provider to another CDN provider. This is basically charged at a rate per GB of data. These costs may or may not be significant.

What is transcoding and encoding?

Transcoding begins when you have a single source video that is going to be the 'mother' of all subsequent video files that you need, as shown in Table 2.4. The problem is ensuring that the right file is set. The original file sent in by the content providers is usually fit for broadcast but way too big for the internet. It takes a lot of storage space (cloud storage is charged on a per GB basis) and takes longer to transcode.

The first step is to create an OVP-friendly version instead. This is where you will hear a term referring to a mezzanine file. The mezzanine file is a conversion of the original source that is large enough to cater to all transcoding requirements and yet not take up valuable space and compute time. Content providers can provide you with the mezzanine but if you are producing your own content in-house, you will probably need to create your own mezzanine. Transcoders are nothing more than servers with the software needed to handle all the technicalities of conversion. They are often grouped together into 'farms' of different sizes designed to handle large volumes of video titles at any one time. This may be the only time you will ever need to host your hardware and software on your premises, although even this notion is being challenged since you could technically do this with a cloud-based transcoding vendor but you would need to rely on dedicated fibre links to carry such large file sizes over from your side to where the vendor is.

Either way, once you can generate the mezzanine version of each of your video titles, you can ingest them into the OVP. The OVPs typically host their own transcoding farms and these could be far bigger than you can imagine, as they churn out the different bitrate profiles for each format that you have specified, plus doing this for various other customers.

Content transcoding also involves images files for the exact same reasons above. Image file resolution has to fit sizes and, again, one size cannot fit all. It will either be too big to be shown on a small screen (where it will simply take longer to load), or most likely just drain your phone's processor.

The terms encoding and transcoding are sometimes used interchangeably when they are actually referring to different ways of converting content. Encoding refers to the conversion of a live source video signal into a web-friendly video stream.

This can be a TV channel being converted for playback on a TV Anywhere service on your tablet. In this case, it's referred to as a linear TV stream. It could also be a one-off event like your company 'town hall' meeting being streamed to your laptop. In this case it's referred to as a live event stream. Encoding requires a special piece of hardware known as, unsurprisingly, an encoder. This device looks like a horizontal-shaped server and can either be controlled via a monitor and a keyboard interface directly, or a browser remotely. The trend is for encoders to be driven by software so that they can easily be upgraded and configured from the browser itself. We'll examine this in more detail in Chapter 8.

Video players

Video players are either embedded into websites or device (native) applications. If you take the example of YouTube, it's easy to create a YouTube account and to upload some videos that you want to share. After that, all you need to do is to get an embedded link (basically the URL that points to the YouTube video player wherever it's hosted) to embed in your website.

Video players used to be developed with proprietary software that needed 'plug-ins' to be installed so that browsers could support them.

Microsoft had its version, called Silverlight. Adobe had its Flash player. Since 2008 the World Wide Web Consortium (W3C) has promoted the HTML5 player, which requires no mandatory plug-in. This also allows the players to be very light and load very fast when you visit a page. In principle anyway. In practice, video players may still make multiple 'calls' to external parties like plug-ins, CDNs, ad-servers, analytics platforms and others when you initiate playback. Bear this in mind when you test your video players before you launch your service.

Your OVP will provide its version of this player, ideally with a graphical user interface (GUI) that you can use to make customisations. If you have customised software development needs you should be able to request – and get – the official player software development kit (SDK). Such kits provide documentation, APIs and other necessary information to build upon and display your player in more flexible ways.

If the above is not available for some reason you can also consider third-party players. The most popular include the JW Player. Invented by Jeroen Wijering, this can be implemented almost anywhere with plenty of libraries to help you with customisation. The JW Player has grown tremendously since its humble beginnings in 2005. For as little as a few dollars a month, you can use its standard 'starter' features. Upgrading to a business plan means you get the equivalent of a lightweight OVP. Other alternatives include Flowplayer and Wistia, both of which claim to be able to load their players very fast and come with a free version too. Just recently, Bitmovin has emerged with the same offerings but claiming specialty for HTML5 players for MPEG-DASH and HLS. Like YouTube, there's no such thing as free without a catch. In this case, you have to put up with the provider's brand being visible on the player when you embed it into your own site.

If that's the case, then people do ask why not just implement a YouTube or Vimeo player? It depends. With YouTube, you'll be creating an account which then allows you to have a hosted page on YouTube's site while you go ahead to embed a player in your own site. This provides the benefit of being able to leverage a large audience that could easily visit your player given some basic promotion on the content you have. However, if your goal is to monetise your videos then you'll have to put up with the fact that YouTube keeps the lion's share of the advertising revenue generated by your content.

Video player features

Video players provide a range of features, some of which require considerable development in conjunction with other providers. For the list of simple features, you may want to consider the following:

1. **Closed captions**: important for live event streaming or linear TV streaming to cater for the hearing impaired (in countries like the US, this is a regulatory requirement). Subtitling is a similar feature but refers specifically to a foreign-language translation of the original audio, hence, it's found only in video on demand content.
2. **Personal video recorder (PVR)**: a must-have for the streaming world but you'll need to acquire additional rights if you're offering premium content with these features. PVRs include the ability to rewind, fast-forward or last title/next title playback.
3. **Video quality option**: this can be used to set your preferred bitrate, or at least with the ability to turn off the high-quality rate, to minimise consumption of internet data. This is particularly important in emerging countries.
4. **Quick rewind or fast-forward**: allows a fast rewind or forward 5–10 seconds to help catch missed dialogue or important information.
5. **Floating player**: ideal for websites that combine articles with video, typically found in news and lifestyle sites. The video is usually placed at the very top of the article for immediate watching. Should you choose to read the article instead and start scrolling down, the player follows you down as it plays, usually in a discreet corner in a much-reduced size.

Video analytics

Video players also contain beacons that collect information about users every few seconds. This information is then aggregated to give you a summary of your audience, either in real time on a dashboard or as scheduled reports. This is vital information that will tell you basics like:

1. **Unique visitors**: how many unique visitors you have over a given period
2. **Visitor location**: where your visitors are located

3. **Viewed content:** what your most popular content is (in terms of views or total hours)
4. **Viewer quality:** how much of the time your visitors are seeing their videos buffer
5. **Stream quality:** how your ABR streams are doing across a given region or time duration

Video analytics are important to gauge how well you are doing. The above also exists for live event streaming where you can literally see how well your service performs over its entire duration. Your OVP should provide basic analytics with its player but if your requirements are complex enough there are dedicated vendors in this space. Make sure you have dedicated personnel helping you to analyse the data and derive insights that lead to further improvements to your service.

Recommendation engine

One of the more impactful innovations has come forth from the introduction of content recommendation engines. These engines filter through viewing data that is available (both individual or aggregated) and detect patterns in usage that might be relevant to end users. Successful recommendations encourage quicker selection and even more compulsive viewing behaviour as opposed to the end user scrolling through a whole wall of images endlessly or frustratingly.

The earliest recommendation engine came from a pioneering team known as Net Perceptions in 1996. They were the commercial arm of GroupLens Research, a research lab in the University of Minnesota. An early customer was Amazon, which used recommendations to powerful effect for its website. Netflix was also at the forefront of recommendations for its content, when it was still only focused on its subscription-based DVD mailing service. The engine, known as Cinematch, continues to be responsible for helping Netflix customers binge-watch shows. The famous Netflix Prize worth US$1 million was even organised so that the streaming giant could find a way to increase viewership by 10 per cent. The reason for this is simple. Any increase in viewing time on your service increases loyalty and translates into more months of subscription. Thus, better recommendations impact on a company's bottom line.

There are various methods used to serve recommendations based on the type of information filtered by the system.

Collaborative filtering

The approach taken by Amazon was to analyse buying data of end users. Let's assume that there were ten people shopping on the website at a particular time. If you just bought a particular horror novel, the engine would find other users similar to you who read it and look for a pattern among them after they read the same novel. If most of them then bought another specific horror novel and liked it, it may make sense that you might like it too. Thus, the engine serves this in an automated way, helping users to feel more appreciated especially if the recommendations seem accurate. Jeff Bezos has credited recommendations with helping Amazon overcome the limitation of physical stores, which only provide titles that are popular, since it only makes good business sense to stock commonly purchased titles that are also the results of 'bestseller lists' that may appear more to be about hype than about individual suitability. But collaborative filtering was only the start.

Content-based filtering

Streaming media sites like YouTube capitalised early on using real-time analytics to alter their recommendations to viewers, typically based on their own viewing history. If you watch a video of kittens playing with babies take note that your search terms are only the start of the YouTube engine's analysis. As you watch and even rate content as likeable, its engine continues to filter that information and rearrange the recommendations accordingly.

Personalised filtering

This takes into account all personal behaviour by the end user, ranging from buying history to ratings and also viewing history. They should be tied to an account or, better still, an individual profile with the account itself. Recommendations based on personal history are powerful because they focus on the individual as opposed to the crowd. They are also obviously the most accurate, if the algorithms are implemented to their fullest potential.

Implementing a recommendation engine

This has traditionally been dominated by a few big players but is becoming increasingly competitive. The current leaders TiVo and ThinkAnalytics have been joined by challengers like Taboola, Yusp, Jinni and Gravity R&D (the winners of the Netflix challenge). None of these may come cheap but the bigger ones certainly have proven engines that have been deployed with broadcasters and streamers around the world. OVPs also provide something as a start but this is likely to be rudimentary. These would manage collections like 'Most Popular' or 'Latest'. Can you build your own? The answer is yes, but you will definitely need to hire additional resources in your technology team for this. It requires a mix of the right level of content knowledge, engineering skills and data science skill sets to build the powerful algorithms that result in accurate recommendations.

Putting it together: a systems integrator (SI)

Now that you have all this technology that you can access and enough money to spend on it, you might be asking, 'How do I assemble everyone together and get it up and running?' The answer is to hire a systems integrator, or SI. These are companies that are specialised in the art of putting technology vendors together and project managing it so that you get something when you want to with the budget you have. Think of them as a contractor who will help build your house. Sure, you have the architect, the builder, the electrician, the plumber and the interior designer. But somebody has to coordinate all these people to make sure that they deliver what they are supposed to. The best SIs to use are also the ones who are specialised in your particular industry. You shouldn't hire SIs that are used to installing your company's human resources software, no matter how affordable they are or experienced they claim to be. Streaming media SIs are usually those that have a lot of experience with broadcast and digital media-specific expertise and know what to expect. When it comes to the crunch time, they will be able to get the testing done much faster as well.

If you are embedding a video player in your website and have no need to monetise the service, you may not need an SI. In this case you can check if the OVP partner you are using will be able to provide what they would call 'professional services' to assist with this. Bigger OVPs will do this but there is no harm asking and they could even provide a referral.

Working with SIs

If you have a budget for your project, set aside up to 10 per cent to give them to get your service up and running. Ensure you also tender this out so that you can get a feel for how much value they can bring to you. Some of the key things you need to consider and allow for are:

1. Industry familiarity
2. Project management methodology
3. Testing expertise
4. Track record in implementations similar to yours

In very large implementations, a good SI will understand not only the requirements but also the weaknesses of some of the service providers you've signed up. They may not reveal this outright – out of respect to the service provider – but they will manage them even more carefully.

Key takeaways

- **For everyone:** online video platforms are, by nature, heavy in hardware, software and infrastructure, so leverage the benefits of a cloud-based solution wherever possible
- **For everyone:** make sure you introduce the people who will operate the platform to the service providers actually providing the platform
- **For everyone:** if you carry a large content library or just want to increase engagement with your service, utilise the power of a recommendation engine to allow your end users to uncover more of the content they love
- **For content owners:** having access to the best technology and service providers won't guarantee success unless you can put it all together. Choose a dedicated, third-party systems integrator if you can

Note

1 Joe Panettieri, 'Cloud Market Share by 2018: Amazon AWS, Microsoft Azure, Google, IBM', www.channele2.com, www.channele2e.com/channel-partners /csps/cloud-market-share-2018-aws-microsoft-google/, 2 August 2018.

3 Protecting your streaming media

Protecting streaming media is vital for any operator in any industry, be it content owners like the Hollywood studios or large enterprise. The primary focus is on the content, and this is important for two main reasons. Obviously, confidentiality of the content is one of them – think of company information being conveyed at employee 'town hall' meetings or 'all-hands' sessions. This involves accessibility of private information to a select few (thousand) no matter where they are in the world. Conversely, when your business's goal is to acquire as many customers as possible, your content then has to be protected from theft or piracy since the accessibility has to be monetised as much as possible in a recurring or sustained manner. Once people find a way to avoid paying because it can be pirated directly from your service – and we all know people will try this – then your business simply needs to prevent that in the first place.

Any plan to ensure secure protection involves four main areas, which are illustrated in Figure 3.1.

Content must also be authorised to the right users only via Identity Access Management (IAM) policies and tools. We will actually focus on this in more detail in Chapter 6 so, for now, our focus will be on how protection is applied to everything else. As a start, storage may seem simple enough. The operators need to store the video files somewhere secure. But there are legal implications and corresponding industry standards to consider. The legal implications are enforced by content owners (the rights holders) when they license content to content aggregators or operators. Since many of you reading this book will come from content aggregating businesses then you'll appreciate the need to fulfil your

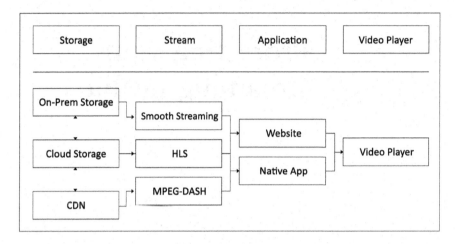

Figure 3.1 Key areas in content protection start from where content is stored up until its delivery to a video player on a browser or device

obligations. The industry response to standardise safe media storage is primarily centred around encrypting the content so that it cannot be stolen at any time.

The basics of encryption

Encryption is based on the theory that messages can, and will, be stolen so it was best to ensure that they should not be legible when read by their interceptors. The Spartan military actually used a form of encryption way back in 700 BC in order to keep battle instructions a secret from the enemy. Modern digital communication continues this practice easily since all streaming content consists of information that can be scrambled and unscrambled. Imagine your content is a file that literally displays '123456789' on it and you wish to share this with your recipient but hide it from anyone else. You could write a program that scrambles the numbers into something else like '478392156'. The program would have used a special 'key' to do the scrambling and you will keep this key for safety. Somehow, you will also have to share the key with your recipient so that they can unscramble the content when they finally get it. The shared key helps ensure that if anyone tries to intercept the file, they simply won't be able to access the content since they don't have the key. Thus, just like in ancient days, the scrambled information is useless to them.

Websites in the Web 3.0 era are complex and don't just load text and images. They serve ads, cookies and play back streaming media, all of which are easily exposed to any entry-level hacker. Since this information can potentially be hijacked and made available for any kind of gain, once again, the need for encryption is present so that tampering is useless.

This starts with your browser.

Browsers used Hypertext Transfer Protocol (HTTP) in the beginning when internet browsing was a lot simpler. As concerns over security grew, Hypertext Transfer Protocol Secure (HTTPS) became a standard using a protocol called Secure Sockets Layer (SSL). In time this has evolved to Transport Layer Security (TLS), which is the current standard since the former is no longer considered secure. TLS is also used to encrypt streaming media in transit. Make sure to adopt it if you choose to encrypt your streams.

With storage facilities, web browsers and streams becoming more secure, media companies are now in a stronger position to also keep their content more secure. The final step is the playback experience and ensuring that the right people get the right content. This requires Digital Rights Management (DRM).

Why we need DRM

Hollywood and other major film/TV studios in the Western world own their content and generate revenue primarily from the licensing of these 'assets' (as they are known). As rights holders or licensors, they cannot afford to see content that they licence out being pirated since it not only creates a loss of revenue for their licensees (the operators) but ultimately themselves too if they cannot find enough licensees to sell to. And this is crucial in a world where it is very easy to find a digital copy of a popular movie, unlike in the old, analogue days.

Let's take a step back in time momentarily and see how content piracy has grown more menacing. Back in the 1980s, video cassettes were the order of the day. They were clunky and easily damaged. They could eventually suffer wear and tear after repeated usage too. For members of the public who wanted to make copies, you had to use the source tape to make a copy which would immediately be of inferior quality to the original. It was also difficult to make copies to dole out to your friends since you had to have two video cassette recorders (VCRs) in order to make a copy (one had the source tape and the other had the blank for copying to). Yes, it could be done but it wasn't easy.

Today, you can download a file and make a copy by pressing the Command-C keys!

The proliferation of piracy and sharing of pirated content is not the only area that is of concern. Even content that is already rented or purchased must be restricted to standard terms (which usually cover requirements like viewing at home as opposed to public screenings, etc.). In summary, a mechanism is needed to help rights owners to manage these terms and conditions of digital content delivery. This is where DRM comes into play.

DRM is relatively new but it can be seen as a generic term that covers a wide range of differing technologies that prevent unauthorised viewing of streaming content. It is also the evolution of technologies that have been in place since Pay TV operators came into being. As the operators of various broadcast channels that package and aggregate content, they are the ones who have to bear the brunt of ensuring compliance. Non-compliance would result in financial penalties and/or contract cancellations. In response, Pay TV operators have long since used a Conditional Access System (CAS) to protect content when it is being broadcast to set-top boxes. CAS prevents unauthorised subscribers from tuning in to channels not found in their subscription package.

DRM works in a similar fashion by creating business policies regarding the access of purchased streaming media and then enforcing it via the technology solution chosen. End users get access to steaming media content but must always abide by the policies that the content owners specify, including the right to share with only a certain number of users and the right not to make copies of that file. For this reason, DRM is also referred to as 'copy protection'.

Simple examples of DRM include being able to download a song after purchase but then being restricted to making only two legitimate copies available on different personal devices. If the user tried to make a third copy the technology would not allow it.

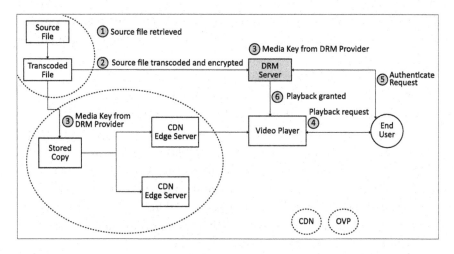

Figure 3.2 The six steps in how DRM works are shown here. It is also possible for the DRM server to be hosted by the content delivery network (CDN) to provide a greater level of protection and reducing delays in authorising playback

DRM *types and uses*

There are five popular DRM systems available in the market today and you may have heard these names before. They are:

1. PlayReady by Microsoft
2. FairPlay by Apple
3. Widevine by Google
4. PrimeTime by Adobe
5. Marlin by Marlin Developer Community

The owning companies above are competitors but they also have a control over certain types of mobile devices and/or streaming media formats. Which is not surprising when you then hear of streaming media companies using a combination of two or more DRM providers. Here's why. When offering your streaming business at your target market, you'll realise that you definitely want to stream to users on iOS devices and, perhaps, customers of Apple computers who use its Safari browser. In this case, you have to use FairPlay DRM since that is precisely what

Apple mandates for its products. Great, so you go ahead and buy DRM for the estimated number of Apple users out there. But then again, the reality is that Android devices are also popular and usually dominant in some markets like Asia. Since Android's operating system (OS) is owned by Google, their mandate is that you then have to use Widevine DRM. So that's two that you have to choose now. But that covers you for the two major browsers out there like Chrome and Firefox.

But if you are using Microsoft Smooth Streaming as your streaming media format to a Microsoft Silverlight player (which was common-place in the past but slowly receding in recent years), then it would be obvious by now that Microsoft will mandate for PlayReady DRM to be supported. That also means, you guessed it, that if you want to stream to Internet Explorer, then your DRM support would come from Microsoft.

Another format in decline is Adobe Flash or Adobe AIR and this requires PrimeTime DRM, again, for obvious reasons. With such fragmentation in the market to note, it may boil down to what devices/formats are more profitable for your service. Obviously FairPlay and Widevine would remain the primary DRM systems needed since they cover you for mobile devices and those using Chrome or Safari. The worst-case scenario for not meeting the requirements of the device or browser is to not be able to play on it at all. You have to balance that against what could potentially be a marginal user experience. Many people have favourite browsers and would be reluctant to switch to a non-preferred one just for one service.

To counter this scenario of proprietary implementations, five major corporations (Intertrust, Panasonic, Philips, Samsung and Sony) banded together in 2007 to announce support for an open-standards concept in DRM known as Marlin. However, it has not had much success due to the dominance of the likes of Apple and Google, so the fragmentation remains. And so will your budget too if you end up supporting a multi-DRM strategy. The less ideal approach is to pick a browser or two that you know the majority of your end users will be using anyway. If this is Chrome and Firefox then we have only Widevine to deploy to solve the problem. Interestingly, as at the time of writing, Netflix had already switched to Widevine after using Smooth Streaming since the beginning of its service.

When and how DRM is applied

DRM is normally applied at the final step of the entire publishing process, just prior to the transfer to the CDN. This is done because content files generally need to be 'clean' or 'clear' when they are being handled early on. You may store the large source file and the transcoded mezzanine file in your local storage but you don't quite know which DRM is being used at that point. Perhaps you've settled on Smooth Streaming for some reason. But one day, you might decide that you'll stop using Smooth Streaming and opt for Widevine instead. In that situation, all you need to do is to access the mezzanine file and apply the DRM after you've carried out the transcoding. If you had applied DRM to the mezzanine file, you'd have to go back one more step to the source file and transcode a new mezzanine all over again.

DRM is managed by a series of licensing servers, which can be hosted on-premises, or in the cloud. When the end user is logged in, a token is stored which identifies them and their entitlements. When the end user presses the play button, the player will first seek to verify that the end user indeed is entitled to watch that title, as per the policy table. It does this by making a call to the DRM licence server, which will check the table and allow playback. All of this is done in less than a second. These servers are usually hosted by your online video platform (OVP) provider, since the latter will manage this as part of their overall service to you.

DRM for free content

You might think that advertising-funded video on demand (AVOD) services don't need to use DRM at all since the content is provided for free. On the contrary, even free content needs DRM to prevent copying and sharing on pirate sites that end up selling their own ads. This happens more often than you think and also dilutes your potential user base since they could end up at those sites for some reason. Since AVOD is all about getting an audience and monetising the views of your ads, this is something you must avoid. In freemium services this is also a no-brainer since you'll need DRM to enforce the policies for paying subscribers as well.

The cost of DRM

It is typical to see DRM sold by OVPs or CDNs to streaming media operators since it simplifies the number or vendors that need to be managed. There are other DRM distributors and these include companies like BuyDRM and Verimatrix. A typical cost involves around US$100–$200 per 10,000 licences (one for each end user), but additional prices go up for every additional 1,000 licences. Plus, there are other fees. DRM costs are material only if you start seeing huge numbers of end users. The challenge is to estimate the number of DRM licences you need from each of the different systems. You do not want to under-purchase since you end up incurring more charges when your DRM provider starts charging you for those overages. But overestimating too much will mean you'll be over-paying for the non-existent users.

As a strategy, ensure you delegate this task to an analyst who can obtain market information about the devices out there and devise a table of users. Then go ahead and buy what you need but only a conservative amount as a minimum. Once launched, you'll be able to find out how much your business is scaling up or not and negotiate additional bulk purchases ahead of time.

Using a digital rights locker

If you've ever bought a Blu-ray disc, you've probably come across the term 'UltraViolet' on a label inside the packaging along with a redemption code. Launched in 2011, it embodies the concept of a digital rights locker, a place where you could store proof of purchase (the redemption code) of a physical piece of content (which UltraViolet calls a 'library'). You could then use that proof to play back the digital version too, as part of your entitlement. It helps you avoid the pain of making your own digital copy but, at the same time, it helps to track how you're making use of those digital copies too, so that you don't exceed your stipulated entitlements.

The only challenge with UltraViolet is that it lacks adoption by some big device players like Apple and Google. Among the major Hollywood studios, Disney was also a non-participant and many studios have since stopped supporting it. Even streamers like Amazon and Netflix also don't support it and that is the biggest hurdle UltraViolet faces. As a 'buy offline, watch online' concept it certainly makes sense but in a fragmented entertainment industry dominated by the streamers, it is considered increasingly irrelevant.

Chances are, you won't need a digital rights locker for your streaming service unless you're working with the Hollywood studios.

Other ways to protect media

Geo-filtering

DRM is not mandatory despite being a highly adopted standard. Using a combination of other measures can be a good alternative depending on how important the content is to you. At the outset, the easiest feature is *geo-filtering*, alternatively known as geo-blocking or geo-restriction (it depends on how aggressive you're feeling). This term really means ensuring that content is available in the right country, seeing as broadcasters or operators usually license content rights on a territory basis. This is normally acquired for viewing in the country they operate in. If they expand to a neighbouring country they will have to ensure that additional rights are granted to broadcast the same content in that country. When streaming content online, the same restrictions obviously apply. While it may seem that websites are 'open' to the whole world, the reality is that IP (internet protocol) addresses are used to differentiate end users and the countries they reside in. These addresses are assigned in blocks by the Internet Assigned Numbers Authority (IANA) to regional registrars, which in turn then assign sub-blocks to telecommunications company providers and internet service providers (ISPs) in particular countries. Thus, a specific range of IP addresses would be unique to a country and possibly to a state or even city. By accessing a database that records these IP addresses, a CDN can help customers by ensuring country permissions are adhered to, and putting other countries' IP addresses in a 'blacklist'.

An example would be a brand wanting to stream an important event live in Singapore. Let's say the only range of IP addresses given out for the country were these:

- Starting from: 64.15.32.0
- Ending at 64.15.32.255

The last block of numbers only goes up to 255, by the way. The above shows that addresses ending in 0 to 255 are within the range. This translates to 256 users. Anyone in 64.15.33.0 onwards would not be considered Singapore so they would be prevented from watching the live event.

A simple analogy would be if you organised a community party and it was meant only for people in your neighbourhood. If your neighbourhood was identified by a specific postal code then you could ask for attendees to show proof of their address as a way to let them in. This would help you keep your costs down and keep the enjoyment to the community folks you meant it for.

With geo-filtering, you can also make individual exemptions, or create a 'whitelist'. These are people you want to give access to but are based in countries that would be restricted. They are usually technical personnel working remotely who need to construct or just monitor your video service.

There are many databases that exist which record the range of current IP addresses around the world, as well as new ones. Your OVPs or your CDNs should be able to recommend the best one and ensure that your business policies are enforced. Because the range of IP addresses is actually offered and re-sold from third parties, it's important to use a database that is frequently updated, especially when important information is available.

Encrypting streaming media

Another layer of protection is in the *encryption* of the streaming media itself. As mentioned earlier, video is delivered in segments. Encryption is just another way to describe the segment's contents actually being scrambled in order and thus being useless for playback. They have to be decrypted, or re-assembled, back in their logical order. Encryption is applied to individual segments before they are streamed to the player and the CDN's servers can encrypt a selected percentage of a video's segments or all of them. To decrypt, a video player must first be verified as authenticated before a 'key' is delivered to it. This is the only way to decrypt the segments. The industry standard is to use 256-bit key encryption.

Player verification

Another alternative to using DRM is *player verification*, a feature for services that use Adobe Flash-enabled video players. This is enabled by creating a list of verified players and issuing licences valid only for them.

When a video is streamed, the server is provisioned to include the licences and these are exposed to the video player. Only a verified player will be able to use the licence, otherwise no playback is enabled. Re-using the earlier party analogy, you could compare it to an invites-only movie screening. The screening party draws up a list of invites and sends them the invitation cards. Only the bearer gets to attend the event, but with the requisite government-issued photo ID of course (see Chapter 6 on IAM).

Since (as we discussed in Chapter 2) Flash players are increasingly being phased out, this is a rarely used feature. The technology itself could be deployed in other types of video players, but since this is used when DRM is excluded for some reason, then other methods should be added for greater protection.

Tokenisation

Then there is *tokenisation*. This is another CDN-enabled technology that keeps a stream from being hacked into and opened in an unauthorised player. In this feature, a token is generated for use by a server within a CDN and a copy is generated for a video player being embedded in a website. When playback is requested the CDN will compare the existence of both tokens. Video players with no tokens to share will be disabled. In the aforementioned party analogy, it would be akin to the screening party putting a serial number next to each invitee's name and then printing them on the invites with invisible ink. When the invitee arrives with the invitation card and presents photo ID, a quick scan also checks for the serial number as a way to ensure that the invite card is authentic.

Digital watermarking

Most of us think of watermarking as copy prevention. This is pretty common when browsing stock images on the internet. The watermark prevents any kind of copying to succeed since it is visible enough to be a visual distraction. But once you purchase it, you can download a copy *sans* watermark.

Digital watermarking on media works primarily as a unique stamp for tracking and is used to track the source of piracy. Watermarking usually involves creating a unique code or ID that represents the end user and this is applied almost imperceptibly somewhere in the image. If this streaming media is then played back elsewhere in an unauthorised manner, it can be used to trace it back to its owner. Whether or not a case can be built against the owner or original end user would be dependent on many variables. Digital watermarking at least allows rights holders to know the source of an illegal stream and take some kind of corrective action.

Preventing insider piracy

Some of the most important areas of content handling by an operator are found in the content operations or content publishing departments. These are the people who actually process and transfer content and eventually make it available to the end users. Thus, this is the area where content leakage is potentially bound to occur. You should put into place a dual approach involving technology-based solutions and organisational policies to counter this threat. In the area of technology, you can prohibit the use of any kind of storage media (thumb drives, portable hard drives, etc.), including the disabling of USB ports in the computers that are used. File attachment can still occur in your company emails but even then, you can get IT's assistance to monitor if video files are being used. Other measures also include blocking access to public cloud-storage sites like Dropbox or Google Drive to ensure content can't be transferred there from a computer. Again, your IT colleagues should be able to execute these measures easily and put tracking mechanisms in place should anyone try to circumvent them. The list of people involved include:

1. **Post-production personnel:** the people who edit programmes you own that are later going to be streamed. The files here are of the highest quality
2. **Content QA personnel:** the people who monitor content to conduct censorship and/or quality assessment (QA) of the content
3. **Content publishers:** the people who enter metadata, select poster images and prepare content to be transcoded before transferring it to the CDN
4. **Gatekeepers:** anyone with access to the storage facilities where content resides

Key takeaways

- **For content owners:** protecting content is not just about your contractual obligations but securing it to prevent piracy and loss of revenue
- **For content owners:** no single solution can guarantee the eradication of piracy but consider different or all forms of protection if you can afford it
- **For everyone:** protecting content is not just about technology; it is a holistic approach that involves policies and organisational behaviour

Distributing your streaming media

How traditional distribution worked

The way we've transformed our media consumption habits from the old physical form to today's streaming alternative is fascinating – it's all happened at dizzying speed in just under 60 years, if you consider it from the perspective of TV alone. For cinema, that transformation period was 110 years.[1] Everything is now either analogue or digital as well as intangible. And we get to choose which one we prefer. But when was the last time you bought a physical CD and played it in your car? And when was the last time you simply plugged your iPhone into it instead?

Before we delve into streaming media's new methods of distribution, it would be good to re-examine how traditional media was recorded, produced and delivered the physical way in the past – chances are, some of you might even remember! The music industry is a good example. A record label would spend a tidy sum of money to produce an album in a studio. Once ready, the vinyl record of the album would be mass-produced and sent to a distributor's warehouse. The distributor itself would have an established business relationship with retail chains (remember Virgin Megastore and Tower Records?), plus smaller chains or even independent record shops. This was the distribution network required to reach any potential buyer. There would also be mail orders direct to consumers if this was considered feasible. But that was it.

Working through this network to reach the buyer required a major effort. If a distributor managed to send out 10,000 vinyl records at a cost of US$10, for example, it would stand to make up to $100,000 from sales. However, it would have to deduct all the costs associated with delivery by truck or van. Going from one capital city branch to another is not all too difficult. It would be the out-of-town deliveries to small retail outlets that would be time consuming. What if there were defects in the records? These would have to be collected back to the distributor warehouse and recorded as damaged and then disposed of. If sales were good in one town, re-orders would be made and then delivered back there again.

In the end, whatever was deducted would be operating profit and this would be shared with the record label on a split-percentage basis. The record label would not necessarily break even if the cost of producing the album was high, but it would possibly have a deal with an international distributor for foreign markets and be able to recoup its investment and possibly start to profit.

For all intents and purposes, traditional distribution was time-consuming, full of manual labour and generated lots of paperwork between the different parties involved (Figure 4.1). This was the case for the better part of the 20th century. The invention of digital media like CDs and audio DVDs might have made storage simpler (due to their smaller physical sizes) but the distribution network hardly changed. It was streaming media that made everything massively different and far more efficient.

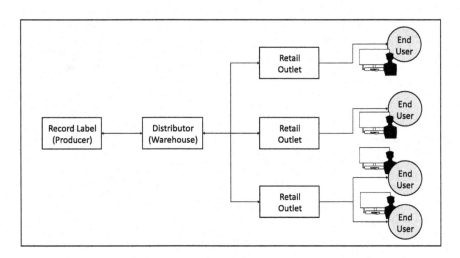

Figure 4.1 A traditional distribution network requires intensive logistical planning. Middlemen and retailers support it

How internet distribution works

The concept that a digital platform could replace its physical version was one of the early opportunities mooted by the internet's emergence, especially in the sphere of commerce. First was the potential that businesses could also reach end users without requiring a middleman. Second was that physical media could also be replaced by digital media and production costs would be eliminated (Figure 4.2).

The simplest form of the new delivery network developed this way: companies stored their media files on a series of large servers known as origin servers (referred to simply as an 'origin'). All you needed was to be able to upload the media file to the origin and make it publicly available through a website, an example of which might be music.com. Then all you had to do was to promote the website's URL to the public and whenever they clicked on the video player, the browser would retrieve it from the origin server. It didn't matter whether an end user was located 2 kilometres or 2,000 kilometres away; when they browsed online and wanted to download a media file, their browser would fetch it from this very server. Obviously, the end user located much further away would have encountered problems since his or her request would

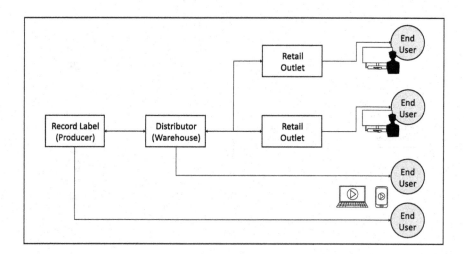

Figure 4.2 An internet-based distribution network shows the 'no distributor' model and also 'no distributor and retailer' model is possible

have to actually traverse through physical routers and internet exchanges along the way and some of these would be congested at some point. But even the end user located nearest to the server would have problems if they had to traverse through a single router and it happened to be congested as well. The dilemma in how best to reach users with this problem is known as *last-mile delivery*. Their experience in getting a speedy or non-speedy response is referred to by a metric known as *latency*.

As this book's initial edition goes to print, I believe that there are many of us who still remember the days when the internet was surfed using low-bandwidth connections and connection congestion described above (often late at night when most people were online), where you literally had to wait up to a minute for a page to load and many more for a file to be downloaded. Latency was measured in seconds, if not minutes. If the file happened to be a movie, it could also be measured in hours!

There were simply too many variables in making delivery of content as speedy as an end user would have liked. These were the original challenges of what was called the Open Internet; the web was designed to promote connectivity thanks to a common set of protocols but not designed to scale up as more and more people started using it. This would pose a serious problem for media delivery that required some creative thinking to solve.

Internet distribution – the online-to-offline model

Netflix, the self-proclaimed 'internet TV' broadcaster co-founded by Reed Hastings, has become a global juggernaut. By early 2018, it already had more than 100 million subscribers worldwide, half of them in the United States alone. However, it is important to remember that its DVD mailing service was its original and sole business model back in early 1998, when DVDs were beginning to take off in popularity versus VHS tapes. It mailed DVDs out and allowed the renter to return it within a month with a reply-paid envelope. All the renter had to do was browse the service's user-friendly website. In the ensuing years, Netflix's biggest competitor was Blockbuster Video and the latter's rent-in-the-store model. Unfortunately, Blockbuster was the first large-scale victim of the internet's promise and by the time it collapsed in 2010, Hastings himself had already become the first technology company CEO to grace the covers of *Fortune* magazine.

Netflix's DVD model is referred to as online-to-offline (O2O), which is exactly how amazon.com works. However, it is nothing more than a sophisticated update of the mail order catalogue that existed prior, albeit with a streamlined fulfilment process that allows the mailing to scale-up to demand. The DVD business still exists today but is declining rapidly as media streaming takes on more subscribers. A purely online model works because it removes any need for dependence on waiting, location or repeat viewing. O2O is a valid business model to consider in areas where the last-mile issues are plagued with internet connectivity problems or where there is no connection at all. A complete distribution model, however, would reach an end user in mere seconds and we will focus on this aspect.

Internet distribution – the P2P model

Napster was a great example of exploiting the pure online model in innovative ways and creating a paradigm shift. Launched by its founders Shawn Fanning and Sean Parker in 1999, it was intended to be a site for users to share music since it would solve one of the greatest problems posed by the physical distribution network that they grew up on: the difficulty of finding rare, niche content since it was no longer sold in stores at present or simply was too difficult to find. One had to travel to specialty stores and these didn't voluntarily advertise the title of every single record they had.

Napster solved this problem by devising a network technology called peer-to-peer (P2P). Fanning and Parker built their own client (which is a software application that you download to your computer) which helped search media files. These were then also downloaded to the end user's computer so that they could be played back at any time. P2P worked on the model that the end users' own computers were part of the distribution network, hence the term 'peer'. Users who downloaded files were basically also turning their clients into a server for another end user. For example, if John wanted to download a particular music file, his client would source part of it from Jane's client. If Jane turned her computer off or her internet connection slowed down, John's client would then source for the remaining parts of the file from Bob's client if it was available and had the same

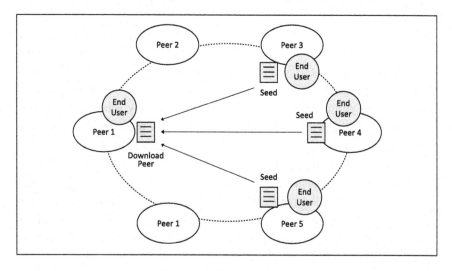

Figure 4.3 The peer-to-peer or P2P model relies on seed peers to help a download peer. The more end users or seeds there are, the better it is for the download peer. Speed or availability is not optimal nor guaranteed

file. Thus, the P2P network benefited its community of users as the community itself grew (Figure 4.3).

Napster was the precursor to an even more famous, or rather infamous client that was exploited to share or deliver media files: BitTorrent. It was originally a P2P protocol created by Bram Cohen in April 2001. Cohen created a client of the same name and made it available in July of the same year for free. By 2004, BitTorrent was responsible for a quarter of all internet traffic, the vast majority of which was illegal music, movie or image media files.

Napster's P2P network was unique and perfect for sharing but not the best way to deliver paid, premium content, especially if one needed to guarantee a certain Quality of Service (QoS). Also, it meant that each person who surfed the internet had to have a copy of the Napster client. For these reasons, P2P will not suit business-to-consumer (B2C) businesses.

It took two struggling MIT academics – Daniel Lewin and F. Thomson Leighton – to develop the technology that formed the basis for the first content delivery network (CDN) in 1998.[2]

Internet distribution – the CDN model

Lewin and Leighton were aware of the problems posed by the Open Internet. They had a potential idea to solve it: caching. This simply meant making copies of original media files or objects and distributing these in multiple servers across a given region. It would allow the traffic of requests from end users to be shared among the many servers rather than just one, and thus, prevent any from crashing. This was theory and putting it into practice as a network that could scale up easily to demand was the big challenge. As a mathematician, Lewin devised an algorithm for intelligent routing of the distributed servers needed to cover the spread of end users while also making scaling-up possible. Better still, it was a dedicated and purpose-built platform that could meet the much-needed QoS metrics that were essential to providing a superior and consistent customer experience. Using the aforementioned analogy of distribution, this platform would provide the equivalent of having mini distribution centres capable of cloning copies of the records. The retail shops didn't have to order from a single head office anymore, they just ordered it from the distribution centre in their same town or one nearby. And the distribution trucks had their own lanes on the highways with their own traffic lights to adhere to. Thus, their company Akamai was born, and with it, the CDN. Many would also argue that the CDN is the earliest incarnation of cloud-based services that are prevalent and commonplace today.

Akamai's network caught the interest of Apple early in 1999 as the latter was looking for a partner to deliver its Apple QuickTime player and streaming media content worldwide. The two key events in March 1999 mentioned in the Introduction had attracted Apple's interest, particularly the Star Wars film *Episode I – The Phantom Menace*. Akamai was contracted to provide the CDN service to Paramount's *Entertainment Tonight Show* website. Two other sites – apple.com and starwars.com – also hosted the trailer but without Akamai. Predictably, it was apple.com that crashed under the weight of the traffic while Akamai had no problem handling the traffic to paramount.com. This caught Steve Jobs's attention. In April 1999, both parties formally announced a partnership. Apple also bought a 5 per cent stake in Akamai for $12.5 million. Other large companies – like Yahoo – signed on to use the service and eventually competitors emerged to take advantage of similar CDN opportunities.

Almost every major site today with a large amount of traffic uses a CDN to ensure it provides reliability as well as speedy delivery of rich media content. End users are not even aware of it.

CDN types

There are different types of physical servers within a CDN. There are servers that simply store media. These are distributed globally for resilience in case of natural disasters. There are also origin servers that pick up incoming/stored media and deliver them to edge servers. The edge servers are critical since they will be delivering media files to the end users. All servers are located in an internet Point of Presence (POP), which is typically a data centre or a telecommunications company (telco) facility. This is critical when we examine the two types of competing CDNs.

The hub-and-spoke model

In this model, shown in Figure 4.4, the CDN's architecture emphasises centralisation of its services but then focuses its edge delivery by building

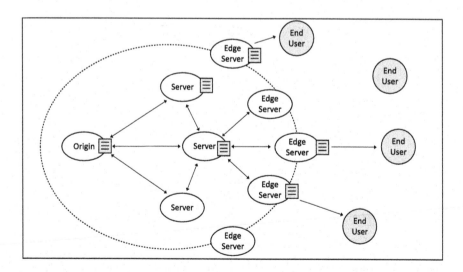

Figure 4.4 A common CDN model relies on dedicated POPs to safely cache and deliver a file to end users in the speediest possible time for a better viewing experience

strategically located 'super POPs' around the world. They focus on reinforcing these super POPs with enough servers to meet demand from end users. Amazon CloudFront and Limelight are examples of CDNs using this model.

The edge model

In this model, shown in Figure 4.5, the CDN's architecture emphasises less centralisation but more on distributing content to the edges of the internet globally. This means building POPs that are co-located with as many network providers as possible, and not just strategic locations. The edge model is more physically demanding simply because more servers are required. But they are also closer to where end users might be. Akamai is a good example of a CDN using this model and is actually the only one to do so. As of time of writing, it claims to have over 200,000 servers around the world.

Basic CDN capabilities

At its most fundamental, a CDN provides storage as well as delivery of media. Some other features that come with the platform include:

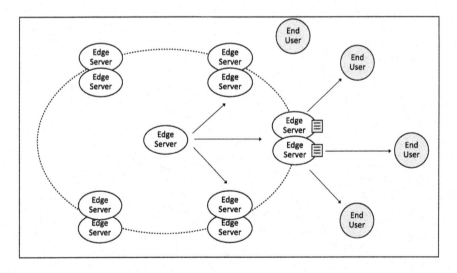

Figure 4.5 An uncommon CDN model relies on vast numbers of distributed POPs to safely cache and deliver a file to end users in the speediest possible time for a better experience

1. Media storage and delivery
2. Media transcoding
3. Media protection
4. Web acceleration
5. Web security
6. Other network services
7. Traffic analytics

Media transcoding

A CDN is not only good for delivering streaming media but also webpages themselves. Both comprise the majority of delivered traffic today. But webpages are no longer simply static HTML (Hypertext Markup Language) code. Sites are increasingly getting 'heavy' as they display many more image files like backgrounds, thumbnails, audio, video plus advertising banners, to name just a few. Consequently, we have all experienced the pain of sometimes waiting for a page to load in its entirety. Or that annoying video that simply won't play even though you pressed 'play' six seconds ago. That's a sure sign of a site not using a CDN! To compound matters, there are many types of devices and screen sizes to cater for when viewing a webpage. One standard image file could (and used to) be provided but it would either be too large or too small a file for a particular device to display quickly enough. Too large and it would take seconds to load. Too small and it would appear fuzzy to the eyes.

The idea of transcoding (or converting) the image into different size and resolution versions would help. End users on small-screen smartphones would simply get the appropriately small image that would load fast. A desktop end user would get the largest. With the myriad device types it would easily take five images to be transcoded from an original high-resolution version, just to satisfy the majority or most popular devices available. But the trade-off was that the website owner would now have ten images to store somewhere ready to be served out when only two would be actually displayed in the end. Most websites have more than three per page today on average, so that means 15 have to be stored. Website owners could make the image transcoding themselves but CDNs quickly evolved to provide this need instead.

Media protection

As mentioned in Chapter 3, content owners are extremely wary of their content being hacked into by content pirates since this poses a major threat to their revenue. While DRM provides a secure way of protecting authorised access to a movie being streamed, it doesn't mean that it is safe. People can still steal credentials and seek to share content. Particularly vulnerable is live streaming content since it can have high peak concurrency viewing at any one time and if premium, paid-for content is leaked at the moment it is available, people can rapidly shift over to the pirated content and leave the actual content owners bereft of viewers. And money. The ideal way is to also protect the stream from being hacked as well.

There are many variants to the above that can be generated but CDNs generally offer plenty of options for protecting media streams. There will be unique situations where contractual, technical, vendor or even cost-based limitations will be imposed and this is where a CDN can help. However, your online video platform (OVP) can also deploy similar features so it is best to discuss what works best with your technical peers. Content studios, especially Hollywood, generally prefer DRM to be used but the above-mentioned alternatives can be applied instead. The level and intensity of protection ultimately depends on how much potential threat is likely to materialise against your service due to its popularity.

Web acceleration

This increasingly important feature from CDNs allows for more rapid delivery of websites, beyond just the standard caching services. These involving a variety of techniques and include:

- Image optimisation: this can mean many things. It can start from prioritising the transcoding of images into versions suitable for popular devices first and then later transcoding versions for older versions (ensuring the majority of users get an optimised image when they make a page request on a popular site). It can also mean transcoding images to the optimal file sizes by compressing them to the exact requirements suited to the end user's device. Be warned though, this means making more versions of an image and leads to increased storage size.

- Enhanced caching: this can include taking origin content and caching these on servers just one level behind the edge servers. This means that the edge servers do not have to travel too far back to request content from the origin, they just go one level back in the network. This is sometimes known as middle-mile caching.
- Compression: this is the use of additional compression techniques to make page headers or other objects aside from images smaller and quicker to deliver.

Web security

Increasingly, CDNs are also being used to make websites more secure from external vulnerabilities. The subject of Cybersecurity is very broad but worth exploring briefly. How are sites vulnerable? Exploitation comes in many bitter flavours and these can be categorised as the following:

1. Social engineering
2. Malware
3. Network attacks
4. Software vulnerabilities

Social engineering

This is quite common and is also known as phishing. This is simply where users try to communicate to you under the guise of someone trusted or even your own financial institution and attempt to obtain customer account information. Customers of financial institutions are frequently targeted, wherein an entire bank site may be faked and customers are targeted with emails linking to the fake website, usually under the pretence of changing their account information and password.

Malware

These are forms of malicious software that are designed to disrupt your site severely once they reside on a networked computer. Users can inadvertently download malware from a malicious website. Other forms include spyware and ransomware, which can remotely lock end users' computers until a ransom is paid. Viruses, Trojan Horses and worms are included here.

Network attacks

These come in the basic shape of a distributed denial of service (DDoS, pronounced dee-doss). This is where someone intentionally makes multiple requests to a single server hosting a website to the point where the server cannot cope with serving to such a high volume and gets bogged down trying to do so. Or it simply crashes. Either outcome brings the dreaded 'Error 404' message on your browser when you try to visit that website. DDoS attacks have become widely reported in the mainstream media in recent years as state-sponsored hackers have resorted to using this method to bring down large multinational corporations or government infrastructure in Western countries.

Software vulnerabilities

As more and more software is downloaded from the internet as opposed to physical discs, the potential for exploitation is prevalent. High-profile incidents are occurring on a regular basis involving large consumer companies.

Web security is largely solved if end users are aware of the potential threats that exist and take preventive action. However, threats can never be totally eradicated so reactive solutions can be sought from CDNs. Some, like network attacks, require the intervention of CDNs. With CDNs fielding thousands or even tens of thousands of servers in their network, they could cache a website and absorb very large attacks without slowing down at all. Some have the ability to also inspect the visitors to discern hostile visitors from normal ones, allowing the hostiles to be traced while the normal ones make it through to their intended webpage. The benefit provided here is that B2C e-commerce sites – which sell across time zones 24 hours a day – cannot afford any downtime (which would be the equivalent of a shuttered shop door in peak hours), since this directly impacts on revenue. For others – like military institutions or public utilities – this could severely impact their ability to perform their vital services.

The mitigation of DDoS threats is arguably the most easily useful proposition that CDNs can pose to potential customers today. It's no wonder that CDNs are – as at time of writing – citing web security or cybersecurity as a growth engine for their business.

Other network services

The Managed CDN model has become more popular in recent years. It was conceived on the idea that some customers can buy their own internet bandwidth but still need a CDN. These companies have access to bandwidth at cheaper or even wholesale prices. Telcos are such companies that fit this profile since they usually already operate as an ISP to their end users. Hence, there is no need to buy additional bandwidth and they remove that requirement from the contract.

Another version of this is the Licensed CDN. This is where the customer also wants to install CDN hardware of their own to effectively build their own physical CDN. This includes the software. The use case for this would be small telcos that operate in a small country, for example, and would see the CDN as an extension of their own telco network. They want to exert more control by operating the network themselves using their own staff, yet lack the expertise to build one from scratch. In this case, the CDN vendor licenses its proprietary software and sells off-the-shelf hardware specified to meet the customer's needs.

Traffic analytics

You should expect a dashboard to access your usage and also see how your CDN is performing. This includes the number of object hits, web visits (if applicable) and data volume stored and served. Even better would be the different types of responses that were also served when visitors made requests from their browsers. How many times were errors reported? How many times did the edge servers have to refer back to an origin for a request? Finally, you should also be able to check the status of your billing and generally get any kind of support you need (from simple queries to creating a support ticket for issues).

It's possible to also get client- or player-side analytics from the CDN and it is a matter of choice, or perhaps a matter of the cheapest cost. Do not fall into that trap. You have to make sure that you get a fair comparison and the best analogy I can think of is, 'Would you want your football club to supply the referee for a match?' No, because there would always be the doubt regarding bias by the opposing team. Chapter 2 should provide the key information to consider before you decide.

Paying for CDN services

Try to take a high-level view of your business needs and define your content delivery strategy first. You may not need a CDN in your initial phase but as you reach a certain threshold, the cost to serve images and streaming media will be critical and be best served by one. Or you will simply need to have one in place from the beginning. You need to decide. The cost-benefit analysis can be served by comparing your traditional web-hosting costs for streaming media and compare them against a candidate CDN's cost. The intersection of both is where you will begin seeing the savings brought on by the CDN, especially when you take note that a CDN allows you to avoid hiring an expensive network engineering team as well as the hardware. However, you will need at least one dedicated engineer since a fair amount of technical work still needs to be handled by customers when performing configuration work of their accounts and maintaining it on a regular basis.

That said, once you do decide that you want to engage a CDN to outsource your web and/or media delivery to, there are basic costs to plan for and make decisions about.

Storage

To begin with, the 'bread and butter' of CDN usage will always be storage and delivery and these are calculated very easily. Storage means that you, the customer, must first upload your media files that you want the CDN to deliver. It is usually done in a selected country in a particular region that you are part of (nominated as the primary region) closest to your operations centre and where files can be uploaded pretty quickly. This is basically a data centre. Storage costs are charged in the number of gigabytes (GB) or terabytes (TB) that are stored per month or per year by the CDN. Usually, a second storage region is provided for redundancy (in case the primary storage region is affected) but this may not always be free. Check your provider's rate card.

If the physical connecting point to the CDN is located at a considerable distance (like a distant country) and time is critical for you, it may be more feasible to consider leasing an 'uplink' line, which is basically a fibre cable that gives you more bandwidth speed and would be dedicated to your needs. It connects you to the CDN. Since many CDNs do not specialise in this you will need to contact your telco broadband provider's enterprise or business account manager for a separate quote.

To summarise how storage works in pricing, imagine you own a streaming media website and you have 1,000 images that are an average of 1 megabyte[3] (MB) in size. You then have a simple total per month as shown in Table 4.1.

Now imagine that you also have 100 videos to offer as a streaming service. These will be far heavier and may average around 10 GB. You then have a simple total per month in your second column. In Table 4.2, you can see how it starts to build up much quicker.

Assuming that storage costs priced to you are $2 per GB per month, your total monthly cost of storing your media is $2,002.

Table 4.1 A calculation of image storage and how it compares to video. It's possible for 100 videos to take up 1,000 times more storage space

	Image file	Video file
Number of files x each file size	1,000 x 1 MB	100 x 10 GB
Equals to total storage, or	1,000 MB	1,000 GB
Equals to total storage	1 GB	1 TB

Table 4.2 A combined calculation of image and video storage costs

	Image storage	Video storage
Space in GB	1 GB	1,000 GB
Costs per GB	$2	$2
Sub-total storage costs	1 x 2 = $2	1,000 x 2 = $2,000
Total storage costs		$2,002

Delivery

Unlike storage, which is simply the cost of keeping static files, delivery is a dynamic activity which requires the consumption of internet bandwidth. Delivery of your media is also charged on a per GB or TB basis and the cost can range from cents to dollars, depending on how much volume of delivery is predicted. The calculation is complex. To understand further, let's compare two types of media.

Image media files are static and simple to store. If your website stores 1,000 images that are an average of 1 MB in size then you have a simple total as shown in Table 4.3.

Assume that you have 10,000 end users who visit your whole website and will see these 1,000 images per month. Assume that 1 GB delivered will cost $0.50. Your cost of serving your media images rapidly and efficiently to your end users is now $5,000 per month.

Streaming media files are different. They are measured by bitrates which are indicators of their video quality. Since the measurement starting point is in bits, they need to be calculated into bytes first. For example, if a TV episode file has a bitrate of 10 megabits per second (Mbps) and has a duration of 1 hour, it will be watched by one person and consume 450 MB in total. The formula to calculate this is shown in Table 4.4.

At a price of $0.50 per GB, the actual cost of delivering the episode to one person who watched it in its entirety is $0.225. However, if the same 10,000 persons as above also watched the episode, your cost of delivering to them now is $2,250. If you had a large audience, you can start to see how this cost could be prohibitive but, in reality, costs are much lower per GB.

Table 4.3 A cost calculation of images delivered to one person each versus 10,000 persons each. This should be used to predict your bandwidth costs in a relatively simple way

	Cost to one person	Cost to 10,000 persons
Number of files x file size x request	1,000 x 1 MB x 1	1,000 x 1 MB x 10,000
Equals to total delivered, or	1,000 MB	1,000,000 MB
Equals to total delivered	1 GB	10,000 GB
Cost @ $0.50 per GB	$0.50	$5,000

Table 4.4 A cost calculation of a one-hour video delivered just to one person versus 10,000 persons

	Cost to one person	Cost to 10,000 persons
Convert bits per second to bits per hour	10 Mbps x 360 = 3,600 Mbps	10 Mbps x 360 = 3,600 Mbps
Megabits converted to MB	3,600 Mbps / 8 = 450 MB	3,600 Mbps / 8 = 450 MB
MB delivered to one person	450 MB x 1 = 450 MB	450 MB x 1 = 450 MB
Equals to total delivered in GB	0.450 GB	0.450 GB
Cost @ $0.50 per GB	0.450 GB x 0.50 = $0.225	0.450 GB x 0.50 = $0.225
Total cost to deliver	$0.225 x 1 = $0.225	$0.225 x 10,000 = $2,250

Forecasting storage and delivery – a note to engineers

Engineers must take note that the tables have all assumed that only one file rendition is used per video. As we discussed in Chapter 2, a video actually comprises several renditions, each of which is transcoded in a different bitrate to accommodate the adaptive bitrate method of streaming. In this case, you must add up all files to calculate the true cost of storage. For delivery – since only one file is used to deliver at any one time – it is slightly more difficult to predict the cost usage. Do you take the average bitrate from all bitrate renditions supplied? Or do you go for the highest bitrate rendition? The answer depends on how well connected your users are to the internet in terms of bitrate. You must match them. For best practices, select the highest bitrate for your forecast and monitor the actual average usage that is streamed. This will help keep actual usage in line with your forecasts.

Using commitments to lock in a specific price

Some CDNs will charge for a minimum commitment of usage each month or each year. This is also known as a minimum guarantee. In fact, this is a standard industry practice for any kind of cloud-based service where there is an element of 'usage'. For CDN services, expect that you will be

Table 4.5 A simple comparison between a minimum commitment per month and actual usage. Given a one-year contract, this wastage would be multiplied by 12, otherwise the hope is that the content library eventually increases!

	Commitment	Actual usage
Cost per GB per month	$1	$1
GB storage per month	20,000 GB	15,000 GB
Calculated storage cost per month	20,000 x 1 = $20,000	15,000 x 1 = $15,000
Potential wastage per month		$5,000

asked for a specific minimum commitment separately for storage and delivery. For example, if you estimated that you will be using 20,000 GB worth of storage per month and agree with your CDN provider on the price per GB, you will be asked to commit to this amount each month. An example should be as shown in Table 4.5.

If you end up using 19,000 GB in a given month you will still be charged for the 20,000 GB x $1 and this will still be $20,000. Ditto if you use even less. Thus, you really should get an idea of how much content is likely to be made available each month so that you can factor in a minimum amount and negotiate a good deal. Then, there's the element of overages or excess usage beyond the minimum commitment. You will most likely also have pre-agreed with your CDN provider on a price per GB once you have exceeded the minimum commitment. This should be lower than your minimum commitment price and should be progressively lower as you cross higher tiers.

Overages

Overages are any usage beyond your minimum commitment specified to your CDN provider. Overages can be priced in the same tier as your minimum commitment but you should be able to negotiate lower prices according to new tiers of increased usage. While minimum commitments provide a guarantee and peace of mind on both sides, it is wise to monitor your usage and how much overage you will incur each month (assuming your minimum commitments are monthly). The ideal situation is that you incur minimal overage. Underutilising your commitment means you have underestimated your usage and are essentially wasting money (see Table 4.6).

Table 4.6 A simple calculation of how storage usage exceeds the minimum commitment per month and goes into overages. If overages continue to increase, the guidance would be to increase the commitment, but at a lower negotiated cost

	Actual usage	Overage
Cost per GB per month	$1	$0.80
Actual GB storage per month	20,000 GB	3,000 GB
Calculated storage cost per month	20,000 x 1 = $20,000	3,000 x 0.80 = $2,400
Combined costs per month		$22,400

As mentioned before, flash crowds will happen and can be predicted. They should be factored in so that you are not caught off guard in your usage. This is especially true with companies that have strict annual budgets to maintain. But if your company is cost conscious and your overages begin to climb higher due to increased traffic (however good that may be), it would be wise to quickly renegotiate a new minimum commitment with a higher threshold and overall lower unit rate. Overages should ideally be a lower unit rate or the same, not higher!

I would advise against setting yearly minimum commitments until you have seen the track record of your site(s) for at least two years and understand the growing consumption needs of your end user base. Usage should be modelled in tandem with expected market growth.

Fees

Other CDN services are charged in varying models, some by GB of usage and some by a monthly fee once it is turned on. Again, check with your provider.

CDNs do not generally provide a ready list of prices. However, Amazon CloudFront adopts a different approach and lists their rate card on their website. Prices are standardised across regions but comparisons with its competitors should be made carefully in conjunction with engineering expertise based on a business's particular requirements. It is still very competitive and many major media companies are using CloudFront.

There are newer models of working with CDNs. In the Managed/ Private CDN model, the customer pays 'rent' each month or year to use a part of the CDN just for them (hence, 'private') and is assured of some service levels from the CDN operator. The customer must acquire their own internet bandwidth but otherwise uses the hardware and software of the operator.

In the Licensed CDN model, the customer also pays a licence fee to the CDN operator, either monthly or yearly. Internet bandwidth can either be purchased through the CDN or independently.

Another way is to delegate your CDN concerns to your OVP provider. This is common if you don't have very specific needs or do not experience very high traffic. Or perhaps you just don't want the hassle of managing a CDN and its related issues yourself. The benefit is that the OVP will use their house account to re-sell your preferred CDN's services to you. You should not worry about cost since most OVPs would have obtained wholesale rates, but it makes sense to get a comparison if you wish. Then decide. One important trade-off is that if there are issues that affect your end users, the OVP will need to work with the CDN to resolve this and there may be extra delays related to the back-and-forth communication that results.

It is difficult to assess which type of CDN is superior but Akamai may argue that the distributed POP CDN is superior when it comes to a live streaming media event watched by a high number of end users. The higher number of servers provides strength in numbers, it would seem. This may seem to have been validated recently when India's Hotstar video service streamed one of its exclusive Indian Premier League cricket matches live and reported 8.26 million peak concurrent users across the region. In case you still didn't get it, those people were watching at the same time! Another fact important to note is that the vast majority of the viewers were watching from smartphones. That is a world record for now and, with more and more cricket-mad Indians having access to cheaper smartphones as they come online, it will continue to be surpassed and be seen as both a measure of growth and a measure of Akamai's perceived platform superiority.

Professional services

Most technical-based cloud services provide some kind of professional services quote and whether or not you need it depends on your requirements. If you are new to a CDN and prefer to outsource some of your config-uration work, you may need your CDN to help. Or, you may conduct complex streaming products that require third-party integration (i.e., a customised video player or live streaming encoding with another vendor). It's best to consider an allowance for a set number of hours each month and increase it once you ramp up your service and require-ments. Professional services do not include ongoing support, so keep that in mind.

Support

As discussed in Chapter 2, OVP vendors provide support in different service tiers, each catering to a specific service level agreement. If you run live events it is highly advantageous to opt in to a dedicated CDN support engineer – you never know what can go wrong during such time-critical moments.

Bundled pricing

If you are using a lot of services, do think about how much cost you will incur on usage of a CDN plus the actual fees for other services. Fees are not part of your monthly commitment but may be included as part of your annual commitment. A CDN may welcome that since you are guaranteeing a fixed amount of compensation per year.

Minimum terms

Most CDNs require a minimum term to lock you in. Don't confuse this with the minimum commitment, which can either be monthly or yearly. A minimum term is preferred – usually another year – and your CDN provider should give you discounts based on longer terms. Some CDNs provide month-to-month pricing but this should be avoided since there are no commercial advantages to be gained here. Why not try to build a relationship with your CDN instead?

When renewing, it is common to do so for another minimum term of one year. In exceptional situations, monthly extensions are provided if contract renewal negotiations take up a lengthy period.

> ## Key takeaways
>
> - **For everyone:** the internet has re-imagined the retail model and with the introduction of e-commerce in streaming media, this has resulted in distribution that goes direct to the consumer
> - **For everyone:** any serious streaming media business must employ a CDN (and do so effectively) to enhance content delivery and protect its business at the same time
> - **For everyone:** understand what your CDN expenses are so that you can manage them prudently

Notes

1 For TV, this is defined from the first commercial radio broadcast in 1947 to the launch of Hulu in 2007. For movies, it is defined as from the time when the Lumière brothers premiered their cinematograph for commercial use in December 1895 to Netflix beginning its streaming service.
2 Akamai was originally known as Cachet and the team behind it was bigger.
3 The calculation used in these examples uses the decimal number system 1 = 1,000 (not 1 = 1,024) which is standard in data communications.

5 | User experience

If this is a book about streaming media then you might be thinking why is this chapter being included? What does streaming media have to do with knowing how someone experiences a service? The answer is simply because a better experience with using something results in more usage of it, or a better engagement with that service. I truly believe that you can only build a successful online service – any service really, not just streaming media – by being focused on meeting and exceeding the needs of your potential users. And you achieve that by understanding how they use your service from start to end. Or, how they would journey through the use of your product as they try to satisfy what they want out of it.

What is UI?

Let's start with the term *user interface* (UI) since it may be used often by engineers and web designers when they talk about the products they are working on. But it can be confusing in its meaning. It isn't about how a TV's screen menu looks when we turn it on. It isn't about just aesthetics. It can, in fact, be described as the way we work with machines when we operate them, and is seen as a design discipline that is multifaceted in its approach. As TV users, the traditional sense of a user interface was the portion of the TV where the channel dials were. Watching TV itself was quite simple: we controlled it via the dials to select the channel we wanted. We could also control the dials for the volume of the sound. That was pretty much all you needed. The TV screen and its speakers were the results or outputs of what we controlled by hand. Then came the remote control, which was a major innovation in how we watched TV. For the first time, we operated the TV with a specific input device from our seats and it provided a bigger convenience in our enjoyment of TV itself. This remained the default or primary interface with TVs for decades.

Three things changed the experience. Firstly, the advent of Pay TV increased the availability of many more channels, introducing the terms *channel surfing* and *couch potato* into modern culture. Pre-internet era, video on demand-like services were also introduced, as well as pay-per-view events and channels. Secondly, the availability of the internet, not just for streaming media, but helping Pay TV users in making content selection easier. With set-top boxes connected to the internet, a vast amount of interactivity was now popular. Thirdly, the rise of smartphones and tablets also allowed for companion devices to be brought into the living room to help control the TV (more on that later this chapter).

With the advent of streaming media, a computer or a smart device now becomes a potentially key part of how we find our favourite shows, and a keyboard, mouse or our fingers become the new input devices. The screen menu also becomes a major point to interface with. The greater convenience allowed by all this means that the end user is spoilt with options on how to watch TV, yet the end user still has one simple goal: to just watch TV easily. What's the best way? Pressing buttons? Using swipe gestures with fingers or thumbs? These are all new UIs for modern TV and the permutations for using them are tremendous.

Yet, the art of UI design should focus on the sole aim to help the end user enjoy TV better by finding the shows that they love as quickly as possible.

With all this in place, the discipline of making sure that the end user's needs are satisfied is the responsibility of a specific department known as Product Management. In truth, product management is a challenging but very important role within media organisations.

The leadership in product management must balance basic needs of the company's business teams (for example: 'this new app must generate more customer loyalty towards our service'), with that of the end user (which always is: 'help me watch TV easily'). With this in mind, UI design is very much part of the department.

What is UX?

Many people confuse the term UX with UI. The former stands for *user experience* and is actually the overall set of experiences an end user has with your service. It is usually end to end, meaning it should start from when an end user signs up for a service (in a retail environment, at home over the computer), to actual usage and right until the moment when they decide to cancel. UX is broad but is increasingly being practised by customer-centric organisations as well to comprehensively understand how an end user may find potential 'pain-points', that is, the moments when using the service results in a negative experience. This is known as the customer journey map. Importantly, this map is also drawn in a way to show how your company stakeholders will interact with the end user at each stage. The goals of customer journey maps are to understand what can be improved for the end user and who plays a role in resolving this. Sometimes, the mapping activity is used to re-imagine how a process should be, as opposed to what it is. Are there entire parts that are even necessary for the end user? All this needs to be managed by a UX designer, again, sitting within product management. Mind you, in small organisations it is the product manager who assumes the role of UX designer but this is not recommended. Product managers deal with myriad roles and UX should always be kept separate, for clarity and objectivity. The old adage that two heads work better than one applies in this sense. When working, a UX designer's customer journey map might look something like Table 5.1. In this case, the main elements to note are:

1. Customer personas or actors
2. Customer journey phases
3. Customer pain-points
4. Stakeholders

Customer personas are detailed portraits of who your customers are. These are written after extensive user surveying has been done so that you understand their actual needs or wants. Nothing else should provide the data, nor should you guess. Only market surveys. These should ideally be qualitative instead of quantitative, meaning you've focused on asking a few people very detailed or deep questions rather than asking many people simple questions. Personas will include who the buyer is as

87

Table 5.1 An example of a user journey map for a B2C company and how pain-points could be captured and shared through an organisation for improvement

	Purchase	Register	Use	Troubleshoot	Billing
Customer (buyer and/or user)	Cannot find pricing page easily	Confirmation email arrives late	Videos are always buffering	Can only email my issues, no phone support	Doesn't understand the charges
Our company representative	UX designer to re-examine user journey	Back-end engineer	Systems engineer to check network	Customer support to investigate alternatives	Product manager to re-examine bill literal
Affected system/ process	Web CMS	Cloud-based registration vendor	CDN or connection to it	n/a	Billing system inputs

well as the decision-maker. Also, is there an influencer? Ultimately, who is the user of the service? These four personas can be merged where suitable (like buyer and user being the same person), but should be captured with some detail.

What is product management?

Does your organisation have a product manager? A product manager plays a multifaceted role. This person represents the voice of the customer but balances that with the needs of the business he or she works for. They then combine that with domain expertise which will be related to the industry they are in. Almost every customer-facing organisation has a product manager today and they can handle several areas of responsibility along the value chain of developing a product and managing it. Some focus on development and the 'building' part of it. Some focus on its management as a business. Many do both of those roles.

Traditional media never needed a product manager. Radio sets were built and sold to millions with limited functionality (the radio dials) and some kind of aesthetic appeal (usually a box shape). TVs fared a little better but people still only had to tune in to watch a channel. Everything changed when the essential viewing device became a little more interactive and complex. Like the set-top box that Pay TV operators built. They introduced interactive menus and programme guides which re-imagined that idea of channel browsing. Features like recording functions required some way to educate the customer and that could only happen if you learnt how to observe and get insights from their daily use. Then came devices that were a little more personal and portable, like the personal computer or the smartphone respectively. As entertainment and productivity found their way into these devices, the requirement to really cater for a great experience became the tipping point for product management to become a sought-after role. Someone had to look after the customers' needs and communicate that throughout the organisation. A product manager is the most customer-centric person and may often struggle with parts of the organisation that want to have as little to do as possible with the customer. Thankfully, more companies are adopting a customer-centric mindset in every department and every role.

If you are a business owner of any streaming media service – whether internal or external – you should be looking at adopting a product manager as the very first hire in your team (besides you)! Is this outsourced to a vendor who's also making the product for you? It can be but it shouldn't. It should be a dedicated team of people as is the case with mature industries like broadcasters, telecommunications, financial services and fast-moving consumer goods. Product managers and those assisting them help translate business requirements into the necessary documentation that can then be conveyed to technology or engineering teams to be built. This intersection of business objectives, end-user needs and technological feasibility usually results in thorough planning and a commitment that a product will be launched and then improved as it becomes bigger. Normally, this is captured in a document called a product roadmap. It is then further broken into an actual schedule where the actual product is built incrementally over a regular development cycle, called a sprint. These are where product features are built and tested thoroughly.

Still not convinced that product managers are needed? Then take end-user needs as an example. The use of streaming media is complicated – unlike that of simply reading an online article. Swiping, touching, scrolling gestures are part of a discovery journey where the content has to be curated as well since there is so much to read and watch. Where does the user begin? How are the categories chosen and laid out for easy representation? How many clicks/presses do they have to make in order to find the title that they love? If they have an existing Pay TV account, how do they register to get their shows online? Do they need their account number and where will they find it? Streaming media publishers have had the responsibility of taking their entire business onto a digital platform and ensure relevance as well as, ultimately, customer loyalty. With competition coming from many sources like free media and social media, any organisation needs to ensure a great viewing experience. Even the *Daily Mail* and *Wall Street Journal* have employed product managers, as they move from using print to more use of streaming media. The mix of hybrid text and video content makes a coherent experience even more important.

Even when it comes to internal uses of video, a great experience is required. Employee engagement with enterprise software (covering human resources, training and others) has been traditionally time-consuming and frustrating. They were developed to cater to processes and not necessarily a better user experience. But the result has been that much time is wasted through trying to understand how to use something. However, I won't stress the point more since these kinds of improvements are more difficult to drive as opposed to external ones so let's focus on those. Since anything customer-facing is critical, the point is, a product manager role is a must-have.

Product management is also critical since it comes at the intersection of business needs, end-user needs and technological feasibility. This is also then balanced with time and budget availability. But once gathered, the primary drivers are the user needs since their adoption is all that matters. Product managers ensure that enough research is done with customers to understand and capture their feedback. These are represented as 'user stories' and presented as companion documents to the business requirements. Combined, these feature requests are then agreed upon and developed in batches, or regular software releases. Software is normally developed in a staging environment and tested once completed. Product managers must run the tests against the original user stories to ensure that these are correct (Figure 5.1).

Think about your business's own strategy and its direction, and decide if this is required. If you do think that your organisation deserves to have the ideal structure, consider one like Figure 5.2.

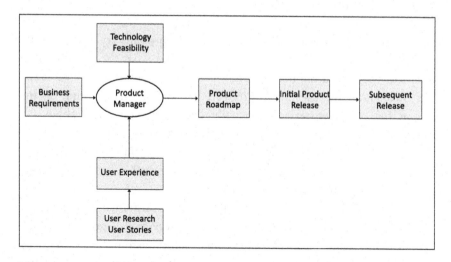

Figure 5.1 An example of a product manager's role within a media organisation (assuming the product manager is a sole contributor or it is a fairly small organisation)

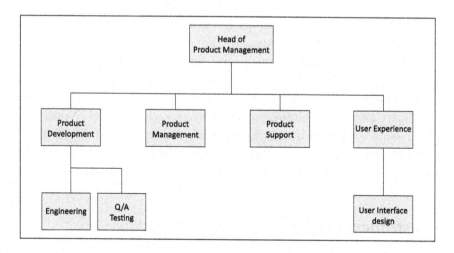

Figure 5.2 An example of a product management organisational chart. This may vary considerably depending on the organisation's culture and size

For many organisations pursuing streaming media, you may decide to outsource the development of the product itself, at least as an initial step. However, if your needs are expanding rapidly or the digital business is growing then this should not be the case.

Pain-points vs friction-points

In product management, pain-points and friction-points could be one and the same thing. But it's important to understand what these really mean and how they affect the take-up of your service. Pain-points are generally felt throughout the use of the product. It could be that waiting on the phone for customer service to finally deal with you takes about ten minutes. That's obviously a major pain-point. Would customers leave your service? Probably not since they may not call you often enough, but fixing that long waiting time next time may give them a better experience that leaves a positive view of you as a brand.

Friction-points are areas that frustrate the customer experience in generally signing up for and also using your service. It's arguable which area is more important but I would opine that if customers don't sign up then you don't have to worry about them watching your service. Therefore, signing up becomes a major focal point for most businesses and their product managers. It would be crucial to map how someone signs up and then signs in. These are sometimes known as activation flows. How many steps did that take for a consumer? How easy was it to find the button to get to the next step? Anything remotely frustrating risks the possibility that a customer might give up and not continue with your service.

Pain-points and friction-points should be continuous areas for product managers and product teams to focus on, for clear results. Neglecting them would result in a negative business impact. Thankfully, there is a framework that can be applied with the collaboration of both the UX designer and the product manager. That's the Customer Journey Map.

Customer journey mapping – B2C

Customer journey phases are the steps taken when a service is first discovered, purchased and billed right until it is cancelled. The stages must be identified. Often, the support part of the stage is mapped since it is important to understand what happens if an end user needs help. Let's look at how business-to-consumer (B2C) companies approach this. The full spectrum of journey mapping can sometimes take on the following terminology:

1. Purchase
2. Register
3. Usage to Cash
4. Trouble to Resolution

The purchase phase is required if the monetisation is by transactional purchase or recurring subscription purchase. If the customer has to go into a retail outlet of an affiliate to buy the service, that would be separate from one that allows the customer to go a website. This is also sometimes referred to as the 'sign-up' process.

Registration is used when the end user identifies him or herself to the service and is granted an entitlement to watch the streaming media videos. Once a customer has placed an order for a service, it needs to be physically activated or provisioned. In Pay TV, this is akin to having your set-top box activated to receive the subscribed TV channels by satellite, fibre or cable. For mobile companies, this is where the customer's SIM (subscriber identity module) is turned on and recognised by the mobile operator's own network. Potential pain-points include late activation, partial services/channels being activated, or being overcharged for usage.

Table 5.1 could be split into different stages, depending on your product or service and how it is sold. In Trouble to Resolution the mapping is around scenarios where a customer may misunderstand how to use something and not be able to solve this intuitively. Or worse, there may be an outage on the video platform or the CDN. What are the avenues for resolution? Is it via email only? Or phone and chat? Or all three? Picking one as the only choice might have implications but at least these need to be mapped out. If customers object to email or find the process painful then this is a red flag to resolve.

The troubleshooting phase is the first real test of customer service. It might be that your video platform has suffered an outage. Or that one of the main internet service providers (ISPs) itself is down. Or your service has an unexpected bug in it from the latest software release that went out 24 hours ago. But you won't know that unless you are equipped with the tools to make such a diagnosis and also dedicated people who can respond to customers to assist them in some way.

Finally, in the Usage to Cash stage, the process is simply to document how the customer will receive their bill and pay it, or how they will receive credits if there was a credit issued for some reason. You might be surprised but potential customers will often put thought into this stage at the buying decision. An example is if a free trial is given. Does the customer automatically roll over into a paid month or do they need to be prompted (this is known as 'opt-out' since the customer has to specifically say so before a certain date)? The best practice shows that customers want to be emailed a few days before their free trial ends or at least be prompted to confirm that their subscription should commence. For this and many other reasons, important consideration is paid to the bill since it needs to be straightforward and contain descriptions of the service that match the contract form. More importantly, bills are the easiest way to provide clarity to end users and to avoid them calling up customer service for clarification. The description – known as the bill literal – should accurately match the name of the product and include terms that are natural and user-friendly. What if the customer decides to churn, which is the industry term for cancelling their service? Will you offer any win-back promotions to retain the customer or at least seek to understand why they want to cancel?

As you can see, the B2C journey map of a potential customer forces you to make important decisions and rules pertaining to your service and how it is experienced. This is why product managers are needed by organisations. No one will have the customers' best interests at heart as much as them. No one will have an opinion about each customer touch-point as much as they will.

Customer journey mapping – B2B

The business-to-business (B2B) world can be vastly different. When businesses buy from each other, especially larger enterprises, everything slows down in terms of the cycles. A good example would be Amazon Web Services, or AWS, which is Amazon's cloud computing platform for businesses. They've taken the complexity of hardware purchasing and eliminated that with a proposition that cloud computing is easier to manage. Even though large companies may need time to make the right purchase decision, they offer a straightforward account set-up process and quick activation. You can start using their service literally within minutes. But there's adequate documentation and resources to support someone who needs multi-stakeholder buy-in. AWS make it extremely easy for the customer, no matter what their buying style is, and it is no wonder they've been able to generate billions in revenue in a relatively short time. In business, a customer journey map also starts when a service is first discovered through advertising, is then purchased, then billed correctly and eventually cancelled. The support aspects of the journey are also mapped since this is absolutely vital for the buyers – they are also focused on serving their end users and will be held accountable for any service faults. The full spectrum of journey mapping may take on the following terminology (with minor variations from company to company):

1. Prospect to Order
2. Order to Activation
3. Usage to Cash
4. Trouble to Resolution

If you're working in the B2B space, it is still critical to map the above so that you have something that resembles Table 5.2. Let's take a look in more detail from your perspective as the customer. Let's assume you are selling online video platforms (OVPs) to broadcasters who want to produce their own TV Anywhere service.

Table 5.2 An example of a user journey map for a B2B company

	Prospect to Order	Order to Activation	Trouble to Resolution	Usage to Cash
Customer (buyer and/or user)	Slow turnaround for customised requirements	Account logins don't work	Customer support doesn't know details about account	I don't understand the charges
Our company representative	Sales representative needs better pricing tools and faster approvals	Customer success manager and back-end engineer	Account manager to upload contract and account info into support system	Product manager to re-examine bill literal
Affected system/ process	Improve internal processes and introduce pricing calculator tool	Update onboarding checklist to include prior testing	Update onboarding checklist and support system	Billing system inputs

Prospect to Order

Like in B2C, there is an initial stage when your target market or segment is identified and then prospects – TV broadcasters – are sought as potential customers. Advertising is generally executed in the trade presses or business journals to create awareness of your OVP. If this is done online, a target customer can respond easily by clicking on the ad to visit your (the advertiser) site. Usually, some form of content marketing is also created instead, usually by way of a useful industry report or white papers given freely to any prospective customer willing to register their contact details online. Their information is then sent to someone in your marketing team as a generated 'lead'. Once some basic credibility checking is ascertained, this is then passed on to the relevant salesperson who will initiate contact and try to understand the customer's needs better. This is the qualification stage. If discussions progress, a proposal may be sought. This is known as – unsurprisingly – the proposal stage. If the customer is further impressed, some kind of negotiation may be made on pricing. This is the commercial stage. If a sale is concluded, then the phase closes with the contract being sent for other stakeholders to view and prepare for.

Order to Activate

In B2B, especially software-as-a-service (SaaS) products, this could be as simple as ensuring that the customer's account is created and access to an OVP is granted. But first, the customer needs to be activated and access needs to be given according to what they paid for (e.g. did they pay for gold-level support instead of silver or bronze?). It's important to ensure that you, as a customer, are onboarded the proper way. All essential contact information should be exchanged on both sides. Training on how to use the OVP is given to the operational teams. Using the graphical user interface (GUI), the customer's operations teams (also known as publishers) can now start to orchestrate workflows involving their media files. They retrieve the source files and send them to the cloud for transcoding in the smaller, mezzanine formats. They can enter metadata into defined fields. They can set content protection rules.

Trouble to Resolution

This process journey involves understanding how a particular issue might turn into a customer requesting assistance. This normally means someone in operations raising a support ticket and then working to ensure the issue is resolved in a timely way, on a pre-agreed timeline.

Finally, stakeholders are a key element. They are your own constituents that have ownership of a process stage or the specific touch-points that are providing the negative experience.

Many companies have proven to launch similar products much later than their competitors but with a much better approach in terms of UX and, consequently, better UI. Google Search was a great example. This can prove to be a differentiator in your business too.

Usage to Cash

B2B platforms pioneered the ability for customers to self-serve their account needs and this has become another important area that must serve customers well. Again, in the case of OVPs, the portal dashboard becomes the go-to destination to check usage of the platform, make service requests and download bills too. The billing details, or the bill literal, must take great care to mention your company, as well as the services you are using.

Paying for UX/UI

Paying for UX design

Most people perceive that a UI services company would be best placed to produce the UI interfaces as well as map the UX journey. I would caution on this. Separate UX work from UI work in order to get a fully objective perspective on the customer's needs. This checks-and-balances approach also helps provide two lenses on customer pain-points, potentially doubling your solution options. UX design teams can be easily found in major capital cities these days and even major consulting firms provide these specialised services. Fees vary but reputable ones can start from US$5,000 a day and upwards. So, how many days do you need? The answer would be to try a Google design sprint. They are designed to be completed in five days and I've personally had success with this. A well-organised five-day sprint will be enough to get stakeholders to map the customer journey and agree on the personas. Only one or two days are needed to then create a prototype and show that to the 'customer' (internal or external). You might need to allow another day for the design team to produce the final artefacts as well, so all in all it should take eight working days.

Take note that customer journey maps are living documents. They need to be updated regularly as your market landscape changes. Customers' needs change from time to time and these need to be captured again to ascertain if your service provides new pain-points or gaps for them. With enough acquired skill you and your team can do these yourselves collectively.

Paying for UI design

Once you've completed your UX customer journey maps, these become inputs that you can feed to your UI team. Similarly to the UX process, you can outsource this to a partner or you can decide to absorb this in-house but it would depend on the complexity of the work involved. If you have more than one application or one that is very comprehensive then you should opt for the latter. There will always be a need to tweak designs, cater to hardware updates or even new ideas that should be adopted. Like UX design, it is imperative to get a good head start and an outsourced partner with best practices gleaned from many other products is more than helpful. Companies well known in the design and development space in media include Accedo, Flow Left, Massive Interactive, Ratio and Tiger Spike. Once you've launched in the market, you should be able to take it in-house to manage the incremental changes needed with a smaller, core team.

At the very least, if you're running a small team from the outset you can simply decide that getting customer feedback is important before you start and every time you have just shipped a new build of your software. Talk to customers and give them mock-ups to gain a feel for how your product works. These can be as simple as Microsoft PowerPoint designs that look and feel like a website. There are also services like Wix or Netlify that offer a fast but beautiful way to create websites. Use these too if you want in order to get a very accurate representation of your product. No coding is required.

Multi-device management

This has become a serious issue with the proliferation of operating systems (OS) and devices. Of the major mobile operating systems, currently there are only iOS and Android. However, iOS itself has several device types to manage when designs are updated. There are several iPhone and iPad versions with different screen sizes. Android has many more manufacturers with their own screen sizes – Samsung, HTC and Xiaomi to name a few. Then there are Smart TV types and streaming device types like Roku, Apple TV and Amazon Fire. These are on a different OS each. Operators these days must choose to either manage these device changes with a team of additional persons or use configuration platforms. Of the latter, Accedo is again the best known, offering a cloud-based product known as Accedo Control. Operators using this can make certain changes and deploy them to the numerous apps they've created in a seamless experience. However, there is an extra cost to using a service like this so the balance is between hiring people to manage this or automating it. I would advise automation only if you are publishing to so many devices that this becomes too tedious and menial for one person. Human talents are better put into time spent perfecting the end-user experience and research required around that.

Key takeaways

- **For everyone:** succeeding in streaming media means focusing on what the end user's needs are and exceeding those needs
- **For everyone:** it takes a dedicated product team to unearth customer needs/feedback for product improvements
- **For everyone:** map the customer journey and document it so that you can continuously revisit and improve how the journey should be

6

Identity access management

Registering on websites is a standard experience today, particularly if you are accessing important news, premium content or just vital business information at work. It is easier, thanks to the convenience of using our social media accounts as well. The cost and effort of managing it isn't quite that easy. It has spawned an entire industry known as Customer Identity and Access Management (CIAM) or just Identity Access Management (IAM).

The reason is that businesses have to move beyond just 'clicks' on a website to be truly effective. And beyond simply registering people. At the most basic, it is about being able to identify your customers in order to provide them with the service they need in a personalised way. This gives them a better experience too. Key to this is giving certain users *authorisation* to use your service and then levels of *entitlement* to appropriate features. Hence, you will need data to reveal:

1. Who these end users are
2. Where they are located
3. What they like in general
4. What they like from your service
5. What they have purchased from you
6. What they are entitled to watch (if they have a Pay TV account)
7. What they have watched and are likely to watch more of in future

Since personal data is the most sensitive part of managing any streaming media service, you are using IAM to generate a win-win outcome for end users and your business. Not exploitation of them. But let's start with how you register your end users the right way.

Identity data

An end user's identity data can come from a variety of sources. We can basically break this down to belonging to these three categories:

1. System data
2. Registration data
3. Behavioural data

System data

This is essentially information that comes from your IP (internet protocol) address, your device or your browser. In the case of IP address, a fixed IP is always associated with you. Thus, it can reveal things like your country or state and even down to which town you're in. It's not personally identifiable but the same service provider that knows your IP address is usually your local internet service provider (ISP) or telecommunications company (telco). So, they do know who you are. When IP addresses are dynamic, i.e. not fixed, this can be a bit of a problem in terms of identifying users on the internet. This occurs when IP addresses are limited and are usually re-issued to different end users. In this case, the media access control (MAC) address, which is an ID for your device, comes in handy. Finally, there is the dreaded tracking cookie. These are used by sites and get deposited into your browser each time you visit a site. Tracking cookies are effectively a form of ID tagged to you to understand your needs better.

Registration data

This is the all-important data that you'll need up front in order to successfully set up accounts for your end users. Best practices for registration can be divided into the following three areas: traditional registration, progressive profiling and conditional profiling. Traditional registration aims to just get enough details, short of payment information, and the basics are shown in Table 6.1.

If you want more, consider getting it progressively. For example, the user's date of birth and gender are additional data that is important in

Table 6.1 The essentials for registration are just these, especially if payment isn't required

First name	This is used for correspondence salutation
Last name	Used in the database if the first name is common
Email	The unique identifier or unique ID of your user
Password	Password
Confirm password	Good to capture it again so that the user knows it
Company	Only if the website is catering to business customers and if so, the email should be from a work domain, and personal ones (Gmail, Hotmail, etc.) be disallowed

understanding overall user demographics. So is their city/town location if you're operating internationally. You may want to wait for the user to log in five times before coming forth to ask for gender. And maybe five more logins before asking for the rest. This proves that you're eager to build trust after the user is becoming more engaged with your website. It is important to build trust and the user will give it to you if they feel that you are trustworthy. Anyway, if a user doesn't come back then you saved yourself and them some time. Progressive profiling is ideal when you run an ad-funded service since you can subsequently specifically target advertising at end users who are only female, for example.

Conditional profiling is when you potentially gather new data as a result of a specific action that an end user makes. In a business-to-business (B2B) example, if a registered user downloads a specific white paper or report on a new product, you could ask if they are intending to make a purchase soon or still evaluating based on specific criteria. In a business-to-consumer (B2C) example, it could be asking certain lifestyle questions.

Behavioural data

This data could come from a variety of observations, many of which are not truly perfect. Here is a list of the key behaviours that are obtained after some time:

1. Purchase history
2. Viewing history

3. Likes and queries
4. Browsing history
5. Search history

The first three are called explicit or declarative behaviour. These are clear indications from the end user regarding their preferences. The best source is purchase history, which is supremely helpful in transactional video on demand (TVOD) services and the hybrid TVOD/SVOD (subscription video on demand) equivalent. Buying implies a commitment to something (although I'm sure we all remember that we've regretted a purchase in the past or just recently). But it is still definitive of an end user's taste. That's why it is best paired with another desirable behaviour trait which is literally the watching of individual media titles, which becomes a powerful trait to exploit. In SVOD or advertising-funded video on demand (AVOD) services, a watch history is the only way to determine an end user's preference.

Netflix pioneered the practice of 'seeding' preference. By asking new subscribers to describe their favourite genres or actors up front, it was clearly signalling its intentions to help personalise content. This has to be handled delicately since not everyone can easily describe a favourite and many people are guided by group decisions as well as their own moods. That's why Netflix pioneered the art of recommending based on a user watching a particular title. It's an easy way to start the personalisation from the outset but limit the chance of early errors.

Other behavioural data is usually related to end users' 'liking' or 'rating' of content. Titles that are rated as favourable or unfavourable by the end user show a definite intent towards watching something similar or avoiding it, although that 'something' is not usually clear until multiple purchases reveal a pattern. A 'watchlist' or 'watch later' list is just as valuable since some users prefer this to liking content. Again, it is the pattern which is more valuable than just the individual titles themselves.

Then comes implicit or non-declarative behaviour. Clicking on 'more info' can be classified in this category. Then there is information like categories that a particular user browses through consistently or titles that a user clicks on but doesn't act on. Search results are important since they can reveal a lot about a product or service that you've just launched. The more ambiguous attempts are when systems try to tell users apart by time of day (e.g. the mother watches in the daytime and the father watches late at night), or by the speed of keystrokes being typed (a reference to people who are older).

The best way to ensure accurate observation of behaviour is to create separate viewer profiles. Netflix has pioneered this towards ensuring that its service is truly personalised. Not only do users get even more accurate recommendations, but they create a space that is truly meant for them. It's beneficial for parents because children also get to see content that is only meant for them. Profiles are almost considered sub-accounts within the main account and can be complex to manage. But this will give you the best and most granular access to viewing data.

Browse and search history work well, even as aggregate data. Examined at regular intervals, this can provide insights into what content is in demand. What are the more popular search terms each day and week? What are the trends? If people are seeking content that you are not surfacing through your recommendations or curation, is there an inherent flaw in your discovery experience?

Authorisation of users

Many services allow unfettered access to some content as a way to giving them a sample of how the service works. Even some sites that flourish on subscription payments tend to allow a certain amount of content to be consumed before requesting payment. In the industry (and to be discussed in depth in Chapter 7) this strategy is known as a *paywall*. After all, content comes at a great cost and needs to be monetised at some point. Thus, the registration feature of your site is meant to identify those customers with whom you want to build a meaningful relationship. For a reasonable fee, they can access what you offer. For such paying custo-mers, registration is one way to make sure you know who those people are when they come visiting.

Registration and authentication

The first step is to register your customer or end user and grant them access. But you'll need basic information about these users in order to easily communicate to them. This is known as *first-party data* since end users are providing it willingly as part of registering. As mentioned before, an email address and password are usually enough to begin with. Email addresses are unique already so don't force a customer to provide a separate user ID. They might give you a miss altogether. However, since anyone can impersonate people by just using an email address, it is standard practice to require a validation check, ideally with something that the end user has close to him or her, like a mobile phone. This is usually executed via an email sent to the user's own email address with a request to respond back by clicking on a shared link. And this link should have an expiration date to make sure the verifier doesn't forget. This almost guarantees that the person who offered the email address is actually confirming who they are. Sometimes a mobile number is also used as a contact and a one-time password (OTP) sent. The user has to key that OTP into the browser as confirmation. This additional request does not replace the email link verification, it acts as a mandatory backup or a second layer of authentication. Officially, it is also known as two-factor authentication (2FA) due to the two ways needed to verify a user's identity. If not already doing so, your organisation should be employing 2FA.

For those who want something a little bit more secure, you can also opt for knowledge-based authentication (KBA). This is executed by simply asking the end user to save one or two (or three!) questions with answers that the end user simply cannot forget. This can replace 2FA but is vulnerable to hacking if the answers are stored somewhere or available on social media (including answers that are provided to obvious questions like 'Where were you born?'). KBA can also be considered intrusive by customers. Furthermore, I don't encourage both KBA and 2FA to be instituted in your service since this is a high-friction experience and will deter many would-be registrants of your service. You're supposed to acquire as many customers as possible and many services believe that this is justifiable against the risk that a small set of customers may try to commit fraud.

For public services, you also need to ensure that you are protecting the personal details being provided by the user and this means obtaining consent for at least two reasons. The first is the consent to your standard terms and conditions. The second is for situations where you might need to share their personal details with a third party. This is explored in more detail below (see the section covering personal data protection). Suffice to say, once you've obtained consent, you can allow your customer to use your service. For this reason, registration is also known as 'signing up', whereby the customer signs up to use a service after agreeing to the relevant conditions (except that they tick a box instead of physically signing anything).

Registration may or may not involve payment but if it does then this is succeeded by the payment method registration and provision of a billing address. This is where you ask for more information, so go ahead and do so. But if you aren't asking for payment then make sure your registration details cover only what you need.

Single sign-on (SSO) registration

Single sign-on is an extension of registration's powerful capabilities because it solves the problem of users having to register when they visit several sites that may belong to one parent organisation. It would be unpleasant to re-register another username and password and then go through the login steps each time you visited those sites. End users would often create the same credentials but be frustrated at the need to duplicate their registration. SSO was created as a solution for this. A good example is when you visit your organisation's various intranet sites. Perhaps it is your human resources administration portal or a finance portal or an online library offered to employees. Perhaps they were commissioned or deployed in the company at different times by different vendors. But since employers have a unique ID (the employee ID), it quickly made sense for employees to be able to register that and be remembered every time they visited an associated site. Best practices also dictate that they should be logged in to the new site as long as they've already logged in elsewhere. For consumer sites, it could be a telco that offers an online video service to watch content and then also has a site where users can check their personal telco bills. Both are different sites but can use the same user ID, thus allowing SSO to be utilised.

Social login registration

Social logins extend the concept of SSO by using social media logins. In this case, their favourite social media site has verified them and is a possible identity provider. Plus, end users get to choose the social login that they prefer. If an end user creates a Facebook account, the user is assumed to be authenticated by Facebook. Later, when the user visits another site to read some content and Facebook is allowed as a social login, it would be easier to just let the site contact Facebook (with the user's consent) and then log the user in. It's extremely quick due to the frictionless user experience and the user doesn't have to worry about creating another password to remember. The double convenience is highly compelling.

The trade-off is that users agree to share the personal data already given to Facebook as first-party data to your service. So, right away, you're getting access to more information with just once click. Some social media sites gather more details than others. Either way, as you can see from Table 6.2, there is a rich set of available first-party data. Your development team will be able to access the social media site's developer documentation (also called *software development kit* or SDK) to access the application programming interfaces (APIs). Again, social login is great for easy access and more suited to websites that are ad-funded or have a freemium model. In the latter, you can start with social media as

Table 6.2 A comparison of first-party data potentially available via social media networks

	Facebook	Twitter	LinkedIn
First name	x	x	x
Last name	x	x	x
Email	x	x	x
Birthday	x	x	
Gender	x	x	
City	x	x	
State	x	x	x
Country	x	x	x
Postal code	x		
Interests	x		
Likes	x		
Activities	x		x
Education	x	x	x
Work	x	x	x
Relationship status	x		

a login and then ask for the necessary extra details when an end user decides to upgrade. But should a customer revoke permission to use their social identity on your service, you'll have no choice but to comply.

Data privacy of users

In the early days of the internet people were generally naive about how their privacy could be invaded via simple scams. Identity theft gradually became a focus topic. If you watched the 1995 movie *The Net* you'd have been surprised at how easily this could occur and what the implications were. Even worse, personal contact details like phone numbers or emails would be collected by a site and then illicitly passed on to third parties who would then try to sell all kinds of products. Hence, spam was born. Today, most countries have enacted regulation that covers such personally identifiable information (PII) and this is commonly known as personal data protection (PDP) and is governed by a personal data protection act (PDPA). It sets a baseline for minimum standards and may be superseded by other types of regulation. Consult your legal counsel about how this applies to your service, especially if you're making it available in multiple countries, since each country has unique requirements.

If you're thinking and feeling alarmed at the need to collect information, you can rest assured that company employees generally are exempt from this. Business contact information is also exempt. Certain public bodies may also be nominated as being exempt from PDP compliance. Again, check your country's actual PDPA clauses or consult your internal legal counsel.

However, all the above aside, it is important to understand what your needs are before approaching CIAM service providers to propose and quote on your offering. They will be able to tell you what's possible with their services.

The recent introduction of the General Data Protection Regulation (GDPR) has introduced more concern among businesses whose end users reside in the European Union (EU). GDPR provides just one set of regulations covering data protection in that region but it has very stringent requirements beyond that of a PDPA. For the first time, the general public not only has a right to inspect how their data has been used by collecting bodies (your company) but they also have the power to revoke that right and have the data deleted. In your specific region or country, new regulations may surface. GDPR is discussed separately below.

Entitlement of users

Once registered, it is then important to consider who gets access to what. Due to your own policies, some of your end users may have access to a certain type of content or features and others may have unlimited access. It is important to deal with such entitlements. They can take the following forms:

1. Offer entitlements
2. Premium entitlements
3. Flow-through entitlements

Offer entitlements are those based on a specific market offer chosen by an end user. Take Dropbox, for example. They offer a free service, a premium service and also a business-needs service. Each is priced differently and actually progressively higher since it supports more complicated or high-usage needs. It makes sense if customers start out using only a little of a service or are still experimenting with it. If you took the low offer, at some stage you might decide to upgrade. Or you might be content with the low offer for the foreseeable future.

Premium entitlements can exist where there is a freemium model. The non-paying customer gets the basic, free service and may put up with ads from time to time while using the service. But at least, by logging in, they will be able to be identified and served somewhat relevant ads. Customers who are willing to subscribe will get the benefit of an ad-free, or premium experience. Your service's registration feature will need to store those differing entitlements. Spotify is a great example of a service that leverages this. But advertising doesn't have to be the differentiator between two offerings. Some websites like LinkedIn make the distinction between basic user profiles and those that provide better insights and exclusive features. This commands a premium.

Flow-through entitlements are designed to protect a purchase that is made offline or from a different sales channel but is still attributed to and enjoyed by the same end user. This is typically found in the Pay TV industry. Broadcasters provide subscribers with online access to their TV packages and these mirror that of what's available on their TV package. This is part of the TV Anywhere concept that is so often talked about in the broadcast industry. One of the benefits of this is a feature known as Catch-up TV. If you missed the latest episode of your favourite TV show you can 'catch up' on it right after it ends by watching it online. But if you subscribed to the sports package on TV but not the movies package, then you just have access to the sports channels. That is also what you get when you browse your smartphone app and log in. If you choose a rental or TVOD movie from your TV service, it shouldn't just be available on your set-top box. You should also be able to watch it on your device whilst commuting on the train.

How entitlements work

How an entitlement works technically is that when you've registered and logged in, the registration system actually has access to your Pay TV account number from the registration data (which you would have provided) and is capable of 'looking up' in a database to see what packages you have subscribed to. Then whenever you press play, the video player makes a call back to the database to determine whether or not that video belongs to the TV package you've subscribed to. If the answer is yes, then that's good. It will also check to see if your account is in arrears. If the answer is yes, then you can't watch anything since non-payment usually overrides any other rule. The video player then displays an error message meant just for you.

Operators should also be able to understand why end users watch what they watch, so that they can improve the service to the end users with recommendations and other levels of personalisation. That's the basic need. The benefit to your business and your end user has to be weighed against the safeguards that you must put in place. These comprise both legal requirements and also industry requirements, both of which may change from country to country. You really need to understand all this before you launch something.

The last is pertinent since it allows ad-funded services to run targeted advertising. The last thing people want is to be shown a video pre-roll that is advertising something totally irrelevant to their gender or basic needs. People expect advertising to be intelligent enough (paid-for sponsorship announcements are excluded from this though). The higher standard is that relevant advertising is just better for everyone since it might actually find a more receptive audience that will result in better ad click-through rates. And that's what all advertisers prefer. A more benign advantage of knowing what you've watched is to allow content recommendations to be offered. This is possible and even desirable since it helps people find more content that they care about. Also, a viewing history is helpful in terms of vetting a complaint. If a customer bought a video rental and claimed a refund citing download issues, a brief check might reveal if the customer actually did watch it, and at what time. This allows services to defend their revenue.

Aside from this, your end users should only access content based on specific policies in place. Maybe some content studios haven't given you access to download rights but some do. Storing these policies in a look-up table will then allow them to be viewable and enforceable.

Let's get a little deeper.

IAM for better customer engagement

Once you have the ability to collect and connect the right information, it is important to be able to leverage what you have and convert as many of your customers as possible into loyal ones. You already have the tools to be able to understand what they like or want. In marketing, this is known as Customer Relationship Management (CRM). What does IAM have to do with CRM? A lot. A fundamental aspect of marketing strategy is to identify market segments and target the ones that you believe will be receptive to your value proposition. Within broader segments, there will be many more that you identify based on their use of their product. Who are the loyal users? Who are on the fringe? Who are not engaging with you at all? With data from IAM on hand, you'll be able to identify these segments and then communicate to them in the right way – whether it be to provide useful onboarding information or to announce newly arrived content that they might like. CRM systems comprise deployment tools that allow you to send text messages, in-app/browser notifications or emails.

Compliance

As we already know by now, IAM is an industry that deals in highly sensitive information. With that comes an ever-increasing need to be aware of industry and regulatory compliances that exist. Let's examine these from a high-level view.

Protecting children

One of many key concerns that can be addressed by IAM is how to ensure children are catered for and protected as end users of your service. From a registration perspective it is important to note that most services are only available to adults, with 18 years being the most common minimum age for allowing registration. It may also be a regulatory requirement, so take note that this is usually accompanied by a need to either prove your age or at least capture your date of birth at the very outset with your consent. It's difficult to prove age so it's normally just a formality. Some countries issue identification cards so it's possible that more stringent methods like 'liveness' detection is paired with the identification card. This requires a 'selfie' to be taken with a mobile phone, then uploaded with the photo of the card itself. Technology detects that the selfie and the photo are the same person.

Firstly, if your service is targeting tweens then your success with them will be setting them up as potentially loyal users. What many sites do is allow a parent to nominate a second user or sub-account holder and assign that to their child. That's a great practice since you can allow the parent to monitor usage while exerting a level of influence. But that still means learning how to cater to the child's needs successfully.

Secondly, you're solving genuine parental concerns about what their children are capable of watching/reading. For streaming media companies the solution is easy: enforce the relevant content classification guidelines pertinent to each country. Where content is restricted, it is customary to allow parents or account holders to set viewing controls. The most common is the verifying code feature. This is usually a simple four- or six-digit code that the account holder sets as a prerequisite to playback starting. The request for the code is invoked when certain classified content is selected and you can even let the account holder determine what level of classifications are suitable. Would it only be for titles rated R18/R21? Should it apply to titles rated PG-13? You get to decide. Even if you think access doesn't need to be controlled by a parent, take note that regulatory bodies often decide otherwise.

General Data Protection Regulation (GDPR)

As mentioned earlier, data privacy and protection has been strengthened in the EU with the introduction of GDPR which became public law in May 2018, replacing Data Protection Directive 95/46/EC. That also includes better enforcement of the new regulations. As long as your service has an office in the EU region and you process data on just one EU citizen, GDPR applies to you. In the light of recent controversies surrounding the social media giant Facebook and the shadowy Cambridge Analytica, this is a pertinent issue today. People are a lot more concerned about how their data is used for any kind of gain, and are mistrustful of data gatherers. Businesses have to be more diligent to avoid massive fallout that could have implications on their bottom line. In simple terms, Table 6.3 shows the changes.

It would be prudent to read the entire legislation and retain legal advice on how to best comply with GDPR. Unfortunately, that isn't all of it. Countries also have anti-spam or opt-in and opt-out regulations that you have to comply with. These cover a variety of use-cases right down to how often you can contact someone to compliance with do-not-call databases.

GDPR makes a clear distinction between data processes and data collectors. A controller is defined as the organisation that determines the purposes and means of processing personal data. As a media company with IAM in place, it is obvious that your organisation would be classed as a data controller. You will be required to implement the appropriate level of technical and organisational measures to be compliant, while your service providers would be data processors by definition. Data processors handle the data for analysis and insights. Both parties can be penalised for non-compliance and, at the time of writing, the penalties range from €20 million to 4 per cent of global revenue, whichever is higher.

The best way to handle GDPR and any kind of personal data policy is to remember why such regulations exist. Other than to obtain consent

Table 6.3 A summary of GDPR changes over existing regulation in the EU region

	Before May 2018	Today
Clear language	Often businesses explained their privacy policies in lengthy and complicated terms	Privacy policies will have to be written in clear, straightforward language
Consent from user	Businesses sometimes assumed that the end user's silence meant consent to data processing, or they hid a request for consent in long, legalistic terms and conditions – that nobody reads	The end user will need to give an affirmative consent before his/her data can be used by a business. Silence is no consent
More transparency	The end user might not have been informed when his/her data was transferred outside the EU	Businesses will need to clearly inform the end user about such transfers
	Sometimes businesses collected and processed personal data for different purposes than for the reason initially announced without informing the end user	Businesses will be able to collect and process data only for a well-defined purpose. They will have to inform the end user about new purposes for processing
	Businesses used algorithms to make decisions about the end user based on his/her personal data (e.g. when applying for a loan); the end user was often unaware	Businesses will have to inform the user whether the decision is automated and give him/her a possibility to contest it
Stronger rights	Often businesses did not inform end users when there was a data breach, for instance when the data was stolen	Businesses will have to inform end users without delay in case of harmful data breach. This is usually within 72 hours
	Often the end user could not take his/her data from a business and move it to another rival service	The end user will be able to move his/her data, for instance to another social media platform
	It was difficult for the end user to get a copy of the data businesses kept about him/her	The end user will have the right to access and get a copy of his/her data that a business has on him/her
	It was difficult for an end user to have his/her data deleted	End users will have a clearly defined 'right to be forgotten' (right to erasure), with clear safeguards

(*Continued*)

Table 6.3 (Cont.)

	Before May 2018	Today
Stronger enforcement	Data protection authorities had limited means and powers to cooperate	The European Data Protection Board grouping all member data protection authorities, will have the powers to provide guidance and interpretation and adopt binding decisions in case several EU countries are concerned by the same case
	Authorities had no or limited fines at their disposal in case a business violated the rules	The member data protection authorities will have harmonised powers and will be able to impose fines on businesses of up to €20 million or 4 per cent of worldwide turnover

fairly, companies should demonstrate that there is a legitimate need to collect the information. The legitimacy must be seen as a win-win for both the end user and yourself. If both parties agree with that when your site is visited for the first time, chances are that you'll be registering plenty of friendly people in no time.

Other compliance

Don't forget accessibility compliance. The visually impaired also use the internet and may not be able to participate fully in certain registration flows. Overarching guidelines governing the internet come in the form of Web Content Accessibility Guidelines (WCAG). There are variances in other countries or jurisdictions, like the Americans with Disabilities Act. With so many countries to think of, take note of major territories and their needs. India – with its 1.4 billion population being the world's second largest – is considering legislation that protects data sovereignty. This mandates any personal data of its population being kept within the country itself. Just think about that as a consequence if it passes into law. If you had a dozen data centres around the world, you potentially couldn't do business in India unless you had a data centre there as well.

Federated identity management

If you wanted to take SSO one step further, your organisation and other like-minded ones could allow SSO to extend to each other as well. It is rare for enterprises to actually do this and the use-case applies to government departments in allowing citizens to easily use various e-government sites easily. In Singapore, all government services allow the national ID to be used as a unique username (albeit with 2FA) to access important needs like checking tax assessments, paying fines or applying for licences.

In your situation, you may be working with content partners who provide channels on TV but access to video on demand in their own website or app instead of yours. You may decide to not host the content yourself. However, a federated identity management allows your users the flexibility of using their username and accessing the service as a TV Anywhere feature, particularly if they've already paid for the TV subscription. Some technical integration is required since your content partner will need to also check the normal entitlements like payment status.

Paying for IAM services

As part of the fundamentals espoused in this book, the decision to use cloud-based service providers is the default decision, with the reasons for choosing an on-premises or 'on-prem' solution the exception. In the case of IAM, there will be a range of reasons to lean towards the cloud model.

First of all, the cost of hardware and security will be difficult to predict and scaling up at the outset is always difficult to forecast. Do you over design your hardware needs? That would potentially waste money. But you can't under-design since if people have trouble signing up then you'll get a backlash on social media.

Secondly, the stringent requirements for storage and protection of data are even more difficult. This is all the more critical if you operate in multiple countries worldwide. Regulatory landscapes change overnight with new governments or the whims of politicians. It is best to let a service provider be accountable for this and so they will; their commitment to their many clients will be dictated by this. Best practices can also be shared with your team, especially in relation to the use of analytics stemming from the data itself. How can you best use it? How will you integrate with your CRM systems?

Cloud-based CIAM providers typically charge an annual licence fee for the basic service, which is typically only for registration. You will come across the term registration-as-a-service (or RaaS). Expect the licence fee to rise as you add SSO and social logins. Additional fees would be charged for the number of users that you end up registering. Professional services also come into play when it comes to any integration with your own system or other vendors like CRM providers. In this situation, the golden rule applies: the integration fee should be negotiable if both parties have done the integration elsewhere before. But for companies that also need some form of 'hand-holding', expect to use a set number of professional services hours per month for knowledge transfer to happen as you grow your business and try to make sense of how to take action on the data. CIAM providers have their own dashboards, their own unique way of representing data and reporting it to you. These types of services fees should be limited to a set number of hours in a set time frame that allows you to flexibly consume it (like within months instead of weeks).

Additionally, make sure that your CIAM provider is also GDPR-compliant, as the ability to hold or delete data – as well as to reveal it to its owner – is mandatory. When in doubt, go for the best, first and strongest at meeting compliance, as well as proving global coverage. There is nothing more frustrating than growing faster than your service provider and having them hold you back for lack of preparedness or simply in meeting new jurisdictional requirements. In this case, CIAM is one area of streaming media where that need overrides the cheapest options. The risk to your business is far too great.

Key takeaways

- **For everyone**: registration helps in identifying and managing your users in return for giving them a better experience with your service
- **For everyone**: seek to provide a frictionless experience as much as possible, including using methods or registration like progressive profiling

- **For content owners**: strive for family accounts with parent-friendly controls. Respect content classification guidelines and regulatory bodies, whichever is more stringent
- **For everyone**: work with service providers who are experts and can hold you up to the highest standards of personal data governance (like GDPR), as well helping you scale across jurisdictions when you need to

Commercialising your service

The commercial model for public-facing streaming media services is still one that faces the greatest scrutiny. Some regions can be highly lucrative but also highly competitive. As we've read in Chapter 3, piracy is also a major influence. That doesn't mean you can't pursue successful strategies that are profitable.

How 'windows' affect content availability

We definitely aren't referring to the operating system here. Content can command a high price if it is considered either new or premium. Or even better, both! To understand how this strategy works, it is best to take a look at how Hollywood and other media owners in entertainment handle their 'distribution windows'. Distributing their titles isn't just about finding ways to get out to the public, it's about ensuring each distributor has enough time to monetise one window before a distributor handling the next window takes their turn. This naturally has a better financial outcome for the studio while making all their distribution partners a lot happier as well.

Cinema window

The global cinema box office is still where most revenue for a movie is generated and a sign of prestige. While the title is en route to cinemas or currently showing, it will be generating plenty of publicity. Making it big in the box office means you can reasonably expect that the other windows will perform well. Cinema windows are generally no more than two months for the average movie since attendance often starts strong before petering out to such a point that it is no longer beneficial to the cinema exhibitors.

Standard DVD window

The next stage is the home or DVD window. Plenty of homes in developed countries still have DVD players so this is potentially another big revenue earner. Plus, if a movie has been a box office hit, it is still fresh in the minds of the public at this stage. The DVD window usually lasts from two to 12 months for rentals, with retail continuing as long as there is market demand for it.

Transactional video on demand (TVOD) window

This specific window was created to initially cater for Pay TV companies wanting to augment their subscription revenue. Movies can either be rented by accessing near-video on demand (NVOD) channels (which play back a movie repeatedly) or downloaded into the set-top box for playback during the specified rental period. It has, however, grown and become an established window that is highly prized by various operators, from hotels to airline in-flight entertainment systems. Apple has since claimed a strong reputational, and arguably, market-leading role in this window thanks to the dominance of iTunes. It is the default platform to purchase audio-visual entertainment from Apple, including movies and TV shows, from any device but with the added ability to then share across multiple devices.

Pay TV window and subscription video on demand (SVOD) window

In developed markets, the penetration of Pay TV services in homes is high, ranging from 50 per cent to as high as 90 per cent even. This particular window is where the majority of TV users will fall in, despite the trend of 'cord-cutting' that's been espoused by researchers and the industry alike. Most Pay TV operators have reacted to ensure that they provide great, if not exclusive content, as well as excellent TV Anywhere experiences.

The Pay TV window is usually where premium linear channel premieres, like an HBO or a Fox Movies channel, get to showcase the movies to a larger market of audiences. This market is far larger than TVOD since the audiences have already paid for the subscription and may be looking forward to the Saturday night premiere of a movie (plus, remember that TVOD is a transactional model and not highly consumed by subscribers). This is also where SVOD rights are tied to when it comes to the streaming media players like Netflix and Amazon Prime.

Broadcast window

The final TV window goes to free-to-air TV, which traditionally is seen as the poorer relative to Pay TV, for obvious reasons. Broadcasters are ad-funded so only the ones with national coverage and high viewership will have the ability to screen movies. Licensing terms and window periods are flexible but generally very few movies make it to this stage unless the broadcaster feels it can find the right advertiser and the right time slot.

Release windows have been increasingly disrupted in the internet age, not just with shrinking windows, but with simultaneous or near-simultaneous releases. For the former, this first occurred in Hollywood when Steven Soderbergh's indie movie *Bubble* was released in cinemas, on DVD and on Pay TV in January 2006. It is unlikely that this will be common as cinema exhibitors continue to command leverage over the Hollywood studios when it comes to major blockbusters. The most commonly seen today are movies going to TVOD very soon after a cinema release and before the Pay TV window. But such opportunities command a premium and remain exceptions to the norm. Even rarer is if a movie goes to SVOD very soon after a cinema release.

Exclusivity and holdbacks

Content exclusivity is an important bargaining factor in any operator's strategy since this creates a unique selling proposition. For example, at the time of writing, *Game of Thrones*, the worldwide hit TV series, is so popular that it has provided Pay TV operators with a way to avoid customer churn. If it isn't available on Netflix and is hard to source on the internet, then sticking to your Pay TV provider might be the best choice for the fans. These companies know that and continue to invest in exclusive live events like major sports tournaments or the Olympic Games.

Exclusivity in a certain window also allows you to then enforce hold-backs. A good example is if an operator gets TVOD rights for a particular studio's current titles. It may decide that it wants to negotiate holdback rights so that the first Pay TV subscription window is delayed further. This gives the operator maximum opportunities to maximise its own window, which can be deemed anti-competitive. This fact was proven in 2012 when the UK's Competition Commission ruled that satellite-based Pay TV operator Sky had such a stranglehold on exclusivity of movies on its linear channel and its SVOD offering during the Pay TV window that consumers would have no choice but to sign up with them to get access to fresh titles. This effectively constituted an anti-competitive advantage over rivals like Virgin Media and BT Vision.

Studios are not afraid to strike exclusive deals that are beneficial and in their interest. In 2012, Netflix made such a deal with Disney to bring major titles to the platform during the first Pay TV window.[1] This included first-run live-action and animated feature films. In an interesting twist, only a few years later, Disney signalled that they would not renew their deal in anticipation of their own foray into streaming media.

The advertising model

The basics of video advertising

The primary means of advertising are within the player itself, or in-player. They are usually referred to as 'rolls'. These are literally videos and can be classed with the prefix of Pre, Mid or End. Media planners in the marketing world also call them 'spots', an inheritance from the broadcast TV world. The pre-roll was the earliest version and virtually guaranteed a 'view' from the audience since you couldn't skip past it. But it annoys people (depending on length) and the increase in this annoyance factor can be measured by how many people cancel their intention of viewing the original video instead. This is known as 'drop-off'. The pre-roll has evolved to allow a 'skippable' view, or greatly reduced duration to maintain a 'non-skippable' view. If you follow the latter, it is highly recommended to make the pre-roll last no more than five seconds. Even a 'skippable' ad shouldn't last more than 15 seconds.

End-rolls were the next evolution of in-player advertising and seem to be the most innocuous to customers. You only see it when the video ends but that really means there are two factors that will affect its success. Firstly, viewers may be unlikely to view it if they have dropped out of the video before it ends. Secondly, viewers may tend to be distracted by searching for the next video or doing something else away from it. And there's no guarantee they'll view the ad until the end if it's too long.

Mid-rolls have come about in a contentious manner. After media planners realised that they were limited by the amount of advertising opportunities to just two spots (and thus, with no way to increase revenue possibilities), it was decided that mid-rolls were the next step. In theory, mid-rolls are a great idea since the ad can be placed in strategic areas that allow for a suitable pause or timing with a product placement. You can also create opportunities for as many mid-roll spots as you wish, which is good for longer-form videos that are popular. The downside is that too many ads will just create potential points for viewers to drop off the player altogether. You have to strike a delicate balance between the number of ads (and hence your revenue) and your audience churning out in droves.

All advertising in a player should come with a timer countdown so that viewers understand how long an ad will command their attention. The primary goal is making sure your ad is reaching the right person. The secondary goal should be the message and the level of creativity executed to gain that person's attention.

Interactive Advertising Bureau (IAB) for standardisation

The IAB was founded in 1996 and its efforts enable standardisation within the media and marketing industries that allow them to thrive in the digital economy (take note that in this context the word media refers to any site or digital space that provides advertising opportunities, and not any traditional or streaming media service). As of 2018, its membership comprises more than 650 leading media and technology companies that are responsible for selling, delivering and optimising digital advertising or marketing campaigns.

Among its most important standards that affect streaming media today are VAST and VPAID.

VAST stands for video ad-serving template. This simply refers to an XML file that contains various metadata (specifically tags) that come from the ad decision server, describing the ad itself. These tags will have bearing on what the video player can do when it receives such an ad.

VPAID stands for video player-ad interface definition. This simply refers to a standard for communication between the ads and the video players. This standard was an important introduction since it allowed all ad servers to operate on a common framework for advertising, which could then be extended to the video players too. Without this, every ad network would create ads using its proprietary technology and then embed that technology in the video player. That would effectively mean that ads would need to be created to cater for different platforms and that would be a huge burden on the ad decision services.

Together, VAST and VPAID are standards that have been accepted by the majority of the industry vendors. Making sure your video player, and your advertising model in general, is compliant with both standards ensures that you can maximise your ability to find media agencies or advertisers and, hence, your revenue.

YouTube advertising overview

With the acquisition of DoubleClick (an ad-serving platform) Google started to build an advertising ecosystem on YouTube and beyond that made sense for users, partners (broadcasters) and advertisers. This was obviously pre-rolls to begin with, but even then, the innovation that was introduced was always user-centric. In 2009, it tested skippable pre-rolls, integrating Google products like AdWords and enlarging the pool of advertising campaigns that focused on using video ads. The brand has come a long way in its offerings and its video advertising capabilities. Its huge audience base and near-zero-cost model (no content delivery network – CDN – or storage fees, for example) make it a compelling platform for some broadcasters and brands to consider.

YouTube video ads

Their video ads today are called TrueView in-stream and are worth dissecting. Based on an opt-in model, TrueView ads are run where the first five seconds are compulsory but the viewer is given the option to skip the next 25 seconds with the 'skip' button displayed. Should the viewer actually watch for 30 seconds or stay to the end (whichever is longer) or take some kind of action, the advertiser pays Google. Besides the usual pre-roll and mid-roll videos (they don't offer end-rolls), True-View in-stream offers the ability for customers to take action on a video, taking them to a page that the advertiser nominates (known as a landing page). The caveat of this business model is that, in the case the users skip the video ad, such a view is delivered free for the advertiser and, hence, the YouTube partner and YouTube would not make any money.

YouTube display ads

Display ads typically take up space in the bottom or top third of a video player and can either be clicked away or will disappear after several seconds. They are also considered a more effective version since the video isn't stopped by the ad but merely visually interrupted. If the video player has a large 'skin' around it, it is preferable to actually put the display ad in this area instead.

Google's addition to this are their TrueView video discovery ads. These are advertiser videos that appear in various sections of YouTube, including:

1. Homepage
2. Search results page
3. Watch page (when video is not in full-screen mode)

The ads might appear to be seamlessly displayed alongside videos but they are identified by an 'ad' mark which is a yellow box and the words 'ad' in white font. Slightly larger ads placed at the very top of results are more visible, not only by their size, but also with icons in the top-right corner. The first is an 'i' icon that allows the viewer to know more about why the ad is being displayed to them. Next to it is an 'x' icon that allows the viewer to also dismiss the ad.

Google aside, virtually any advertising-funded video on demand (AVOD) service will have similar advertising opportunities, and thus will have their own versions of the TrueView in-stream or TrueView video discovery ads. Publishers can get creative in how they wish to satisfy some customised needs by an advertiser, while still being true to the standards set forth by the IAB. The challenge is to do so without infuriating the viewer. In such situations, it is best to keep in mind the following principles:

1. Keep ads, even skippable ones, to short lengths. Nothing really needs to be more than 15 seconds if you can really craft a compelling proposition about your product.
2. Avoid site-takeovers (those pesky ads that interrupt your attention with a full-screen pop-up) unless you can provide a 'dismiss' button immediately. The worst offenders are the ones that lack a count-down timer, and thus infuriate viewers even more.
3. Keep track of how many times a viewer is seeing the same ad and limit their exposure to it. By the same token, keep track of the ads they have skipped and try not to show them again (there's a reason why they skipped the ad in the first place). Nobody likes to be besieged by the same advertiser.

Measuring advertising success

The potential reach of online advertising in general is usually measured on the metric of 'impressions served'. This refers to how many times the ad server that hosted the ad, sent it to a video player. Impressions have been criticised as an insufficient metric since it is possible that viewers don't end up actually seeing them on the browser or the app. For example, it could be that the ad was placed at the bottom of a browser and wasn't noticed by the viewer until he or she scrolled down further. Or it could be that the ad failed to load at all. This has given rise to another metric: viewability. The rationale behind this is that for an ad to be really effective, it must be displayed on screen for enough time that a user will reasonably notice it. For video ads, viewability is still a concern since it is possible that the ad itself may not load. The IAB defined viewable impression guidelines as an extension to the original guidelines by addressing a new level of quality for ad impression measurement – whether or not the ad was in view by the end user. A lot can happen between fetching an ad and actually displaying it. In addition, even after the ad is loaded, site elements or browser window size can interfere with the visibility of the ad. These guidelines define a general standard for measuring viewable impressions displayed on websites and in videos. It is important to note that there are guidelines for different settings, such as desktop browser, tablet browser, mobile browser and even mobile apps, etc. But reach is only one part of measuring online advertising's effectiveness.

The IAB also sets definition of audience reach related to internet-based content or advertising (or also referred to as 'unique' measurements), including appropriate controls, filtration procedures and disclosures associated with this measurement. Included in these guidelines, because of the closely related processes involved in measurement, are supplemental guidance for metrics like visits and time spend (as a measurement for attention and effectiveness). A common reference of reach is 'unique users', but there is a never-ending debate on how to normalise numbers when the audience is anonymous. For example, the same end user can access your service or content using different browsers or devices.

One of the true metrics for advertising effectiveness is the 'click-through rate' (CTR) to the advertiser's landing page. This is calculated by dividing the number of clicks on an ad by the number of impressions measured against it. This signals actual interest, or intent to understand more about the product. The general trend is for CTRs to be measured at 1 to 2 per cent of the ads' impressions. Working backwards, your service and its content have to be sold as inventory to advertisers in order to gauge interest on them to spend. This means employing a sales manager or an entire sales team if you intend to monetise in the first place. The downside is that you also need to generate sufficient viewability of your content in order to make the sales team's job easier. The benefit to this is that you will be able to sell your advertising inventory for higher prices. The industry standard is to create a price based on every 1,000 users that you get as viewers, known as *cost per mille* (CPM) where 'mille' actually refers to 1,000. There is no standard price or rate card. If you have compelling content that is generating high amounts of traffic you can generally put a premium on your CPMs. Low-value or stale content may, in turn, attract low CPMs. Factors like 'non-clickable' versus 'clickable' ads make a difference since the former obviously don't have CTR as a relevant measure of effectiveness: every ad is considered a click. Hence, a lower CPM is mandated instead of the 'clickable' version. Table 7.1 illustrates how YouTube makes its money as an AVOD player.

Table 7.1 An example of how an AVOD platform like YouTube or others would potentially share revenue with its creators

Cost per mille (or CPM)	Number of views accumulated	Total cost	AVOD platform share (45%)
US$5.00	100,000	$500	$225

It doesn't look like a lot. But it's just an example. For all services, what would make the example variable is the CPM. Large AVOD services will take advantage of the content's earlier window of availability by putting a premium on the CPM. Typically, this will involve special deals with certain advertisers to take up an advertising package of various ad properties and other 'offline' opportunities (yes, salespeople can get creative too).

Delivering video ads to end users

Given the fact that the online world is all about being able to identify end users, advertisers can be very specific about who they want to target their ads at. They can specify that ads are shown using various parameters like time of day, channel, user profile and geographical data. For example, a beer advertiser may decide that it wants to advertise to males only in the evening, just before it is time to actually enjoy a beer. Once it has found the video sites that it feels will be representative of its target audience (young, working men who are professionals), it can decide that the ads can only run between 5.30 pm and 8.00 pm, specifically to men and only in the country where it is running its promotion. The advertiser needs to then take its requirements and input them into two types of advertising services: ad decisioning and ad insertion.

Ad decisioning

The advertiser's ads are generally stored or hosted in an ad decision service that itself is maintained by the digital media agency they have appointed. These are basically servers with specialised software that allows them to deliver the ads to the precision that the advertiser wants, hence the name. Because of this they are also known as an ad decision manager. The ads reside here in different bitrate profiles and will be 'served' once the targeted viewer has opened a page containing the video player, and pressed the play button.

Ad insertion

How ads are delivered to the player will be determined by the two types of insertion technologies available today. The first is server-side ad insertion (SSAI) or dynamic server ad insertion (DSAI), and the second is client-side ad insertion (CSAI). Each has its benefits.

Why they exist lies in the nature of streaming media itself, especially so with live streaming. When end users are watching a live stream, they will usually oblige by watching an ad (especially if it is a short one). But they usually expect a flawless response from the moment they press play, receive the ad, see the ad being dismissed and then see their anticipated content appear. This requires a fair bit of effort in streaming media as compared with traditional broadcast TV. There's the issue of buffering and dealing with the different bitrates that should be used for a specific end user. It goes without saying that the ad also must be served in the right bitrate.

With SSAI, the technology actually takes the pre-roll ad (as an example) and 'stitches' it with the actual video that an end user requested and makes this one seamless video itself. It would also do this if it was a mid-roll or an end-roll. With SSAI, the CDN is also involved. But importantly, the video player itself is ignorant of what is happening and merely plays back the content. The fans of SSAI cite this as one of the technology's best features since any heavy processing that the players must do often may result in buffering as well. More devices can also make use of SSAI since their video players don't need to be developed further just to receive the ads. With ad and content video stitched together, it is also very difficult for ad-blocking software to detect the ad, allowing the ad to be passed through in the end. This is controversial since, on one hand, SSAI promises a better end-user experience, but on the other hand, if end users are keen to not see ads, what is the use of forcing these ads through? The end user only ends up blaming the video service in frustration for this.

One crucial pain-point is that the ad-stitching did not work with VPAID until the IAB released VAST 4.0 in early 2016. SSAI now seems to be the more favoured approach.

With CSAI, the video player takes full responsibility for coordinating the playback of the ad and the actual video content. The heavy resources potentially mean that video buffering is more likely to occur here. This is amplified during a live stream since the ad must be fetched rapidly. Any issue with latency would mean that the ad could be delivered too early or too late. Also, since the player must be developed further, anyone deploying CSAI will need to bear with changes to their devices and video players as a prerequisite step. Finally, because the ad is delivered separately from the video content, it is highly susceptible to being successfully targeted by the ad-blocking software that an end user has installed.

Ad exchanges

Ad exchanges help advertisers meet potential buyers of their spots in a 'marketplace' environment. This platform is critical because streaming media services cannot possibly meet every potential advertiser in the market unless they have a large sales team. And advertisers need to make sure they are finding the right website to acquire their own customers. Exchanges bring everyone to the same marketplace and set up the right systems for both parties to promote themselves, negotiate and ultimately benefit. Bidding often occurs if multiple parties compete, which might sound counter-intuitive to the sellers, who want the best price. But bidding does help when sellers have a hot piece of content that is exclusive to them. In return, they take a small commission for every successful transaction.

Scaling advertising with a supply-side platform (SSP)

If your service has an audience that is large enough, you will want to keep all your inventory of ads in one system that can be plugged into the various ad networks out there. This is called an SSP. The benefits of SSPs are that they allow publishers to automate the selling of their inventory whilst optimising the CPM rates they are charging. Better still, they are plugged into exchanges that ultimately connect to the buyers, who themselves use a platform known as a demand-side platform (DSP). This is where real-time bidding (RTB) of ad spots can be generated and has given rise to the term 'programmatic trading', in reference to the world of financial shares and commodities trading.

With an SSP, you can sell your inventory and collect revenue without having to invest in a large ad sales team. But to get to that stage, you'll need to show that you're getting a lot of impressions, often in totals of a million per month and upwards. There are many out there but an example of an SSP is Google Ad Manager. It also contains its own ad exchange, and thus helps large business-to-consumer (B2C) brands get set up easily with AVOD models and find other advertisers.

The subscription model

The success of Netflix and Hulu naturally has resulted in references to their monthly subscription model, with almost every streaming media platform owner taking on assumptions that this model can be used in their own target market. Away from streaming media services, it seems like every second website uses this model as well, many with cheaper annual terms thrown in as well. This is natural since everyone – including your senior management – loves the idea of a business with recurring monthly revenue. Better still are the ones where annual licence payments are due up front. Finance folks call these 'annuities due' and they look great against your cash flow key performance indicators.

Monetising with subscriptions can be difficult in emerging markets. Both iflix and HOOQ (based in South-East Asia) started with an SVOD model before semi-pivoting to a freemium version instead. Many others have failed in SVOD outright.

Taken in context, Netflix's and Hulu's success was the result of their subscription plans not being bound to any kind of contract or multi-bundling requirement that cable TV providers traditionally offered home viewers. With high credit card adoption and high-speed broadband, conditions were ripe for viewers already frustrated with these bundles to 'cut the cord' (as the industry phrase goes) and switch to something entirely streaming-based.

But having spent many years in media and telecommunications companies (telcos) in South-East Asia working within the subscription business model, there are many challenges. Here are six fundamental rules that I believe will make you successful at using this model.

Have an outstanding value proposition

Firstly, have an outstanding value proposition for your target customer segment. No surprises here. Millennials are getting more cynical after seeing their parents spend exorbitant amounts of money on print publication subscriptions and heavy Pay TV bundles over the years. With lock-in terms to boot. They see subscriptions for what they are: a great way to make money at their expense. So if you can't articulate why you deserve to be paid – especially when there are free or cheaper alternatives – you're heading towards doom. And no, having a great user experience (UX) is not a value proposition. It helps. But get your content or your service serving a purpose first.

Provide a proper free trial

It depends on what industry you're operating in. It is imperative in the business-to-business (B2B) world to allow sampling since business users and decision-makers rarely decide on a sales pitch. They buy in committee and they compare against other products to complete their due diligence. In B2C, you need to do this unless you're absolutely sure that you provide benefits no one else does. If your UX is great you can steer their way to a subscription. In a way, a free trial provides validation with your market if they really like your product enough to commit to it. And don't be stingy with a seven-day trial. No one has that short a time to do anything substantial with your service; 30 days is the minimum. And yes, if you're going to implement an 'opt-out' mechanism, consider being courteous enough to send an email reminder. It tells your customers that you care more about them then about making money.

Provide a transparent and flexible price plan

Start with, and promote, your monthly plan. As mentioned earlier, people are wary of being locked in to terms. But always offer a good deal in your pricing plan. Everyone appreciates a good offer. If they enjoy what you have, encourage them to upgrade to an annual plan to achieve a slight discount. Make this the surprise option, not the default option when you sell. Auto-renewal terms should also be clearly explained and the charges shown in no uncertain terms. Making cancellation easy, as opposed to a labyrinth of an experience, will augur well should the customer ever decide to come back. However, it is also important to consider (given your market coverage) how flexible you want to make pricing for your customer segments. Consider daily or weekly plans, since in emerging markets not everyone gets paid monthly. Some simply can't afford a monthly price point. Furthermore, it may not be feasible to apply uniform pricing across geographies. End users in some countries will not provide parity, with a classic example being India. Annual SVOD pricing here is the equivalent of a yearly plan in the United States!

Payment methods matter

Just because you have a credit card doesn't mean that your customers will too. In South-East Asia, card adoption rates are relatively low, especially in countries like Indonesia (try 2 per cent) or the Philippines (3 per cent), according to a report by carrier billing company Fortumo.[2] To run subscriptions as a model means having to judge the best non-card options out there. An inevitable fallback is carrier billing. The telcos take a cut as a billing agent but now you have greater coverage and a marketing partner to work with. And yes, carrier billing even works with mobile pay-as-you-go (or prepaid) customers provided there is a minimum balance when deductions are to be made.

Be prepared for great service

We've all been through it. The moment payment is required from a site we immediately start to process a range of decisions about the value of what we might be getting. Do I really need this? Should I wait for a promo deal? Is there a way to get it for free? Once they get it, they will be even more demanding that you live up to your bargain. Make sure your customer support is top-notch. Articulate added benefits prior to the 'checkout' page so that they are aware. Onboard them with personalised newsletters and relevant notifications so that they understand how to get the most of what they've paid. Otherwise, they will churn in a heartbeat and leave unflattering reviews in the App Store.

Track your customer's journey with data (fanatically)

Finally, if you're not using a sales funnel view to track your visitors' conversions to subscriptions then you had better start doing so. Once you set your measurable goals, you need to be absolutely data-driven about how you convert your customers. This should be a weekly, if not daily, ritual. Every registration or sign-up step is a data point that tells you something about how customers feel about the process. That's where a good data science team will ultimately help you with success in building a dashboard view and the right reports. This is the final step in ensuring you're ready for a subscription-based business model.

The transaction model

For those used to the traditional video store concept, rentals were a commonplace model to encourage movie consumption by the public, as opposed to buying a title for higher price. With video on demand (VOD), the rental concept became even more attractive since the transaction was still continuous but there was no physical tape to manufacture. As an end user, you also never need to walk out of the store. You just rent from your cable set-top box or the hotel in-room service. This can be as profitable as the traditional SVOD distribution model itself. However, it depends on how much market share you have and whether or not your content is exclusive to you. Apple's iTunes service is still the best example of a thriving TVOD store for anyone with an iTunes account (and there are upwards of 500 million if investment firms like Credit Suisse[3] are to be believed, and possibly close to 1 billion already as at the time of writing).

How TVOD works

The industry norm, as dictated by the content owners, is for rentals to be purchased and be available for viewing for up to 30 days. Once viewed, the norm is also for the renter to have 48 hours to complete watching the title. If you try to watch again after 48 hours, access will be denied so you'll have to pay the rental price all over again. This window is sometimes shortened to 24 hours but this is a rare occurrence.

Rentals are normally associated with fresh and/or premium titles, referred to in the industry as 'currents'. This is the opposite of the much older titles which are usually referred to as 'library'. On some occasions, it is possible that a Hollywood studio assigns exclusive rights to distribute its library titles to one operator for SVOD rights only, and can then only assign TVOD rights to a competitor.

Rental prices also vary, but can range between $1–$6, with fresher and premium titles commanding the higher end of the price.

Pros and cons of TVOD

A chief benefit for the TVOD model will be how you attribute revenue to content owners. You can link it back directly to purchases on a per-title basis and see which studio's title is performing or not. You can subsequently renegotiate terms with your studio/distributor to your betterment. This is not to say that you can't measure SVOD effectiveness – video analytics can be shared to show who's watching what. But from an accounting practice, TVOD success is a lot easier to measure.

The primary drawback of TVOD is that it doesn't allow for any free or trial period. This is a restriction that is controlled by the studios, who can also determine the final price at some stage. But without any trial, the movie title itself must be compelling enough to create demand. This is the greatest risk since TVOD costs are so much higher when compared to SVOD and results in price sensitivity.

The secondary drawback is that it will not encourage repeat purchases and loyalty, compared to SVOD. End users will more likely go in and out of your service at will, driven only by what is new or popular. This is only natural since mainstream end users rightly view TVOD as a premium service to be accessed only sparingly. It will be up to you to ensure that your service can deploy great Customer Relationship Management (CRM) tools to engage previous users in what is new or what curated offers you have. On curation itself, you will have to focus on curating in a timely manner to exploit real-world events or trending topics.

Setting up a billing engine

If you're going to have to start charging customers, you will need to have both an identity management system (to identify and register customers), and then add a billing engine that can process customer orders and manage those with recurring monthly billing (assuming your business is starting out with SVOD) that can then accept major payment methods. Pay TV broadcasters and telcos typically have no problem venturing into this area since they already have the network, infrastructure and processes in place. But as I've highlighted before, there's no reason why your service can't be operated in the cloud purely on software and application programming interfaces (APIs). The service you choose should be able to generate transactional billing as well as longer-term billing (e.g. annual fees), whilst taking into account the different types of tax implications across an entire region.

Working with cloud-based billing providers is getting easier, with a variety of players already in the market. Simple providers that help you get started easily include companies like Stripe. You can get started straight away with card-based payment methods. If you want a full-blown, multi-currency set-up to power a premium service you could look at companies like MPP Global or Vindicia (recently acquired by SAP).

Hybrid models

You can offer a hybrid commercial model for your service if this makes sense. Essentially, this is a freemium service that offers cheap content without payment, SVOD for users who expect premium titles in the Pay TV/SVOD window, and TVOD for users who will prefer the fresher titles that are available in that window. With this, you could theoretically offer an end-to-end suite but you would really need to be able to afford large annual budgets. Your content offering would also need to be highlighted to users properly.

There is another point to consider if you're including TVOD in your offerings. It really works if that is all you do. But if you operate a hybrid SVOD-TVOD model, it is best to draw the line that TVOD is reserved for fresh titles and SVOD is for library titles. I have seen examples where certain studios have already sold library SVOD rights on an exclusive basis and only TVOD rights are available. It can be confusing to the layman to see some older titles requiring to be rented.

As you can see, hybrid services add complexity to the management and you really need to have a passionate and responsive content curation team.

Key takeaways

- **For content owners:** understand how windows work and where your service is placed in those windows. It becomes part of your value proposition, and hence your ability to price your service to either end users or advertisers appropriately
- **For everyone:** an ad-funded model is complicated and the best results are gained when you comply with IAB guidelines. Great adherence to standards begets more advertisers
- **For everyone:** a subscription model is the ideal one, but one that needs a fair amount of rigour in execution and tracking in order to be a success

Notes

1 PR Newswire, 'Netflix and The Walt Disney Studios Announce Multi-Year Premium Pay TV Window Agreement in the United States', www.prnewswire.com/news-releases/netflix-and-the-walt-disney-studios-announce-multi-year-premium-pay-tv-window-agreement-in-the-united-states-182053971 .html, 4 December 2012.
2 Fortumo, 'Carrier billing in Asia: 2017', www.fortumo.com/blog/carrier-billing-in-asia-2017-market-report-by-fortumo/2017-08-29-carrier-billing-in-asia-2017-market-report-by-fortumo.pdf, 29 August 2017.
3 Leswing, Kif, 'Investors are overlooking Apple's next $50 billion business', www.businessinsider.sg/credit-suisse-estimates-588-million-apple-users-2016-4, 4 April 2016.

8   Live streaming media

The previous chapters of this book gave you a complete yet concise view of streaming media's technical building blocks. As a final chapter, we'll focus on live events and linear TV streaming since this is where a lot of innovation is being seen. Fundamentally, we are seeing linear TV streaming being adopted increasingly by broadcasters' TV Anywhere services. Coupled with better search, personalised recommendations and interactive TV guides on mobile devices, this is bringing the old experience of watching TV into a better light and is continuing to keep viewers engaged. However, linear streaming of TV channels is also encroaching on several pure-play streamers around the world as these players pivot to a freemium business model, channels as part of the free layer itself. Live event streaming is becoming more prevalent among enterprises for a variety of reasons, both for internal and external uses. Again, better end-user engagement is the goal.

In these services, a good-quality viewing experience is critical to credibility and fosters loyalty.

Live streaming media is still dependent on hardware in the very initial, or upstream stage of the process. Since it begins with video being recorded, you already need basic hardware that a typical video production set-up requires: cameras, dollies, audio equipment, mixers and an array of lights. The goal is to get the highest-quality video signal that you can afford. The second stage is to convert that signal into an internet-ready stream in real time whilst maintaining quality. This requires an encoder. Depending on your workflow, you may need a second encoder downstream in the process and this is known as a packager. To some degree, packagers can be deployed in a cloud environment too but the gist is that you'll need to make some capital investments in hardware to succeed in live/linear streaming. If you're in the IT or technology engineering department and planning a purchase for the very first time you should approach this diligently. If you're concerned about quality and you've invested in a premium video production, that could all go to waste if your beautiful video signal fails because your encoder can't convert it anywhere close to real time or simply fails at the wrong moment. Yes, there may be other dependencies further downstream but hardware should be a priority. Let's look at the various use cases internally.

Live internal communications

Employee 'town hall' meetings or 'all-hands' gatherings in a global company have always been traditionally difficult. You either brought in senior or long-serving employees or you rotated people each year. If you really had money, you paid big bucks to bring everyone together in one location. To augment this, some companies would also have department 'all-hands' to focus on departmental goals and issues. The issue has always been to share the experience with those who couldn't make it for some reason. With this in mind, live streaming has been a great solution to catch these events 'in the moment'. In the usual set-up, a physical event still occurs, but the on-site production changes to add streaming media capabilities.

A live event streaming media solution simply plugs into what you already have on-site: the video production crew that's recording the event. The production crew will normally be able to provide an output from the camera or the video mixer and this will need to be plugged into an encoder. The encoder will convert the high-quality video into what is known as an internet-ready stream. This single stream is ready to point to another downstream encoder known as a packager, which will reconvert the high-quality video into what is known as profiles. And later enter a packager into various streaming formats. These are then ready to be sent to your video player via the help of a content delivery network (CDN) which was explained in great detail in Chapter 4. All you need to do then is embed your video player into your company's website. Ideally, all this happens with minimal latency, i.e. in a few seconds, so that employees are able to see it live on their desktops or devices.

To increase engagement by employees, introduce a series of useful playback features and make sure you promote it ahead of time. This includes the ability to rewind or just 'scrub' back on the video player's progress bar at any time if a moment was missed. Employees having trouble joining on time will love this. You can also ensure that an on-demand video of the event is made available right after the live stream ends to facilitate engagement while the event is still fresh in people's minds. All this is possible either with the help of your online video platform (OVP), or CDN or any other cloud provider. Your employees are also diverse in their challenges or spoken languages. Add closed captions to aid the hearing-impaired or in cases where viewing may be done in noisy environments, but don't forget to also add subtitling options. Cloud provider Amazon Web Services (AWS) boasts a complete platform for live video to be captured, transcribed into text and that same text to be translated into different languages for increased effectiveness across your sphere of operations. It's not a fantasy, just speak to your internal IT/technology partner about it.

Additional features to consider include slide-show presentations from the event on a second screen so that users can easily toggle between it and the speaker, just as the live audience would. A chat functionality is desirable if there's a need for some kind of questions and answers session, but bear in mind that this will require moderation. One option is to also embed the video player in a corporate social media site since it will natively allow chat and other forms of interactivity. The choice is yours.

Live event streaming is amazing because nothing beats the ability for an employee to join in with thousands more colleagues the moment an important announcement is made. It can be anywhere and anytime. It doesn't need to be an expensive solution since you don't need expensive integrations like Identity Access Management (IAM) or monetisation options. The assumption here is that your organisation will use its single sign-on (SSO) for registration and the site is hosted on an intranet.

Live external communications

Major events are always managed with the highest of expectations, particularly if you're targeting a large public audience. With live events streaming, the audience – and expectations – increase to a potentially global reach. Any sub-par experiences could result in swift negative publicity. Thus, while any brand can access a live audience, it really means you need to raise the bar on streaming as high as possible.

Be prepared for flash crowds. Ensure that your CDN partner is informed in advance (more on this further below). Rehearse for a live event if you can. Mistakes cannot be undone easily once you go live for real.

Consider broadcasting different angles of an event simultaneously and let your viewers decide which angle they want to focus on. Whilst streaming live, you can also consider clipping highlights and converting those into on-demand clips instantly. Your OVP should provide the tools to do this within your content management system (CMS) easily.

Either way, professional hardware-based encoders should then be used to encode your video into a streaming media source. A high-quality baseline results in a high-quality viewing experience that should befit your brand. Figure 8.1 shows a simple live streaming set-up for reference.

Linear TV streaming

With TV broadcasters capable of transmitting their signals 24 hours a day across satellite or terrestrial antennas, the challenge has always been to accomplish the same feat across the internet itself. In such a situation, encoders also need to be resilient enough to process video and output them in real time without any technical glitches. And do this virtually non-

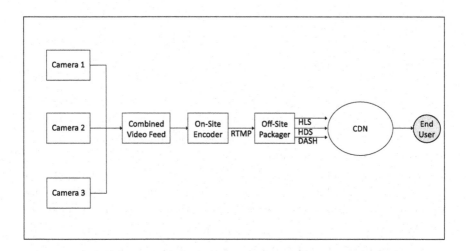

Figure 8.1 A typical live streaming workflow. The packager can be a complement to the encoder and this can be hosted on-site by you or your cloud encoding/CDN provider

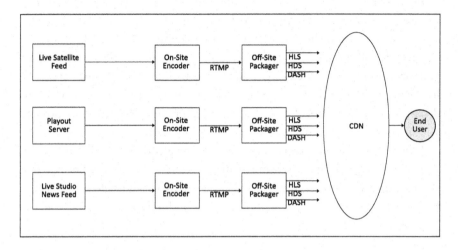

Figure 8.2 A linear streaming set-up would look identical to a live event set-up except that the cameras would be replaced by individual 'playout' video servers, incoming broadcast feeds and/or even a live studio feed. Each would then feed a dedicated encoder which would have to run 24 hours a day

stop. Video can come from a variety of sources. Figure 8.2 shows how this would differ from a live event.

The first crucial step to understand is why you need a piece of hardware known as an encoder.

What is an encoder?

As mentioned in Chapter 2, encoding and transcoding refer to live streaming media and on-demand media content respectively. With live streaming, the challenge is to convert video for the internet as seamlessly as possible via an encoder, and in real time.

Encoders, depending on the processing power of a particular unit, can accommodate several inputs of video, the most common of which is a serial digital interface (SDI). Other inputs, like high definition multimedia interface (HDMI), can also be supported but aren't considered a professional or broadcast-grade input. Traditional encoders were primarily 'dumb' encoders that relied more on their brute processing power. Modern versions are software-driven, providing flexibility amid the rapidly evolving landscape of industry formats, codecs (compress-decompress) and customer requirements. These can be accommodated by the vendor releasing an appropriate version update on the encoder itself. These encoders can also be maintained remotely after being installed in their location. This is perfect for customers who already hate paying high prices for hardware and don't want their investments being rendered obsolete overnight because of new innovation.

In live streaming, encoders also handle one important feature: the handling of encryption, which was explained in Chapter 3. This in itself adds to the complexity of the processing so encoders have a lot to handle in literally each second of video.

If you work in a broadcast operator, chances are you've heard of the term Headend, which refers to a dedicated room where encoders are installed. Since encoders resemble a modern-day server, they can be fitted in server racks and kept from overheating by constant air-conditioning. This can be, in fact, an actual data centre. Headends typically contain broadcast encoders, which broadcast to homes. But modern, 'unified' headends broadcast to streaming platforms too and basically become a centralised venue for easy maintenance.

Live streaming encoding protocols

The standard video protocol used by most encoders for a live video stream primarily was, and still is, known as Real Time Messaging Protocol (RTMP). It was developed by a company called Macromedia and was first used in its proprietary Flash video streaming servers sold to customers. Adobe bought Macromedia and made Flash video a popular standard for many years. As we read in Chapter 2, RTMP has not survived as a preferred delivery protocol to consumer devices. Hypertext Transfer Protocol (HTTP)-based streaming is far cheaper, better suited for adaptive streaming. However, RTMP's positive attributes still make it a good protocol when you're creating the 'first mile' stream from your encoder which you then send to a packager.

What is a packager?

A packager is a complement to an encoder, designed to do the specific job of re-packaging the RTMP streams (inclusive of all bitrate renditions) into the various HTTP-based adaptive bitrate (ABR) formats that exist today for consumer devices. After you've decided on your chosen flavour of formats, the packager does it in real time. Once done, the packager completes the final step of the live streaming process (and probably the most important), which is to apply any required Digital Rights Management (DRM) encryption. Thereafter, off to the CDN it goes.

Packaging is only performed if your business needs and your workflow require it. For example, you could only be streaming to a website using Dynamic Streaming over HTTP (DASH). In that case, your encoder could just convert the video signal in DASH, plus the various bitrate renditions, and send that straight to the CDN's origin server.

Cloud encoding

Operating your streaming media business can be a very expensive affair if you start buying your own hardware. It's not just about the encoders and the packagers. You need back-ups for these plus spare parts in case of critical outages. You need to account for cabling, server racks and other network peripherals, plus the added cost of overheads like electricity and redundant power supply. Most of all, you need manpower to look after these.

The smarter move seen by many is the move to cloud encoding so that you only pay for what you actually use. Cloud giant AWS anticipated the entire industry's need for pay-as-you-go IT services many years ago. Having acquired Elemental in 2015, it is now doing likewise with the broadcast and streaming media with an entire offering of services in the cloud, from live encoding, transcoding, to packaging and even server-side ad insertion (SSAI). If you're looking at a dedicated media provider, encoding.com is another option, having been an early pioneer in this space since 2007.

Architecting live streams

Important terms you'll hear throughout your organisation are 'architecture' or 'systems design'. You'll even come across people called enterprise architects, but who don't seem to carry building blueprints with them. The reason is because they don't design anything physical, rather they design the way the company's IT and technology systems work, and how they should be connected together if they are a combination of different platforms that already exist.

The enterprise architect looks after a company's overall IT systems and decides what are the best systems that could be designed to support the company's business and operational goals. One step down is the solution architect, and we'll focus more closely on this role. The solution architect is usually focused on one specific area and, in the case of this book, this would concern the company's streaming media services. The end result of his or her work is what is called a solution architecture design.

Solution architects work closely with business owners and product managers to make a vision a reality. Basic knowledge must be applied to ensure that nothing fails and stops 'the show'. In the context of live streaming, if one encoder is needed to ingest a video signal to convert it to an internet stream, a good architect looks at placing a second encoder nearby to take over in case the first one fails.

If packaged streams are being sent to a CDN, they should ideally be sent via a high-speed fibre link. But is one link enough? Why not a second link that is maintained by a separate internet service provider (ISP)? Which public cloud provider will be required to store the media content? What's the best way to create a personal video recorder (PVR) experience for customers if they want that on their device? All these must be weighed up as inputs. Ultimately, it is the solution architect's design that is going to be built and launched by the company.

Live streaming monitoring

Live streaming success comes from being obsessed with quality. This includes monitoring what is being transmitted as well as what an end user receives. Encoders, packagers and even CDNs need to be monitored proactively to avoid nasty technical surprises. There are even solutions that help you probe and test every part of your streaming media platform that is either outputting video or is making an application programming interface (API) call. Meaning, it is either delivering the video stream or delivering information that is crucial between various systems or platforms. Such probes can determine if something is working by simulating a request and capturing the response. In capturing, it also performs analysis to see if the response is complete and what is missing. All this data can be visualised on a dashboard for engineers. If anything goes wrong, it is their job to troubleshoot the issues and try to fix them quickly before potentially escalating to the service providers.

Companies that provide these critical solutions include Touchstream, and Video Assure. However, you will still need to provide the relevant manpower to perform the monitoring.

Paying for live streaming

Live streaming solutions can be found in many forms, to suit your organisational size and specific needs. If you are still learning and experimenting with streaming media, it makes sense to start with service providers that offer a full, managed solution that can be customised in some way.

Quick-start solutions

Companies like Ustream provide this, with simple monthly plans to get you started. All you need is a camera or a webcam and you can stream video without having to build anything from the ground up. Ustream incorporates allowances for content storage and content delivery via a CDN based on viewer hours. You get some extra video features as well and you get to embed your video player in your own website. If you download the Ustream mobile app you basically have the video camera and the encoder all set up in your phone and can start a live stream! Competitors like Livestream simply help you stream to YouTube or Facebook Live which absorb the CDN costs. And they will also sell you the camera hardware to get you started. You can also work directly with sites like YouTube if you're savvy enough and believe it's the right platform for your needs. You'll need to shop around to really understand what you can get. Free trials or extended demos should be leveraged so that you can share these opportunities with your colleagues and facilitate better discussions.

Professional solutions

If you're focusing on premium or entertainment content to the public, you'll find that an OVP-led live streaming solution is a great addition.

Companies like Brightcove and Deltatre can easily make this a total offering and include more advanced features like automated closed captioning, syndication to other partner sites and social media tools. The more granular video analytics will be useful to your team to analyse content and quality metrics in real time. Ad monetisation will be much simpler with the addition of SSAI or client-side ad insertion (CSAI). Pay-per-view or transactional/subscription-based models should be easily integrated too. Depending on the complexity, adding live streaming to your existing on-demand platform shouldn't be a problem but if you're starting from scratch, you'll need to work closely with your procurement and finance colleagues to run a tender process.

Premium or broadcast grade solutions

If your focus is primarily on live and linear streaming and less on on-demand content, with complex needs, it may be viable to create a bespoke solution in partnership with public cloud providers like AWS and Microsoft Azure and their suite of media-specific products. Taking the former as an example, you could leverage the full capability of encoding and packaging your streams with ad-insertion capability (using AWS Elemental) and then bundle that with their own CDN product (CloudFront). Need a high-speed uplink to send that video feed to them in the first place? They can even offer that via AWS Direct Connect. Integrating everything would then be something they would offer via their preferred systems integrator partners or developer partners, who have expert knowledge of the AWS APIs, and help build you the tools to manage everything.

So, it really depends on the need at hand. Taking the above example a bit further, Amazon owns the streaming platform Twitch, which is highly popular in North America and Europe for its live gaming-centric focus and chat interactivity. It's not unusual to occasionally see AWS events being live-streamed from their Twitch account and promoted to the public as such. In this case, simplicity and interactivity win out over form. But you can rest assured that an AWS Elemental Live server was probably being used at the event! Similarly, expect Google 'town hall' meetings to be streamed live using YouTube's own platform and branded player.

Parting thoughts

High-profile glitches still happen these days and they're mostly entirely preventable, especially with cloud-based solutions that can scale to meet unexpected surges in traffic. When done well, like major sports tournaments and pay-per-view (PPV) events, they look spectacular. A great live event stream is as exciting as a TV broadcast. There's nothing better in streaming media than experiencing something personalised for you, from the device you choose, that you can interact with in real time and through which you can socialise with people you care about. And the best part is that you can enjoy the event or the highlights you love whenever you want to.

Just press play again.

Key takeaways

- **For everyone**: live streaming requires some technical understanding and hardware. Don't skimp on price if you're looking to make an impression
- **For corporates (internally)**: live streaming solutions come in all shapes and sizes. Start small before expanding your ambitions or you'll get lost in technical clutter
- **For content owners**: don't underestimate the value in good architectural design of a live streaming solution, prior planning and on-site support

Bibliography

Bowen, Jonathan. *Anticipation: The Real Life Story of Star Wars: Episode I – The Phantom Menace.* iUniverse, Inc., 2005.

Brandt, Richard L. *One Click: Jeff Bezos and the Rise of Amazon.com.* Penguin Group, 2011.

Competition Commission. *Movies On Pay TV Market Investigation: A report on the supply and acquisition of subscription pay-TV movie rights and services.* Competition Commission, 2012. www.competition-commision.org.uk

Gorchels, Linda. *The Product Manager's Handbook.* McGraw-Hill, 2012.

Keating, Gina. *Netflixed: The Epic Battle for America's Eyeballs.* Penguin Group, 2013.

Knight Raskin, Molly. *No Better Time: The Brief, Remarkable Life of Danny Lewin, the Genius Who Transformed the Internet.* De Capo Press, 2012.

Miller, Luke. *The Practitioner's Guide to User Experience Design.* General Assembly, 2015.

Mowbray, Thomas J. *Cybersecurity: Managing Systems, Conducting Testing and Investigating Intrusions.* John Wiley & Sons, 2013.

Nagel, Wolfram. *Multiscreen UX Design: Developing for a Multitude of Devices.* Morgan Kaufmann, 2016.

Negre, Elsa. *Information and Recommender Systems: Advances in Information Systems Set.* John Wiley & Sons, 2015.

Simpson, Wes and Greenfield, Howard. *IPTV and Internet Video: Expanding the Reach of Television Broadcasting.* Focal Press, 2007.

Van Tassel, Joan. *Digital Rights Management: Protecting and Monetizing Content (NAB Executive Technology Briefings).* Focal Press, 2006.

Velte, Anthony T., Velte, Toby J. and Elsenpeter, Robert. *Cloud Computing: A Practical Approach.* McGraw-Hill, 2010.

Young, Jeffrey S. and Simon, William L. *Icon. Steve Jobs: The Greatest Second Act in the History of Business.* John Wiley & Sons, 2005.

Index